# *it's* Not Me *it's* You

Mhairi was born in Scotland in 1976 and her unnecessarily confusing name is pronounced Vah-Ree.

After some efforts at journalism, she started writing novels. *It's Not Me, It's You* is her third book. She lives in Nottingham with a man and a cat.

Also by Mhairi McFarlane

*You Had Me At Hello*
*Here's Looking At You*

# MHAIRI McFARLANE

## *it's* Not Me *it's* You

HARPER

*Harper*
HarperCollins*Publishers*
1 London Bridge Street
London SE1 9GF

www.harpercollins.co.uk

First published by HarperCollins*Publishers* 2014
This edition published by *Harper* 2015

2

Copyright © Mhairi McFarlane 2014

Mhairi McFarlane asserts the moral right to
be identified as the author of this work

Graphic novel illustrations © Chris King

A catalogue record for this book
is available from the British Library

ISBN: 978-0-00-811621-7

This novel is entirely a work of fiction.
The names, characters and incidents portrayed in it are
the work of the author's imagination. Any resemblance to
actual persons, living or dead, events or localities is
entirely coincidental.

Set in Bembo by Palimpsest Book Production Ltd,
Falkirk, Stirlingshire

Printed and bound in the United States of America
by RR Donnelley.

# Acknowledgements

It would've been impossible to think at the start of this year that we'd say goodbye to my incredible literary agent, Ali Gunn, but we did, and the loss is still taking some getting used to. RIP Ali, I owe you so much and the world is duller without you.

In her absence, Doug Kean at Gunn Media has been even more heroic than he usually is, and a lovely friend as well as a dynamic repping force.

Huge thanks as always to my wonderful editor, Helen Bolton: it's now our third rodeo and my gratitude for your dedication to making the book the best it can be only increases. This time I also benefited from the skills of Martha Ashby and Kimberley Young at HarperFiction: thank you for your hard work! Keshini Naidoo's copy edit was, as usual, brilliantly effective and entertaining and the art department did me very proud with this cover. A big cheers to the whole HarperCollins family for such enthusiasm and support. And the parties, with all that champagne.

Thanks to Chris King, whose illustrations brought The Fox to life so brilliantly: I'm lucky to work with such talented people. I also work with people, like my screen agent Mark Casarotto at Casarotto Ramsay & Associates. (Haha! Only kidding, Marco. Oh come on, don't sulk. Thanks to your big talent too.)

People who read early drafts and say nice things help me more than they know: cheers to my brother Ewan, Sean Hewitt, Tara de

Cozar, Jenny Howe, Jennifer Whitehead, Mark Casarotto, Tim Lee and Kristy Berry. I bare-thefted a joke from Tom Bennett, the super teacher – let me know if you ever need me to do a lesson plan in return or whatever. And one from James Donaghy, TV critic extraordinaire. I couldn't do Aerial Telly reviews justice though, so I'll send you some dusted Lindt truffles.

Thanks to Andy Welch, top journalist and all round good egg who kindly and very entertainingly helped me with the world of press and PRs.

Computer genius and definite Welshman Colin Jones aided me with the practicalities of writing Peshwari Naan; thank you for covering my shame with your big brain.

Bon viveur and proper restaurant critic Jay Rayner provided the idea of the superb pizza-ordering stunt; I owe you, sir (and for what it's worth, I think you should definitely do this).

Serena Mandair gave me her lawyerly counsel on the logistics of reporting an imaginary flasher, and never said: 'Are you sure this is for a book, V?'

Cheers to the gorgeous Fraser Wilson for his brainwave that Andrew was, in fact, Adam.

Thank you to Rachael Burns, who doesn't even know she helped by liking Cherry Amaretto Sours, cooking lots and generally being cool and Delia-ish, and similarly, Katie de Cozar Rushforth for being wildly Emma-ish, even if she is the enemy of livers.

Lastly but mostly, thanks to Alex, whose assistance in the 'creative process' this time round has been amazing.

And thank you if you bought this! Having readers is the most amazing privilege, and I try not to waste your time if I can possibly help it.

For Tara
One of the most heroic women I know

# One

Ann clomped over in her King Kong slippers, with a yoghurt, a spoon and a really annoyed expression.

'Is that stuff in the Tupperware with the blue lid, yours?'

Delia blinked.

'In the fridge?' Ann clarified.

'Yes.'

'It's stinking it out. What is it?'

'Chilli prawns. It's a Moroccan recipe. Leftovers from what I made for dinner last night.'

'Well its smell has got right into my Müller Greek Corner. Can you not bring such aggressive foods into work?'

'I thought it was just confident.'

'It's like egg sandwiches on trains. You're not allowed them on trains. Or burgers on buses.'

'Aren't you?'

It was a bit surreal, being snack-shamed by a woman who was 1/7th mythical monkey. Ann wore the slippers because of extreme bunions. Her feet looked like they didn't like each other.

'No. And Roger wants a word,' Ann concluded.

She went back to her seat, set the contaminated yoghurt down and resumed typing, hammering blows on the keyboard with stabbing forefingers. It made her shock of dyed purple-black hair tremble. Delia thought of the shade as Aubergine Fritter.

Ann's policing of the office fridge was frightening. Despite being post-menopausal, she decanted her semi-skimmed into a plain container and labelled it 'BREAST MILK' to ward off thieves.

She was one of those women who somehow combined excess sentiment with extreme savagery. Ann had a framed needlepoint on her desk with the Corinthians passage about love, next to her list of exactly who owed what to the office tea kitty. For last year's not-so-Secret Santa, she bought Delia a rape alarm.

Delia pushed out of her seat and made her way to Roger's desk. Life as a Newcastle City Council press officer did not provide an especially inspiring environment. The pleasant view was screened by vertical nubbly slatted blinds in that porridge hue designed to make them look dirty before they were dirty, to save on cleaning costs. There were brown-tipped spider plants that looked as if they were trying to crawl off the shelving and had died, mid-attempt. The glaring yellow lights, built into the ceiling tiles' foamy squares, made everything look like it was taking place in 1972.

Delia got on well enough with the rest of the quiet, predominantly forty-something staff, but geographically she was trapped behind Ann's wall of misery. Conversations conducted across her inevitably got hijacked.

Delia crossed the office and arrived at Roger's desk at the end of the room.

'Ah, Delia! As our social media expert and resident sleuth, I have a game of cat and mouse for you,' he said, pushing a few A4 printouts towards her.

She wasn't sure about being christened the office's 'resident sleuth,' just because she'd discovered the persistent odour in the ladies lavatory had come from an 'upper decker' left in one of the cisterns by a discontented male work experience placement who might have deep-rooted issues with women. It was a *eureka!* moment Delia could've done without.

Roger steepled his hands and drew breath, theatrically. 'It seems we have a goblin.'

Delia paused.

'You mean a mole?'

'What do you call a person who goes on to the internet intentionally trying to annoy people?'

'A wanker?' Delia said.

Roger winced. He didn't do swears.

'No, I mean a concerted irritant of a cyborg nature.'

'A robot?' Delia said, uncertainly.

'No! Did I mean cyborg? Cyber*space*.'

'Being rude to people online . . . A troll?'

'Troll! That's it!'

Delia inspected the printouts. They were local-interest-only stories based on council reports in the local paper. Nothing particularly startling, but then they usually weren't.

'So this individual, rejoicing in the anonymous moniker "Peshwari Naan", starts trouble in the conversations underneath the *Chronicle*'s online stories,' Roger said.

Delia scanned the paper again. 'We can't ignore it? I mean, there are a lot of trolls online.'

'Ordinarily, we would,' Roger said, holding a pen horizontally, as if he was Mycroft Holmes briefing MI6.

He took his job deathly seriously. Or rather, Roger took nothing lightly. 'But it's particularly vexatious in its nature. He invents quotes, fictitious quotes, from members of the council. It makes a mockery of these councillors, damages their reputations and derails the entire debate, based on a falsehood. The unwitting are sucked into his vortex of untruths. Take a look at this one, for example.'

He tapped a piece of paper on his desk – a recent story from the *Newcastle Chronicle*.

'*Council Set to Green-light Lapdancing Club*,' Delia read the headline aloud.

Roger picked the printout up: 'Now, if you look at the comments below the story, our friend the sentient Indian side order claims—' he put his glasses on, '*I am not surprised at this development, given that Councillor John Grocock announced at the planning meeting on November 4th last year: "I will be first in the queue to get my hairy mitts on those jiggling whammers."*'

Delia's jaw dropped. 'Councillor Grocock said that?'

'No!' said Roger, irritably, taking his glasses off. 'But that false premise sparks much idle chatter about his proclivities, as you will see. Councillor Grocock was not at all happy when he saw this. His wife's a member of the Rotary club.'

Delia tried not to laugh, and failed when Roger added: 'And of course, the choice of Councillor Grocock was designed to prompt further juvenile sniggering with regards to his name.'

Her helpless shaking was met with disappointed glaring from Roger.

'Your mission is to find this little Cuthbert, and tell him in the most persuasive terms to cease and desist.'

Delia tried to regain her self-composure. 'All we have to go on are his comments on the *Chronicle*'s website? Do we even know he's a "he"?'

'I know schoolboy humour when I see it.'

Delia wasn't sure Roger could tell humour from a shoe, or a cucumber, or a plug-in air freshener for that matter.

'Use any contacts you have, pull some strings,' Roger added. 'Use any means, foul or fair. We need to put a stop to it.'

'Do we have any rights to tell him to stop?'

'Threaten libel. I mean, try reason first. The main thing is to open a dialogue.'

Taking that as a *no, they had no rights to tell him to stop*, Delia made polite noises and returned to her seat.

Hunt The Troll was a more interesting task than writing a press release about the new dribbling water feature next to the Haymarket metro station. She flipped through further examples of Peshwari Naan's work. Mr Naan seemed to have a very thorough knowledge of the council and a bee in his bonnet about it.

She toyed with the phone receiver. She could at least try Stephen Treadaway. Stephen was a twenty-something reporter for the *Chronicle*. He looked about twelve in his baggy suits, and had a funny kind of old-fashioned sexism that Delia imagined he'd copied from his father.

'Ditzy Delia! What can I do you for?' he said, after the switchboard transferred her.

'I was wondering if I could beg a favour,' Delia said, in her brightest, most ingratiating voice. Gah, press office work was a siege on one's dignity sometimes.

'A *favour*. Well now. Depends what you can do for me in return?'

Stephen Treadaway was definitely a little Cuthbert. He might even be what Roger called 'a proper Frederick'.

'Haha,' Delia said, neutrally. 'No, what it is, we have a problem with someone called Peshwari Naan on your message boards.'

'Not our responsibility, you see.'

'It is, really. You're hosting it.'

Pause.

'This person is posting a lot of lies about the council. We don't have any argument with you. We'd like an email address for them so we can ask what's what.'

'Ah, no can do. That's confidential.'

'Can't you just tell me what email he registered with? It's probably Pilau at Hotmail, something anonymous.'

'Sorry, darling Delia. Data Protection Act and all that jazz.'

'Isn't that what people are supposed to quote at you?'

'Haha! Ten points to Gryffindor! We'll make a journalist of you yet.'

Delia did more gritted-teeth niceties and rang off. He

was right, they couldn't give it out. She didn't like being in the wrong when tussling with Stephen Treadaway.

She tried Googling 'PeshwariNaan' as one word, but she got tons of recipes. She attempted various permutations of Peshwari Naan and Newcastle City Council, but only got angry TripAdvisor reviews and a weird impenetrable blog.

She had welcomed a challenge, but this was suddenly looking like a nigh-on impossible task. She could go on the message boards and openly request him to contact her, but it wasn't exactly invisible crisis management.

And *was* he a crisis? Peshwari was active but hardly that evil. Scrolling through the *Chronicle*'s news stories, it was clear that most people got he was joking and the replies were similarly silly.

Under a report about 'Fury Over Bins' Collection "encouraging rats"', Peshwari claimed that Councillor Benton had started singing 'Rat In Mi Kitchen' by UB40.

Delia sniggered.

'Something's amusing you,' Ann said, suspiciously.

'It's a troublemaker on the *Chronicle* site. Roger's asked me to look into it.'

'New frock?' Ann added, uninterested in Delia's response. Her eyes slid disapprovingly over Delia's dragonfly-patterned Topshop number.

Ann clearly thought Delia's outfits were unprofessionally upbeat. Aside from medicinal novelty slippers, she believed in simple, sober attire. Delia wore colourful swingy dresses, patterned tights and ballet shoes, and a raspberry-pink coat. Ann wore plain separates from Next. And gorilla feet.

People said Delia had a very distinctive, ladylike style. Delia was pleased and surprised at this, as it was mainly borne of necessity. Jeans and androgyny didn't work well on her busty, hippy, womanly figure.

Years before she reached puberty, Delia realised that with her ginger hair, she didn't have much choice about standing out. It wasn't a tame strawberry blonde, it was blazing, rusty-nail auburn. She wore her long-ish style tied up, with a thick wedge of fringe, and offset the oyster-shell whiteness of her skin with wings of black liquid eyeliner.

With her wide eyes and girlish clothes, Delia was often mistaken for a student from the nearby university. Especially as she rode to work on her red bicycle. At thirty-three, she was rather pleased about this error.

Delia drummed her fingers on the desk. She had a strong feeling that Peshwari was male, bored, and thirty-ish.

His references were songs and TV shows she knew too. Hmmm. Where else might he be online? In her experience, message board warriors had always practised elsewhere. Twitter? She started to type. Wait. WAIT.

Yes – complete with avatar of a speckled flatbread, there was a Peshwari here. And he mentioned being a Geordie in his bio. (*Snog On The Tyne.*) She hit the GPS location on the tweets, praying to a benevolent God. They were sent from the web, and not only that – BAM! – a café in the city centre, Brewz and Beanz. A most distressing name for likers of proper spelling and good taste, she'd always thought. She knew the place – her boyfriend Paul called it Blow Your Beans.

She scrolled through the Naan's timeline and noted they

were usually posted at lunch hours and weekends. This was someone in an office, firewalled, annoyed, bored. She empathised. Project Naan kept her occupied for two hours, until the weekend's start point arrived. Friday afternoon productivity in her office was never Herculean.

Well, Monday's lunch destination was assured. A stake-out, that was much more exciting than the usual fare. She wouldn't tell Roger just yet: no point bragging and then realising she'd happened across a different talking Naan altogether.

Delia headed into the loos to get herself ready for her evening out. She'd left the bike at home and got the bus in today. She changed into a small heel and a 50s-style rock'n'roll petticoat she'd brought with her to work, stuffed into a plastic bag. She shook it out and wriggled it on under her date-night attire dress.

The ruffled taffeta was a dusky lavender that poked out an inch below the hem and picked up on the pattern of the fabric. She was self-conscious once back among her colleagues, and bolted for her coat.

But not fast enough to evade Ann's gimlet gaze.

'What *are* you wearing?!' she cackled.

'It's from Attica. The vintage shop,' she said, cheeks heating.

'You look like a Spanish brothel's lampshade,' Ann said.

Delia sighed, muttered *wow thanks* and grimaced. Nothing between nine and five mattered today, anyway.

Today was all about this evening: when life was going to take one of those small turns, a change of direction that led onto a wide, new road.

# Two

'If he's making stories about the council worth reading, they should pay him, not sue him,' Paul said, wiping his paratha-greasy hands on a paper napkin.

'Yeah,' Delia said, through a thick mouthful of spicy potato. 'But when a councillor gets upset, we have to be seen to do something. A lot of the older ones don't understand the internet. One of them once said to us, "Go on and delete it. Rub it out!" and we had to explain it isn't a big blackboard.'

'I'm thirty-five and I don't understand the internet. Griz was showing me Tinder on his phone the other day. The dating app? You swipe left or right to say yes or no to someone's photo. That's it. One picture, Mallett's mallet. Yes, no, *bwonk*. It's brutal out there.'

'Thank God we did dating the old way,' Delia said. 'Cocktail classes.'

They smiled. Old story, happy memory. The first time they met, she'd swept into his bar on a cloud of Calvin Klein's Eternity with a gaggle of friends and asked for a

Cherry Amaretto Sour. Paul hadn't known how to make them. She'd volunteered to hop over the bar and show him.

She still remembered his startled yet entertained expression as she swung her legs round. 'Nice shoes,' Paul had said, about her Superman-red round-toe wedges with ankle straps. He'd offered her a job. When she said no thanks, he'd asked for a date instead.

'In the current climate, we'd be marginalised freaks who'd have to be on a specialist site for gingers. Gindar.'

Delia laughed. 'Speak for yourself.'

'If there's no female of my species on Gindar, who am I dating? Basil Brush?'

'What a fish for compliments,' Delia said. 'You should be slinging a rod in the Angling Championships, Paul Rafferty.' She giggled and glugged some beer.

Delia was biased, but he wasn't short of appeal.

Paul had dark-red hair, a few shades less flaming titian than Delia's. He had the lived-in, 'all night poker' fashionably dishevelled look, a permanent five o'clock shadow, and worn jeans that dragged on beer-slopped floors. There were no jokes about both being ginger that they hadn't heard – the worst was when they were taken for brother and sister.

Paul caught the waiter's eye. 'Two more Kingfishers when you're ready, please. Thank you.'

Paul's manners when dealing with members of the service industry were impeccable, and he always tipped hard, largely as a result of running a bar of his own. *Pub*, Paul always corrected Delia. 'Bars make you think of tiny tot trainee drinkers.'

Delia thought it'd be most accurate to say Paul's place straddled the line between pub and bar. It had exposed brickwork, oversized pendant lamps, and sourdough bread on the menu. But it also had real ales, a no dickheads policy and music at a volume where you could hear yourself speak. It sat between the stanchions of the Tyne Bridge and in the Good Pub Guide, and was Paul's beloved baby.

'I'm grinding to a halt here,' Delia said, surveying the wreckage of her dosa.

'I'm still rolling, I'm a machine. A curry-loving machine,' Paul said, poking his fork into some of her pancake.

They had pondered expensive, linen tablecloth restaurants for their ten-year anniversary and then admitted they'd much prefer their favourite Southern Indian restaurant, Rasa. It was a treat to have Paul out on a Friday night.

Perhaps it was daft, but Delia still got a thrill whenever she saw Paul in his element behind the bar; dishrag thrown over shoulder and directing the order of service with the confidence of a traffic policeman, pivoting and slamming fridges shut with his foot, three bottles in each hand.

When he spied Delia, he'd do a little two-fingers-to-forehead salute and make a 'one minute and I'll bring your drink when I've served the customers' gesture, and she'd feel that familiar spark.

'How's Griz's search for love going?'

Paul was always quite paternal towards his staff – Delia had turned her spare bedroom into a recovery ward for an inebriated youth more than once.

'Huh. I don't think it's love. He's bobbing for the wrong apples if so. Seriously, Dee,' Paul continued, 'there are some weird generations coming up underneath us. Girls *and* boys wax their pubes off and none of them listen to music.'

Delia grinned. She was well used to this sort of speech. It not only amused her; Paul had special dispensation to act older than his years.

It was in the first flush of passion that Delia had found out Paul's past: he and his brother Michael had been orphaned in their mid-teens when a lorry driver fell asleep at the wheel and piled into their parents' car on the A1. The brothers reacted differently to the event, and the inheritance. Michael disappeared to New Zealand by the time he was twenty, never to return. Paul put down all the roots he could in Newcastle – bought a house in Heaton and later, the bar; sought stability.

Delia's tender nature could not have been more touched. When he'd first revealed this, she was already falling in love, but it pitched her head-first down the well. He'd been through such horror? And was so amiable, so fun? She knew instantly that she wanted to dedicate her life to taking the sting away, to being all the family Paul needed.

'Ah, it was a shitty thing. No question,' Paul always said whenever it came up, rubbing his eye, looking down, partly embarrassed in the face of Delia's lavish emotion, partly playing the wounded hero.

'Who's written lyrics like Joy Division's "Love Will Tear Us Apart" in the last ten years?' Paul continued now, still on modern music in the present day.

'What's the one about "that isn't my name"? Na na na, they call me *DYE-ANNE*, that's not my name . . .'

Paul made a sad face, and a gesture to the waiter for the bill.

'You love playing the codger, despite being the biggest child I know,' Delia said, and Paul rolled his eyes and patted her hand across the table. *Kids*. She imagined Paul as a father, and her heart gave a little squeeze.

They settled up and stepped out into the brisk chill of an early Newcastle summer evening.

'Nightcap?' Paul said, offering her the crook of his arm.

'Can we go for a walk first?' Delia said, taking it.

'A *walk*?' Paul said. 'We're not in one of those films you like with the parasols and people poking the fire. We're going to walk to the pub.'

'Come on! It's our ten-year anniversary. Just onto the bridge and back.'

'Oh no, c'mon. It's too late. Another time.'

'It won't take long,' she said, forcibly manoeuvring him onward, as Paul exhaled windily.

They set off in silence – Paul possibly resentful, Delia twanging with nerves as she wondered if this surprise was such a good idea after all.

# Three

'What are we going to do when we get there?' Paul said, with both humour and irritation in his voice.

'Share a moment.'

'I could be sharing the moment of being in a warm pub with a nice pint.'

Paul didn't do showy romance or *I love you*s. (Delia had to ask him, months into their relationship. He blanked. 'Why else did I ask you to move in?' *Because my lease was up on the other place*? Delia had thought.)

Simple, self-evident, uncomplicated affection was all Delia needed, usually. Solidity and companionship mattered much more to her than bouquets or jewellery. Paul was her best friend – and that was more romantic than anything.

And she loved this city, with its handsome blocks of sandstone buildings, low skies, rich voices and friendly embrace. As she tottered down the steep street to the Quayside, breathing the fresher air near the river, clutching Paul's arm to steady her, she knew she was in the right place, with the right person.

The sodium orange and yellow lights from the city tiger-striped the oil-black water of the Tyne as they arrived at the mouth of the Millennium Bridge. The thin bow, pulsing with different colour illuminations, was glowing red.

It felt like a sign. Red shoes, red hair, red bicycle. For some reason, the phrase *date with destiny* came into her head, which sounded like an Agatha Christie novel. There weren't many people about, but enough that they weren't alone. Whoops, why hadn't Delia thought of that? All they needed was some persistent hanger-abouters and this plan would be sunk. But in this temperature, loitering on bridges at pushing nine o'clock was not a particularly popular choice.

She felt her heartbeat in her throat as they approached the midway point. The moment was arriving.

'Do we have to walk the whole way or will this do?' Paul said.

'This'll do,' Delia said, disentangling herself from his arm. 'Doesn't the city look great from here?'

Paul scanned the view and smiled.

'How pissed are you? Hang on, it's not the time of the month? You're not going to cry about that lame beggar seagull with one eye and one leg again? I told you, *all* seagulls are beggars.'

Delia laughed.

'He was probably faking.' Paul squeezed one eye closed and bent a leg behind him, speaking in a squeaky pitch. '*Please give chips genewously to a disabled see-gal, lubbly lady. Mah situation is mos pitiable.*'

Delia laughed harder. 'What voice was that?'

'A scam artist seagull voice.'

'A Japanese scam artist seagull?'

'Racist.'

They were both laughing. OK, he'd perked up. Deep breath. *Go.* It was stupid of her to be nervous, Delia thought: she and Paul *had* discussed the future. They'd lived together for nine years. It wasn't like she was up the Eiffel Tower and out on a limb with a preening commitment-phobe, after a whirlwind courtship.

Paul started to grumble about the brass bollocks temperature and Delia needed to interrupt.

'Paul,' she said, turning to face him fully. 'It's our ten-year anniversary.'

'Yes . . .?' Paul said, for the first time noticing her sense of intent.

'I love you. And you love me, I hope. We're a great team . . .'

'Yeah?' Now he looked outright wary.

'We've said we want to spend our lives together. So. Will you marry me?'

Pause. Paul, hands thrust in pockets, squinted over his coat collar.

'Are you joking?'

Bad start.

'No. I, Delia Moss, am asking you, Paul Rafferty, to marry me. Officially and formally.'

Paul looked . . . discomfited. That was the only word for it.

'Aren't I meant to ask you?'

'Traditionally. But we're not very traditional, and it's the twenty-first century. We're equal. Who made the rules? Why can't I ask you?'

'Shouldn't you have a ring?'

Delia could see a stag-do group approaching over Paul's shoulder, dressed as Gitmo inmates in orange jumpsuits. They wouldn't have this privacy for long.

'I know you don't like wearing them so I thought I'd let you off that part. I'm going to get a ring though. I *might've* already chosen one. We can be so modern that I'll pay for it!'

There was a small silence and Delia already knew this was not what she'd hoped or wanted it to be.

Paul stared out over the river. 'This is a lovely gesture, obviously. It's just . . .'

He shrugged.

'What?'

'I thought I'd ask you.'

Hmmm. Delia thought the sudden insistence on following chivalrous code was disingenuous. He didn't like being bounced into it, more like.

She fought the urge to say, *sorry if this is too soon for you. But we've been getting tipsy on holidays and talking about it happening maybe next year for the last five years. I'm thirty-three. We're meant to be trying to start a family straight after: on the honeymoon, hopefully. This is our ten-year anniversary. What were you waiting for? When were you waiting for?*

She shook the irritation off. The mood was already strained and she didn't want to shatter it completely with accusations or complaints.

'You haven't given me an answer,' she said, hoping to sound playful.

'Yeah. Yes. Of course I'll marry you,' Paul said. 'Sorry, I didn't see this coming at all.'

'We're getting married?' Delia said, smiling.

'Looks like . . .?' Paul said, rolling his eyes, grudgingly returning her smile, and Delia grabbed him. They kissed, a hard quick kiss on the lips of familiarity, and Delia tried to keep still and commit the feeling to memory.

When they moved apart, she said, 'And I have champagne!' She knelt and fumbled in her heavy bucket bag for the bottle and the plastic flutes.

'Here?' Paul said.

'Yeah!' Delia said, looking up, pink with exhilaration, Kingfishers and cold.

'Nah, come on. We'll look like a pair of brown-bag street boozers. Ground grumblers.'

'Or like people who just got engaged.'

A look passed across Paul's face, and Delia tensed her stomach muscles and refused to let the disappointment in.

Maybe he noticed, because he pulled her up towards him, kissed the top of her head and said into her hair: 'We can go somewhere that serves champagne and has central heating. That's my proposal.'

Delia paused. *You can't try to run the whole show. Let him have his way.* She took his hand and followed him back down the bridge, arm once more through his, their pace now quicker, thoughts buzzing. *Engaged.*

Paul had once said to her, about the loss of his parents:

you can still choose whether you're going to be unhappy or not. Even in the face of something so awful, he said he'd started to recover when he realised it was a choice.

'But what if so many bad things have happened to you, you're unhappy and it's not your fault?' she said.

Paul replied: 'How many people do you know where that's the case? They've chosen gloom, that's all. Every day, you get to choose.'

Delia realised two things during that conversation. 1) Part of the reason she loved Paul was his positivity. 2) From then on, she could spot Gloom Choosers. Her office had one or two.

So tonight, Delia thought, she could either dwell on the fact she'd never got a proposal, and that her offer to him instead had been met with some reluctance. That Paul was simply never going to be the kind of man to gaze into her eyes and tell her she set his world alight.

Or she could concentrate on the fact that she was walking hand-in-hand with her new fiancé to a pub in their wonderful home city to drink champagne and chatter about wedding plans, on a stomach full of coconutty curry.

She chose to be happy.

# Four

'They only do champagne by the bottle,' Paul said, after they burst in to the warmth of the Crown Posada. Paul didn't drink in places that hadn't won CAMRA awards. They rubbed their hands and studied the laminated drinks menu as if they were at The Ritz.

'Shall we bother with the fizz? Booze is booze is booze,' Paul said.

Delia realised the evening as she'd imagined it wasn't quite going to happen, but don't force it, she thought to herself. You have your wedding day planning for all this stuff. (Wedding day planning! It was possible that Delia had a secret Pinterest board, covered with long-sleeved lace dresses and quirky licensed venues in the Newcastle area, and hand-tied bouquets of peonies, paperwhites and roses in ice-cream colours. At last, she could now go legit.)

She acquiesced cheerfully and Paul readied sharp elbows among the crowd to get their usual order, a bottle of Brooklyn Lager for him and a Liefmans raspberry beer for her. Paul sometimes worried they were ageing hipsters.

He motioned for Delia to grab a table and she retreated across the room to watch him waiting his turn at the bar, one eye on the action, the other playing with his phone. Nat King Cole's 'These Foolish Things (Remind Me of You)' was crackling on the Posada's ancient gramophone, competing with a roomful of lively inebriated conversation.

Paul's scruffy good looks were even better when offset by something smarter, she thought, like tonight's fisherman's coat. She had an idea for a Paul Smith suit, tie and brogue combination for the wedding (the Pinterest board was busy), but she'd have to broach it carefully so Paul didn't feel emasculated. She wanted him to be completely involved.

She knew the right way to pull him in – interest Paul in the drinks, then the music, and finally, the food.

Think of it as dinner at theirs, writ large, she'd say. Paul and Delia were big on having people to dinner. When Delia had moved into the house in Heaton, she'd been free to indulge all her nesting urges. Paul had invested in the house as a blank canvas, but with no particular idea of what to do with it. He liked that she liked decorating, and a perfect deal was struck.

When other people her age were spending on clothes, clubs and recreational drugs, Delia was saving for a fruit-picker's ladder she could paint the perfect sailboat blue, or trawling auctions for mirrored armoires that locked with keys that had tassels. She knew she was an old-before-her-time square but when you're happy, you don't care.

Delia was also an enthusiastic home cook, and Paul always had wholesaler-size piles of drink from the bar.

Thus they were the first among their peers with a welcoming, grown-up house.

Many a Saturday night ended in a loud, messy singalong with their best friends Aled and Gina, with Paul acting as DJ.

In fact, Delia had wondered whether to throw an engagement party. She had recently ordered some original 1970s cookbooks and was enjoying making retro food: scampi with tartare sauce, Black Forest gateau. She fantasised about a kitsch *Abigail's Party* buffet.

Should her family come to that do? Delia would wait to call her parents, leave it until tomorrow. She would love to tell them now, to make it more real. But she couldn't bear the thought that Paul didn't have an equivalent call to make. Not even to his brother, what with the time difference.

Her phone rippled with a text. **Paul**. She looked up in surprise. He was playing it cool, pocketing his phone as he gave their order to the bar man.

Delia grinned an idiotic grin, feeling the joy roll through her. Oh ye of little faith. She had her moment. He'd needed time to get used to it, that's all. There was a romantic in him. She slid the unlock bar, typed her code (her birthday, Paul's birthday) and read the words.

*C. Something's happened with D and I don't want you to hear it from anyone else. She's proposed. Don't know what to do. Meet tomorrow? P Xx*

Delia sat stock still, the weight of the phone heavy in her palm. Suddenly, nothing made sense. She had to work through the discordant information, line by line, as her stomach swung on monkey bars.

'Don't know what to do' punched her in the heart.

Then there were the kisses at the end of the message. Paul was not an electronic kisser. Delia was privileged to get a small one. And she was his closest family.

But what was so frightening was the intimate tone of the message. A voice coming through it that wasn't Paul's, or Paul as she knew him.

She spoke sternly to herself. *Delia. Stop being wilfully stupid. Add the sum up to its total. This is clearly meant for another woman. The Other Woman.*

'I don't want you to hear it from anyone else.' Some faceless, nameless stranger had this size of a stake in their lives? Delia felt as if she was going to throw up.

Paul put the drinks down on the table and dragged the chair out opposite her.

'I like the ale in here but they need to step the service up. They've no rush in them.' Paul paused, as Delia stared dully at him. 'You OK?'

She wanted to say something smart, pithy, wounding. Something that would slice the air in two, the same way Paul's text had just karate-chopped her life into Before and After.

Instead she said, glancing back down at her phone, 'Who's C?'

Paul looked at the mobile, then back at Delia's expression again. He went both red and white at the same time, the colour of a man Delia had once sat next to on a National Express coach who'd had a coronary in the Peaks.

She'd been the only passenger who knew First Aid, so she ended up kneeling in mud at the roadside doing CPR, trying not to retch at tasting his Tennant's Extra.

She would not be giving Paul mouth-to-mouth.

'Delia,' he said, with an agonised expression. It was a sentence that started and stopped. Her name and his voice didn't sound the same. From now on, everything was going to be different.

# Five

Art didn't prepare you for the smaller moments between the big moments, Delia thought. Life had no editing suite to shape the narrative into something that flowed.

If the arrival of Paul's text had happened onscreen, after the close-up of Delia's horrified face there'd have been a jump cut to her bowling away down the street, stumbling on her heels (rom com), slinging plates around their kitchen (soap opera), angrily filling a battered clasp-lock suitcase (music video), or staring out across the blustery Tyne (art house).

Instead, what happened next undercut the momentous awfulness with boring practicality.

It was established in words of few syllables that Paul had sent the message to the person it was about, rather than the person it was for. A fairly common cock-up that usually had less dramatic impact. There was a surreal moment when a wild-eyed Paul rambled about only sending it to Delia the second time when he thought it hadn't sent, or something. As if that could make it better and it could somehow be un-seen.

It begged a lot of other questions and answers, ones they could no longer exchange in a busy pub.

Delia managed to quell her urge to vomit. Then she had to get home.

While she considered leaving Paul on his own, looking at two full glasses and a swinging pub door, he'd only follow her. If she succeeded in storming solo into a taxi, all she'd do at home was wait to confront him anyway. It seemed a self-defeating gesture of defiance that would achieve nothing more than a double cab fare.

So she had to endure a silent, agonising journey in a Hackney, pressed against the opposite side of the seat from Paul, staring through the smudged window, occasionally catching the curious face of the driver in his rearview mirror.

When she put her key in the door, there was the familiar bump, scrape and snuffle of their dog Parsnip on the other side. Paul, obviously glad of the distraction, shushed and petted him, making Delia want to scream: *Don't be nice to the dog, you huge bastard faker of niceness.*

Parsnip was a tatty old incontinent Labrador–Spaniel cross they'd got from a rescue centre, seven years ago.

'We can't place this one, he pisses,' the man had told them, as they stroked the sad, googly eyed, snaggle-toothed Parsnip. 'Could that be because you tell people he pisses?' Paul said. 'We have to,' the man replied. 'Otherwise you'll just bring him back. His name should be Boomerang, not Parsnip.'

'No bladder control and named after a root vegetable. Poor sod,' Paul said, and sighed, looking at Delia. 'I think he's coming home with us, isn't he?'

And right there was why Delia fell in love with Paul. Funny, kind, Paul, who understood the underdog – and was sleeping with someone else.

Delia pulled her clanking work bag from her shoulder and dropped onto the leather sofa, the oxblood Chesterfield she'd once spent all day pecking at an eBay auction to win. She didn't have the will to take her coat off. Paul threw his on the arm of the sofa.

He asked her in hushed tones if she wanted a drink, and again she felt like she hadn't been given a copy of the script.

Should she start screaming now? Later? Was the drink offer outrageous, should she tell him he couldn't have one? She simply shook her head, and heard the opening of cupboards, the plink of the glass on the worktop, the clink of the bottle. The glug of . . . whisky? She could tell Paul took a hard swig before he re-entered the room.

He sat down heavily on the frayed yellow velvet sofa, at a right angle to where she was sitting.

'Say something, Dee.' He sounded gratifyingly shaky.

'What am I supposed to say? And don't call me Dee.'

Silence. Apart from the clatter of Parsnip's unclipped toenails on tiles, as he skittered back from the kitchen and settled into his basket in the hallway.

She was expected to open this conversation?

'How did it start?'

Paul stared at the fireplace. 'She came into the bar one night.'

*The same way I did*, Delia thought.

'When?'

'About three months ago.'

'And?'

'We got chatting.'

There was a pause. Paul had a cardiac arrest pallor again. It looked as if giving this account was as bad as the original discovery. *Good*.

'You got chatting, and next thing you know, your penis is inside her?'

'I never meant for this to happen, Dee . . . Delia. It's like some nightmare alternate reality. I can't believe it myself.'

'How did you end up shagging her?!' Delia screamed and Paul almost started with fright. Offstage, Parsnip gave a small squeak. Paul put his glass down with a bump, and his palms together in his lap.

'She kept coming in. We flirted. Then there was a Friday lock-in, with her friends. She came and found me when I was bottling up. I knew she liked me but . . . it was a total shock.'

'You had sex with her in the store cupboard?'

'No!'

'You did, didn't you?'

'No, I absolutely didn't,' Paul said, without quite enough conviction, shaking his head. Delia knew the answer he wouldn't give: not full sex. But more than a kiss. What Ann called mucky fumbles.

'What's her name?'

'Celine.'

A sexy name. A cool name. Celine created visions of

some bobbed, Gitane-smoking Left Bank beauty in black cigarette pants.

Oh God, this hurt. A fresh wound every time, as if she was being whipped by someone who knew exactly how long to leave the sting to burn before lashing again.

'She's French?'

'No . . .' He met her eyes. 'Her mum likes Celine Dion.'

If Paul thought he could risk cute 'you'd like her, you'd be friends' touches, with information that had come from pillow talk, Delia feared she'd get violent towards him.

'How old is she?'

Paul dropped his eyes again. 'She's twenty-four.'

'Twenty-four?! That's pathetic.' Delia had never disliked her own age, but now she boiled with insecurity at the twenty-fourness of being twenty-four, compared to her woolly old thirty-three. She'd never worried that men liked younger women, and yet here they were, living the cliché.

Twenty-four. One year older than Delia had been when she met Paul. He'd traded her in. Ten-year anniversary – time to find someone ten years younger.

'How many times have you had sex?'

Delia had never wondered if she was the kind of person who'd want to know nothing, or everything, when in this situation. Turned out, it was everything.

'I don't know.'

'So many you've lost track?'

'I didn't keep count.'

'Same thing.'

A pause. So much sex Paul couldn't quantify it. She

32

could probably tell him how many times they'd slept together this year, if she thought about it.

'Where did you have sex with her?'

'Her house. Jesmond. She's a mature student.'

Delia could picture it; she'd lived there as a student too. Lightbulb twisted with one of those metallic Habitat garlands that looked like a cloud of silvered butterflies. Crimson chilli fairy lights draped like a necklace across the headboard. Ikea duvet. Bare bodies underneath it, giggling. Groaning. She felt sick again.

'How did you hide it? I mean, where did I think you were?'

To have had no idea was genuinely startling. She'd always been so proud of the trust between her and Paul. 'All that opportunity, aren't you ever worried?' some women used to say. And she'd laugh. *Not in the slightest.* Cheating wasn't something they did.

'I've been leaving work earlier some nights. Delia, please, can we . . .' Paul put his face in his hands. Hands that had been in places she'd never imagined.

She looked down at her special anniversary dress with the dragonflies. She and Paul shared a home, a wavelength, a pet, a past. They were always honest, or so she thought. Any passing fancies on either side were running jokes between them, and could be admitted in the safety of knowing there was no real risk. There was leeway, trust, a long leash. Paul and Delia. Delia and Paul. People aspired to have what they had.

'What's she like in bed?' Delia said.

'Can we not . . .?'

'Can we not be having this awkward conversation about all the times you've had sex with someone else? That relied on you, not me, didn't it?'

She felt as if Paul had let an intruder into their lives, a third person into their bed. It was a total, bewildering, senseless betrayal from the one person she was supposed to be able to count on. Why? She didn't want to question herself – it was Paul who should face interrogation – but she couldn't help it.

*Would it have been different if I'd been different? Made you feel less secure? Lost a stone? Gone out more? Gone on top more often?*

'When it started, it was like an out-of-body experience,' Paul said, and Delia opened her mouth to say something about it surely being a very in-body experience, and so Paul rattled on fast. 'It was disbelief at what I was doing, that I even *could* do it. I wasn't looking for it, I swear. You and I, we're so solid . . .'

'We were,' Delia corrected him, and Paul looked anguished.

'And – I don't know what happened. It was as if all of a sudden I'd crossed a line and there was no going back. I hated myself but I couldn't stop.'

Yeah, they'd come back to that, the stopping, Delia thought.

'What's she like in bed?' Delia persisted.

Paul squirmed.

'I've never compared.'

'Start now.'

'I don't know.'

'Was she like me?'

'No!'

'So, different?'

'I don't know.'

'Better?'

'*No.*'

'Would you tell me if she was?'

'. . . I don't know. But she isn't.'

'Is this something you've wanted for a while?'

'No! God, no. It just happened.'

'It doesn't happen. You make a decision to do something like that for a reason. I mean, other women must've come on to you and you've said no? You told me you did.'

'I did. I don't know why this happened.'

'She was too attractive to pass up?'

Paul shook his head.

'I didn't see it coming I guess, and then somehow, when I was drunk, it was on.'

'What were you going to say to her tomorrow?'

For once Paul looked nonplussed.

Delia quoted: '"She's proposed and I don't know what to do. Meet tomorrow?"'

Paul looked at the floor.

Right on cue, there was a tiny treacherous little mechanical hiccup from the direction of Paul's discarded coat. They both knew what it was: Celine's reply.

# Six

'Read it,' Delia said, and Paul shook his head.

Delia felt a determined venom pulse through her veins. 'Read it out,' she said, steadily.

Paul pulled the phone from his coat pocket. She waited in case a look crossed his face that told her it wasn't Celine, but she could see from his unchanging scowl of dread that it was.

'I'm not reading this.'

'If you ever want any trust between us again, read that text aloud.'

Paul grimly swiped the text open, jaw clenched. When he spoke, he sounded strangled. Delia knew she'd never forget the strangeness of hearing her fiancé's lover's voice coming through his. She could see him desperately trying to edit it and not quite having the time to do it and still make it sound natural.

'If I think you're leaving bits out, I'll ask to see it,' she said, hearing herself as if she was a stranger. The woman scorned wasn't a role she ever thought she'd have to play.

'*Oh my God, you're getting married to her? What does this mean for us? Can you . . .*' Paul looked over, beseeching in his shame, obviously hoping against hope that Delia would burst into tears and let him off the rest of it. She shook her head and willed herself to wait. He continued in a funereal whisper: '*Can you get away tonight at all to call me? Speak tomorrow. Love you. C.*'

Love.

'How many kisses?'

'Three.'

With a gasp, Delia felt the tears start, warm water that gushed down her cheeks and partially blurred Paul from view. Her nose started running too; it was a full face explosion of liquid. Paul made to get up and comfort her and she shouted at him to get away from her. Delia wouldn't allow him to hug her, to make himself feel better. As if right now, he was the person who could make her feel better.

Delia rubbed at her eyes and when she could focus, she saw Paul was crying too, albeit in less of a fountain-like way. He wiped at his face.

'I'll end it. It's over. It was the most massive, insane mistake . . .'

'What were you going to say to her tomorrow?' Delia said, in a half-sob.

Paul shook his head, looking sorrowful that he kept being asked all these tricky questions.

'Tell me the truth, or there's no point. If you keep lying, there really is no point any more.'

'I was going to say we were getting married and it was time to finish.'

'No you weren't. You said you didn't know what to do.'

'I didn't want to break it off in a text. I was building up to it.'

Delia cleared her throat several times, and mopped herself up as best she could with her bare hands.

'I don't believe you. I think you hadn't decided what you were going to say to her. You don't want to get married.'

Paul muttered, 'It was a surprise, I admit.'

'I can imagine you weren't in the mindset when you were busy throwing your nob up someone else.'

Paul looked at Delia with bloodshot eyes.

'How would you feel if I'd done this?'

'Devastated,' Paul said, without hesitation. 'Gutted beyond belief. I can't tell you this isn't shockingly unfair and awful shitty behaviour, because it is. I hate myself for it.'

Yet – was Delia imagining that he sounded as if he was recovering, ever so slightly? Some of the Paul self-assurance had already crept back in. The worst had happened for Paul – Delia had found out. So now he was already repairing, while Delia was still scattered in a hundred pieces.

Parsnip waddled into the room. For the first time since they'd brought him home, Delia resented their dog; she'd cleaned up a *lot* of piss. Petting him was a way of easing Paul's discomfort, breaking the tension.

'I know it's going to take a huge effort to get past this, but please tell me we can,' Paul said.

Paul wasn't leaving her for Celine? She hadn't framed

the question quite so bluntly until now, but it was the big question, she supposed. However, it dawned on her what he was actually asking. *If I end it with Celine, promise me you'll still be here?* He didn't want to be left with neither of them.

She wasn't ready, not by miles, to decide how she felt. Especially as she didn't believe that he'd planned to end it with Celine. That text spoke of uncertainty, *tell me what to do,* the same way he was asking her now.

Delia saw the light glinting on the unused flute glasses in her open bag. They'd never even used them.

Ten years together, laden with guilt, and he hadn't indulged her enough to drink the champagne. I mean, maybe the guilt was why he hadn't wanted a spotlight on the whole engagement thing, but that hardly made matters better.

'I don't know if we can,' Delia said, standing up, stiff underskirt rustling. She felt like a painted panto dame. 'I'm going to stay in the spare room tonight.'

'You don't have to, I'll stay in it.'

'I don't want to be in our bed. Tomorrow I'm going home to my parents. You can meet Celine and tell her whatever you like.'

'We can't leave it like this,' Paul said.

Paul honestly expected some sort of pledge from her? Delia feared this said something about Paul, and something about her too.

'I don't know who I'm with any more, so how can I know if I want to be with him?'

'I'm still the same, I've just done something that makes me a huge arsehole.'

'No, you're not the same. You're a traitor, who I don't trust.'

Delia left Paul with Parsnip, thundered up the stairs, pulled her dress off and went to bed in full make-up and her new underwear. She didn't cry again. She was numb, only partly functioning: as if a chamber of her heart was no longer pumping blood round her body. Joy Division's 'Love Will Tear Us Apart' looped in her head.

She realised perhaps that failing to set a date wasn't about what Paul was waiting for. It was who.

# Seven

Ralph answered the door to Delia in a t-shirt saying *Colorado Surf Club '83*, eating a floppy buttered triangle of Mighty White toast.

'S'up,' he said, grinning, and then remembered why his older sister was on the doorstep with a trolley case and puffy eyes. 'Ehm. Are you . . . well?'

Delia smiled, despite herself. Ralph didn't quite comprehend the subtleties of conventional interaction. Liberal, well-meaning teachers at their comprehensive had tried to get him diagnosed with this and that, so everyone could label it and feel better, but never succeeded. Ralph suffered from chronic Ralphness. It was a benign condition, in Delia's view.

'I've been better,' she said, smiling, stepping inside and stretching up to make him hug her. Ralph bent his head in an awkward, touching way and circled her with his arms, looking like someone doing an impression of a hug they'd seen once in a Human Beings instruction manual.

Ralph was a mountain of a man, with Delia's carrot-coloured tresses, worn haphazardly tufty.

A cruel onlooker might note that it wasn't only the fact of Colorado being landlocked that'd prevent him being in Colorado's Surf Club. Delia worried about his weight, but he worked in a chip shop and had never met a junk food he didn't like, so it was a futile battle.

'Mum's at the allotment and Dad's out back. Want some toast?'

Delia shook her head. She'd not eaten a meal since last night's curry, so it was just as well that had been huge. Her stomach was now a balloon knot that tightened every time she spent more than a minute in contemplation.

'I'll put my stuff in my room,' Delia said, fake-brightly, bumping her trolley case up the stairs, grateful her parents weren't witnessing this sorry sight. The thirty-three-year-old wanderer returns.

She was supposed to be showing them an engagement ring.

'How's Parsnip?' Ralph asked, to her back. Delia was glad she didn't have to meet his eyes. Leaving wobbly Parsnip was a wrench. He'd been abandoned once and she'd promised him it'd never happen again.

'Good!'

'You could bring him, you know. He can sleep in my room.'

'Thanks.'

Delia's family lived in a semi in Hexham, a market town about twenty miles up the Tyne from Newcastle. Ever since she could remember, the house had looked like this; full of solid wooden furniture, patchwork and crocheted old throws, and rows of herbs in tubs that leaked earth along the windowsills. It was resolutely about function, not form, which was perhaps where Delia's urge to prettify and home-make had come from.

It was welcoming and constant though. On the bricked mantelpiece, there was a framed photo of her parents' wedding in 1971: her dad in giant chocolate-brown bell-bottomed suit, big ginger Open University beard. Her grey-blonde mum in that bowl cut that gripped the circum-ference of your head, and a post–hippy-era trailing veil with daisies.

Her family were . . . *eccentric* was the gentlest word, though Delia felt disloyal even using that. Paul used to sing the theme tune to *Button Moon* as they drove to visit, in affectionate reference to the fact her family home was its own planet, with its own customs.

Paul. Their team of two, that no longer existed. The stomach knot tightened.

Everyone in Delia's family related best to something other than people: her mum to her allotment and garden, her dad to the timber, saws and planer in the shed, her brother Ralph to computer games and the television in his stuffy bedroom.

Delia was loved, but she was – she didn't like to admit this, as she pushed open the door to her old bedroom – a little lonely in their midst. She was the only one with common sense, and a sense of the outside world.

She heaved her case onto the pine single bed and unzipped it, flipping the lid. Looking at the possessions

she'd brought, she felt the tears swell in her chest. Oh God
. . . this was even harder than she'd thought. Delia wanted
to go home to Heaton. But she couldn't. Her feelings
completely forbade it. For all she knew, Paul was with
Celine right this second, telling her he'd marry her instead.
She didn't know where she stood or what he wanted
any more.

She'd got up very early, after a sleepless night, thankful
that she kept lots of her clothes in the spare room and
could pack and leave without seeing Paul. He'd obviously
woken with the closing of the front door and the disturb-
ance of Parsnip though because she'd had a missed call
and a text offering her a lift shortly after, which she'd
ignored.

Again, Delia wished she had someone to tell her what
to do. Was leaving the right thing?

Her mum had made sympathetic noises when she'd
called that morning to say they were having problems and
that she was going to come home for a while, but Delia
wasn't surprised that she was out when she arrived. Her
mum found emotions, especially raw ones, disconcerting.
She would make her a cup of tea and rub her back, but
Delia would know she'd be dying to get out to her cukes
and radishes and not discuss the whole messy personal
business. Ralph and her father were even less use.

No, there was only one person who'd have insight and
sympathy about this, though she dreaded telling her.

Delia's eyes moved to a familiar photo blu-tacked to the
mirror. It was possibly her favourite picture in the world.

It could stay here as she'd had copies made, framing them and sending one to Emma.

It had been taken in their second year at university, by some long-forgotten amorous boy. Delia and Emma wrapped around each other in a cheek-to-cheek embrace, huge Rimmel-lipsticked smiles, plastic pint pots of Newcastle Brown Ale in hands, toasting the camera-holder.

It wasn't that they both had the moonshine complexion of the twenty-year-old, or that they were so happy. It's that they both looked so *confident*. It brimmed with the 'Look out, I'm coming to get you' insouciance she used to have.

Delia wasn't vain, but she thought she looked pretty in it. She had such heavy liquid eyeliner, she was practically in a bandit mask. She'd believed life was going to be full of adventures. Then she met Paul three years later, and was happy to give them up. All that she had, was suddenly his.

'Hello, knock knock,' said Ralph, his unkempt head, with its specs and watery blue eyes, appearing round the door. 'Ehm. Would you like to play *Grand Theft Auto*?'

Delia smiled. Actually, that was exactly the sort of thing she wanted to do. Even though she didn't know what it involved.

She followed Ralph to his bedroom. Ralph's cluttered, natural-light-free, *Star Wars* memorabilia-strewn lair might conceivably be the HQ of some young pop culture website punk, or Pentagon hacker genius. Instead it was exactly what it looked like: the dream timewasting crib for a twenty-eight-year-old man who still lived at home.

He handed Delia a confusingly complicated control

panel and motioned for her to take a place on one of the beanbags. She loved the way the video games reversed the roles between them: Delia asking stupid questions, Ralph gently chiding her for not grasping it fast enough.

It was strangely reassuring, concentrating on clumps of pixels instead of real things, in the bluish haze of Ralph's eternal twilight mole hole.

'Is Paul not coming here again, then?' Ralph said, eyes fixed on the screen, as Delia's avatar crouched behind a car in the middle of a firefight with some Mexican drug lord's gang. Her parents had been licensed to pass this news on.

'I'm not sure,' Delia said. She had a sudden desire to share. 'He's been seeing someone else.'

'Why?' asked Ralph. 'They're dead now, you can move. Fast.'

'I don't know,' Delia pushed a button and head-butted a wall.

'Does he like her more than you?' Ralph said. From anyone else, this would have been wounding. From Ralph, it was artless, childlike curiosity.

'I don't know that either. She's younger than me. She might be cleverer and better and funnier and more attractive and . . . fresher.'

'She's still not The Fox, though,' Ralph said, as he took the controls from Delia and expertly navigated her out of a dead end.

'What?' Delia had not heard that name in so long, it took her a moment to absorb its meaning.

'The Fox. Like, Super Delia.'

'You remember her?' Delia said, taken aback and very touched.

'Course,' Ralph said.

'She was retired a long time ago,' Delia said, sighing and resting her head on Ralph's arm, then realising it inhibited his gaming, and awkwardly moved it.

'It was you who put her into retirement, so you can get her out of retirement. You're in charge, like, here,' Ralph said. 'Oh YES! Let's go rob a plane.'

Ralph had a high-pitched, cawing bird-like laugh that ripped from his larynx with no warning rumble and took people unawares.

Delia smiled. She could enjoy Ralph's games for a bit, then she'd get bored. Ralph's ability to have a complete immersion wallow for days at a time struck her as a male brain thing. Or maybe a Ralph brain thing.

'Do you want a Swiss roll?' Ralph said, and for a second, Delia thought this was gamer talk, but he reached over and picked up a cake box.

'I'm alright, thanks,' said Delia, frowning a little as Ralph unwrapped the cellophane and started eating a whole cylinder of buttercream-filled sponge like a baguette.

Her mum put her head round the door. Her upper half was clad in her grass-cuttings-flecked gardening gilet. 'Oh you're here, love.'

'Yes,' Delia smiled.

'Macaroni cheese for tea?'

'Sounds good.'

Her mum hesitated. 'Are you alright?'

'I will be.'

'Cup of tea?'

'Yes please.'

In terms of maternal advice, that — bar the odd stiff word as Delia helped clear up from the evening meal — would be that. The door closed and Delia turned back to the screen, where Ralph was racing across the fictional city of Los Santos to Aphex Twin's 'Windowlicker', the wind in his virtual hair.

'You really liked The Fox?' Delia said to Ralph. 'I worried it was silly.'

'No way. Best thing you ever did,' Ralph said, wiping some jam from his chin.

There was something to be said for having someone who would, with no spite whatsoever, give you the unvarnished truth.

# Eight

'I see you've got something less smelly,' Ann said, by way of Monday-morning greeting.

A wan Delia was unpacking her lunch on to her desk: cling-filmed ham and gherkin sandwich squares, salt and vinegar Hula Hoops, waxy Granny Smith.

'Oh. Yeah,' Delia said absently, registering Ann's triumphant smile and belatedly remembering the spicy prawn bollocking.

Delia wouldn't be explaining that all her pots and pans and exotic odorous ingredients were back at her house in Heaton which she'd fled on Saturday morning. This was a Hexham cupboards' effort.

She still couldn't eat but she didn't want to worry her mum. She felt her concern when Delia's gluey bowl of macaroni cheese was returned having been vaguely tampered with, as opposed to eaten.

Delia usually turned up with a Ziploc bag of spices to customise her parents' cuisine to her tastes. Her parents obviously wondered who this floppy, quiet, appetite-less imposter was.

She placed her phone on her desk and saw she had a text: the umpteenth from Paul.

*Please answer my calls. We need to talk. Px*

The standard issue one small kiss, Delia thought, remembering how Celine merited the frankly promiscuous hand-in-the-bra quantity of one big, one small. She felt revolted.

Would it always be like this? Could she ever see their relationship free of this stain? She only knew there was a huge hole in her middle that you could see the sky through, like a surrealist painting.

Delia gave thanks that she was nowhere near close enough to anyone in her office to have confided Friday's plan.

No one was asking to see the Art Deco square emerald and diamond cluster she wasn't wearing, no one was demanding to hear how she had worded her proposal, or Paul's reaction, or the hoped-for date of the wedding that wasn't happening.

There was only one person who knew about Delia's plans last Friday, and the inevitable email arrived within an hour. They'd have talked during the weekend, but Emma was in Copenhagen for a whistle-stop three day holiday. She did that a lot. They mostly conducted their friendship via email nowadays.

From: Emma Berry
*Subject: Well . . .?!*

*How did it go, future Mrs Rafferty? (I'd like to think you'd keep Moss but I bet you won't, you surrendered, cupcake apologist Stepford.) Can I see my bridesmaid dress yet? (No bias satin with spaghetti straps that's designed for fatless flamingos, I look like Alfred Hitchcock at the moment.) X*

In another universe, one where Paul had concentrated harder on who he was sending his texts to, or better still, was turning round to twenty-four-year-olds and saying 'Woah, I'm taken,' Delia was giggling in purest delight at these words, rather than wincing.

Delia didn't want to tell Emma. Emma adored Paul, Paul adored Emma. 'Can't you clone him, or do some lifelike android thing,' was Emma's refrain.

He'd sweep her into a bear hug when she visited and make her his special recipe scrambled eggs, always keeping her glass topped up. Delia would spend the whole time refereeing good-natured debate between two highly opinionated people, enjoying every second. There was nothing as satisfying as two people you loved independently, loving each other.

Pulling Paul's statue down was no pleasure at all, although it seemed like the kind of savage cold comfort she *should* be entitled to.

With heavy heart and hands, Delia opened a reply she could scarcely believe she was typing.

*Hi E. It went like this: I proposed. Paul said yes, not particularly enthusiastically. Then we went for drinks, and he sent a text to his mistress saying 'oh fuck, Delia wants to marry me' to me by mistake. Turns out he's been shagging a student for the last three months. So I've moved out to my parents and he's asking for me to stay, but I'm not really sure what's going on. Hard to tell what Paul wants. Or what I want, now. How was your weekend? (BTW, just to be clear – the wedding is off.) (But for the record, I'd never dress you badly, what are we: amateurs?) Xx*

The reply was sent from BlackBerry, within three minutes.

*Delia, what? Seriously? What?! Can I call you? Ex*

*Thanks but maybe not right now. Sour tits Ann would die of schadenfreude earwig joy. Maybe at lunch? 1.30? X*

*Yes. FUCK. E X*

Delia wasn't sure she should be spending her lunch hour sobbing on the phone, but Emma wouldn't be put off for long. Emma was a corporate lawyer for a big firm in London and pursued an agenda with a dedication Delia reserved for pursuing Crème Eggs when in season.

Their lives had taken very different directions since university and Delia was so grateful they'd met in that little window of egalitarian opportunity. That brief space between adolescence and adulthood when it didn't matter that Emma was high-powered alpha and Delia was domesticated beta, only that they'd been put in rooms next door to each other in halls of residence. Delia would be completely terrified meeting Emma, as they were now. As it was, she remembered younger Emma trying to bleach her cut-off denim mini by pouring lemon Domestos over it, or getting off with a gentleman at the Student Union known as Captain Tongue, three Fridays in a row.

Delia stared unseeing at words on a screen about the council's new tree-planting drive until noon approached, and the chance to stalk Peshwari Naan. She'd forgotten about him in all the turmoil, and was hugely glad of the excuse to escape the office and breathe fresh air. It'd be an opportunity to call Emma. Although as soon as she was on her way to the café, she felt the risk of thinking, and weeping. Oh no – and she was passing the university, and its students.

Every single girl who entered her line of sight was a possible Celine. Delia's eyes darted left and right as her nerves snapped. Did Celine know who she was? *Oh my God, you're getting married to her? What does this mean for us? Her. Us.*

Delia nearly broke into a run to reach the coffee shop, wrenching open the door as if pursued by wolves.

She got herself a flat white and took a seat in the window with a good view of the room. There was a trustafarian-looking girl with dreads, typing on a MacBook Air, and three Japanese students huddled round an iPhone – no one with plausible Naan potential. Before, she thought she'd love a stake-out; today, she was listless. It was a count-down to speaking to Emma.

Delia's mind drifted, as she toyed with her sugar wrapper.

Clichés about the aftermath of being cheated on were coming true, she noticed.

For example, she used to think the 'it's the lying that

hurts' line about affairs was slightly wishful. *Really? Pretty sure it'd be the tongues and the hands and the frantic pulling at clothes and the groping and licking and gasping and grasping and sharing a shuddering climax that'd most bother me.*

And while the thought of Paul having illicit intercourse with Celine was so horrific as to make her nauseous, unexpectedly, it wasn't the worst pain. He'd had plenty of girlfriends before Delia – the thought of him having sex with another woman could be assimilated, however agonising it was. What Delia couldn't begin to reconcile was the eerie, disorientating sense that she hadn't known Paul the way she thought she had.

Take the conversation on their anniversary meal in Rasa, for example. He'd blithely mocked the younger generation's dating habits and implied he'd be at sea if he was back on that scene. Meanwhile, he was confidently knocking off a twenty-four-year-old. Oh my *God*: and the remarks about intimate waxing. He knew this from a firsthand encounter with a lady's bald part? Delia couldn't bear to contemplate it.

That discussion had been gratuitous. Paul had voluntarily done an impersonation of a person he wasn't, for her benefit. She tried to tell herself he'd been so scared of her finding out, that he'd overdone it. But it was more than that. It was treating Delia as a dupe.

She now recalled a few times recently that he'd grumped about being left to do all the bottling up at the end of a shift. *I'm too nice a boss.* These were times the too-nice boss had been in bed across town with another woman.

It was accomplished, bravura bullshittery. His deceit had

been conducted so artlessly, all as part of Paul's charming patter. Who exactly was she in love with?

Did any of his staff know? They might've had some idea, at these lock-ins. Did Aled and Gina know? *Aled and Gina.* She couldn't believe it had taken this long to wonder. They'd declined the last dinner party, she remembered.

Had they cancelled out of awkwardness? Had Paul told Aled, in a drunken 'Mate, I've messed up' confidential?

She couldn't pretend she was on her A-game, as time alone meant time thinking about her broken engagement, yet she saw precisely no one who could conceivably be Naan for the hour that she staked out Brewz and Beanz.

The only gang on a laptop now was a shoal of squawky teenage girls in private school uniforms, and whenever she passed them, ostensibly to get a stirrer or a sugar, she saw Facebook on their screen.

The Naan could be a member of staff, she supposed, tapping away out of sight in a backroom office. But his or her activity was unlikely to be confined to between 12 p.m. and 1 p.m., if so. She checked his timeline her phone: no Naan tweets.

The search for answers would continue, in more than one area of her life. How ironic: Delia the 'resident sleuth', who hadn't noticed her other half had another life.

# Nine

'I'm struggling to get my head around this,' Emma said down the phone, as Delia wiped tears from under her eyes and sniffed loudly and snottily as she plodded back to the office.

'Me too.'

'Why? Early midlife crisis?'

'I don't think he's in any crisis. Or he wasn't. I think a hot student threw herself at him and he went for it.'

*How long would it have gone on if she hadn't found out?* Even if he was going to break it off after the proposal, that was led by Delia's decision-making, not Paul's. Perhaps her proposal forced him into ending it with Celine, when he didn't want to.

'Did you see any signs at all?' Emma said. 'I thought everything was as good as ever between you.'

Emma had a squeaky baby voice. Every single clue about her was misleading. The cute name, the cherubic, wholesome tavern wench face with rosy cheeks, the sleek 'lacrosse at Malory Towers' yellow bob. In fact, she was one part raucous socialite to two parts terrifying litigator.

Emma knew that her forcefulness came as a surprise and she used it to good effect in her job. She even played up to it, with her Boden dresses and Mary Jane shoes. 'They think they're dealing with Shirley Temple and discover it's more *Temple of Doom*.'

'Nope, no signs at all. Zero. Which makes it worse. I'm officially stupid and he's a really devious liar,' Delia said.

'You're not the first person to not know your partner's being unfaithful. It's not your fault. Paul, though. I can't believe it. I'm so bloody angry with him. He knows what he's got in you.'

'Does he?' Delia said, miserably. She was ashamed of him, and annoyed she felt the pang of protectiveness. 'Everything I thought I knew was a lie.'

'Not everything. You're staying at home?'

'For the time being.'

'Do you want him back?'

'I don't know,' Delia raised her eyes to the cloudy heavens. 'I honestly don't know. He says he'll end it with her, but I don't know what to think.'

'Does he say it was only sex?'

'Yeah,' Delia said with a shrug. It wasn't how that text sounded. '*Oh my God, you're getting married to her? What does this mean for us?*' Delia had never had an affair – perhaps they were always this febrile and needy, even when they were only about banging.

'But he would, wouldn't he?' Delia continued. 'It's a lot less trouble to choose me rather than her. That's the awful thing. I'm not sure of him in any way.'

'You do have ten years of history and a home. He loves you.'

'Ten years that's culminated in me wanting to marry him, and him wanting to sleep with someone else. The reviews are in.'

'How easy will it be to get your money out of the house, if you do split up?'

Emma knew how much Delia loved the house, and that Delia had co-paid the mortgage for long enough that a chunk of it was hers. Her lawyerly mind usually leaped straight to practicalities.

'Not very. I don't think Paul has the money set aside to give me my equity. The bar's needed a lot of work recently.'

'And then there's calculating what you spent doing it up. Oh, I am so sorry for you, Delia. This is so shit. Can I come and visit?'

'I'd love you to but there's no space in Hexham. Shall I come down?'

'Definitely. As soon as you like. This weekend! I'm so sorry, but I'm going to have to run into a meeting . . .'

'No, go!' Delia made her farewells as her mobile pipped at her with a waiting call from Aled. She switched to answer it before she knew what she was doing.

'Hi, Dee. How are you bearing up?' he said, stiffly.

'Hi,' Delia said. 'So Paul told you?'

'Yeah. Only about a month ago. I told him to knock it on the head.'

Pause. 'I meant he told you I knew.'

'Oh. Fuck,' Aled said.

Unlike his best mate, dissembling wasn't Aled's forte. A big bear of a man with black hair and beard and hands like shovels, he had the unlikely job of wedding photographer. It happened by default: he started as general freelance, then most of the work he got was nuptials. Delia had been going to ask him to cover theirs.

'You knew a month ago, and you didn't tell me?' Delia said, warm with resentment and shame. Here was another stage of the post-revelation process. Humiliation.

'I know, I'm so sorry. He would've killed me. I couldn't get in between you.'

'Why did he tell you?'

Delia could hear Aled's reluctance and discomfort whooshing right down the phone line, but he'd not left himself with an escape route.

'He. Err. He didn't exactly choose to tell me. I saw him with her. Then he had to tell me what was going on.'

'What? When?'

Delia came to a standstill, open-mouthed. Paul had been that indiscreet?

'I caught them in a store room. I went in for last orders.'

'Caught them?' Delia said, feeling faint. 'Shagging?'

'No! Kissing.'

The store room was obviously Paul and Celine's enchanted kingdom. Delia had only been in there when heaving dusty crates full of mini bottles of mixers around. An overwhelming desire to know what Celine looked like gripped her, to complete the picture. The picture of her and Paul locked in a passionate tongue-wrestling session, her back pressed against a shelf of Britvic tomato juice and soda.

Delia was speechless. If she tried to speak, the noises would be hysterical and indistinct.

'Me and Gina both thought he was an idiot.'

Gina knew? Their closest friends in this city? Delia already knew it didn't matter what time passed or what rationalisations they gave her. Nothing would ever be quite the same between them again.

She felt as if everything in her life had belonged to Paul, that she was only sharing with him. In separation, when you had to divvy up your possessions, the fact of his ownership was unavoidable.

Uncovering an affair wasn't a one big fact headline story. It was like Matroyshka dolls, lies inside lies inside lies.

'Paul's told me he doesn't want to lose you,' Aled said.

'Oh yeah, he obviously doesn't want to lose me, you can see that. So, so careful. I feel like a *precious crystal vase.*'

'Gina is worried you'll blame her, too.'

Delia muttered that it was only Paul's fault, while feeling slightly rankled she was doing the excusing and the 'make feel better' of the conversation.

'Really though, Delia, think about it. We couldn't take sides. We had to let Paul tell you.'

'Did he tell you he was going to tell me?'

Aled paused. 'He said he'd finish it with this girl and that was that.'

This answered the question about why Aled was making the condolence call, not Gina. She knew the lack of female solidarity was too glaring. They were both going to keep schtum about this, forever. Sitting there through the speeches on their wedding day, clapping and toasting them and knowing that Delia had been betrayed.

She wanted to say: *You did pick a side – Paul's*. But she didn't have the stomach for more fallings-out.

Then, with nonchalant brutality, Aled added: 'The Paris trip is incredibly stupid, I told him that.'

'The *what*?' Delia said, flat with dread.

'Some plan, Cel— she – wanted him to go to Paris, to get over this. You have to talk to Paul about it. I'm sorry.'

Aled sounded as if he'd have given anything not to have had this conversation now. How did he think Delia felt?

Delia could only make a 'Nmmm, hmmm, yep, bye' sound before she ran to the undergrowth in the gardens by the office and retched black coffee and bile into the earth, hearing birds tweeting around her and the odd murmur from an onlooker.

Somewhere behind her, a middle-aged woman said, 'Monday afternoon! The amount students drink these days is disgusting, Stanley.'

'I've got gastric flu, actually,' Delia said, turning round, eyes pink, but the woman was shaking her head and walking away.

Delia briefly contemplated pulling a sickie – she looked bad enough for even Ann to give her the afternoon off – then imagined going home and staring at four walls in her old box bedroom in Hexham. With her worried parents knowing she was psychically, not physically, ill.

Delia repaired the damage as best she could, squinting into her compact with the sunlight behind her, and rootling out an Extra Strong mint to combat the vomit smell. She drifted back into the office like a pale wraith.

Paul was going to Paris? Did he mean what he'd said about ending it, or did he simply feel he had to say it was her he wanted, when confronted?

Delia had to now admit something else to herself. She'd always sensed she didn't quite have his full attention. She doubted that Paul would have picked her out, or fought for her, or even been too cut up if she'd wobbled on her way in those red shoes, a few months down the line.

Deciding to propose fitted a pattern she'd not wanted to examine until now. She had built a life around Paul, but he hadn't moved an inch. The decorating told the story in microcosm: he was happy for her to get on with it, but that wasn't the same as properly participating.

He was a showman and a show off, and he was a little more in love with himself than he was with her.

It would take something fairly startling to concentrate Delia's mind on her work: a bomb scare, or Ann being pleasant. However, at not long after five o'clock, she got something startling enough. An email so strange, she started in her seat, and turned to scan the room behind her.

From: peshwari.naan@gmail.com
*Are you looking for me?*

# Ten

It was one thing to search for someone who used the phrase 'womble's toboggan' – Delia had to consult the Viz *Profanisaurus* on that one – in comments on newspaper message boards.

It was entirely another thing to suddenly find yourself in the crosshairs of some sort of omniscient online trouble-maker. The back of Delia's neck grew cold and she shivered.

She couldn't think of any possible way this man (was it a man?) had found her. Yes, she'd been in the café, but how had he known she was looking for him? She'd not committed a single keystroke to discussing him online, so even if he'd hacked her email (and how would he do that?) there was no smoking gun. And how would s/he recognise her anyway?

The principle of Occam's Razor, Delia told herself; the simplest answer was usually the right one.

So the Naan could be one of her colleagues, who'd overheard the briefing with Roger?

Only thing was, there was surely no one in this office of long-servers and clocker-offers who had anything approaching that level of disrespect for their salary.

I mean, was it polite Gavin, forty-three, who liked Dire Straits, wakeboarding, his kids, and hated his wife? Nope. Or maybe Jules, fifty-one – married, no kids, saving for a Greek Island hopping month off to celebrate her thirtieth wedding anniversary soon? Hardly.

The idea they were firing up private email in office hours to endanger their income stream was downright crazy. And they certainly weren't *Viz* readers.

And yet. Peshwari Naan's words glowed stark black and white in front of her. Delia could go straight to Roger with this email address evidence, and say 'Voila, here's a way to talk to him.' But something stopped her, and she wasn't sure what. Possibly pride. A little longer, and she might solve this mystery and produce a stellar result.

After fifteen minutes internal debate, Delia opened a reply.

*Yes I am. How did you know I was looking for you?*

No reply, though she nervily hit refresh on her inbox every two minutes until it was time to go home. Home to Hexham.

Her phone rang mere minutes after she left the office, and she realised Paul was watching the clock, anticipating her being free. She answered. They had to speak some time.

'Delia, at last.'

'What do you want?'

'To see if we can meet up.'

'I don't want to. We haven't got anything to discuss.'

'I understand how angry you are but I don't agree that we don't have anything to talk about.'

'Like Paris, you mean?'

There was a rewarding moment of stunned silence, then Paul muttered:

'Jesus, Aled, you absolute twat.' Louder: 'Yes, Paris, we can talk about that. How I'm not going. I've finished with Celine.'

'Sorry to hear. Hope you're both OK. Hugs.'

Paul sounded shocked, and Delia wondered how small a mouse she must've been in this relationship for him to not expect this depth of fury and hurt at him sleeping with another woman. Did he think she'd sling the Le Creuset set about a bit, sob, and then eventually allow him to put his strong arms around her? She felt more like committing a blunt trauma head injury with the cast-iron casserole dish.

'I know you need time. I'm here if you want to talk,' Paul said.

'You seem to assume I'm coming back, one time or another.'

'I'm not assuming anything! I'm letting you know what's happened and where I stand. Glad I did, given Aled's obviously not a reliable go-between.'

So winning, so plausible, so very Paul. The Paul who'd lied through his teeth. What had Aled said? 'I told him Paris was a stupid idea.' It sounded as if Paul had initially told Aled he'd considered going, even if he'd rejected it later.

'Aled said he'd had to talk you out of it.'

'That's . . . ! *What?* I'm so angry at Aled for this. I can only think he blurted and then thought he had to say that to you, to compensate. You know what he's like, tact's like a foreign language to him sometimes.'

'Who knows? Not me. Bye, Paul.'

Delia couldn't act as if she and Paul still had that shared ground, and were confidantes.

She had considered Paul's explanation already: that Aled, conscious he'd put his not-inconsiderably-large feet in it earlier in the phone call, was trying to win brownie points by making Delia think he'd disapproved enough to intervene.

Delia knew what she was doing. She was trying to knit the wound back together almost instantly: to find a way out, so Paul's behaviour wasn't as bad as she feared. Delia wanted to believe him, rather than Aled. She stopped herself, but not before she'd shown that her instincts to side with Paul remained in place.

Delia was going to have to subdue impulses like this. She'd trusted him absolutely, without question, and look where it had got her. Now, she had questions – and absolutely no trust.

# Eleven

Ralph was behind his closed bedroom door, rapping 'Dis dat prime SHIT!' to himself and bumping into furniture, so Delia decided he sounded quite caffeine-wired and was probably OK for a cup of tea.

She would've asked him to help her to track down Peshwari Naan, only Paul had always gently mocked her for thinking Ralph was an I.T. supremo. 'He plays loads of games, Dee, he's not an expert. That's like expecting someone who has the telly on all day to write you *The Sopranos*, or fix the reception.'

As she turned to head back downstairs, she saw that their mum had washed his royal-blue-and-yellow-striped chip shop tabard and left it neatly folded outside his door.

Delia had tried to have motivational talks about seeking alternative employment with Ralph, but they always fell on deaf ears.

'Do you enjoy work?' was one tack she used. 'No, that's why they call it work,' Ralph gurgle-shriek laughed.

'Wouldn't you like to use your brain more?' Delia said, and Ralph shrugged. 'Do you like your work?'

He had her there.

Delia wasn't fired up by writing press releases about school litter-picking drives or changes to the traffic light signalling in Gosforth. Her job paid for her life when she wasn't at work, that was all.

Ralph said he was doing the same, it was just that his occupation involved adding the green dye to vats of grey marrowfat peas, or dunking wire baskets of raw potato slices into bubbling fat.

From time to time, Delia appealed to her parents to help her cause. Their view was that Ralph wasn't in any trouble, and seemed happy: he'd move out eventually. They weren't ambitious for their kids, and Delia usually liked that.

On occasion though, she mildly resented it. A boot up the bum wasn't always a bad thing, but hassling Ralph felt like prodding a gentle creature through the bars of its cage, and it'd never bite you back.

She plodded downstairs and headed towards the sticky-sealed UPVC back door, cup of tea in one hand – tea was the currency at her parents'; like Buddhists bringing gifts, you must always bear tea – and crossed the garden to her dad's shed. It was more of a small summerhouse, and full of the forest floor smell of wood shavings.

Her dad was at his workbench with a piece of oak that had been smoothed and planed into a crest, presumably one day to be part of a bed or a wardrobe.

'Thanks, love,' he said, putting his goggles on his head and accepting a mug of milk–no–sugar with sandy hands.

'Mum's not home yet. I thought I might make spag bol for tea?'

'Sounds nice. Are you OK?' her dad said.

'A bit sad,' Delia said. 'I'll get better.'

'You're always so cheerful, usually,' her dad said. He blew on his tea and paused. 'Did he not want to get married?'

'He said he'd get married,' Delia said, then stopped. She'd only said she and Paul had been arguing and needed some space. (She'd told Ralph the truth, but Ralph wouldn't pass it on, nor would they ask him.)

She was conscious that if she said Paul had been unfaithful, she might never restore his reputation in their eyes. It was one thing eventually deciding to forgive your cheating partner, but adjusting wasn't so easily accomplished by your parents. Better to keep them in the partial dark until you'd decided. Once again, the scorned woman's sour rewards seemed to be denied to her. 'I don't think he was very happy with me. Or as happy as I thought. I'm not sure.'

Her father nodded; perhaps he'd deciphered this code. 'You make everyone else happy though.'

Delia nodded, smiled, and gulped down the threat of a sob.

'You can stay here as long as you like,' her dad concluded, fixing her with watery blue eyes, the pouchier version of Ralph's. 'No rush.'

'Thanks, Dad. Good to know,' Delia said, and she meant it.

Back in the galley kitchen, she chopped onions and garlic, fried mince, and slopped a tin of chopped tomatoes into the pan, rinsing the residue out with water and adding that too – a student 'make it go further' trick that had stuck. It occurred to her how reassuring cooking could be, even though she wasn't hungry.

It was ironic: without her usually very healthy appetite, Delia could feel herself tightening and shrinking inside her clothes. As if she might end up disappearing entirely into a deflated dress, like the Wicked Witch melting at the end of *The Wizard of Oz*.

If she was still getting married, Delia would have been delighted: the corsets on some of the vintage gowns she'd admired looked worryingly constrictive. As it was, it didn't matter. She could be any size she liked – Paul had still slept with Celine.

Once the Bolognese sauce had coalesced into something orange-brown instead of red-brown, she turned the gas down, put a lid on it and went up to her bedroom.

Delia hesitated, once she'd closed the door. She could hear Ralph's singing and her dad's saw. Her mum was at the allotment. She opened the wardrobe. There at the bottom, under the old clothes and mothballed coats, were flat, clear plastic storage boxes with handles.

She slid them out, hauling them onto the bed, and opened the top one. Delia was oddly anxious, excited, and self-conscious. It was so long since she'd looked at any of this.

Delia had started *The Fox* when she was a teenager. It

was an idea borne of daydreaming at school, when life had been getting on top of her. She was teased for her red hair. She wasn't an exceptional student, she wasn't an athlete, or cool, or popular.

She was lonely. So she fantasised another life for herself. One where she was all the things she wanted to be in the real world – special, fantastic, heroic, brave, exciting, useful. As a child, she was fascinated by a fox that visited the family garden, and bombarded her parents with questions. Why did it only come out at night? Did all the foxes know each other? Where were they hiding during the day? Delia had decided her invented answers were preferable to their explanations.

When the idea to draw a comic book occurred in her teens, she knew straight away it had to involve that fox.

As a superhero, The Fox lived in a subterranean lair, travelled on a super-fast bicycle and had an actual talking fox sidekick, called Reginald. Her network of bushy-tailed spies told The Fox what was going on in the city, and she used this information to uncover wrongdoing and fight crime.

When she'd told Paul about it once, he said: 'LSD is a helluva drug.'

Delia had always been creative and never quite known how to channel it: in writing and drawing *The Fox*, she found herself fulfilled in a way she'd never been before. She bought herself fine-nibbed pens and A3 drawing pads with her pocket money and escaped into the frames of the story, spending hours cross-legged on her bed, sketching away. Everyone in her family had their magical outlet from mundanity, and now Delia did too.

She felt too foolish to show any of her friends, but luckily having a brother as offbeat as Ralph meant she had a non-judgemental audience. When she'd first shyly showed him *The Fox*'s escapades, she half-expected even him to laugh at her. Instead, he was fascinated – and with Ralph, you always knew you were getting a genuine reaction.

'Can I see more?' Ralph would ask. 'What happens next?'

*What happens next?* might've been the most thrilling thing anyone had ever said to Delia. Someone cared what might happen in a fictional universe she'd made up, simply to entertain herself, as if it had a life of its own. As if The Fox existed.

Somehow, though The Fox had started as a Delia alter ego, it became instructive to her. If there was something happening and Delia didn't know how to deal with it, she punted it over to The Fox, presented the challenge in a universe where she could make the courageous choice.

She carried on writing and drawing it at university, when she studied Graphic Design, but shelved it when she graduated, lacking the self-belief to launch a career. 'What I learned on my course is that everyone else is more talented than me,' she told Emma, who thought her work was incredible and called her a raving idiot. Delia complained she had all kinds of technical deficiencies compared to her peers. Emma vehemently disagreed. 'You have something very special that sets you apart from most people: you have charm,' Emma had said.

Instead of trying and failing, Delia never tried. She told herself that failure was inevitable and she'd only look silly in the process. It was fear, cloaked in rationalisations and self-deprecation. So Delia fell into the kind of jobs that educated young women with a nice phone manner in the twenty-first century fall into, because that's what she told herself she was good for.

This evening, a dozen years since university, Delia felt faintly daft returning to the escapism of her youth. However, as she turned the pages, she found herself grinning despite herself. It was sparky and joyful in a way you so often weren't, in adulthood.

What did Ralph say? 'You're in charge.' She was surprised at how inspiring those three words felt. Perhaps Ralph was much better at motivating her, than vice versa.

She was lost in re-reading The Fox's adventures until her mum, who'd somehow returned home without Delia noticing, called up the stairs to ask if she should put the spaghetti on.

After dinner, Delia picked up a pen and tentatively began a fresh page of The Fox. It came to her immediately, like mouthing the lyrics to an old song you'd not heard in years, and yet instinctively knowing the next line.

BETRAYED BY THOSE I TRUST....

... MY CITY TURNED AGAINST ME

IS THIS THE END?

DO I HANG UP MY CAPE?

OR... DO I GO ON?

# Twelve

Had Delia not told Roger about Peshwari Naan's surprise appearance in her inbox because the search was a welcome distraction from her misery?

The thought only occurred to her as she turned her computer on the next morning, and felt a shiver of excitement wash up and down her arms. It was an analgesic for the pain of thinking about Paul.

Sure enough, she had a Naan e-communiqué waiting for her, from a Peshwari Naan Gmail address.

From: peshwari.naan@gmail.com
*Why are you looking for me?*

Delia typed:

From: Delia Moss
*You didn't answer my question! Quid pro quo.*

Would she have to wait another day for the response? That would be deeply frustrating. No, she had it within ten minutes. Another thought: the Naan had an office job. The log-off time yesterday had been consistent with that.

From: peshwari.naan@gmail.com
*I knew because I am quite good at this 'computers' thing. Now you . . .?*

Delia wasn't supposed to be hiding her intent, she supposed. She'd better chuck in an emoticon to keep everything friendly.

From: Delia Moss
*That's not really an answer, is it? ☺ I want to discuss why you're so negative about the council. A lot of your comments on the Chronicle site are pretty scathing! (assuming there isn't another potty-mouthed, fruity Naan out there) (why ARE you called Peshwari Naan?)*

From: peshwari.naan@gmail.com
*I'm not negative, really. I post things that make me laugh. (It's the most troublesome of the Naans. Why put fruit in it? I know you'll be with me on this.)*

From: Delia Moss
*OK, but . . . they don't always make other people laugh. Some of the councillors have got quite upset. (Yep, agree on the Peshwari wrongness. Chilli and/or garlic, every time. Coriander for a curveball.)*

From: peshwari.naan@gmail.com
*That's because they're hairy old cornflakes who wouldn't know humour if it dry-pumped them from behind with a strap-on while grunting their name. (I also like cheese, and keema.)*

Delia did a small bark-laugh at her desk, and Ann, busy see-sawing a bent big toe with her special chiropractic elastic band, looked over suspiciously.

'Something on Buzzfeed,' Delia mumbled, while typing a reply.

From: Delia Moss
*Whether that's true or not . . . would you consider toning it down?*

From: peshwari.naan@gmail.com
*Is there any reason why I should?* ☺

Delia drummed her fingers on the desk.

From: Delia Moss
*As a favour to me? I've been tasked with getting you to stop. It'd hugely help me if you did. Or minded your manners a bit more. My boss would be happier.*

From: peshwari.naan@gmail.com
*Maybe your boss should grow a bigger pair of plums and tell these councillors to get a sense of perspective. I'm*

*entertaining people and adding to the sum of bliss in the
universe.*

From: Delia Moss
*You can be entertaining and not go so far as to suggest
Councillor Hammond told the AGM he bleaches his bumhole.*

From: peshwari.naan@gmail.com
*That one wasn't a lie. Check the meeting minutes. He
described it as looking as fresh as a grapefruit half
afterwards.*

Delia nearly guffawed at her desk and stifled it in time, as
Ann's eyes slid towards her again.

Delia reckoned she could talk this Naan round. She'd
established a rapport, now to see if she could gently dissuade
him from *Viz*-quoting anarchy.

The mystery remained: how the hell did he find her?
That part was spooky and baffling.

Her mobile pinged with a text; Emma.

*I will be calling you in five mins. I have an idea. Move to a
secure area and open your mind to incoming magnificence.
E X*

Delia smiled to herself and slipped the phone into the
pocket of her chambray pinafore dress, making her way to
the gardens outside. Park, if you were being fancy: a strip
of green between the council and the rest of the world.

As Delia kicked her heels, she thought how she'd forgotten – to her chagrin – how much she and Emma meant to each other.

Something in Delia's good-humoured unfussiness matched up very well with Emma's ebullient smarts. Delia was all about home, Emma was all about work, yet they equally enjoyed sitting around giggling at stupid things while wearing loose pyjama trousers. They found the bitchier shades of female gatherings hard to take. They weren't snipy, or competitive with each other, and neither of them ever gave the other grief for a lapse in correspondence. They instinctively *got* each other, in the way of great friendships. In their differences, they learned from each other.

So while Delia was wilting and fading in the face of Paul's loss, Emma wasn't saying *poor you* and plumping her cushions and making chicken soup. She was right there in the sinking boat, trying to bale the water out.

It occurred to Delia that she was also part of another long-term double act, a still-devoted couple, and the thought comforted her.

Nevertheless, Delia did worry what scheme this might be. No matter what worked for Emma in resolving a dispute, she was not going to host an air-clearing round table summit with Paul and Celine.

When Delia answered her mobile, she heard a soundtrack of ambient traffic bustle and the heavy breathing of someone walking fast. Emma's whole existence moved at a different mph to Delia's.

'I can't talk long! I've had a huge brainwave. You're going to say no at first and then you're going to think on it and say yes.'

'Oh, kaaay . . .'

'You know we were saying you should come down? Why not move in for a while?'

'How do you mean?'

'I mean, move in here with me. I have a spare room and you could resolve my guilt about not looking for a lodger. I didn't want one and I can afford not to but Dad's been on at me about it. Live here for free, sort yourself out, make me dinner. Do that mysterious thing you do where you make a place feel homely. We could be a comfort to each other, like the two old spinsters in *A Room with a View*. Your room doesn't have a view, by the way.'

Delia hadn't yet seen Emma's new flat in Finsbury Park. With the hours Emma worked, Delia suspected she hadn't seen much of it either. Delia lifted her face to the sun and enjoyed being out of doors, not in her office, a place that smelled of carpet and disappointment.

'The small issue of my employment? I can't leave my job,' she said.

'Why not?'

'Because it's the only job I have, and I need the money?'

'You always said that job wasn't a job for life thing, and how long have you been there now? Seven, eight years? When are you going to leave?'

Delia grimaced. True, but. You didn't get two broken

legs and then decide the time was right to do a parachute jump. Or something.

'I know. However, having lost my home and my partner, I'm not in the mindset of binning the job.'

'I knew you'd say that. It seems like the worst time to do it, when actually it's the best time. Everything's upside down, anyway. Also, if you want Paul back . . .'

'That's a big if,' Delia said, thinking Emma had her sussed. Her eyes drifted to a woman bending down, fussing with a moon-faced churlish baby in a buggy.

'*If* you do want him back, coming down here will ensure you have his complete attention. Trust my instincts. I know the difference between a small fix and a big fix. What's happened between you and Paul needs a big fix. Make him miss you.'

'Won't I clear a path for him and the shag piece?'

'False. You're already out of the way, if he wants that. But while you're in Newcastle, you can return to him any time. In London, you're suddenly out of sight and very much in heart and mind. If there was maybe a little too much routine before . . .'

Delia's stomach flexed. She'd thought that routine was what happiness felt like.

'. . .You doing something dramatic and unexpected will completely focus his mind. He'll be running after you. You'll have the proof it's you he wants.'

Delia tried this idea on for size. Paul would be startled, it's true.

Domesticated Delia disappearing to the Big Smoke. She

wasn't sure that doing rash things because of how they'd look to Paul was very healthy, mind you. And it could backfire spectacularly.

'My boss has a saying,' Emma said. 'When the fight comes, don't turtle up.'

'Turtle up?'

'Go into your shell.'

Emma loved management-speak neologisms.

'So you want me to be your housekeeper?' Delia said.

'No! Well, yes. If you want to be. Mainly I want you to keep me company and put yourself back on track.'

'I couldn't not work and live off you. That's mad.'

'Then look for a job! You're qualified in comms, PR. There'll be tons more opportunities here. I'll start sniffing around.'

Delia nearly said they were plenty of jobs in the north too, they weren't living in black and white. But Emma didn't generally do that London superiority thing, so Delia forgave her the odd slip.

'Don't! I'll think about it,' Delia said, 'I promise.'

She wouldn't, she was pacifying Emma. It was nice to think she was wanted. And it had been nice to toy with the idea of making Paul sit up and take notice. Realistically, there was no way Delia was adding 'unemployed' to her tick list of life achievements. London intimidated her. It was so gigantic. You were supposed to feel like you were in the middle of things, but you were never in the middle of it.

As she rang off and raised her eyes from the ground, they met those of a girl with a liquorice-black pudding basin haircut, bright pink lippy and a nervous, expectant expression. She'd been waiting for Delia to finish her call. She could quite conceivably be twenty-four.

Delia felt she might faint. *Not here. Not now.*

'Excuse me?'

Delia's mouth was dry and her heart pulsing: zha-zhoom zha-zhoom zha-zhoom zha-zhoom.

'. . . Yes?'

'Where did you get your dress? I love it.'

Relief flooded out of Delia like rainbow cosmic energy.

'URBAN OUTFITTERS! IT WAS AGES AGO THOUGH, SORRY! Hahahaha,' she squealed, while the girl looked politely startled at Delia being drunk. 'Maybe try eBay?'

The girl smiled, clearly thinking: and maybe Betty Ford for you.

Even if she wasn't going to London, Delia thought, as she trudged back into the office, shaky with fight-or-flight adrenaline, she couldn't pretend Newcastle felt the best place for her either.

# Thirteen

Delia lay in the avocado bath and braced her toes on the taps, as she'd done a thousand times in her youth, looking at her burgundy nail varnish. She always wore dark red on her pale feet; it reminded her of a childhood fairy story about drops of blood on snow.

The house was quiet: Ralph was on a shift and her parents were at their weekly pub quiz.

In her reflection in the plastic-framed mirror at the end of the tub, she could see the hollows of her eyes as charcoal smudges, after flannelling off her black eyeliner. She'd worn make-up like it for so long, even she thought she looked peculiar without it, like a newborn mole.

Hmmm. Not so newly born any more. Not long till thirty-four. Delia hadn't wanted to think about this until now, but there was something about being naked that forced her into stark honesty.

Here was the thought that had buzzed like a wasp at the edge of her thoughts, ever since the revelation about Celine.

If she wanted kids, Paul was still probably the safer option than re-launching herself back into the dating scene in her mid-thirties, hoping to find another solid prospect.

Even if Delia met someone else soon – and this seemed unlikely – she had to factor in the time to get to know and be sure of him, before taking the step into parenthood. She hated to give in to outmoded ideas about being a single woman of a certain age – no choice should be made in desperation, or it wasn't a choice at all. She'd be the first to tell a friend she had all the time in the world. But you said things like that to make those without a choice feel better. If she was honest, her situation as it stood felt perilous.

As she and Paul discussed the other night, where would you even start, dating now? Deeply unfairly, at thirty-five, he was still young enough to be the cool rather than creepy older guy to a twenty-four-year-old. He could wait till she was, say, thirty and ready to be thinking about a family.

Delia didn't have similar leeway.

She'd been out of circulation so long, the mindset required to make polite conversation over a gin and tonic with a stranger you might want to sleep with seemed utterly alien and overwhelming.

Before Paul, she'd pinballed from boyfriend to boyfriend without ever having to consider the getting of them. They'd always been there when required, and sometimes when not required. Modern dating, it needed practice – it wasn't something you could start from cold and expect instant success. You weren't without baggage, and neither were your prospectives.

Emma was long-term single, with the odd dishonourable

exception of posh, brusque men she met through work and had brief, brusque flings with. Delia had always shivered slightly at the brutality of it all. Emma had been dumped a couple of times by social media, seeing Harry or Olly with someone else in a ski resort selfie. (Though Delia put these cruelties down partly to Emma's self-confessed questionable taste in men.)

Emma had been looking for her Paul online and through friends-of-friends all her life, and had yet to encounter one.

Then there were further hurdles, if Delia miraculously hit it off with a potential in a drink at The Baltic. New person sex. *Gulp.*

Delia looked down at her body.

She hadn't needed to assess its aesthetic value quite so bluntly before: it did its job, and it was loved. She might want a flatter stomach, but as long as there were A-line skirts, creamy blue cheese and Paul around, it wasn't a priority.

Now she wondered at what restoration work might be needed before it could be opened to the public again. She gazed despondently at the white orbs of her breasts, bobbing in the water. In clothes, they got a fair bit of interest. Double D-cups were popular enough with menfolk.

However, cosmetic surgery had come in during Delia's decade off the market. Frighteningly, she had seen the word 'saggy' cruelly hurled at women she thought of as aspirationally pert. A larger chest size inevitably meant she had some 'hang', when out of a bra. The thought of pinging the clasp on one and being assessed by someone she didn't know all that well was frightening.

Delia shivered: Emma had once been hard-dumped right after the first time with someone. Imagine that. Even Emma's buoyant demeanour had taken a bad knock.

Delia wasn't thin, or sculpted. She had little silvery shoals of stretchmarks on her hips. And she had hair.

Would being a natural redhead startle some? Given that extreme waxes were the near-norm? She used to get teased for having a Ronald McDonald wig in the games changing rooms at school. She didn't fancy discovering the prejudice was alive and kicking, two decades later, right when she and what she could quaintly call *a new lover* were about to get down to it.

A new lover – it seemed impossible. Paul and Delia. Delia and Paul. They belonged to each other. Yet he'd loaned himself out.

She added more scalding hot water to the bath, to make up for how cold she felt.

Was this how it worked, coming to terms with an affair – like passing through the stages of a death: anger, denial, bargaining, acceptance?

Yes, a bereavement was exactly what it was. Accepting that the old relationship with Paul, the one where he'd never be unfaithful and she had unshakeable belief in him, was dead. If they got back together, it would be a new relationship. Many features of the old, but not the same. Realising that gave her much sadness, but some peace.

What if she went to London? Got away from all this and gained some perspective with distance? Only that would mean becoming unemployed. As much as she was indifferent towards her job, Delia couldn't quite countenance it.

Delia dipped her head under the water and let her hair float in a warm halo of snakes around her skull, thinking of herself as a modern-day Ophelia, submerged in Radox pine bubbles. Her feelings for Paul hadn't vanished over the course of one ugly evening.

She could see a time she would go back to him. She also knew she had a giant lump of stone inside her stomach, a dead hard weight of hurt and resentment that would have to dissolve, slowly, until she could feel love towards him again.

Delia didn't know how or when or if she'd be able to rid herself of it. It seemed a big enough challenge to have admitted that she would try.

# Fourteen

'We've had a major security breach and this Peshwari Naan pest has ratcheted up to Threat Level: Amber,' Roger barked at Delia, causing everyone to look at them both, obviously wondering how words in their native language could be strung together to form something so incomprehensible. 'There have been some developments.'

Delia looked at him blankly.

'Are you, or are you not meant to be updating and monitoring our Twitter feed?'

'Yes,' she said, bewildered.

'When did you last tweet?'

'Erm, an hour or so ago?'

'Then log on to our account,' Roger said, leaning over Delia and heavy-breathing decaf Caffe Hag down the neck-line of her sweater. He adopted the hand-on-hip lean-in pose, with the self-importance of a security spook briefing the POTUS at a COBRA meeting.

Delia obliged, feeling a significant prickle of fear. Should she mention the Naan emails yet?

She brought up the council's timeline and instantly clenched her jaw to keep the muscles in her neck from spasming in laughter.

It was full of fake tweets.

*Comrades! It's Awards Season Again! Please nominate in the following categories . . .*

*Ugliest Planning Decision*

*Most Harrowing Public Toilet Experience*

*Hottest Councillor*

*Best Dogging Spot*

Delia said: 'Oh dear,' and cleared her throat. *Do not laugh, do not laugh . . .*

'You hadn't seen this?'

'Of course not!' Delia said, hastily moving to the Edit Account Settings section. 'I'll change the password right now.'

'We've been hacked?' Roger said, pushing his science teacher glasses up his nose.

*No. I thought it might be fun to pretend the council has an award for Most Specific Graffiti.*

'How do we know it's Peshwari Naan?' Delia said.

'Same M.O.' Roger took the mouse from Delia and scrolled down the page. 'The fictionalised quotes.'

*Coun. Janet Walworth said: 'The awards are a chance for you to tell us which of our policies really twat you off.'*

'This has never happened before. That password change may hold him off for now but in light of this, I wonder how many vulnerabilities the system has. I will put our I.T. team on it. Now, please take a look at what's happening over at the *Chronicle*.'

Roger was absolutely loving this, Delia realised.

Delia pulled up the *Chronicle* site and under Roger's guidance, put 'city council' into its search engine. The first story that came up was about an unemployment seminar.

Delia scrolled the comments, not expecting to see anything, but there, third down was Peshwari (did this person really have a job?).

*Hey guys: got to let you know that the Powers That Be and pen pushers up at City Hall are on to me. Guess some people don't like The Sheeple to see with their own eyes. I've been asked to 'mind my manners'. Well, this truther won't be silenced! The chief executive sits on a throne of lies. And signs off expenses for big platters of Ferrero Rocher at receptions. This genie is OUT of the BOTTLE.*

Roger's lips moved as he read the words, and cogs turned. He looked at Delia with scarily maniacal eyes, like a Blue Meanie in *Yellow Submarine*.

'Thoughts?'

Delia had very little time to decide what to do. In the brief window afforded for calculation, she concluded that playing completely dumb was not going to work. The Naan was describing her approach, right after Roger had asked her to make it.

'I had . . . opened a dialogue,' she said.

'How?' Roger said. The air of menace could be cut with a potato peeler and Delia knew every single one of her colleagues were watching the show avidly.

'On email. I . . .'

'Forward me the correspondence!' Roger bristled. Literally bristled. He looked like a Quentin Blake illustration: scribbly hair, beard made of hay, thunderous brow, pinprick eyes, magnified behind thick, square teacher glasses.

He stalked back to his screen to await the evidence and Delia felt sick.

The playful exchange between her and Naan only looked acceptable on two conditions: 1) she had time to present it carefully and sympathetically and 2) Naan had indeed backed off.

Given neither applied, she was fucked.

She looked at the discussion again and tried to tell herself, well at least you're not outright saying HAHAHA GOOD ONE STICK IT TO THE OLD SCROTES. She didn't think she came off as issuing the sort of schoolmarm admonishments that Roger's wrath demanded though, to put it mildly.

Delia hit forward with the heavy heart of the condemned woman and prefaced it:

*Hi Roger. As you can see, I am making the first steps in gaining his trust here.*

It was a craven 'Please do not bollock me' plea. She also offered a brief explanation of staking out Brewz and Beanz. It didn't really help Delia's cause that the whole interaction started with the Naan spotting her, not vice versa. Or that Roger's testicular fortitude as a boss was alluded to.

Some extremely tense minutes ticked past. Roger was hunched over his screen, Delia trying not to look over at him.

Ann said: 'Was that to do with the things you kept laughing at?' loud enough that Roger's head jerked up.

*What an absolutely traitorous cow,* Delia thought. Ann probably only found natural disasters and jihadist attacks funny.

The appearance at her shoulder took less than fifteen minutes. It felt as if Roger appeared with a gust of icy air and the opening chords of 'Enter Sandman'.

'Follow me,' he said.

Roger took Delia into an airless deserted office down the corridor, full of filing cabinets and an old whiteboard, with FUNDAMENTAL PRINCIPLES = ACTION? -> FACILITATION marker-penned on it.

'Any idea what I want to talk to you about?'

'Peshwari Naan?' Delia said, hoping her tone didn't sound insubordinate.

'I'd like you to explain the rationale behind the informal correspondence you've entered into with someone who is a declared enemy of this organisation.'

*Oh for goodness' sake, why did Roger always have to talk as if he was in a Tom Clancy? The battle fleet will never be ready!*

'I was winning his trust by speaking to him in his own language,' Delia said.

'The impression you gave the Naan – and myself – was that you found the tenor of his contribution acceptable. No doubt emboldening him to commit his latest infraction.'

He was officially the Naan now, like the Zodiac or the King of Pop.

'I had to be careful about steaming in and saying "You can't do that," because technically, he *can* do that. I thought the softly-softly approach would work better.'

'We've seen how well it worked. Sorry if I wasn't clear enough, Ms Moss, but as a representative of the council you were not expected to engage in ribald badinage and casually ask he "tone it down a bit".'

This was so unfair. Roger had said: *any means, foul or fair.*

'I don't think he would've responded to a simple cease and desist request or I would have made it.'

Roger's nostrils flared.

'You could've come to me at several points to have me sign off on what was best to do. Instead you saw the trust I placed in you as licence to indulge in sophomoric sniggering and inflame the situation further. Do you have any idea how this is going to look when I have to explain it to Councillor Grocock?'

And there it was. Roger had a flea in his ear, so he was

bloody well going to pass the flea on to Delia. Only by this time, the flea had become the size of a walrus.

'Do we have to say we've been in touch at all?' Delia said.

Roger went puce.

'Yes, we do. Your attitude towards what constitutes proper disclosure is extremely worrying. I'm giving you a written warning and it will go on your file,' Roger said.

'That's not fair,' Delia said. 'I was working undercover with special rules . . .'

'You were not undercover when he contacted you on your email here! Do you have any idea how he knew you were looking for him?'

Delia miserably shook her head.

'Your achievements are exactly nil. Game, set and match to the Naan.'

It occurred to Delia that the Naan might not have finished making her look bad. The Twitter account hack signalled unlocking a new mischief achievement level.

When Delia got back to her desk, she started as she saw she had an email from the Naan waiting for her. She felt considerable anger towards this invisible architect of her misery, and had absolutely no freedom to say so.

*Hey: what if Councillor Hammond meant his bleached bumhole looked like a RUBY grapefruit? Make you think.*

She hit delete.

# Fifteen

Delia doubted her day could get any worse.

Then mid-afternoon, everyone uncharacteristically got out of their chairs. Delia glanced around in confusion.

'Fire drill?' she asked Mark.

'Team-building thing,' he mumbled, apologetically.

Delia noticed he was sheepish because she was getting the *sotto voce* tone reserved for someone in trouble. She had been branded with The Dark Mark, and no one wanted to be seen colluding and fraternising with her for the time being. It was vaguely ridiculous.

Roger might favour a degree of quivering melodrama – Delia wondered if it was his way of offsetting a very quiet life of chess and golf – but she didn't see why proper adults had to play along.

They trooped down to a meeting room on the next floor. There was another whiteboard at one end, this time with a list of commandments, an agenda for discussion. (No.4 was 'Overcoming Diversity', which Delia was pretty sure was meant to be 'adversity', but she wasn't going to mention it.)

Once they'd all been herded in the doorway, a woman in a plum two-piece skirt suit with a badge bearing the name LINDA addressed them all. She had the air of worn down but persistent jollity that could only have come from twenty years ploughing the ever-decreasing returns of the regional training circuit.

They couldn't sit down because the desks had been dragged around into a formation that Delia couldn't fathom, with one sat on its own in the middle.

'Good afternoon! Are we happy campers?'

Muttering.

'Oh dear, that's not very upbeat. I said, ARE we all HAPPY campers?!'

Slightly louder mumbling.

'We're here today to run a workshop that's going to leave you all with an invigorated sense of what you do, and who you do it with!'

Delia glanced sidelong at Ann. She didn't want an invigorated sense of Ann.

'First up, the purpose of the Table Fall exercise is to create a sense of trust in co-workers.'

Oh God no, they were doing the 'falling backwards and being caught' trust thing? Had the city council finally got wind of this decade-old fad?

'This is about how we support each other and co-operate to create a real physical sense of togetherness as a team.'

Delia didn't want that either.

'Who would like to go first, and win extra bravery points?' Linda twinkled merrily, in the manner of all perky sadists.

Delia's colleague Jules put her hand up.

'Right, so if we have the volunteer step onto this chair, and everyone else stands like so, with arms outstretched and linked, to create a net . . .' Roger said, suddenly Linda's helper. Delia betted he'd done that to distract from the fact he wouldn't be doing it, and risking them all dropping him.

Delia reluctantly joined the group who'd made a hammock with overlapped arms and winced at how embarrassing this was going to be. She was in a flared cotton skirt, what if it flew up when she flew down? She had a phantom shiver at the memory of aggressive, knicker-flashing birthday bumps at primary school. In fact, this situation bore uncanny resemblance – the pretence of positivity masking intent to humiliate, with no option to decline.

Nice, obliging Jules was helped onto the chair, and the desk.

She looked nervous. To be fair, everyone looked nervous; Jules had done Lighter Life last year and then relapsed badly.

Jules turned round, tried to lean back. Everyone tensed. She squealed: 'I can't let myself!'

'Harder than you think, isn't it!' trilled Linda, delightedly. 'It can be surprisingly difficult to let go.'

'It's not advisable to mimic fainting from furniture, is why,' Delia said. She knew she was getting herself into more trouble but she felt too mutinous to care.

Linda turned the swivel eyes of a fanatic upon her.

'Exactly! Unlearning our inhibitions is real work. De-inhibitisers bring us closer together: emotionally, socially, even spiritually.'

'I'm the only Christian,' Ann said.

'Spirituality can take many forms,' Linda said, sweetly.

'That stuff with the aliens that the actors do isn't religion,' Ann retorted. 'Jesus was the son of God, not the son of Zod.'

Linda looked confused and Delia found herself unexpectedly giggling at a bona fide Ann zinger.

After two false starts, Jules let herself drop backwards onto their arms, the slippery sweatiness among the interlinked hands palpable.

As Jules fell towards them, Delia had an awful premonition they'd fail her and she'd perish in the world's most ludicrously unnecessary death. Spin that, council.

As it was, they staggered slightly but they supported her with ease. Or, they thought they had, until a bloodcurdling scream was emitted.

At first, Delia thought it was Jules, but Jules was still horizontal, blinking up at them. She looked as frightened as everyone else.

As they set her on her feet, Delia turned to see Ann sat on a chair, holding her arm out in front of her, face contorted in a rictus of pain.

'My arm! My arm!'

'Heavens above, what's the matter?' Roger said.

'It's a fracture. I've not got the support bandage on today.'

Someone stepped forward to try to examine Ann and she let out another howl.

'Don't TOUCH IT!'

'What did you do to it?' Delia said.

'It got shut in a fire door in Chapel St Leonards,' Ann said. 'It's never been right since.'

Delia remembered that tale. The gruesome incident happened in 1989. Ann was only obsessed with expiry dates for food, obviously.

'Was I that heavy?' Jules said, quietly, and Delia said quickly, 'Not at all! Not even slightly! Ann has an old injury.'

Yeah, a sprain of the manners.

'Do you need First Aid?' Roger said to Ann.

'No, I am used to pain,' Ann said, with a whiff of burning martyr.

'Who's our next volunteer?' he said, trying to restore focus.

'Shouldn't you do exercises where I can take part?' Ann said, beady eyes on a wary Roger. His eyes were suddenly full of: *oh my God, I am going to be sued up the pipe on a discrimination and disability ticket*.

Delia nearly laughed out loud. Ann truly was a rattlesnake in a Per Una waterfall cardigan.

Roger went into hushed conference with Linda and when they concluded, Linda said: 'OK, we're going to move on to a great fun exercise, my favourite. We all tell everyone one fact about ourselves that the group doesn't know, for discussion! Here's mine, to kick you off. I've seen Del Amitri nearly fifty times in concert and am a founder member of a fan club, The Del Boys and Girls.'

'Never heard of them,' Ann said.

# Sixteen

After the excitement of Ann squawking, Delia's hot resentment of the team-building games returned with full force.

Then irritation turned to boredom. Feigning interest in a colleague's car-booting hobby or childhood sporting achievement wasn't easy.

As they discussed her diffident gay colleague Tim's trip to Reykjavik, Delia's mind roamed the room and wandered out of the window. And then – KABOOM – something suddenly burst into her front brain at the most inappropriate moment.

Like a music hall act leaping through the curtains with splayed jazz hands – *ta dah!* – while an audience sat in sepulchral silence.

It had happened in the first days of February, earlier this year. Paul had slung his fisherman's coat over the banister and Delia had seen a card in an inside pocket slide out. She wouldn't usually have been nosy, but she could spy a teddy bear face. It couldn't have been for Paul's nephews – Delia ran the birthday admin for him.

'What's that?' She'd tweaked it out, and found a Valentine's card, a tooth-rottingly sweet, teenage sort of one with teddies stood in a pyramid formation, their rounded bellies each carrying a letter B-E-M-Y-V-A-L-E-N-T-I-N-E.

Paul had blushed damson. Paul *never* blushed.

'For me? Aww! Getting slushy in your old age,' she teased him.

She'd thought it was odd – Paul thinking of Valentine's Day for once, the choice of that card. He sometimes came home with a bottle of Amaretto on the 14th of February, the choice of beverage in honour of their first meeting, but cards and flowers weren't Paul's way.

'I'll get you a different one. Not much of a surprise,' he'd demurred. Sure enough, Delia received Monet's lilies instead, although she insisted she liked the cheesy teddies.

Delia added the clues together. It had been for Celine. She had been getting romantic gestures long denied to Delia. And February to May: they'd been seeing each other longer than three months.

She felt as if she'd been disembowelled with a melon baller.

'Delia. Now you,' Roger said, turning to face her.

'What?' she said, blankly. It wasn't meant to be insolent; she just felt so howlingly empty. She thought it didn't matter that work didn't mean anything because home was everything. Now, she had nothing.

'Please tell everyone here a fact about you we don't know.'

Delia blinked. That they didn't know? Her life?

Her mouth was dry.

'Last Friday, I proposed to my boyfriend. Then he sent a text meant for another woman to me. It turned out he's been having an affair. We've split up.'

The circle of faces registered a mixture of fascination and astonishment.

'That's hardly appropriate,' Roger said, into the ensuing silence.

'You said something you don't know?' Delia said.

'Yes! Something we don't know. Not . . . that.'

'Was it meant to be something work related?' Delia said. She was in a space beyond caring about professional interests or social embarrassment. It was like that time on a campsite when she was so hideously ill with flu she didn't care about doing a noisy Portaloo poo.

'No!' Roger said.

She dispassionately noted that even though she wasn't trying to be clever, he looked wrong-footed and maybe even intimidated.

'It should be something innocuous. We don't need to know about your dirty laundry.'

*Dirty laundry?*

Delia swallowed and assessed her surroundings. This room, these people, this job. What was it all *for*, this putting up and shutting up and sucking up? Where did it get you?

'Well, that's bullshit. You asked for something personal you didn't know and I told you something. Now it's not good enough. Being cheated on isn't good enough either but I have to live with it. Don't play stupid "getting to know you" games and then complain about getting to know someone.'

Roger boggled. Everyone else sat bolt upright and poised, perfectly immobile, like Red Setter bookends. Linda looked like she'd been slapped. Ann was enthralled, having forgotten about her osteopathic agony.

'Here's something else you don't know about me. I'm leaving.'

Roger snorted. 'Then I need you to follow me upstairs and we'll discuss your notice period.'

'I've saved all my holiday for the honeymoon I'm not having any more, which is offset against my notice period. So I don't have a notice period. This is it.'

Silence.

Roger stared at Delia. The room's attention had now switched to him, like Centre Court at Wimbledon, to see his return volley. Roger pushed his glasses up his nose. He cleared his throat.

'The council has only just paid to send you on that health and safety course. We've nursed a viper at our breast.'

# Seventeen

Delia was going to call ahead and say 'Surprise! I've left my job and will be walking into our house at an unusual time of day,' then asked herself why she was doing it.

She didn't owe Paul the courtesy. In fact, who was Delia really protecting? If there was anything to interrupt, she needed to know. She didn't think Paul would risk doing it in their bed when she still had her key, but her parameters for what was or wasn't Paulness had changed.

Delia felt cold trepidation as she opened the front door, but there was no noise inside. No Parsnip to greet her, either. Paul must be walking him, or he'd taken him to the pub. Delia wondered if Celine had ever petted him, and the rage surged again. She'd be checking Parsnip's fur for any unfamiliar perfume.

Her phone beeped – a nervous text from Aled's partner Gina, asking if she was OK. *Too little, too late.* Delia fired off a brief reassurance that didn't invite more conversation.

Delia had asked herself what she'd have done if she'd had word of Aled cheating on Gina, and she decided she'd have insisted Aled tell her. She certainly couldn't have sat there with them and run double books. And condolences-wise, she wouldn't have limped in with a text, days after the fact, either. It would've been bringing a bottle and a box of pastries, and swearing, like a proper friend.

Delia avoided looking round the house, and bolted up the stairs. She heaved the largest trolley case out of the wardrobe, the dark blue one with the hummingbirds on it that Paul complained made him look unmanly in the arrivals and departures hall. A notional unmanliness, as they never went abroad. Parsnip's infirmity and the pub were powerful draws to stay home.

What should she pack? Delia started flinging underwear and clothes into the case. *Had she really left her job? Had the Paul shock made her manic? Was she going against the advice she'd heard more than once, about not making any major decisions in the first six months after a life-changing event?*

The front door banged and gave her a thunderclap of the heart. Paul was home, chatting to Parsnip. She heard their dog yap and do his usual three revolutions, chasing his own tail, before settling in his basket. Parsnip didn't so much sit down as let his legs collapse underneath him.

Delia paused over the suitcase. She knew Paul was staring at her discarded pink coat.

'Delia? Dee?' he shouted up the stairs.

She zipped the case and heaved it off the bed, her work bag on her shoulder. Along with everything she had in Hexham, this would do for now.

She pulled it along the first-floor landing as Paul bounded halfway up the stairs.

'Delia,' he said, line of sight dropping to the suitcase as he eyed her through the banister spindles.

He looked tired, with a shaving cut on his chin. He was wearing that grey John Smedley jumper that Delia bought him to match his grey eyes, but he wouldn't win any brownie points because of it.

'You're going to Hexham for longer?'

It was strange – Delia realised she hadn't definitely decided, until that moment. Seeing Paul standing there, she knew she had to leave Newcastle. There were so few certainties now, Delia had to rely on the rare convictions she had. She surprised herself with her resolve.

'I'm going to London.'

'What? For the weekend?'

'For the foreseeable future. I'm going to stay with Emma.'

'How long have you got off work?'

'I've left my job.'

'What?'

Paul's aghast expression was sour satisfaction. She could do surprises too.

'How come? Are you OK?'

'Because I got told off for how I run social media and participate in team-building events, and I needed to leave anyway. I haven't been OK since our anniversary.'

Delia left her luggage trolley for the bathroom raid, filling a toiletry bag with jars and tubes. Paul and his confusion loitered behind her.

'Do you not think we should talk before you move to the other end of the country indefinitely?'

'Do you?' Delia said. 'Is there new information?'

She zipped up the vinyl flowery wash bag, then did a mental inventory: favourite dresses, liquid eyeliner, laptop. Those were the can't-live-without essentials, she could buy anything else.

'We've been together ten years, yes, I think there is more to talk about.'

'So, talk,' Delia said. 'I'm going to call a taxi.'

She produced her mobile and booked one for 'as soon as possible' while Paul frowned.

'Come downstairs while you wait for it?' Paul said.

Before she could stop him, he'd darted round, got hold of her trolley case and bumped it down the staircase, standing it upright in the hall.

Delia followed him and bent down to pet Parsnip in his basket, making it quick so she didn't cry. She kissed the top of his head, rubbed his ears and inhaled his biscuity smell. He blinked baleful chocolate eyes and did what passed for a wonky Parsnip smile, before resuming snoring. Paul would take good care of him in the interim, she still trusted him that much.

'Are you leaving for good?' Paul asked, once Delia had made it clear she wouldn't be sitting down.

'I'm leaving for a while. I don't know how long,' Delia said.

'Does this mean you don't want to stay together?'

'All I know is, I can't live here with you for the time being.'

'. . . OK. Can I call you from time to time?'

'You still have my number.'

'You'll be looking for work in London?'

'Yes.'

'You'll probably be there for a while, then.'

Delia simply shrugged.

'Can I ask you some questions?' she said, after a short pause.

Paul nodded.

'When did you start seeing Celine?'

Paul coloured, instantly. 'As in a date . . .? I don't know . . .'

'You went on a date?' Delia said, to increase the discomfort, folding her arms.

'No. I mean as in, the day it started.'

'Was it before February this year?'

Paul frowned. 'No . . .?'

'Later, then?'

'Yeah. Like I said, about three months ago.'

'You bought a Valentine's card. I saw it, and you never gave it to me.'

Paul frowned. 'You saw one before you were meant to, so I had to buy another one. You still got one.'

'You never buy me Valentines' cards.'

'I know. It being the twentieth anniversary with my parents . . . it made me more sentimental than usual.'

If he was invoking his parents' death to get Delia to back down, it was the most craven gambit imaginable. If he wasn't? Delia's former feelings finally stirred.

'So, what date did you get together with Celine? I find it hard to believe that it wouldn't *stick out* in your memory.'

Paul ruffled his hair, shifted from foot to foot.

'Late March,' he said, gruffly.

'You know that, how?'

As with the text, Delia had the sense that Paul was trying to edit his reply to filter out sensitive content, but had no time.

'It was Mother's Day, the next day.'

'You said you never even noticed when it was Mother's Day. Did you go to the graves after all?'

She and Paul had a whole conversation about how he never celebrated Mothering Sunday when his mum was alive, so it had no particular meaning for him. They'd planned to do something for the anniversary of the crash, in November, though it had been fraught, discussing it with his brother. Michael felt differently about that date: he saw marking it as according importance to a senseless, horrible event.

Delia didn't know how it felt to lose your parents but suspected you never get to choose which dates in life are significant for you, bar your wedding.

'No. We talked about it. She asked if I had got my mum a gift.'

Ah. Now Delia got it. Paul's emotive orphaning had got Celine into bed? The idea that Paul might've seduced Celine occurred for the first time, and she couldn't believe she hadn't properly considered it before.

'Where did it happen, the first time? The store cupboard? It's your happy place.'

'No, I told you. I'd never . . . do that, in the pub. It was at hers.'

'She said, fancy a nightcap?'

'Not exactly. I was locking up on my own after that . . . and she came back. I was outside.'

'You went home with her, that easy?'

'It had been building up. Then there she was.'

'I need the words. I need to know what was said.'

Paul cast his eyes heavenwards and ground his teeth. 'Dee, I get this is the grimmest thing. Why torture yourself with the details? It doesn't matter. None of it matters.'

'It matters, because it's the only way I can start getting my head around how you could do this. It's such a mystery to me, I need to know how you went from "I don't shag twenty-four-year-olds I meet in my bar" to, "yeah sounds fun, whereabouts in Jesmond?"'

Delia hated how bitter he'd made her sound.

'She came up and said she couldn't stop thinking about me and we should do something about what was going on between us. She said you only live once.' He rattled it out.

Delia sensed what wasn't being said.

'She used your parents' deaths as an argument for why you should cheat on me? I assume she *knew* there was a me.'

'Yeah, not much, but she knew.'

'That is . . .' Delia shook her head, 'Tasteless isn't even the word, is it?'

'It sounds worse than it was. Pissed people talking nonsense . . .'

113

'Nonsense that was good enough to see you going back with her.'

'Yes.'

Paul looked beat. Not much hope of polishing the turd.

'And that was enough, what she said?'

'In that moment, yes. It was a *take the red pill, follow this thing and see where it leads*. It was about risk taking, I guess.'

'Was it monkey sex?'

'What?'

Paul looked befuddled.

'Was it wild? Give me some idea of what you did.'

'It was sex. Plain, average sex.'

'Who on top?'

Paul's jaw tightened further.

'Her on top.'

Delia's stomach contracted.

'Lights on? Off?'

'Off. Well, she had some of those lights on a string, they were on.'

Delia felt the triumphant sizzle of being proven right.

'Why did Aled say he talked you out of a trip to Paris?'

'I honestly have no idea,' Paul said, visibly relieved at being allowed his own anger at last. 'I'd already finished with Celine by the time I spoke to him about it. If he ever answered my calls, believe me, we'd have words.'

Outside, there was the roll of a car's engine and a beep.

'Look, Delia . . .'

'What's Celine's last name?' Delia said, to cut Paul off.

'Roscoe. Why?'

114

'In case I ever need to know,' Delia said. 'Look after Parsnip.'

She reclaimed her luggage trolley and flew out the front door before Paul could persuade her to stay. Before she could see her dog wake up, before she could look around and think about what she was leaving behind, possibly forever.

Halfway to Hexham, her phone pinged.

*I got you the Valentines card on impulse, thinking about how much my mum would've liked you. Please come home. Px*

# *Eighteen*

In that moment between sleep and wakefulness where you remember who you are, where you are and what you do, Delia spent longer than usual arranging all the pieces. It made a strange picture.

As the sun leaked through her bedroom blinds and she sensed she'd slept beyond nine, Delia felt the weightless weirdness of having no job to go to.

She imagined her old desk with the pink Post-its framing the computer screen, the photo of Parsnip in the paddling pool no longer there. Life continuing without her. Delia felt oddly bereft – it'd be strange not to, she thought, after seven years at the same office.

Then she thought of how Ann would still be wailing about her arm and Roger glowering at her, and told herself better late to leave than never. She had no wedding to be saving for, any more. Someone else could do battle in the middle ground between the Naan and Roger.

She'd had a big glass of red before she told her parents the night before, and gave them some white lies. *Her boss had known of her intentions for a while, everyone was fine with it.* She had savings, she reminded them. The wedding fund was a pretty healthy size, in fact.

Nevertheless, their uneasy expressions communicated: *Should we be paying more attention to you? Are you unravelling before our eyes?*

For all her efforts to act casual, obviously most people who moved from one end of the country to the other didn't usually make the decision in the space of an afternoon. Or go the next day.

Delia got herself together for a mid-afternoon departure, thinking, at least hanging around workless in Newcastle is of short duration.

She knocked and pushed her head round Ralph's door.

'See you later. I'm off to London to stay with Emma for a bit.'

'Cool. Go to Big Ben!'

'Is it a favourite spot of yours?'

'It's where they fight the Ultranationalists in *Call of Duty: Black Ops II.*'

Delia laughed.

'You could come visit me, while I'm there?'

Ralph shrugged and made non-committal noises. Ralph didn't travel. Neither did her parents. There was an annual tussle to get them all to come into Newcastle city centre for a birthday. Last time they went to a nice restaurant, her mum had complained at the plate having 'cuckoo spit and frogspawn' on it.

'Wait. Take this,' Ralph said, rummaging around his

fold-up sofa and producing a slightly crushed box of Fondant Fancies.

She gave him a hard hug and a kiss on his soft cheek and didn't meet his eye.

Her dad was in the kitchen, having a cup of tea as her mum bustled around finding the car keys. Delia got the feeling she'd been spoken of, before she entered the room.

'Off then, Dad! See you soon.'

He gave her a kiss on the cheek and then held out two twenty-pound notes.

'Oh no, no no,' Delia said, as her throat and stomach tightened. 'I've got plenty of cash, Dad, honestly.'

'You might want a sandwich when you get there,' her dad said, and Delia realised he'd feel better if she took it.

'Be careful. London's full of thieves and chancers, and they'll see you're a nice girl.'

It was such a kindly fatherly idea that London would see anything about Delia at all, before it spat her back her out again.

Delia smiled and nodded.

'So you're staying with Emma?'

'Yes.'

'She lives on her own?'

'Yes.'

'You're not . . .' he hesitated. 'There's not a young man involved, is there?'

It was so unexpected a question that Delia had to stop herself snorting.

'Of course not!'

She looked at her mum, who was fussing with her handbag and avoiding Delia's eyes. This was what they'd come up with, in their concern. She was chasing a boy.

'I promise you, there's nothing to this but needing to get away for a while. I've barely seen Emma in the last few years, let alone had time to get to know anyone else.'

Her father nodded. As they hustled out of the hallway, her dad huffing and puffing, holding her case at waist height – fathers didn't acknowledge the wheels on trolley cases, they had to be picked up – Delia felt sodden with guilt for worrying them like this.

Her mum drove her to the station in the old Volvo, with Delia anxiously trying to play down the whole unemployed peril with nonsensical chatter. If she talked fast enough, surely her mum wouldn't notice.

'This whole break Paul and I are having, it was the right moment,' she said, hoping echoing Emma would be the charm.

'You're moving to London permanently?' her mum asked, timidly. Her parents pretty much never lost their tempers or exerted their will. Something in their quiet forbearance was so much more shame-inducing than any shouting or outright disapproval.

It was a good question. It gave Delia stomach snakes. It'd been her right to be vague with Paul, not with her mum.

'No! I don't know. It's more to get away from things for a while.'

The parental relationship loop: fibbing to protect them

from worry, and them sensing being fibbed to, and worrying. The truth — that she had no idea what she was
doing — would be more worrying, so Delia had no choice.

On the train she sat next to a short old man in a bulky
coat, who started a conversation about pollution, which
Delia politely tolerated, while wishing she could listen to
her iPod.

As they got to Northallerton, he pointed to the tracks
and said: 'See those pigeons?'

'Yes . . .?'

'Pigeons know more than they're letting on.'

'Do they?' Delia said.

'Think they carried all those messages and never read
any of them?' the man said, incredulously.

Delia said she was going to the buffet car and switched
carriages.

Arriving in London, she taxied from King's Cross to
Finsbury Park and told herself she'd definitely economise
from tomorrow onwards. It was late, she was tired, and full
of Fondant Fancies, cheese toastie, acidic G&T and a mini
tube of Pringles, all picked at in nerves and boredom.

As Delia left the station, the evening air in the capital
smelled unfamiliar: thick, warm, petrol-fumed. She was hit
by a wave of home sickness so hard it was in danger of
washing her away.

# *Nineteen*

Emma's flat was the first floor of one of those haughty, draughty Victorian houses with drama in its high ceilings and cold in its bones. There were bicycles crammed under the plaster arch in the narrow hallway, and subsiding piles of mail for the various residents stacked on a cheap side table by the radiator.

It was a leafy, residential street, yet still felt slightly overrun and run down.

Delia had warned herself not to be shocked by the space that a wage as intergalactic as Emma's could buy here. But she still was.

She bumped her case up the steep worn-carpeted stairs to the door that separated Emma's territory from the rest of the building and knocked. Music was humming on the other side and she hoped she wasn't arriving into a cocktail party. She didn't feel up to meeting the London society yet.

The door was flung open and all five foot three of Emma Berry filled it to the jambs, in a pale green party dress with circle skirt, pointy salmon satin heels and bouffanted Marilyn-blonde hair. Despite constantly bemoaning imaginary obesity, she had one of those Tinkerbell figures where any weight gained went to the pin-up places.

'Hey there, Geordie girl!' she sing-songed.

Delia grinned 'Hello!' and did an awkward fingertips-only wave, with her luggage.

There was some fussing and clucking as Emma tried to reach round and take Delia's case on the vertiginous steps and it became obvious Delia would probably be killed in the attempt. Emma shuffled back into the flat to allow Delia to make a very laborious entry instead.

'I'm not interrupting anything, am I?' Delia said.

'No, I was waiting for you! I admit I possibly started on the booze a bit early. Let me get a hug at you! This is so ridiculously exciting.'

Emma smelled of gardenias and her dress had watery silver sparkles across knife pleats. It rustled with the crispness of new and expensive fabric as Delia leaned in. To Delia's fairly expert eye, it was not of the high street.

'I can't believe you're here!' Emma squealed and then it settled in both their faces that it was incredibly well-meant but possibly not the most tactful thing to say.

Delia replied: 'Neither can-fucking-I,' and they laughed, breaking the tension.

'It's going to be so great.'

Because Delia couldn't share her confidence but didn't want to offend with a lack of enthusiasm, she said: 'Your dress is spectacular.'

'It's a Marchesa design.'

Delia gasped. 'Like the Oscar dresses?!'

'It's a replica I got on Etsy for a song. It smells a bit dodgy. So I've covered it in Marc Jacobs,' Emma said. 'The hair's backfired a bit too,' she said, stroking it. 'I was going for Doris Day bubble flip, I think it's more New Jersey mob wife.'

Delia giggled.

'Do you want the tour? It takes less than two minutes.'

'Yes!'

Delia followed Emma — noisy on the hard floors in her clippy-cloppy shoes — around the flat. It was so very Emma to dress up for Delia's arrival.

Delia's weary soul gave a little sigh of relief that the flat was nothing like as ragtag and anonymous as the hallway downstairs.

In fact it was tiny, but beautiful. The floorboards were stripped and varnished Golden Syrup yellow, and the doors were an artfully washed out, distressed chalky aqua with Mercury glass handles.

The bathroom screamed 'no man lives here' — a white roll-top, claw-foot bath, Oriental silk dressing gown on a print block hook, thick white towels, a pile of water-wrinkled glossy fashion magazines. And one of those free-standing glass bowl sinks that look like a giant's contact lens.

'You've done all this?' Delia said, in awe.

'Nah, have I bollocks. The last girl had good taste and massive budget. Do not piss your money away on something that isn't broke, I say. It cost me enough to buy it. I've run a J cloth over it and that's it.'

The front room was another stunner – vaulting ceiling with original plaster rose and ruby-red Murano chandelier dangling from it, deep emerald velvet L-shaped sofa and huge, trailing swathes of Liberty print curtains.

Delia had a little covetous pang about a girls' place. Paul mostly gave her free rein, but drew the line at 'busy fussy old teashop spinster' patterns.

'Where's your . . . things?' Delia said, nailing what had confused her. It was as clutter-free as a photo shoot.

'Got rid of things from Haggerston and stored a load with my parents back near Bristol.'

Slight worry still tickled at Delia. *Emma was clearly never here.*

They thundered up the small flight of hollow wooden stairs leading to the sleeping quarters. Delia was braced for the spare room to be the size of a margarine tub. Actually, it was well proportioned and there wasn't much between it and Emma's room – the main difference being Delia's had a futon, while Emma's had a wrought-iron princess bed. Both filled the floor space, leaving room for a shallow wardrobe only.

Emma had propped a framed print of David Bowie on the cover of *Low* on the spare-room windowsill. 'Do you still like him? To make you feel at home.'

'Oh, Emma, thank you! It's all amazing.'

'It'll do,' she agreed. 'Given it's broken me for savings.'

Emma had wealthy parents and even wealthier grandparents, the latter having obligingly pegged and left six-figure sums to her and her sister right when they wanted to get on the property ladder. It was still only a third of the cost of this flat, Delia guessed. The sums made her dizzy.

Emma led Delia into the kitchen last, which was a sleek white gloss space-agey fitted affair, with yet more sea green as accent colour.

A large twisty modern halogen light fitting, like a pipe cleaner animal made of a tungsten filament, hung low over the rustic wooden table in the centre. It was covered with dozens of foil trays of food with cardboard lids.

'I got Thai,' Emma said. 'I didn't know how hungry you'd be so I ordered everything. And I've got fizzy! I don't have an ice bucket though.'

She lifted a bottle of Taittinger out of a washing-up bowl full of ice cubes and slopped it into a wine glass.

'This fuss for me?!' Delia said.

'Who else would I make more fuss for? To Delia Moss's London adventure!' she said, and Delia accepted the glass and toasted.

Delia didn't think she'd be having any adventure, nor did she much feel like one. But she felt so grateful, and humbled, because she'd managed to forget how fun her best friend was. Or 'a certified loon', as Paul had always said, fondly.

Emma had this hedonistic knack for making life more exciting. It wasn't to do with her income; she'd been the same at university.

She was the person who produced cheap seats in the

gods to a Shakespeare matinee that afternoon, and had been to a market and bought a whole octopus for dinner, its tentacles waving out of the bag. Or came back from the bar with a surprise round of Sambuca sidecars in espresso cups. (Her capacity for any intoxicant was fairly legendary.)

The odd thing was, if you tried to replicate an Emma gesture at a later date, it was never quite the same. There was something in her spontaneous, generous joie de vivre that made it entirely of the moment, and it lost something in efforts to copy it. An Emma idea lived only once and shimmered briefly, like a sandcastle, or a rainbow.

Or in this case, *pork larb*, *khao pad* and massaman curry.

Takeaway food, foaming alcohol, cackling laughter, and Delia's surroundings made sense. Her appetite had come back.

After half an hour, she knew she was soaring high on the back of the eagle of booze and would no doubt crash hard on to the rocks of a hangover, but she didn't care.

As the night wore on, Delia and Emma slumped side by side on the sofa, Emma occasionally reaching down to top up glasses from the third bottle.

'We won't finish it, obviously,' she'd said, solemnly, shortly before firing the cork at the chandelier with a soft *phut*. 'That would be madness.'

By the time it was pushing midnight, they'd covered Delia's exit from the council, and Emma's ill-fated entanglement with pitiless but vigorous Richard from Insolvency and Restructuring.

'Rick the Dick, as he's known to the secretaries. Sadly

with that nickname, I got the wrong end of the stick, literally and figuratively.'

And Emma's sister's forthcoming giant folly of a wedding.

'Ten days in Rome for the hen, Delia! *Ten days*! Count them! They add up to ten.'

'But you're all for that non-stop party stuff,' Delia said, holding her glass out for a refill, loving being the Delia she was with Emma again.

'Not with Tamsin's friends I'm not,' Emma said, twisting the bottle away expertly before the glass frothed over, 'Like Salem's Lot, in Joules Breton tops and Hunter wellies. I was hoping for Bath tearooms and a spa, two nights, in and out. Everyone knows what happens on hens, you get wasted on the first night and phone in your performance on the second. Imagine doing that as rinse-repeat for *ten days*. Ugh.'

Delia laughed. Emma topped her own glass up. Like a proper friend, Emma had clearly sensed that Delia needed time to work up to discussing Paul.

'Do you think you'll go back to him?' she asked, eventually.

'I don't know. Maybe, yes. When the rage at the thought of him with Celine has subsided. If it ever does.'

'*Celine*,' Emma said, trying it out. 'Oof. He could've at least been poking a Hilda. Or an Ethelred.'

'Ethelred's a man's name, isn't it?'

'Exactly.'

Delia was reminded of the calming effect of someone not doing what they were supposed to, like Ralph.

'Any idea why he did it? I mean, *because sex*. Paul doesn't seem the type though.'

'I think he wanted to try it out, take a risk. We'd been together for ten years.'

Delia hated herself a little for sounding as if she was making excuses for him. She tried a different tack. Total honesty.

'You know something I never admitted to myself, until now? I made it easy for Paul when we got together. I knew that if it was hard, he might not have bothered.'

'What do you mean?'

'He was never that crazy about me . . .'

'Oh that's not true!'

Delia took a deep breath. She'd always shoved this knowledge into a cupboard and shut the door on it, and Paul's affair now brought the contents cascading out.

'It is, Em. I don't mind, or I didn't. I know he loved me, and he liked my company, and he fancied me enough. It was fine, we still had a great life. But that extra-special thing that makes you lie awake and watch someone sleep in the early days, or want to kill your rivals with your bare hands? That kind of passion, it's never been there for him, like it was for me. I wanted Paul, so I built it all around him. It's why I was so good about him spending all hours at the pub. It was going to be the same way with the wedding. He only had to show up and say his lines.'

'That's Delia-ish caringness. You'd be that way with anyone.'

'I wasn't trying that hard with men before Paul, though.

I usually had the upper hand.' Delia swiped her travel-greasy fringe out of her eyes, 'Am I allowed to say I was quite a bit in demand, now it's so long ago?'

'You completely were,' Emma said. 'I remember in the union bar when you wore your hair in those buns which had all the boys sighing. You were one of those manic pixie dream girls. Without being a twat with a ukulele.'

What was different about Paul? It was his wasn't-much-fussed nature, the carelessness. It made Delia determined: you WILL notice me, you WILL want me.

'Maybe Paul being half-hearted is why I wanted him so badly. How messed-up is that? I knew I had to strive for him. I was so demented about winning him over, I never considered if I wanted to be with someone who needed convincing.'

The truth of the last line landed heavy. Delia felt depressed. Accepting she'd got something so vital wrong filled her full of regret. Would she wish the last ten years away? No. She should've walked into them and through them with her eyes open, though. She encouraged Paul's complacency.

'I never thought of you as unequal,' Emma said, adjusting the stem of her glass on her glamorously girdled stomach. The shoes had long been kicked off, her flesh-coloured tights pouching at her toes.

'We weren't in a day-to-day way. But his house was my house. His lifestyle was my life. His friends were mine. Parsnip is the only truly joint project we've ever had, come to think of it.'

'You feel like now you've thought this, you can't un-think it?'

'Kind of. I have to face it and it has to change, if we're ever going to be together again.' Delia absently touched the edge of her glass against her lips, in contemplation. 'You know all the things you never have to ask yourself, because you *know*? In your gut?' she said. 'This might sound odd but whenever I popped into the bar unexpectedly, Paul always looked pleased. Instantly. You know that split second when you can't disguise how you feel? Like when you see someone you know in the street at the same time, and you think "Oh shit now we have to chat" and you both see it on each other's faces, just for a moment? Paul never did that with me, not even through the Celine months.'

'Maybe he's always pleased to see you. As they say.'

'Yeeaah, but never to show any concern I might run into the other woman? It turns out he's also really good at lying to me. That's what I can't un-think. I'm not sure I know him as well as I thought I did. It's almost like, if I suspected, it'd be easier. Now I think, it could all happen again. Because I didn't spot one clue.'

'You and Paul had a good life together though. I know it's tempting to see everything through this massive mistake, but it doesn't undo everything you have together.'

'I know. All I can do is wait to see how I feel after time's passed.'

Emma nodded.

'And another thing,' Delia said, conscious she didn't want to alarm or cast judgement on Emma's singleness, 'I have to accept that if I don't go back to Paul, I might not meet someone else who wants a family in time.'

'Yeah,' Emma sighed. 'I can't lie to you, dating over thirty is full of that fear. Sometimes I worry I'm too fussy. I mean, look at Dan. I got bored, but maybe that was my fault.'

'Which one was Dan?'

'The one with the rich family in Hertfordshire who turned out to have the raging coke habit that day at the races.'

'Oh yeah,' Delia said, not sure she remembered him. Wealthy drug taker and a trip to Ascot wasn't really pinning it down in Emma's romantic CV.

'The cocaine might've been a problem if you'd spawned.'

'I know. But compared to the usual idiots I meet, he wasn't a git. He was pleasant. He was . . . benign.'

'Tumours can be benign.'

'That is so fucking deep! Write that down,' Emma said.

After so much chatter they lay in peace on the sofa, watching a small breeze move the curtains, listening to an argument taking place outside the flat between a taxi driver and his fare. It was like being back in halls again.

'You know what annoys me?' Emma mumbled. 'When people act as if not having your personal life sorted out by our age is some sort of failure of paying attention. Like if you want it, you can automatically have it. As if it isn't mostly down to luck. We've both gone at it in different ways and here we both are. On my sofa.'

'On your sofa,' Delia agreed.

'I read this interview the other day. You know that blonde woman . . .'

'That blonde woman?'

'You know. Used to do that telly thing in the nineties, I forget. She was all "Women should remember that they're less fertile after thirty-five and remember to get pregnant by then." Remember?!' Emma roared. 'Yeah thanks, it had totally slipped my mind. And where did I put that perfect father material partner? Must have left him in the pub with my umbrella. What a shitcranker.'

Delia laughed. Not for the first time, she imagined Emma as a formidable opponent in a boardroom.

'Don't you need to get to bed?' Delia said, twisting her watch round.

'I'll inject Costa Americanos. Two of them and I'm riverdancing these days. No major meetings tomorrow. And, on the subject of the opposite sex: I have to share something so awful it can only be with my best friend,' Emma continued. 'Rick the Dick did this freaky thing. Oh God it's so awful I can't even tell you! I'm not exaggerating when I say it's the worst thing to ever happen to anyone ever.'

'You said that when you were bought gift vouchers for Zara Home and couldn't swap them to Zara fashion.'

'Worse even that that.'

'Did he bring out spiky toys? Like a rubber prickly pear?'

'When he reached his . . . conclusion, he said stupid stuff.'

'What, dirty talk?'

'Kind of . . .'

'You filthy slut, dirty whore, sort of thing?'

'No, I could've coped with that! It was surreal, irrelevant.'

'I'm not sure I get what you mean . . .?' Delia said.

'He came out with nonsense-speak. Gibberish. I can't tell you!' Emma covered her face with her arms and her voice came through muffled. 'I let this man into my bed, I'm implicated.'

Delia sat upright.

'Emma Berry, tell me what he said!'

'The first time he said "*Fuerteventura*!"'

'What?' Delia sat stunned, then clapped a hand over her mouth. 'Ahahahaha . . .'

'Another time it was "*Drambuie!*" The worst was,' Emma was hyperventilating in the attempt to get the words out now, '"*Charles Dickens!*"'

She did an overbite face when she said the words. Delia was utterly destroyed, face down in the cushions, shaking with whole-body laughter.

'Did you ask him why?' Delia gasped, face wet with tears.

'How could I? Why did you mention the greatest novelist of the Victorian period when you spaffed?'

They collapsed into more howling and weeping.

'Must be some very specific form of Tourettes,' Delia said, wiping under her eyes. Why did laughter with Emma feel so therapeutic? She wanted to send Richard a thank you note. Signing off: *Emily Bronte*

There was a pause, where they watched lights from

passing cars strobe across the darkened room and sigh-giggled, pondering the mysteries of love and relationships. Delia opened her mouth and thought she might be about to give birth to a profound thought.

'Where do I go from here? I can't date. I mean, thongs have come back in, for God's sake. I look like my dad in a thong.'

# Twenty

As she woke in the eerie stillness of the empty flat, an incredibly saddening thought occurred to Delia. She lay on the futon, examining the cobwebbed nooks and gulleys of a ceiling that didn't belong to her.

She and Emma had talked about falling in love the night before and Delia had relived that gut-wrenching sense of your world pivoting around one person. She'd only ever had this strength of feeling lopsidedly with Paul, so the chances of doing it all again, and fully reciprocally, seemed slim.

It was very possible, she thought, that it was only a feature of your twenties. When you had time, self-obsession and innocence enough to make heartsick compilations of *please sleep with me* songs and stare forlornly out of rain-spattered windows.

Your twenties were a time when you were passionate about being on the brink of blending with another soul. And going at it like weasels being suffocated in a pillowcase.

But in your mid-thirties? It was hardly old. Yet you were considerably less open to it all. It *wasn't your first bar mitzvah,* as Emma liked to say. The ratio of head to heart was going to change, because you could spot potential problems and predict outcomes a lot more clearly.

You'd plan embarking on a serious relationship more like buying a house – undertaking searches of the structural solidity, haggling over the price of acquisition.

She and Paul had dated because he liked her legs and her sense of humour, and she liked his smile and his charisma. Everything else they could figure out later.

Nowadays, maybe he'd want to know how soon she wanted kids and she'd want to know if the bar was bought with a bank loan. He'd wonder if her office job and love of soft furnishings meant she'd nag him about late nights; she'd fret about whether his love of parties was a sign of a perpetual man-child.

Ack. Delia had a stern word with herself.

It's half nine: stop wallowing, get up and face the day. You're bound to be blue, booze is always a depressant.

In the quiet of the flat, she padded to the kitchen and switched the kettle on. A set of keys sat on top of a note.

*SO MY HEAD FEELS SHOCKING. That champagne must have been corked* ☹ *Have a lovely day, it's the two gold keys for the Yale lock and the one below. If Carl downstairs asks who you are say you're only visiting. You'll know who he is, he looks like a boil in the bag Michael Barrymore. E X*

Delia's work bag was in the hallway. She found it and slid her laptop out, setting it up on the dining-room table.

There was an item of business she'd been putting off but

it needed doing, a strange twenty-first century necessity. She opened her Facebook page. Her profile picture was one of her and Paul on holiday in the Yorkshire Dales. She was grinning into the lens, Paul was pulling a face as if he'd fallen asleep on her shoulder. In the upper right-hand corner of the shot, a cow could be seen defecating. A proper raised tail action spurt.

It was funny, unplanned and perfect, and it had to go. Delia wasn't going to change her relationship status for now, and suffer a barrage of inquiries from the nosy. But she couldn't have herself presenting a perfect united front with Paul online either.

She uploaded her new picture. It was Delia as a toddler: still with ginger fringe, plus bunches. She was wearing her dad's carpentry goggles as a superhero mask and her mum's daisy wedding veil as a cape, standing serious-faced in the middle of the kitchen floor, looking up at the parent photographing her.

She flipped her profile to the new image and sat with chin propped on palm, gazing at it. Little Delia. What did she want for herself, and how much of it did she achieve?

Her Facebook inbox showed a message. She clicked on it and saw, with a spike of adrenaline, it was from Peshwari Naan. From a Peshwari Naan Facebook account, with a naan as a profile picture.

OK, now she was scared. In the seclusion of the flat, she felt her heart rate leap and skin crawl.

*Hi Delia. Please don't think I'm stalking you, you're easy to find on here. You've gone very quiet on your work email and*

*I wondered why? Sorry if the anal bleaching jokes were a step too far. PN.*

Delia read and re-read as her heart rate slowed. She didn't like this man pursuing her. Nevertheless, she was being given a chance to vent some spleen.

*The reason I'm quiet is, I left my job. Partly because of the trouble you caused, which I got blamed for. Please don't bother me on my personal account. Cheers. Delia.*

Delia checked his profile. It was anonymous and had no friends listed – it had obviously set up purely to message her. She felt some nerves return before thinking: he surely won't hunt me down here.

She drummed her fingertips, made another cup of tea and waited for the response. Her mind wandered to other things and other people.

A terrible, terrifying, yet irresistible prospect suddenly raised itself. She had the full name now. Delia tapped it into the Search For People field, feeling giddy and hoping it'd return no matches.

'Celine Roscoe' came up instantly. There was only one, and the line of biography Delia saw made it clear she'd found the right one: *student at University of Newcastle.*

The profile picture was of a lightly tanned girl with amazing legs in jelly shoe sandals, sat on the floor, pretending to drink from a giant inflatable bottle.

Delia breathed hard, smelling so much danger and

competition from that tiny thumbnail image. Sylphlike beauty, youth, high spirits, confidence. Delia had wondered if she simply wasn't enough fun for Paul any more? Seeing Celine made it fully real.

She clicked through to the page, again hoping that Celine would have tight privacy settings that saved Delia from herself. She didn't want to know and equally she had to see everything. Sadly, Celine had virtually no padlocks. Delia could see her photo albums, her status updates, everything.

A sick, ugly compulsion gripped Delia. She hammered through picture after picture, update after update, in determination and increasing pain. The virtual version of cross-hatching her inner arm.

Celine was beautiful. Not perfectly, conventionally so, but that only made her more compelling. Delia could quite easily see how Paul had fallen under her spell. She had rich dark chocolate hair, a long, aquiline nose, slanted eyes ringed with kohl, and a swipe of claret lipstick.

Her figure – this made Delia feel almost lightheaded with jealousy, imagining it unclothed, wound round her boyfriend – was naturally slender and graceful. She looked like the lines of a fashion designer's sketch.

But most of all, Delia felt threatened by the attitude. The larky, humorous, totally-at-ease-in-her-own-skin swagger. Every single image brimmed with the subtext: SCREW YOU, I SCREWED HIM.

Had Celine ever looked Delia up too? She must have done. What did she think of her? Did she ever feel guilty?

Then, combing the comments on her page, she saw something that stopped her breathing. Someone asked Celine if she was bringing her 'boyfriend' to a house party.

Another person had said 'C's boyfriend is MR MYSTERY.' Celine had replied NO COMMENT, and it had 11 Likes. *Eleven.* A dozen people who knew the owner of the bar was sleeping with her on the side. Delia was a laughing stock among strangers.

*Boyfriend*? Celine considered Paul her boyfriend?

Delia jumped up and leaned over the sink, holding her hair to one side. Emma's lovely deep Bristol sink wasn't meant for vomiting at ten a.m. She heaved, twice.

*Turn it off turn it off turn it off*, she told herself. Finding Newcastle's spectres on the internet is not healthy or helpful. You're in London – you can step outside that door and see no one you know. You're safe.

As she went to close the laptop screen, she saw Peshwari Naan had replied.

*Seriously?! Oh my God, I am so so sorry. I had no idea you'd get in trouble for anything I was doing, it was a bit of fun, I thought. Please tell me if there's anything I can do to put this right. Burning with shame and guilt. Honestly, sincere apologies. PN.*

Delia thought for a moment.

*If you mean 'anything', then I'd like to know how you tracked me down in the first place. And who you are.*

# Twenty-One

Delia was lonely in the following week. She was surprised by how much, before she reminded herself: no shit, you lost your partner and your job, you left your home and dog, and have moved to a city of over eight million people where you know only one person.

Wake up and smell the . . . well, the Café Direct java roast and the interestingly barbecue-smoky pollution, which she was slowly growing accustomed to. The aroma of so many bodies and vehicles and buildings packed into such a tight space.

Less easy to accept was the stark reality of Emma's schedule, which took Delia aback. Delia was barely awake at the hour Emma left the flat, and she routinely fell through the door at gone nine in the evening.

Delia shopped for food and flowers, prepared things that kept in the oven well like stews or moussaka, lit tealights in the Moroccan-style lanterns and waited. And waited. Did lots of waiting.

On arrival, Emma would try to look suitably thrilled when she could obviously only cope with warm bowl on lap, cold glass pushed into hand, small talk and hot bath before the whole process started again.

Meanwhile Delia, after eagerly awaiting her return all day, desperately tried not to irritate with her need for attention and chatter. It was like being a housewife in the 1950s.

She was also getting a crash course in speaking 'London'. Emma had amusing but obscure rants about the difficulties of life in the capital. It contained all kinds of knotty practical problems to do with travel and parking spaces that Delia hadn't contemplated, and the tribal rivalry was a surprise. It wasn't one city, it seemed. It was five or six soldered together, and they all disliked and mistrusted each other.

Take Emma's friend who was having a flat-warming in Brockley – something which was apparently catastrophic. It was as if Emma was discussing the Uruk-Hai of Isengard, as opposed to residents of South London.

'Brockley!' she said, waving a fork over her goat's cheese and spinach pie with homemade puff pastry. 'I work in west London. How the hell do I get to Brockley? It's not on the Tube! The *bus*? Me, at my time of life, a bus!'

'How do people in Brockley get into London?' Delia asked.

'The overground,' Emma said, with a shudder. 'Brockley sounds like it should be in Kent, which it practically is. Do you want to come?'

'Maybe another time.'

Delia didn't feel up to meeting new people. But she was surprised to find she had two non-physical friends keeping her company in her first fortnight. Firstly, Peshwari Naan. He'd replied. She'd softened.

*How I tracked you – remember like explaining any magic trick, it's always a let-down. I set up a Googlewhack. PN*

*A what? I appreciate the irony that I could Google it. D*

*It's a unique combination of words hidden in a site that means any search for those words will bring up one result. I guessed I might be looked up online. Once you'd hit my blog, an IP trace showed that the visit was from council HQ. Boom. PN*

Ah: Delia remembered the odd blog with its gibberish copy and thought, yes, this checks out. However, the *Found You!* email came direct to Delia. She knew very little about the mechanics and specifics of IP traces, but Delia knew enough to know it wouldn't tell the Naan it came from the computer of the redhead in the pinafore, to the left of the angry woman with knobbly feet.

*But how did you know that was me in particular? Also, you didn't tell me who you are? D*

*The answers to these questions are connected. Go on. One guess and then I'll tell you. PN*

Delia was glad of the chance, that day, to think about something other than Celine's photo album 'Gurlllls Go To Crete 2011 aaaaargggh' and its plethora of bikini shots.

She pondered. The Naan identifying her must be

something to do with her trip to Brewz and Beanz. That's how he'd know it was her. Yet he recognised her? The council website didn't have headshots of the press office staff.

Aha! Her original theory returned.

*Wait. You know me. Which means I know you?! D*

*4.5/5! I don't know you as such. I know 'of' you. I know you always wear a good dress to the Christmas party, and don't like fruit in salads. (Buffet small talk.) (I once hinted that we'd had this conversation! Amazingly enough, I don't think I stuck in your mind.) And yes, thanks to the Googlewhack tripwire, I knew to be wary at Brewz that day. Didn't go in. You shouldn't have sat by the window. Surveillance 101. PN*

*Oh my GOD. I can't believe you work at the council! D*

*Neither can I. PN*

*So why the trolling, the mayhem, the havoc, the antagonism towards the council? D*

*Because I work at the council. PN*

In the quiet of Emma's kitchen, Delia laughed out loud at her laptop screen.

*Haha! You really hate it that much? D*

*It's not hate-hate. I have a low boredom threshold – idle hands, the devil, and all that. Truth be told, I never meant to make it a regular thing. Once I heard the councillors were getting their pants in a bunch, I couldn't resist carrying on. I'm like that. If there's mischief to be made online, I often make it. PN*

*But what about your job if you'd been caught???! D*

*I'm never caught at the scene, I'm like Macavity the Mystery Cat. With broadband. But I def went too far, not least as it came back on you. I never meant it to get nasty, in my head it was only anarcho-lols. Sorry again. PN*

*Oh, no worries. Which department are you in? D*

*Would you mind if we didn't divulge those details right now? I know you say you've left. For all I know, you're on annual leave and this is some new stage of the press office investigation ☺ Sorry again if you've left though. PN*

Delia relaxed. She believed him. This was someone who'd been chancing his arm, he wasn't outright dangerously reckless.

*Hah! OK. Though I am sure Detective Donkey Saddle could easily check I've definitely left. D*

*. . . Donkey Saddle? PN*

*A big naan! You never heard that description before? My fiancé always used it. (I say fiancé, he was only engaged to me for an evening before I found out he'd been shagging someone else. Is an ex-fiancé still an ex-fiancé if they were only your fiancé for under an hour? If a tree falls in a forest, etc. etc.) D PS Can't believe I don't remember you.*

*As I said, I'm not very memorable TBH. Sorry about the former fiancé, sounds a fool if you don't mind me saying. PN*

*I'm sat here looking at the profile of the girl he was/is sleeping with on here. You can say anything you like, frankly. D*

*Do you want me to erase her Facebook account? Because I can do that. PN*

*Can you?! D*

*You'd have to give me a War Command room, some tin soldiers to push round a map, a set of marker pens, a flipchart, and a box of Krispy Kremes. I'd probably penetrate Zuckerberg's fortress full of flip flop-wearing douchebags in Palo Alto in a week. He said, modestly. Hey, I have plenty to be modest about, otherwise. PN*

*If you're so good at computers, why not work for GCHQ or the FBI? D*

*Ah. That'd be lack of confidence and motivation, and doggy paddle being easier than the deep end. Then getting to an age where doggy paddle is all you do. (An ancient 31.) PN*

*I'm 33 so shut your filthy mouth!* ☺ *D*

She wasn't usually so rude – or at least, not when sober – but she'd somehow fast-tracked straight to a mate-in-the-pub intimacy with the Naan.

*Well. You don't look it* ☺ *PN*

Delia had never been one for actually socialising on social media. Selling her life in its shop window had never appealed. Uploading albums titled '*Big Bite Out Of Big Apple With Team Hello Kitty*' – really, Celine sounded a total idiot – had always seemed faintly narcissistic to her. She was superstitious about showing off: even the best-looking lives could come apart at the seams. As she could attest.

Yet right now, she got the lure of the digital age. She had a new sort-of-friend who lived in her screen, behind protective glass. Peshwari seemed genuinely regretful at causing Delia trouble, and she relented and admitted he was only one part of hustling her towards a door she should be heading for anyway.

They began chatting during her first days down south, about life, the universe, the differences between Newcastle and London, the fears that could hold you back and the things that could push you forward. She could be a different Delia online: more flippant and funny, and less sad and careworn.

Her second friend was The Fox. On her third day of solitude, Delia went to an art supplies shop. It was a gorgeous place, with rainbow galleries of glass jars of pure powdered pigment, planks of hard pastel crayons and thick paints in fat tubes you were *itching* to squirt. She bought new pens, brushes and pads and got back to the flat with the excitement bubbling. Sat in Emma's front room, the only sound the scratch and swipe of her tools across the paper, Delia covered acres of cream cartridge with the story of her superhero alter ego moving cities. She started in soft, feathery swoops of pencil, then inked it in.

There was something about being in charge, as Ralph said, that was so exhilarating. Delia hadn't drawn in so long and felt oddly shamed at having been so lazy. Lazy, or scared? She was worried what others would think of the results, so much so she'd forgotten the effect that doing the drawing had on her. She went into a sort of trance, absorbed by the alternative universe. Telling this story was soothing and enlivening, at the same time.

The Fox wasn't frightened of her new terrain. She was sailing through the streets at night, or sitting on the edge of a rooftop, scenting the air, enjoying the glittering possibilities spread out before her. No one and nothing could scare her, she had battles to fight.

On her fourth night, Delia realised The Fox was telling her something.

AFTER SEEKING SANCTUARY
WITH AN OLD ALLY,
I BEGIN TO CONSTRUCT A NEW BASE....

... SLOWLY,
I HAVE
REBUILT MYSELF

THERE,
IT'S READY.
TIME FOR
NEW
ADVENTURES.

WHOOSH

# Twenty-Two

'What makes you think you're right for this role as a junior account manager?' Delia thought she heard a satirical inflection in *junior.*

The immaculately made-up Indian girl, Tori, had thin, perfectly threaded brows, the width of matchsticks. The sharp eyes underneath communicated pity and irritation in equal measure. They spoke volumes, in fact.

*Why have you come here? What made you think you were qualified? Why is your foundation a shade too pale so you look like a ginger geisha, didn't you do that jawbone test in natural light? When can I finish this depressing conversation and get my low-carb salmon from itsu?*

Delia could answer those unspoken questions more easily than the spoken. 1) Panic 2) Desperation 3) Trying to economise and use the rest of the bottle. The saleswoman in Fenwicks bamboozled me, I look like a mime artist 4) As soon as you like, how in the hell can you Londoners justify five quid for some fish though? I'd be starving an hour later.

'I'm very motivated and enthusiastic and I have good writing skills,' Delia said.

Tori did a quirk of the lip and a near-imperceptible shake of her head.

'That's true of many of the candidates.'

'I have very good social skills and fit well into a team.'

Oh no, she was on the verge of doing the *works well on her own or part of a team* cliché. Tori ignored it.

'Do you have any questions you want to ask me?'

Delia had spent the last half hour trying to cover her shame that she'd only done a smattering of bar jobs, maternity cover in admin at SpecSavers and eighteen months at a boring PR firm – mainly construction industry clients – before landing her plum role at the city council. PR and comms weren't interchangeable, Delia knew that, nor were Newcastle and London. Just because she could draft releases trumpeting good or bad news, didn't mean she was an automatic dab hand at 'starting dynamic conversations' and 'engaging target demographics' to launch clients and/or products and services into the saturated news cycle in the capital.

Delia didn't understand how she'd got the interviews if her CV's scant contents consistently ruled her out. Didn't her interviewers read it first, to save them all the time and the trouble? The answer seemed to be a firm no.

Delia was all too aware how her employment history should look: bouncing every two years between increasingly well-known companies, her job title getting more impressive with each move. Instead, her CV was the equivalent of a comb-over – a few desperate strands arranged to try to conceal the glaring bald pate, and fooling no one.

This interview had now entered the purely face-saving rigmarole phase. It was her fourth of these moments in as many days and Delia's will to pretend had left her.

'. . . No. It's fine, no questions from me. I think I've got the idea,' she smiled, and glamorous, twenty-eight-year-old-at-the-most Tori looked embarrassed for her. Delia had ruined the gloss and cool of the place with her sweaty honesty. Tori's face as she ushered her out said that Delia had to leave before it became contagious.

Confidence: how did you get it? How did you come by that extraordinary, life-transforming quality?

Emma had once told her about being offered a raise at her last firm that was more than she expected. Yet she still screwed her face up and told her bosses: 'What? This is an insult.' And they doubled it. Emma whooped with laughter. Delia had been incredulous. 'But. How do you *dare*?' Emma shrugged. 'It's the game, isn't it? It's only money. They can only say no.'

Delia had repeated this mantra to herself constantly as she hurtled around London, in her third week as a sort-of Londoner. She meticulously planned all her Tube stops and routes in advance and yet it still became a scary logistical nightmare, relying heavily on Google Maps.

The PR company offices she'd visited so far were typically light, air con-chilly shrines full of vases of amaryllis and trilling phones and the bustle of proper people going about their brisk necessary business. Meanwhile, Delia sat in reception feeling like a spare part, holding a silly coat.

Call Delia a quitter, but she couldn't see any of this changing. She'd thought she could at least score a summer job. She was going to tell Emma tonight this had been a nice experiment, but after two weeks of dud interviews, she was back up to Newcastle at the end of the month. Fox tail between legs. Hoping to evade her foes with similar vulpine cunning . . .

Delia was too frail to cope with more rounds of rejections and in worklessness, she had started to feel like a teenage mope, sponging off Emma.

She'd live in Hexham, hunt for another comms job – temping if needs be. She'd draw in her spare time. She was ten years too late to apply her Graphic Design training, but perhaps she could catch up with a night class . . .?

If only Tori had been the end of it. The last dignity ransacking was due to be at three o'clock in an office off Charing Cross Road, at a place called Twist & Shout. She couldn't remember if she or Emma had shortlisted it as a possible – Emma had been browsing during her lunch and emailing her with suggestions, a generous gesture when Emma got what seemed to amount to twelve minutes' break.

The jumpy, dancing website told her it was looking for someone with individuality and a fresh mindset, which was much more important than experience. *LOL, sure it is*, Delia thought.

Earlier that afternoon, the sole company director, one Kurt Spicer, had messaged her. Due to the delivery of new office furniture, it might be easier to rendezvous in a nearby Starbucks, was that alright?

Makes no difference, Delia thought. Literally. None.

# Twenty-Three

Delia was early. Wonderful. She could get her drink, choose a seat and gird her loins.

She saw something move on the edge of her vision. A middle-youth-ish, hefty man was waving at her from across the room. In front of a table strewn with paper, a laptop bag by his legs. Balls. She wasn't early enough. She made the 'tipping cup to lips' gesture that meant 'drink?' and the bespectacled man shook his head. She hoped the done thing was to get herself one, then present for inspection. Delia queued, feeling the coins in her hand grow greasy, telling herself not to be nervous. She just needed to get through this final rejection, then her London 'adventure' would be over.

She got her coffee and wound her way over to his table.

'Hello, Kurt?'

'Delia, right?'

'Yes,' said Delia, trying to divest herself of her coat in an elegant, job interview worthy way, and instead feeling like a fumble-fingered Mrs Tiggywinkle.

She could see a printout of her limp application on the table in front of him and cringed slightly. Inshallah, this would at least be brief. She hadn't chosen a small one-shot latte for nothing.

Kurt was fleshy, spiky-haired, forty or so, with the soft burr of an Australian accent and rimless glasses. He had a certain scrubbed media polish. He looked like someone you might see as a business correspondent on the twenty-four-hour news.

Delia said she hoped his office furniture had all arrived and Kurt blew on the surface of his giant black coffee.

'Howay the toon! Like the accent.'

'Thanks,' Delia said. 'I started speaking and there it was.'

'You're from Newcastle?'

'Near enough, a place called Hexham.'

'So give me The Delia Moss Story. You have a mainly comms background, for the local council?'

'Yep, that's right,' said Delia, stoutly, thinking sod it. Let's wring the chicken's neck and get this over with.

'Why are you in London?'

'Personal reasons, really. I have a good friend here and needed a change of scene.'

'Messy break-up?' Kurt said.

'How did you know?'

'I've seen that look. I've got an ex-wife who sits at the right hand of Satan. If she was on fire, I'd dial 998. Luckily she's still in Canberra and we couldn't have kids. Sometimes God knows what he's doing, right?'

'Right,' Delia said, thinking, *help, what's happening?*

'And what makes you think you can make the transition to PR down here?'

'Uh. Confidence. Life is all about confidence, isn't it? I know I have the ability. I lack the experience.'

'Experience is overrated. Experience is what no one has to begin with, no matter how good they are. Attitude is everything. Can you write me a press release I want to have sex with?'

'Um . . .' Delia tried not to laugh, 'Er. Depends on your type?'

'When it comes to skills at selling in, I look for raw humpability. Don't give me missionary position. Go all out. Seduce the shit out of me, sideways. In suspenders.'

Oh yuck, Delia thought. The 'lecher' warning light flashed urgently on her internal dashboard.

'Can you stir up interest and generate publicity? That's all I want to know. The phrase is "grab attention". You don't ask for it. You *grab* it.'

Delia opened her mouth and it dawned that Kurt was someone who liked to speak in rhetorical question, mission statement bumper stickers. She didn't have to say anything, merely nod enthusiastically while narrowing her eyes a lot.

'In fact I nearly called the company *Smash & Grab.*'

'But the criminal connotations weren't ideal?' she said, sipping her coffee. She'd tried to park her usual Geordie dryness so far in London interactions, but here she thought: in for a penny.

'Precisely. After the riots, the whole thing took on an

element of ram-raiding Tesco for a sack of Value Basmati Rice. What a waste.'

'The name you went with was good, too,' Delia said, wondering at how the conversation had turned so weird, so fast.

'I meant the rice. What were those shitrags going to do, make a huge paella? The whole caper made me sick.'

Delia nearly laughed until she realised she wasn't meant to. She also refrained from pointing out you'd want Arborio in a paella. Basmati was more of a pilaf opportunity.

For someone who said so many amusing things, Kurt delivered them in a completely deadpan fashion, leaving Delia unsure how much humour was intended.

'I like to do PR for notable individuals, I shade into what you could call a publicist. I do consumer, if it's interesting. Occasional bits of crisis management, spraying foam on the fire. No business to business, I'd rather watch cement set.'

'Right.'

'Tell me. What's the worst day you had at your last job?'

'Well, the day I left, I called a team-building exercise bullshit.'

'Team building,' Kurt snorted. 'Did the Avengers assemble to fight evil and then do an egg drop?'

'Hah!' Delia said, thinking, she'd never heard of an egg drop.

'And what was the best day?'

'Oh! Er . . . there was a sculpture in a local park that looked quite phallic, which was under construction. There were some complaints from the Why Oh Why Oh Why types. We knew the eventual outcome would be less . . . willy-like but the artist was being a diva about secrecy and not discussing a work in progress and wouldn't be quoted. So we couldn't definitively say so. My contact at the local paper stitched me up, said he'd wait and then ran the headline What A Cock Up!'

Delia had no idea if this was the right anecdote, but Kurt was nodding.

'Anyway, it was a "modern take" on a maypole. The Mayor did the official unveiling with lots of schoolchildren running round. We were one short at the press call, so I made the reporter who'd done the cock-up story join in the dancing, as revenge. He's very small. It was a bit harsh perhaps, but very funny.'

'Love it.'

Kurt sat back in his seat.

'OK. This is on,' he said.

'Uh . . . Sorry?' Delia said.

'You're hired. Start Monday at nine. I'll be in for a team briefing and we can sign contracts then.'

'Oh, wow. Great!' Delia said, wondering if he was winding her up. Kurt scrutinised her, in a slightly uncomfortable way.

'Your accent says trustworthy, your face says friendly and your art college clothes suggest creativity. Clients will like you. And frankly when it comes to account management, I'd rather train you my way.'

'Oh. Thank you,' Delia said, thinking this sounded ominous.

'I warn you now, I'm unconventional. I like to jump out and pull the rip cord at the last minute. I'm not the guy who says "why", I'm the guy who says "why the fuck not?" I take a dump on the rulebook, basically.'

Delia thought there might be hidden filming going on. She was going to end up on *Britain's Baddest Bosses* or similar, surely.

They said brisk farewells and Delia wondered how it was possible she'd secured herself a job in one eccentric exchange in a café, and what sort of job it might be. Wow. The thing about succeeding as soon as you weren't trying held true. Delia was pleased, and mildly stunned.

Still, it was definitely cause to return the champagne arrival favour to Emma. One of the boons of living in London, Delia had discovered, was incredible takeaways. When Emma staggered through the door, Delia had a washing-up bowl full of ice and Moët and two thin crust pizzas the size of dustbin lids, steaming gently inside cardboard.

There was much squealing and Delia could see Emma was overjoyed at Delia being pinned down to stay for longer.

Emma fired up Delia's laptop, a sagging triangle of chorizo and green chilli in one hand, to conduct her own inquiries.

'Twist & Shout looks kind of mysterious from the website, doesn't it, but then it's a new company I suppose?' she said. 'Oh, Deels, well bloody done. I knew someone would see you're special.'

MHAIRI McFARLANE

Delia slopped more fizz into Emma's glass and, as she felt a small explosion of nerves, tried to quell them; she had Monday morning to be apprehensive. For now, it was time to celebrate.

As Emma closed the browser window for Twist & Shout, she saw an open email with a large CONGRATS banner across it.

'Well-wisher?'

'Peshwari Naan.'

'You talk to him now?!'

'Yes, he keeps me company. He's really funny.'

'But you've never met him?'

'No. I don't even know his real name yet.'

'Be careful.'

'I don't think he's dangerous.'

'I don't mean for your safety. I'm saying don't fall in love online. It's all smoke and mirrors.'

Delia giggled, high on new jobs, alcohol and general novelty. 'Hardly!' And yet it wasn't entirely true that it was wide of the mark. After a few weeks of correspondence, she'd often caught herself thinking about Peshwari Naan, giving him imaginary physical form. She'd get up looking forward to their interactions, crafting her messages to him in her head. It was like having a diary that talked back to you. He was an unexpected treat, a new ally who had sprung from the unlikeliest of origins.

So much of her life in Newcastle was enmeshed with Paul. She was Paul With The Pub's Partner, and everything orbited around Paul, as the planets did the sun. The Naan was hers alone, nothing to do with that life. As she typed replies, she could be whoever she wanted to be. His was a funny, irreverent voice, and Delia felt her heaviness lift whenever she corresponded with him.

Paul texted her fairly often, sometimes with minor news, asking for hers in return. And he called, explaining he just wanted to chat. Delia ignored the calls, or made excuses. Only when necessary did she give intermittent, terse responses that provided basic functional intel, merely the co-ordinates from a submarine, but no narrative or emotion. The channels of communication remained open but nothing much was travelling down them.

'Someone at work, she met this guy in a chatroom . . .' Emma said.

'And he turned out to be a con man? I'm not about to give him three grand when he says his American cousin needs a new kidney.'

'No, worse. She met him after about a year of emailing and she didn't fancy him.'

'Doom!' Delia said, mocking.

'Honestly, she was gutted! They'd got married in her head, moved to a farmhouse in Shropshire with good garage space she'd seen on Rightmove and had three kids. Imagine the scale of the disappointment. All I'm saying is, if you start to feel something, meet him, as soon as possible. Otherwise it's like you're locked in that moment with someone right before you kiss, for far too long.'

'That's very poetic.'

'I'm quite pissed. Also, I met this guy when we worked on a big contract . . .'

'Oh . . .?' Delia suspected this advice had the sting of personal injury.

'He emailed me after we closed the deal. I don't mean the sex deal, I mean the literal deal; we never slept together. He emailed me every day for a month. It got completely het up, like we were soulmates. Then he stopped. That was it, gone, mid-conversation. I sent a few "Where did you go?" messages but he ignored them, so that was that.'

'Maybe he left the firm? Or died.'

'Negative, Ghost Rider. He's still on their website. You don't promote a dead man to run your Intellectual Property department. What I learned was this: if something rolls to you too easy, it can roll away again just as easy. Is there any *Quattro Stagioni* left?'

# Twenty-Four

Inside the solid stone portico, Delia scanned the list of company names next to the buzzer and couldn't find Twist & Shout. *Was she in the wrong place?* Oh, wait – there it was, right at the bottom. Hand-scribbled on a scrap of paper: 'Twist & Sharp'.

She pushed the stiff bell of a dirty-cream, boxy Georgian building and waited. As full of trepidation as she was, it had been enlivening to be part of London's ebb and flow this morning. In a city full of get up and go, it was impossible to feel part of things when you woke just as everyone had gotten up and gone.

And although Delia still didn't see Emma, she was, for the first time, among the commuter crush. She'd tried to act as if she'd always used an Oyster card (Hang on, it worked through wallets? Witchcraft!), all the while waiting for someone on the Piccadilly Line to tap her on the shoulder and say 'Never seen you here before? Can I see some sort of ID?'

'. . . 'LO?' a female voice boom-crackled over the intercom.

'Hello! Delia Moss for Twist & Shout,' Delia said, feeling as stupid as you always did when talking into an intercom.

There was some static, it switched off and the heavy door with one of those Hobbit hole, Bag End-ish central metal knobs was dragged backwards over thick carpet. A short, late middle-aged woman with a severe grey bob and spectacles on a string confronted her.

'Twist & Shout?' Delia said.

The woman glared at her in suspicious incomprehension.

'Kurt Spicer . . .?' Delia added.

'Oh! Kurt,' she relented, letting Delia in. 'Downstairs.'

'Thank you,' Delia said, thinking welcomes had been warmer.

She picked her way past cardboard Lever Arch files and unplugged landline phones and down precarious narrow squeaky steps to a basement. This wasn't the ice-palace, Fortress of Solitude type of PR office of her recent experiences.

At the bottom, there was a corridor that led to, on one side, a cramped kitchenette with the standard-issue soggy bag of granulated sugar and ugly mugs, plastic kettle, fridge. Beyond that, she saw a cupboard-sized toilet with a torn-open twelve-pack of Andrex dimpled. OK, Delia had gone the wrong way but now she knew where the essentials were.

At the other end, she found an office with an old metal filing cabinet, cheap desks, a landline and a whiteboard. The only decoration was a gold figurine of a Japanese Lucky Cat, on top of the cabinet, waving paw rocking back and forth. Delia always found them faintly macabre. Didn't Kurt say he was getting furniture delivered? By a time traveller, it looked like.

Delia ducked her head out of the doorway and couldn't see any more rooms. No. This must be it.

She felt foolish and unsure, and recalled this was why new jobs were so absurdly stressful. It wasn't the work, it was all the tiny procedural unknown things that left you standing around cluelessly like a goon.

'Hello!'

A female voice right behind her.

'Are you Delia?'

She whipped round. A girl – for once a girl who wasn't patronising – was grinning broadly at her.

She looked early twenties at most, with unruly long brown hair held back from her sweetly pretty, unmade-up face. Had Kurt really chosen two such very prima facie atypical-for-PR types?

'I am! Hello,' Delia stuck out a hand, thinking that this girl had an expression and demeanour where you knew immediately she was wholesome and kind. Something in the smile going all the way up to her eyes.

'I'm Steph.'

Oh my word. And she was Scouse?!

'A fellow northerner!' Delia couldn't help herself exclaiming.

'The Wirral.'

'Have you been here long? At Twist & Shout, I mean.'

'No, I'm starting today too. I think it's only us.'

Delia could've thrown her bag and coat down, grabbed her and waltzed her round the room. She had been imagining the aloof intimidatresses she might be dealing with. Instead it was Steph, who wore Doc Marten shoes with sheer black tights, like a nurse, and was pulling her ponytail out of her duffle coat hood, saying: 'Think there's any form of caffeine on the premises? I left it too late to get to Caffè Nero.'

Delia felt like she'd made a friend on the first day of school.

They bonded in the traditional British way, making cups of tea. Steph was a recent media studies graduate and she'd found Twist & Shout in the same way as Delia, via the website. She was doing a tough commute from her aunt's in Essex in each day and Delia thought how lucky she was, billeted at Chez Emma in Zone 2.

Almost strange that Kurt would hire two such similar candidates, Delia thought. She wasn't about to argue, though.

They carried their drinks back in and surveyed the bare space.

'Brought a laptop?' Delia said. She had hers, in a new school 'belt and braces' spirit.

'Yeah, good job too,' Steph said. 'Why didn't he tell us the computers weren't here?'

They set them up – Delia on the old Dell she'd originally inherited from Ralph, covered in Marvel stickers – and logged into the WiFi, drummed their fingers and chatted as they awaited their new boss.

Ten minutes later, and suddenly Kurt was in the room.

The temperature, volume and crowdedness seemed not to triple but to increase tenfold.

'Ladies!' he barked. 'Day one of the new dawn. Let's get going. Client list, strategy notes,' he said, throwing a ring-binder folder onto each of their desks.

'I prefer to work with hard copies, they're less easy to share or duplicate. This is our company bible. Protect it like a newborn. Don't show it to anyone outside this room.'

Delia and Steph both tried to look suitably fascinated as they flipped through the pages.

'Save it for later!' Kurt said. 'I'm out for a meeting on the hour, read it then. A few things first, to explain what Twist & Shout is all about.'

He pulled a chair out to the centre of the room and sat down on it, as if they were a panel interviewing him.

'Something about me,' he said, with the weight of intro-ducing a big revelation. 'I don't queue.'

A tense pause. Delia felt, as the older employee, it was her duty to step up.

'You don't queue?'

'No.'

Another pause.

'What do you do when you want to buy something which is being served, on an, um, sequential basis?' Delia ventured.

'I find another way. Or I don't bother. What I'm saying is, there's people in life who stand in line, who let other people set the pace and the terms. Then there's those who take charge.'

Delia had absolutely no idea how this mantra translated to actual situations. *Hello. I don't recognise your being ahead of me in the queue for the checkout. Stand aside.* She imagined Kurt being removed by Sainsbury's security, shrieking '*Carpe diem.*'

'You'll start to understand how I operate as we go along. You'll see clients come to me because I don't think like all the rest. My campaigns are shock and awe. I'm a rainmaker.'

*I'm more of a tea maker,* Delia thought, dismissing all expectation of Kurt making any sense.

'I go out there, and things happen. You are my Girl Fridays. I need you to do the admin, keep the clients happy, answer the phones, write the press releases, manage the media inquiries. Some of our adventures will require ingenuity and flexibility . . .'

Delia hoped that wasn't the literal sort.

'. . . But I promise you, we'll have fun. Any questions?'

Delia felt she should have three thousand questions, but none were coming to her.

'How should we get started this morning?' Steph said, politely.

'Read the files, get to know the notes. Give me ideas about how we can tackle various clients, if you like. That's all. Go for lunch and do some girly bonding. We can start slowly. I'm going to need you to pull an evening, now and again.'

They both nodded.

Kurt stood up and spun the chair back in its place.

'I'll be on my mobile if you need me, but I airplane mode when with clients. They need to know they have my fullest.' As he exited, he threw up a hand: 'Shalom.'

There was a pregnant silence as Delia tried to work out how irreverent she could be with Steph.

'Is it me or does he talk in *riddles*?' Steph said.

A combination of the Liverpudlian accent, and the relief, made this incredibly funny to Delia, and they both corpsed.

Steph leafed through the pages.

'I've heard of some of these people!' she gasped.

Delia shared her surprise at its respectability. It was partly the contrast between the clients' profile and the down-at-heel offices and haphazard way Kurt ran things.

He didn't return for the rest of the day, and at half twelve, Steph said: 'Shall we get that "girly" lunch we're supposed to? I think the word bonding is clear approval for us to get a pint, too?'

Delia was falling in love.

# Twenty-Five

*What are you doing today then, Dynamic Delia? PN*

*I'm meeting the Evening Standard restaurant critic for lunch. Apparently Kurt has big plans for him. Although I'm only there to take notes because Kurt says it'll lend him greater importance to look like he has assistants. Not sure this is dynamism. Or feminism. D*

It was lucky that Delia had managed her expectations with regards to the pleasure of Gideon Coombes, because there was absolutely no pleasure to be had.

A long wiry creature who wore owlish, oversized, very round glasses, with an expensive-looking grey flannel suit and a gingham shirt, he had a reputation for completely destroying establishments he disliked. His was a poison pen, wielded by a puff adder in Paul Smith.

She and Kurt met him in a modern Italian trattoria near Soho. Having thought it was a shame she was being treated as Kurt's sidekick, she soon found herself deeply grateful that the bulk of the conversation didn't require her input.

At first Delia assumed this was simply London-ish behaviour from Gideon. But as time wore on, her instincts told her she was in the company of a giant helmet.

Every so often, Gideon would break the conversation mid-sentence and mutter comments about the food into his Dictaphone. There was no reason that Delia could see to allow it to interrupt conversation, other than as an affected flourish.

Kurt was discussing Gideon's wish to transition from print media to television, and suddenly Gideon held up a finger. *Click.*

'Not one of my strongest gnocchi experiences to date. Gluey consistency. They should float like tiny clouds, not pebbledash the bowl. Compare here with Bocca, Locanda. Things improve with floral notes of fennel and muscular flavours of borlotti and boar sausage. Something about tart's knickers underneath a Laura Ashley dress. Mention curious smell in the men's. Incense should not be found outside shops that spell the word magic with a K.'

He pressed the stop button and smoothly returned to the discussion at hand. Kurt was unfazed by it – but then unfazedness by clients' eccentricities was his job. Delia goggled.

'. . . So you need a fight with a top chef,' Kurt concluded. 'After all, who was Gordon Ramsay before he threw AA Gill out of his joint? Some guy with saucepans and a face like a tortoise's scrotum.'

Delia was fairly sure he was a Michelin-starred tortoise scrotum, but didn't mention it.

'. . . That fracas was a 360-degree win. Ramsay looks like the tough guy, Gill looks like the most controversial critic in the country. Everyone goes home more famous.'

'You want me to give a Ramsay place a drubbing? It's not that controversial any more. His brand of staid neo-classicism for golden anniversary celebrations is distinctly tired. He's got himself into *airports* for goodness' sake.'

'No, there's no point re-running it with Ramsay. You're the *enfant terrible* of critics, you need like-for-like. I was thinking Thom Redcar.'

Gideon Coombes put his head on one side.

'I give Apricity a bad review? I suppose some of his dishes do err on the side of post-Blumenthal innovation for its own sake. At times his spicing is positively thuggish. Apricity is solid, however. I gave it four out of five, despite the sea trout sashimi misstep. I compared that experience to a sex act in a morgue, but subs lost their nerve and took it out.'

Delia was only dimly aware of Thom Redcar from a piece in a Sunday supplement, months back. One of those slightly annoying spreads where a ruggedly handsome sleeve-tattooed cook is posed like a rock star in his chef's whites, holding a giant cleaver, biceps like bags of walnuts, hair teased with wax. The strapline telling you he's a young hothead who's going to cook the fuck out of shit and generally mess you up with his iconoclastic approach to scallops.

After training under various big names, Thom Redcar had recently opened his own restaurant, Apricity, in a derelict rail shed near King's Cross. It had a star dish involving a smoking duck egg on hay and a waiting list for tables longer than those for a donor liver.

'We don't leave it to chance to get you thrown out. I say we get Thom in on this. That way we can tip the paps off. It'll be endless publicity for this Apricity and he'll come out of it looking like the big I Am, too.'

Gideon forked some subpar gnocchi round his plate. Delia noted despite comparing them to droppings, he could still finish them.

'What if someone decides to squeal it was a set-up? I'm a little antsy about these very contrived things backfiring.'

'That's the beauty of bringing Thom in. He's not going to tell on you if it means telling on himself.'

'What if he says no at the first hurdle, then tells on us?'

'Hah!' Kurt leaned back in his seat. 'Trust me, that's not how I handle business. He won't know you've said you're in until he's said he's in.'

Gideon wiped his mouth on a napkin.

'Then I'm in. What was the artichoke like?'

Delia was startled by Gideon addressing her directly. He'd barely acknowledged her since her arrival.

'Uh. Nice,' Delia said.

'*Nice* doesn't butter critical parsnips, darling. Don't mind me,' and with that, Gideon had dug his fork into her pasta.

It wasn't often Delia's heart sank at the mention of having desserts.

As they left Gideon in the street, he was muttering: 'Partially redeemed itself with an efficient if uninspired *tartufo*,' into his Dictaphone.

'What did you think? To Gideon?' Kurt said, as they strode through Soho, lest Delia think he wanted amateur views on the *pomodoro* sauce.

'Uhm, he's very . . . on the ball,' Delia said, congratulating herself for finding something positive to say that had a vague sheen of truth.

'Haha! He's a ball *ache*, that's for sure.'

Delia allowed herself a small guilty smile. 'Is he?'

'He's got these ambitions about television. Trouble is, he wants to be a media personality, and his personality is his weak point. We need to make him a Simon Cowell, Mr Nasty-type hole.'

'Or just a hole, with a lid,' Delia said, before she could stop herself. Kurt boomed with laughter.

'How are you finding Steph?'

'She's great. I love her,' Delia said.

'Hmmm. I'm not sure she's distinctive enough.'

Delia was disquieted by this. It didn't fit the 'easy breezy, let's all get to know each other' tone of days prior. Also, she wasn't so egotistical or naïve as to think Steph wouldn't be asked the same about her.

One of Delia's life rules was, if you condone someone treating someone else badly, it will come right back round to you and roost. She couldn't say she *liked* the fact that Paul was friendly with his exes, whenever they'd called by, but she respected what it told her.

'She's finding her feet,' Delia said, but Kurt wasn't listening.

'I'm getting coffee, if you can find your own way back,' he said. How Kurt didn't race off his tits on the amount of Americanos he inhaled, Delia didn't know.

'Kurt,' she said, as he made to go. 'How will you get Thom Redcar to say yes, without telling him Gideon's involved?'

'Oh, I'll tell him Gideon's involved,' Kurt said nonchalantly. 'I only told Gideon what he wanted to hear to put some steel in his backbone. Golden rule, Red: tell the client what they want to hear.'

But what if it backfired, the way Gideon said? What about the risk? Delia walked the rest of the way back to the office thinking she was too sensitive for this world.

When she got back to the office, she was relieved to have lurid tales of how Gideon Coombes spoke to waitresses to regale Steph with – something to distract her from Kurt's small effort to divide and conquer. She didn't like to think of what his comments meant for Steph; surely he wouldn't fire her on a whim? She was the perfect officemate: down to earth, fun, and staunchly observant of proper tea-round etiquette.

At the end of the day, the landline rang while Steph was brewing up: Delia could hear her tapping a tune with the spoons on the Formica (Steph played drums and was gutted to leave her kit behind in Birkenhead).

'Hello, Twist & Shout,' she said, with sing-songy confidence.

'Kurt Spicer, please,' said a confident, fairly youthful male voice.

'I'm afraid he's not here at the moment. Is it anything I can help you with, or take a message?'

'You are?'

'Delia Moss, account manager.'

'Hello, Delia Moss, account manager. It was a meet and greet I was after. A chat through Twist & Shout's clients and future opportunities. Is that something you could help with?' Brisk, bit posh.

'And you are?'

'Adam West. Journalist. I'm freelance. Mainly a business writer.'

'Was it consumer stories you're looking for?'

Delia balanced the receiver between her shoulder and cheek and silent-typed his name into Google, with business reporter after it. A variety of national newspaper stories sprung up.

'I'm easy really, what with the freelancing. You know, if you've got anything compelling, perhaps we could come to an agreement.'

'OK, we could meet up,' Delia said. She wanted to feel capable in the face of this man's bumptiousness, and fancied the feather in her cap of making a useful contact. 'When were you thinking?'

'How about tomorrow? Brunch at Balthazar? Eleven?'

Delia had only a faint idea of where or what that was, but brunch sounded good.

'Fine.'

'Great. See you there.'

Delia rang off, and put the meeting in the office diary that no one really checked.

Feeling buoyed at the prospect of bringing in a contact of her own, she thought: I am getting to be alright at this. Maybe confidence is all about simply pretending, until it's not a pretence any more.

Delia felt a swell of excitement, and pride.

Her staid old office, Ann's right-angled big toes, and Roger's *Patriot Games* with Peshwari Naan, and even Paul and his pub, seemed so very many miles away.

Could it be this easy, after a lifetime of doggy paddling, to jump in the deep end, and swim?

# Twenty-Six

The buzzing brasserie of Balthazar in Covent Garden looked like a posh Café Rouge to Delia. She appreciated that they were both an Anglicised version of a Gallic original, but she'd never been to France so it was her only point of reference. She pushed all thoughts of Paris out of her mind. Paul was never far from her thoughts.

Inside the doorway was an explosion of a flower display the size of a tree, in a giant urn. She was well ahead of time and asked for a table for two, trying to act like she belonged.

Delia slid into a lipstick-red booth under a gigantic silver-misted mirror and ordered a hot chocolate. She pulled the client folder out, shrugged her coat off and thought: business brunching. Respectable. Even chic. I am officially part of the rhythms of industry in this city. Perhaps London wasn't so bad after all. You needed to start putting pins in the map, creating fixed points of familiarity you orbited around.

In the rattle and hum and coffee machine hiss of the

morning service, she had a moment of contentment. This was perhaps what it was like, when you were forging forward and doing scary new things, acclimatising. You were briefly in sync with the environment – for a few seconds, it all started to make sense. As time went by, hopefully these moments would become more numerous until they strung together like a paper chain, and you simply felt at home.

She flipped open the Twist & Shout folder, her as-yet-unfinished homework. She was enjoying plans for Marvyn Le Roux, an old-school, end-of-the-pier-style magician who Kurt was apparently determined to re-design as some dangerous psychological trickster.

She soon forgot to examine the client notes in favour of people-watching. There was a large mother-daughter duo from the States, who were the spit of each other. They were talking at that loud American volume about having been to the cutest places in Florence where they got their matching silk scarves. Delia found them touching: it must be lovely to be that close to your mum. She wasn't about to start wearing fleece gilets though.

Across the room from her, a table of twenty-something spivvy suits were having a meeting, clearly all trying to outdo each other with braying witticisms. The laughter rolled round the group at perfectly spaced intervals.

Her eyes moved to a male customer who had been sat down, and was now in conversation with the keeper of the Bookings Book. He didn't look like ordinary people: more like he was in a film or TV drama, discussing his role with the director.

He had mussed, short dishwater-blond hair and one of those classical faces with pronounced cheekbones and brow, and a strong, straight nose. It was a brook-no-argument A-list handsomeness that could change the air pressure in a room, causing women's heads to rotate like owls.

He was the kind of person you were more likely to see in London, Delia thought, peacocking about as if he owned the place. No other city would've been big enough for them.

Delia found his appearance interesting to admire, in a safari trip sort of way, through binoculars. She couldn't say she particularly liked it. She preferred Paul-style good looks: unassuming, characterful. Looks that stole up on you, instead of slapping you around the face. That made you feel drawn to him, rather than intimidated. But then, Delia always preferred worn, pre-loved things to gleaming, sharp-edged perfection.

She had a pang of missing Paul. He'd try the Bloody Mary if he was here. He was a connoisseur and had to have one everywhere he went. She hadn't thought this 'absence making the heart grow fonder' deal might work both ways.

Blond Man wore a gumshoe's beige trench coat, hands shoved in pockets underneath it. He rocked back on his heels as he spoke, the very picture of entitled, metropolitan self-confidence.

He turned and scanned the room, as if looking for someone. *Oh, wait? No you don't. Not you.* Delia realised she'd been expecting a Stephen Treadaway-type little oik from the *Chronicle*, but this Dorothy was no longer in Kansas.

His eyes snagged on her and her spirits plummeted. He stared hard, as if she was an anomaly in this universe, in her pink checked gingham. She loved her diner waitress dress, but under this man's gaze she felt instantly uncomfortable. Delia had been found out. She didn't belong.

As she swallowed hard and hastily stuffed the folder full of secrets out of sight, he strode towards her.

'Delia. Twist & Shout?' he said, with a note of question in his voice, when he reached her. She nodded and he did a mechanical lift-and-drop smile that didn't reach his eyes. Delia's previous burst of happiness was shredded, in ribbons at her feet.

'Adam West.'

He thrust a hand out and Delia shook it. It was a cool, confident palm of course, and Delia was grateful hers hadn't had the time to get clammy. Why did he have to throw her off-balance with his blinding genetic superiority? It wasn't fair, the beautiful automatically outranked you.

'I'd booked and they said you weren't here. I didn't realise you'd taken a different table,' he said.

'Sorry,' Delia said, unsure if she was being accused of something.

'Did you want to eat?' he said. *Well, we did say brunch.*

'Not really . . .' Delia lied. She wanted the double eggs on muffins with yellow sauce or even steak *au poivre* with shoestring fries – and for the man opposite her not to be there.

'Sure? They do a good waffle, I'm told.'

'Are you eating?'

'No.'

'I'm fine.'

If this was some sort of waffle-based power play, Delia wasn't biting.

'I'll get drinks, then,' he said as a waiter appeared at his side. 'A black coffee for me, thanks, and . . .?' he looked to Delia.

At that moment, a hot chocolate arrived, complete with whippy cream. Yes, of course she'd ordered a childish drink. Adam West stared at it as it was set down and said: 'Right,' absently.

'Did you have far to come?' Delia said, in a bid to distract him from the beverage.

'It's all quite far in London,' he said. Delia was immediately irritated at his assumption that her accent meant she didn't know her way around. 'How long have you worked for Kurt Spicer?'

'Uhm,' Delia didn't want to give an answer that screamed NEWBIE, but short of outright lies, she had no choice. 'Almost a month.'

'A month?' Adam said, accepting his coffee as it arrived. 'And before that you were, where . . .?'

'Sorry, how is this relevant?' Delia said, terse, and embarrassed.

'Just "getting to know you" chat, Delilah,' Adam said, accepting his coffee.

'It's Delia,' she said, to the top of his head.

'Delia.' No flicker of embarrassment for the error. She was starting to really dislike this man.

'I've recently moved down from Newcastle,' she conceded. 'I worked in comms.'

'This is a bit of a change then,' Adam said, regarding her over his cup as he sipped.

Delia bridled at this. It was code for *underqualified hick from the sticks*.

'Not really. Same principles.'

At this, Adam West broke his first genuine smile. 'Principles.'

Delia stirred her hot chocolate to make the embarrassing cream disappear and decided it was time to change the subject. 'So what can I help you with today?'

'I thought you could talk me through who you have on your books and we could go from there.'

'Er . . .? We don't give out the client list like that.'

Delia got a whisper of danger to add to the instinctive dislike. He must know she wouldn't do that. What was he up to?

Ah. Experience. Here was where it might come in handy.

Customers arrived at the table next to them and Delia had to move her coat and bag. She welcomed being able to break eye contact with this man; he really did lower the temperature.

'As I said, I'm very open to any kind of story. Good ones. Something with a bit to go at. Not so much frothy world of showbiz, unless it's got some heft,' he said.

'Business?'

'Yeeeah,' Adam said, with the insouciance of someone completely-at-ease-in-his-skin. 'Business. Consumer stuff. Politics.'

'Where are you working? I know you said you're free-lance; where are you selling most of your stories?'

'Didn't you Google me?' he said, looking up from under his brow. A look that had no doubt worked on a lot of women. That said, he was shit out of luck with this one.

'Yes,' Delia said, curtly, 'most of the bylines were from a few years back.'

'Alas, I've not yet made the *Daily Star*. But I dare to dream,' he said without a flicker of a smile and without answering the question. 'Do you have any start-ups? Entrepreneurs?'

'Uhm . . .' Delia immediately thought of one which was wildly inappropriate, but her mouth started to move without getting approval from her brain. 'We've got something quite light and novelty in the consumer realm. Nothing hefty . . .' Delia muttered, wishing she'd kept her trap shut and hoping she could put him off.

'Try me.'

Oh, no.

'Er. It's an aromatherapy bathroom thing. The client is looking at rolling it out to higher-end hotels. You . . . er. Spray it in the loo.'

Adam's eyes widened. Delia wanted to dissolve.

'You're offering me hippy Air Wick?'

'Shoo Number Two is different because it doesn't mask smells, it neutralises them.'

Adam choked on his black coffee with laughter and Delia thought, the only tiny piece of dignity to be reclaimed was to act as if she was deliberately trying to derail the conversation.

'I think we've established we've nothing for you at the moment.'

'I'm not so sure. Do you have anything for making farts glittery?'

# Twenty-Seven

When Delia walked back into the office, Kurt was chatting to Steph. He was on his way out, but clearly in no hurry. Rats. Delia had hoped to kick this particular meeting under the rug.

'Where have you been, Red?'

'Coffee with a freelancer who wanted to say hi,' Delia tried to do a blinding smile and hurry back to her seat.

'Who's that?'

'Uh. Adam West.'

The atmosphere changed abruptly.

'What did you meet him for?' Kurt said, sharply.

Steph looked up.

'He asked to meet. He said he might write about consumer clients but he didn't seem interested in anything in particular. A bit of a time waste.'

'Never, ever meet that dickfag again. Or so much as speak to him.'

'Is he bad?' Delia's heart sank into her stomach as she realised her first bit of initiative had gone horribly awry.

'Is he bad?! Just so you know, Adam West works for an investigative website, a little online agitational free-sheet aiming to stir shit for people who work for a living. He's nothing but trouble.'

Delia gave a small shiver at how close she'd skated to disaster. 'Understood.'

'Did you find out who his boss is?'

'No.'

'Hmmm. I'd like to know who's pulling the strings there. Follow the money, always.'

Kurt's eyes stayed on Delia after the conversation was over, and she had a horrible sense of a black mark next to her name in the imaginary ledger.

An hour later, Delia got two missed calls from Adam West. As she looked at her flashing phone screen she thought, hah. Think I'm going to be stupid enough to ever talk to you again? Think again.

But within minutes, an email arrived too.

*Hello Delia,*

*You don't seem to be answering your phone. A quick FYI to say you left your folder behind. Thinking you might want it returned? Have a great afternoon.*
*Adam*

Delia's stomach contents dropped through the floor. Oh no, no, no — she'd left the client folder with him?! She grabbed her bucket bag as if she'd been stung with a bolt gun, hoping in vain that he was winding her up. As she desperately rummaged through the cavernous bag, she quickly knew her search was fruitless. It was stubbornly empty of its most valuable item.

She looked around the room, as if it might offer up the answer. Think. *Think.* If Kurt found out, he'd sack her. Without a doubt. That said, she might sack herself for rank stupidity and carelessness.

With heart pounding, giving Steph a nervous smile and saying yes thanks to a tea, she tried to stay calm and carry on.

*Adam,*

*Yes I would, thanks. When can I collect it?*

*Regards,*
*Delia*

Oh God, he'd probably only send one of those flashing skull and crossbones that come up in movies when the terrorists have hacked the mainframe.

*How about you meet me at the greasy spoon caff on Endell Street – tomorrow at 4 and we hammer out a deal?*
*Adam*

She couldn't leave the office to see him again! That was sack-worthy too. Her fingers skittered over the keyboard before she had thought it through.

*Hi Adam, I'm very pushed for time tomorrow, could we arrange a handover? I can come to your office.*

*Thanks. D*

Wait. And wait.

'You OK?' Steph said.

'Oh. Yeah!' Delia said. She couldn't confess to her. It wouldn't do any good and it'd make her a collaborator.

'Don't worry about that Andy West thing. How were you to know he was an enemy of the state?' she said.

'Yeah. Thanks,' Delia said, with the world's fakest and queasiest smile. She saw a new email arrive, out of the corner of her eye and opened it, with due sense of dread.

*Dear Deidre,*

*You seem to have mistaken me for a dumb chump. Or you're the world's worst hostage negotiator. Hope no one ever hands you the loudhailer.*
*The way this works is I have something you want and you have nothing I want and no leverage, as yet. So, see you there at 4, or I keep the folder.*

*All best,*
*Adam*

Utter, *utter* wankshaft, Delia thought.

When Delia could bear it that evening, i.e., after a stiff gin and tonic, she looked up Adam West online. This time, properly.

He had indeed racked up plenty of bylines in nationals. However, if she'd bothered to read more thoroughly, she'd have seen he had been involved in a series of reports about white-collar corruption. It had led to a libel case his paper won.

Her stomach tightened as she read the plaintiff's words in reference to Adam:

'Demeaning and invasive coverage . . . attack dog, bully boy tactics . . .'

He was now on a website. It was called Unspun. A cross between *Private Eye* and a Drudge Report for business, media and politics, lots of longform articles, emphasis on the kind of lengthy, painstaking investigations that broadsheets didn't do much of any more. Annoyingly respectable and intimidating.

How was it possible that Delia had pitched propeller-first into the sea, so soon after feeling she was flying high? What a moron. She could kick herself.

When Emma got in, Delia was morose, channel flipping, on her third Gordon's, to which she'd barely shown the tonic bottle.

She filled Emma in.

'What's he going to do with this file?'

'God knows. It's everything. It's all in there. PR firms are very secretive about who their clients are, and this not only lists them all, it has strategy notes and ideas for coverage, autobiographical detail, and so on. It's a Twist & Shout blueprint. The possibilities are endless.'

'I don't get it – it's a new company. What's his problem?'

'I have no idea. Adam's a nasty piece of work and muckraker, probably. I mean, look at these stories about him. He's got form for completely ruining people,' Delia said, turning her laptop screen towards Emma.

'Oh my God,' Emma said, after a few minutes.

'See?'

'No, have you seen this photo of him? I'd like him to demean and invade me, preferably three times in a row. Then come at me like an attack dog bully again next morning.'

'Oh for fuc—'

'You've met him? Is he fit?'

'He's vile and completely your type. Horrible *ruling class, might wear a wax jacket at the weekend, charge your father a tithe of corn for living on his great estate*, sort of bossy . . .'

'Nnngggg, keep going, I'm nearly there.'

'Emma!' Delia shouted, but laughing. 'I can't believe I left the file lying there,' she groaned. 'I'm so angry at myself.'

Emma squinted at the screen and closed the laptop, before taking a swig of Delia's gin.

'If he's that ruthless, he might've lifted the file when you were looking the other way.'

Delia sat up slightly. 'Oh yeah.'

The thought made her positively boil. That was illegal – although in reality she knew she was grasping at straws. Still, someone with any sense of British fair play would've picked it up, riffled through it at most, then chased her down the street to return it.

'What sort of deal do you think he's going to offer?' Emma said.

'No idea. An awful one.'

'OK, I am putting Lawyer Emma hat on. There are very few situations that can't be turned to your advantage if you hold your nerve. This is a stage in the game, that's all. Walk in there, see what he's got to say and remember this is not life and death. The time may come when he's at your mercy.'

'Heh. Mmm. Thanks, Em.'

There was a pause during which Emma looked as though she was working herself up to saying something.

'Have you spoken to Paul since you came down?' Emma said, taking another sip of Delia's drink. The thought of men being at Delia's mercy, or not, had clearly turned her thoughts northwards.

'No. He's called me a few times but I haven't called him back. I replied to a text and said things were OK.'

Delia was avoiding Paul, she didn't know what else to do. She had to wait until she was ready to deal with him, and if she was never ready, that was an answer in itself.

'Did you tell him you've got this job?'

'Not yet.'

Emma looked at her and said nothing.

'Top up – gin with a hint of tonic?'

'Yes, please.'

Not for nothing was Emma a lawyer. Delia knew she perfectly understood the situation from that much information.

Delia was still giving Paul ice and a slice of cold shoulder, but to tell him about the job was to suggest she was gone for good. And she wasn't ready for that yet.

# Twenty-Eight

'I'm off then, see you tomorrow,' Delia said to Steph.

'Have fun with your flat feet,' Steph said, raising a palm, cheerily.

Delia decided to cover Adam West with a doctor's appointment, for a problem with fallen arches that might – but not, it was going to turn out – need a referral to a chiropractor. 'From wearing these ballet shoes all the time,' she said, unnecessarily, in the way of embroidering all lies.

Delia hoped and prayed that Kurt didn't see her with Adam – the only result of that would be an insta-sacking.

In the bright summer sunshine, she scuttled into the caff under its awning, chin angled into chest, as furtively as someone having an affair. She wondered if Paul had ever taken Celine anywhere. She imagined him, hand on the small of Celine's back as he ushered her through a doorway, eyes darting up and down the street as he followed her inside. Anger rose inside her at the thought that he'd taken her to dinner at any of 'their' places . . . but no. He wouldn't have. Apart from anything else, the risk of discovery would be too great.

The caff was a far cry from Balthazar – china plates of full Englishes with orange lakes of baked beans, bowls of toast and mugs brimming with brick-red tea. The air was alive with the waft of fresh buttery grease and the sound of sausages and bacon spitting and sizzling as they hit the pan.

It was as if Adam West was unsubtly communicating: yesterday was for show, today we get real. Delia felt dislike, anger and fear in equal measures.

Across the room, an unsmiling Adam raised a hand in a wave.

He looked completely out of place in a stockbroker-pink shirt and Delia suddenly decided she hated blond men who wore pink shirts, especially in greasy spoons. Why couldn't he be in his proper place, precipitating another banking crisis, rather than precipitating a Delia one?

A white coffee was in front of him. No sign of file.

'Tea? Coffee?' he asked.

'I'm fine, thanks,' Delia said, tersely.

Adam raised his eyebrows in an *Oh, that's how you're playing it?* way.

'Can I have my belongings back, please?'

Delia was itchy with nerves and hadn't consciously decided on dispensing with all diplomacy. She simply couldn't bear the anticipation of finding out what she was in for.

'Yes. Eventually.'

Adam West's blond hair, blue eyes and chiselled sort of evil would see him work nicely if cast as a Nazi, Delia thought.

Also, on reflection, Delia decided he had not one feature that was particularly distinctive or appealing. They all simply hung together in a way that technically 'worked'. He wasn't attractive, as such. He was blandly, boringly competent at having a face.

'What does that mean?' she said, returning to the situation at hand.

'It means I want something in return.'

Delia glowered fiercely and Adam let go a contemptuous bark of a laugh.

'Oh, come on! As if you wouldn't use this if our positions were reversed.'

Confusingly, Delia wouldn't. She also knew it wasn't in her interests to hammer the point home that she was a fish out of water. Getting a midget reporter to hop round a maypole was starting to feel distinctly tame.

She had an uneasy sense that Adam heard her thoughts.

'Exactly how much do you know about your employer?' he said.

Delia hesitated. Since yesterday, she'd been on the back foot in this dance more times than a ginger Ginger Rogers. She shrugged.

'He's from Canberra, he does personal and consumer PR. He's divorced . . .'

'I meant his other business interests.'

'I work for Twist & Shout. What's this got to do with anything?'

'Once again, not exactly done a deep-carpet clean on the internet have you?' Adam said.

Delia shook her head, reluctantly. She'd looked Kurt up, but had seen nothing startling. LinkedIn, trade press articles, affiliations with some of the big firms.

'Then it falls to me to tell you what kind of man your boss is. You know when you get those "please help, send cash" emails from abroad, with sob stories about very very sad situations involving "knived robber bandits"? The crooks that always take wallets but never passports, for some reason? You'd be better off responding to one of those than a press release from Kurt Spicer.'

Delia feigned eye-rolling contempt, while her skin prickled.

'PR man in Not Somalian Aid Worker shocker,' she said. In order to fight fire with fire, Adam West made her talk like him. Another reason to loathe him.

'Much as I dislike your trade, I recognise some PR shills are better – or worse – than others. Kurt Spicer is an Olympic sprinter in the race to the bottom. He's a blagger and a bullshitter and someone who will bend truth till it snaps. Or a liar, in old money,' Adam said, sitting back, fiddling with his spoon and surveying Delia's reaction to this.

Delia remembered what Kurt said about Adam being nothing but trouble. Adam, who was holding her to ransom.

'You're doing a hatchet job on Kurt?' Delia said.

'Hatchet job's very value-laden language. I prefer "exposé".'

'Exposé of what? PR firms pull strings to get coverage? I think that might be less of a surprise to people than you think.'

'Yes, thanks.' Adam West pulled a face. He obviously didn't like being hit with the patronising stick in return. 'It's looking at the problems with modern media through the progress of one person. You know, the whole world on the head of a pin. Or a pinhead, in this case.'

'Maybe the public aren't very interested in press shenanigans,' Delia said, thinking that would've been a stronger observation without the word shenanigans. 'All the back-room bargaining that goes on.'

Adam shrugged.

'Maybe not. But I bet the same was said of phone hacking, or MPs' expenses. The main thing is, put the truth in front of people, then they can make up their own minds. That's the only obligation of journalism as I see it.'

'The truth as *you* see it.'

'No, the truth. Facts. Not spoon feeding them confected nonsense like fat babies trapped in high chairs who deserve no better than pre-chewed pulp.'

'The truth, well known to be on every page of those red-top tabloids you worked for,' Delia said.

'Ah, but I'm not writing for them any more.'

'What do you want from me? I'm new. I don't know any dirt.'

'Now *that* I'm prepared to believe,' Adam said, with a tip of his head. 'But, you will find out more. My deal is this: I'll return your file. You meet me every so often and give me the information I request on particular clients. Wait for the bat signal in the night sky.'

Delia turned this proposition over.

'You want me to be a . . . double agent?'

'Precisely.'

Adam reached down and produced the file from his briefcase, pushing it across the table at her.

'There you go.'

'How do I know you haven't photocopied the contents?'

Adam laughed out loud, showing white teeth in his Nazi commandant head.

'I have! Dear oh dear, you're a proper greenhorn, aren't you?'

'Then what's the value in you giving it back?!' Delia near-shrieked at him.

'You have your file, I don't dob you in with Spicer for mislaying it. If it all pans out for you, there'll be nothing I write that can be traced back to my having seen it.'

Great. Very reassuring. Delia stuffed it into her bag.

'What if I say no?'

'Then I call Kurt and say you left it with me, and I imagine you'd be out of a job. Are you irreplaceable? Sorry to be frank, but you don't seem it.'

Delia twitched with hatred.

'Consider this, however – I've no motive in losing you your job while you're useful.'

'A huge comfort.'

'With that in mind, you might want to give me your

200

personal email address. And if you haven't already, I'd delete the messages we've sent so far. Kurt will be a snooper.'

Adam pushed his notepad and pen over to Delia. She could refuse. But he was right, using her work email would imperil her, not him.

'Thanks for the advice,' Delia said, as she scrawled, resentfully. 'Perhaps you can tell me how to wipe my arse too. Is it front to back or back to front?'

Delia surprised herself with how crude that was and realised she was scared, and it made her judgement wobbly.

'I'll leave that to your discretion,' Adam beamed.

It was pointless trying to be nasty. It only made him happier. He had her in a cage and she could jump up and down all she liked; it was just further entertainment for her captor.

'Can I ask you something? Why were you calling up trying to speak to Kurt when you knew he wouldn't talk to you?'

'I knew I wouldn't get Kurt, he doesn't answer his own landline. I got your Scouse friend before you, she took a message for him. Luckily, you were more helpful.'

Great. Delia had eagerly walked into this trap.

She knew there was only one card left to play. It was humiliating and antediluvian, and appealing to someone's humanity was pretty pointless when they appeared to have none. Delia was firmly in 'can't get any worse' territory.

'You know, I've got this job by the skin of my teeth, I have rent to pay and I didn't move to London for . . . happy reasons. Losing me my job would ruin things for me. I am asking you, as a fellow human being, not to do this.'

Adam leaned back in his chair.

'As a *man* human being? I didn't have you pegged as someone who'd pull a Penelope Pitstop.' He stirred his coffee and tapped the spoon several times on the cup. 'Even if I was the kind of slow wit to fall for the damsel in distress routine, I think I'd be doing you a huge favour if I lost you your job, Daisy. You'd be better off on benefits than doing Kurt Spicer's grubby bidding. Ditto getting rid of the bilge pump that is his fiction factory.'

He paused. 'Nice touch with the thing where you made your eyes look even bigger though,' he mimicked cartoon cow eyes, pout and exaggerated blinking.

Well. Here was an intangible landmark in her time in London.

Delia had made her first enemy.

# Twenty-Nine

Kurt twirled his chair from side to side in the centre of the stuffy basement office.

'Come at me.'

He'd announced a 'thought-nado' – a brainstorm, in old money, Delia thought – about a client.

She was actress Sophie Bramley, a cherubically pretty blonde C-lister. Attractive, but not threateningly so.

Sophie was currently a supporting player in a medical series, *The Golden Hour*. Set in an A&E department, it was distinguished for its unusual levels of 'business end' gore.

It was the kind of show where people in green scrubs shouted 'I need fifty ccs of oxytoxycontalin NOW, dammit!' There was lots of defibrillating, heartrending bedside confessions, arguments with arsehole consultants and out of hours inter-medic romances.

Sophie was thirty-one, a mother of one, and was regularly being passed over for more interesting – read, 'grown-up, prime time, possible nudity' – roles. In the fight to be better known, she was ready to take the surgical gloves off.

Kurt was trying to come up with a battle plan for Sophie and had just used the phrase 'sex up her dossier'.

'We need raunch, with maybe some overcoming adversity element thrown in,' Kurt was saying, while stretching an elastic band between his hands. 'I'm thinking along the lines of "Tiger Mom Lapdanced Her Way Out Of The Projects".'

Delia looked at her notes.

'She's from Ashby-de-la-Zouch.'

'Does it have mean streets?'

'It's a village near Leicester. Not really.'

'Hmmm. Not sure about playing up the single mother angle, actually. I don't want the complication of the dad getting involved.' Kurt frowned, flinging the bands onto a nearby desk. Notionally his desk, as he rarely used it. 'There were some custody issues. Last thing we want is to bait Fathers 4 Justice and the ass clefts who dress up as Spiderman, dicking about on rooftops.'

'I think Fathers 4 Justice disbanded,' Delia said.

'Surprising, because when it comes to being seen as responsible people to be in charge of kids, their PR was watertight. What we need for Sophie is a good old-fashioned pants-off scandal.'

'Like an affair with a co-star?' Delia asked.

'I've explored that with her, there's no one convenient at the moment. Plus anyone in the same show is low-hanging fruit. We don't just want people to think about her, we want them to think about her *differently*. Anything else?'

Freed from the constraints of the by-the-book stolidity of the council, Delia tried to get into the spirit, but it was proving difficult. *Don't hanker for a job that gives you creative, off the wall and fun, and then whinge*, she thought, having a stern word with herself. Even though this felt right on the line between frivolity and vulgarity.

'Accidentally uploading a nude photo on Instagram?' she said, remembering an incident with one of Paul's barmaids. (Although Paul had said: 'She told every one of the staff and five of the regulars before she took it down. I think it was an accident in the same way they're all accidents once the camcorder's definitely running on *You've Been Framed*.')

Kurt rubbed his chin, thoughtfully. 'Not bad. Only it puts all the weight on the client to deliver. We want something we can justify getting paid for.'

The clock ticked.

'A sex tape?' Steph said, glancing nervously towards Delia.

Kurt put his head on one side.

'Ooh. *That's* calling to me.'

'You mean, get her to make a sex tape?' Delia said, doubtfully and fearfully. OK, this was full-on tacky. Come back Roger the jobsworth and Ann the joy thief, all is forgiven.

'No!' Kurt said. 'Walk the gangplank and get on the boat here, Red. Free your mind and the rest will follow.'

Delia translated this as: nothing needs to be true. Adam West's words rolled round her mind.

'Sex tape, good start.' Kurt interlinked his fingers behind his head, rocking on the back legs of his chair. 'OK, OK. So a scumbag ex-boyfriend is hawking this tape around the papers. We put out a release saying we condemn his actions. No one should have anything to do with him. Equally, Sophie's not ashamed of her past.'

'Which ex-boyfriend?' Steph said. Delia was grateful to her for taking over the Bleeding Obvious Question Asking task.

'We won't dignify that question with an answer,' Kurt said. 'We won't give this turd any more publicity. They'll find out if he makes an approach. Which they should be strongly warned not to entertain.'

'But he won't make one . . .?' Delia said, trying to catch up.

'No. Because he doesn't exist,' Kurt said, looking at Delia as if she was a blade-of-grass-chewing simpleton.

Delia sensed she and Steph very much wanted to share a look of distress, but didn't dare.

'Y'see, a lot of people would stop here,' Kurt said.

*A lot of people would've stopped before here*, Delia thought.

'. . . I think bigger. How about if Sophie had a secret adult movie career? Did a few amateurs with the boyfriend, and then went semi pro? Sold a few, at the corner shop? White paper covers and all that.'

Delia didn't understand how Kurt could 'imagineer' so recklessly.

'How do we invent that history? Wouldn't there be a record?'

Kurt shrugged. 'Small distributor, went bust? Let's see if the papers go for this first, then worry about that. Personally, I love it. The Linda Lovelace of Leicestershire. Cheap Throat. Delia, you write me the press release on this. I'll get Sophie to sign off on her quotes. Do NOT give me grey. Give me purple prose. Purple, veiny and throbbing.'

*Yeuch.*

'. . . Whizz it over as soon as it's done and I'll check it on the BlackBerry. I like to strike while the iron is hot.'

'Does she want to be associated with having made porn?' Delia said, worrying Sophie would be offended by something Delia had been told to write. She still hadn't forgotten the false assurances that Kurt gave Gideon.

'Do you know much about acting? It's only one notch up from prostitution as it is.' Kurt slammed back down on his chair legs and stood up.

'Friend of mine from school, good-looking guy, talented. Thought he was going to be the next Jimmy Dean. Talking about which directors he'd work with, he'd be all about art instead of money. Five years later he's in a shopping centre dressed as an onion ring and he'd give his left nut to be third possum in Awesome Possum: The Musical.'

Kurt shook his head.

'What's he doing now?' Steph said.

'No idea,' Kurt said, looking surprised to be asked. 'Not in Scorsese's latest, that's for sure.'

Kurt picked up his coat, doing a fingers-to-forehead salute. 'Good work, ladies. Onwards and upwards.'

Delia and Steph waited several beats to be sure that Kurt wasn't coming back.

As the sound of his footsteps faded, they turned to stare at each other with wide eyes, before bursting into laughter.

'This is well mental,' Steph said.

'Shouldn't we have something to stand it up before we test interest?' Delia said. 'Shouldn't it have a *bit* of truth to it?'

'The aroma of truth!' Steph laughed.

'With truth-style flavourings. Reality-free. Safe for truth allergy sufferers.'

Delia had flutters of concern, which she wasn't mentioning in so many words to Steph. She felt sure that if this story went tits up, it wouldn't be Kurt spluttering and stuttering on the phone to a journalist and tarnishing their name. Still, you had to buckle down in your first weeks.

Hopefully, Sophie Bramley was going to take one look at this 'story' and say 'no way'.

With this in mind, Delia tried to dispense with self-consciousness and write the kind of press release that would be overheated enough to please her boss. Delia had always found inventing procedural quotes for councillors vaguely uncomfortable, but this was excruciating. BBC ACTRESS SLAMS EX PARTNER TRYING TO CASH IN ON ADULT MOVIE PAST. Delia angled it on the modern peril of 'revenge porn' and Sophie's (synthetic) outrage at this unprincipled mercenary, going behind her back.

'*I'm appalled someone I was once close to would betray my trust like this,*' *Sophie said.* Delia wondered who Sophie should be appalled at. '*It was a long time ago and while I am not ashamed of my past, the particular films he is offering were strictly for private consumption and something we did as a couple.*'

She sent it to Kurt, waiting to be told it wasn't nearly outrageous enough, or that Sophie hated it.

*Red. LOVE IT. Sophie's good with it too. Get it out there. KS*

Delia didn't know whether to be pleased, or to believe him. She hit send with a sense of squeam. She now had dirty hands.

# Thirty

Delia had dodged a few nights out since she arrived, but her defences were never going to hold for long against the march of Emma.

To quote her hostess: 'You're not Julian Assange and this isn't the Ecuadorian Embassy.'

Emma got Delia to 'keep Thursday free' – as if all Delia's evenings weren't free.

'You've got to see this speakeasy bar, Mayor of Scaredy Cat Town in Spitalfields. You'll love it. The entrance is through a Smeg fridge door. The cocktails are lush.'

She was so enthusiastic, Delia didn't have the heart to tell Emma that the last thing that appealed was sitting somewhere self-consciously fashionable, necking drinks with ironic paper umbrellas at ten pounds a pop.

She wanted a standard-issue pub with textured wallpaper, jars of glacé cherries and morose older couples with halves of mild and lager blackcurrants who'd run out of conversation twenty years ago. She needed plain comfort, not spicy novelty.

To make it even less possible to say no, it was the night before Emma disappeared for the hen marathon in Rome. She had to be up at Oh Fuck o'clock to go to Stansted, and yet she was out on the lash. Emma's energy reserves were truly Herculean.

As expected, the bar was a posers' paradise. It had all the hallmarks: Stygian gloom, barmen in braces who looked like D.H. Lawrence, a disco ball and signs saying No Heavy Petting.

They had the first half an hour to themselves. Delia told Emma about the Adam West encounter.

'This double-agenting is very good news,' Emma said, handing her 'Basil No Faulty' cocktail to Delia to try, wiggling Delia's appropriate 'Red Lady' towards her.

'Is it?' Delia said, trying to connect mouth with straw. 'It feels like a total disaster.'

'Oh yes. There's all kinds of room for manoeuvre here. What if you give him bad intel?'

'Then he eventually realises, and drops me in it?'

'Depends on the information. He's not going to be able to hold the folder thing over you forever. This has a lifespan. A few big wins at work and it'll be old news.'

'That relies on me having big wins.'

'Ah, they're here!' Emma waved at a crowd of shiny-haired strangers who'd poured through the door.

Delia put her game face on and tried to make a polite effort with a group who were, with the best will in the world, only feigning polite interest in her.

Jessie, Tallulah, Sarah-Louise and her boyfriend Roan – and someone who might actually be called Bounty, as in bar or hunter – didn't want to make an effort with the odd one out, given a choice of that or a catch up with the people they'd come out to see. She couldn't blame them.

Every so often, Emma would shriek a remark in her direction, having found a helpful detail to draw Delia in to the chatter. She smiled and made efforts but no topic sparked, caught light and developed into natural conversational momentum. Delia was reminded of her parents' old oven in Hexham that needed the dial holding in for minutes on end to get the hobs going: clack clack clack.

She fell between stools, and was able to sit in her own little bubble of aloneness, feeling sorry for herself.

Frustratingly, alcohol wasn't helping. Eventually, Delia decided to hell with the cost and knocked back postmodern cocktail after postmodern cocktail. The booze only deepened and lengthened the shadows inside, instead of brightening her up.

When she went to the loo, she saw a missed call from Paul. An accompanying text said: 'Hey, just calling for a catch up/chat if it's a good time. Px' She'd lost count of the number of times over the past four weeks that she'd seen his name flash up on her phone – she wasn't strong enough to resist returning it, this time. She wanted to speak to someone who wanted to speak to her.

She slunk out and stood in the street with the smokers. Taking a deep breath, she pressed his name.

'Hi. Paul?'

'Dee! Thanks for calling back. Where are you?' Paul said.

'Outside a bar, why?'

'Sounds noisy, that's all.'

It wasn't noisy, but Paul could tell she wasn't in the flat and wanted to keep tabs. He had some nerve if he was going to get suspicious about Delia enjoying herself, she thought, however misapplied a suspicion it was in this situation.

'How are things going?'

'Good,' Delia said. 'You?'

'Same old, same old.'

'What did you want to talk about?'

'Nothing in particular. I wanted to hear your voice and know how you're doing.'

This was why she was dodging Paul. She couldn't be bothered with small talk and she wasn't ready for big talk yet.

'How's Parsnip?' she said, poking a burger wrapper with the toe of her patent shoe.

'Y'know. Widdly and rickety. Missing you. You alright for money?'

'I have a job.' Delia couldn't avoid admitting that, if Paul was going to turn paternalistic provider on her. 'Not sure how long it'll last.'

'What sort of work?'

'PR. A small PR firm.'

'Wow. Delia.'

'What?'

'You've really gone, haven't you?'

'I told you, it's more like . . . a sabbatical. I haven't made any long-term decisions.'

Paul was quiet and Delia began to feel sorry for him; old habits died hard. But then she recalled Celine calling him her boyfriend and the sorriness was obliterated by a flood of liquid fury and insecurity. In sobriety, she'd stem the tide. In ebriation, she carried on.

'Did Celine call you her boyfriend?'

'Sorry, what?'

'I saw her referring to you as her boyfriend on Facebook . . .'

'Eh? How can you even see that?'

'She has no privacy settings. Maybe in life as well as social media.'

Paul fell silent before saying, 'Maybe she was seeing other people too. She must've meant someone else.'

'I suppose we should both get tested then.'

It was an ugly thing to have to say, and Paul mumbled, then said: 'Look. Maybe she did call me her boyfriend. The truth is, I don't know. I wasn't her friend on there.'

'So she did or she didn't?'

'Not to my face. It is how she talked, though. It's the kind of thing she'd say.'

'What does that even mean? You just keep lying and lying, don't you? Listen, Paul. I've got to go.'

'Delia, don't—'

Delia cut him off and, taking in an inadvertent lungful of Camel Lights, felt the force of her folly. These skirmishes got them nowhere. She wanted him to take back what he'd done, and he couldn't. She called him because she felt lonely in the bar downstairs, but talking to Paul made her feel lonely in a different way.

Delia was trapped between worlds, worlds with a Smeg fridge door as portal. Hipster Narnia.

# Thirty-One

'Hi. This is Freya Campbell-Brown from the *Mirror*. This story about Sophie Bramley . . .'

Delia, alone in the airless office, had a whisper of fear. The press releases had been released into the wild.

'Yes?'

'Can we have a name for the ex-boyfriend?'

'I'm afraid we can't give it out. We don't want to give him any more publicity. Sophie's adamant.'

'Riiiight,' Freya said, in a languorous and contemptuous drawl, with a rising inflection. 'It's just that without that, this isn't a story?'

Delia paused.

'You have Sophie's quotes.'

'Yeah. But nothing about the films. You're saying she made them for sale? Where were they sold?'

'Local outlets, I think . . .' Delia mumbled, feeling her face heat.

'You *think*?'

'Obviously it's a painful memory for Sophie.' Oh God,

this was excruciating. Delia wasn't Kurt. She couldn't build magical citadels out of untruth, in unconstructed dream space. She squirmed.

'How do we know the films exist?'

'Why would Sophie comment on them, if they didn't?'

'Don't get me wrong, we're interested. But not without something more to stand it up. There's nothing on her IMDb page . . .'

'She's hardly going to put it on her IMDb page,' Delia said.

Freya stopped speaking for a three-second beat, to make it abundantly clear she did the insults, not the other way around.

'. . . There's nothing on her IMDb page. So, yeah. Call me if you have anything more, otherwise no go. Ta.'

Click. Brrrr. Delia could pretend that conversation had never happened. However, since she became an involuntary informant, creating more situations that could bite her on the arse was not wise.

Delia rang Kurt and updated him on the troublesome but not unexpected burden of proof.

'Horseshit. Say they can have a nice exclusive interview, photos and all. Tell them if they want to see the films, they can do a public appeal. See if anyone who bought home-made bongo in the East Midlands in the Noughties would like to come forward. And let us know how that goes for them. Har har.'

Delia rang off, deeply downhearted. She was between a rock and a hard place. As she'd sensed from the start, conveying Kurt's nonsense to the press was not easy.

A bout of fretful procrastination was necessary before steeling herself to doing humiliating battle with Freya again. Worst of all, she had no one to commiserate with – Steph was out doing her silent sidekick duties with a new Twist & Shout client.

She opened her email and told Peshwari Naan of her woes. It was ripe stuff, but the Naan didn't colour inside the lines himself.

*Tricky. You think they know it's not true? PN*

*It's stranger and more complicit than that: they probably know full well it's not true. The deal is, we have to give them enough 'proof' that they can say they did believe it, if there's any fall out from it. Plausible deniability. D*

*Hmmm. Then how about a link to the website for the defunct adult film distributor? PN*

*That would be good – there is no distributor though, and no website. D*

*DERK! Keep up. What if there WAS one? Do you see? PN*

*. . . Not really? D*

*I could knock you one up. PN*

*You can do that?! You'd do that for me? D*

*Emphatic yes times two. I think I owe you a favour. And as I'm off this week, you'll have it in no time. PN*

Delia was starting to have serious affection for this man-slash-oven-baked flatbread. She and the Naan traded ideas about the site design and she felt as if she was actually doing something creative and useful, however bizarre and twisted it might be.

When Kurt and Steph came back to the office, she said, casually: 'I've got a friend who's a bit of an IT genius who owes me a favour. He suggested he puts together a landing page for the film distributor for Sophie. What do you think?'

Kurt made a 'why not' face. 'Sounds good. Let's see what he comes up with.'

A few hours later, Peshwari Naan sent a very humble 'Is this OK?' link to a completely plausible, Technicolor tacky, cleverly outmoded and highly detailed fake distributor website, complete with spoofed versions of real films.

*Howard's Ending* was Delia's favourite, but *Ed Gets Wood* and *Schlong Good Friday* deserved honourable mentions.

On the list of actresses was one 'Sophie Sweeney', her suggested former alter ego. Delia called Kurt over to see it and watched with a strange satisfaction as he did a double take.

'*Shazam*. And this is some friend of yours? Does he want a job?' Delia belatedly realised the cost: Kurt would want the Naan effect again.

As Kurt wandered off, she emailed her effusive thanks, amazement and admiration.

*All in an honest day's work! Or a dishonest one. But, it's done and hope it helps ☺ PN*

Delia emailed 'does this help' to Freya, who came right back: *Thanks for this. We'd like to arrange an interview with Sophie.*

Across the room, Kurt was doing overarm bowling gestures.

'Sophie's OK to talk about this in an interview?' Delia said. Kurt wasn't kidding when he said they'd learn how he worked.

'She's an actress,' Kurt winked.

Delia felt like she needed a shower; but in work rather than moral terms, it was definitely one of those big wins that Emma had been talking about. Even when values had been turned upside down, the instinct to please the person who paid your wages stayed in place.

And maybe as time went on, Delia would be able to shape and handle events so that fake-a-roo web pages weren't required?

But a couple of hours later, she might've known who'd be the day's Captain Buzzkill – in like a bullet to her Gmail by 5.30 p.m.

*Hi Delores!*

*So here's a rum thing. I've been shooting the shit with my friend Freya over on the Mirror and she tells me about this SLIGHTLY WHIFFY story about an actress who's suddenly got this new past making blue movies. Imagine my surprise when she mentioned the PR firm behind it! And your name! What a fine accomplishment.*

*Anyway, like all great predators, my vision is based on movement, and it reminded me that we should meet up. How's tomorrow?*
*Adam*

*Adam. I couldn't care less what you think. OK, tomorrow, but nowhere central this time, and after 5.30. Delia (that's 'Delia')*

*The forecast tomorrow is for sunshine. How about Hyde Park, by Speakers' Corner at six? Adam (that's 'Herr Adam')*

# Thirty-Two

In the mellowing heat of the early June evening, low sun filtering through the trees, Delia found the right spot at Hyde Park.

People wearing much less than her rollerbladed past, creating a pleasant breeze. Delia hadn't quite nailed dressing for London. Everything had to cross longer distances and straddle more occasions; nipping home and coming back out again wasn't an option.

Delia steam-cooked in her black popper-studded body, which reminded her of her old ballet leotards, floral midi skirt and opaque footless tights.

Ten minutes passed; Adam West was late. She had a ripple of apprehension – was he playing her? She put nothing past him. Then out of the periphery of her vision, she saw him waving at her.

He was in rolled-up pale blue shirtsleeves, buying ice creams from a van.

'Sorry, I had an urge. Funny Foot?' he said, holding two

Elastoplast-pink lollies, brandishing one at Delia when she reached him.

'No thanks,' she said, arms folded.

'Ah, you miserable sod! It's going to melt and dribble down my hand now. Who doesn't like a Funny Foot?'

'Me.'

'Liar. You don't like me, it's not the Foot's fault.'

'I wonder why I don't have warm feelings towards the man trying to lose me my job,' Delia said.

'I'm not!' Adam said, through his first mouthful of ice cream. 'I'm endangering you keeping your job as a by-product of getting what I want. Gedditright.'

Delia sighed and then, hating herself for her love of ice cream and dislike of food waste, swiped the lolly from his left hand.

Adam grinned.

'Let's do a walk and talk and eat.'

If the ice cream was a device to make her feel even more compromised, it was working. It was difficult for Delia to maintain any sort of hauteur as she gnawed the toes off.

As they entered the park, a group of women with a picnic basket passed them. Delia noticed all eyes move to Adam. Then to her, and back again, trying to figure out why Mr Blond Ambition was with a grumpy-looking busty ginger in leg-shortening hosiery.

'What have you been doing today then? Apart from basking in the glow of faking Sophie thingy's porn career?

The website was slick work, by the way. I think I'd have enjoyed *Piledriving Miss Daisy* more than the original.'

'Are you doing a piece on Sophie? Because you said "no showbiz" when we met. Was that not true?'

'I'm merely making conversation.'

'Then I'd rather not discuss it.'

'I have seen the client list you know, being ultra-Masonic isn't necessary. Hey, how's Marvyn Le Roux doing? I loved the plan to make him "bigger than Derren Brown", haha. Marvyn looks like someone who'd wave a rubber chicken around Longleat Center Parcs.'

Marvyn had been Kurt and Steph's meeting the day before. Steph reported he had a waxed quiff, watery eyes and kept finding coins behind her ear. Kurt wanted him to claim borderline supernatural powers off the back of a few weak parlour tricks.

'. . . Squeaky charlatan. Be wary of him and his *and you're back in the room* routine. I hear he likes his bananas green.'

Delia frowned. 'I'm not a green banana. I'm lightly browning, if anything.'

Adam guffawed.

'I more meant be on your guard in general, as his rep. Did you persuade any casinos to ban him for doing a Rainman routine at a table in the end?'

'Do I have to tell you, or is this optional too?'

'Yeah,' Adam said, producing a paper napkin from his pocket and wiping away melted ice cream from his left hand, 'I'm not much bothered about Marvyn, per se. I'm sure Kurt wouldn't be either, if Marvyn wasn't scion of a Scottish shortbread biscuit fortune.'

Adam handed her a paper napkin and she accepted it, without thanks.

'Is he?' Delia said, forgetting she perhaps shouldn't show she knew less about a client than Adam West. 'Le Roux isn't a very Scottish heir name.'

Adam looked at her with pop eyes and burst out laughing.

'You think Marvyn Le Roux is his REAL name? You do kill me, Dina.'

'My fucking name is Delia!'

'Your *fucking* name. One Funny Foot and you're anyone's, eh. Yeah, I think he calculated that saying *hoots mon, what you're about to see will confound your very eyes* as Tavish McTartan wasn't going to have the same effect.'

Despite her anger, Adam's terrible Scottish accent made this even funnier and Delia broiled and tried not to laugh. This man *really* did not deserve her laughter.

'How was I to know it wasn't his real name?'

'It's so obviously a twirly-wurly silly abrakebabra magician name.'

'I'm not as cynical as you.'

'Well, working for Spicer, you need to be. Given Marvyn's a flagrant no-hoper, Kurt will have other uses for him and his money. And I'll tell you something, Kurt Spicer won't be his real name either. Kurt *Spicer*. It hardly has the ring of reality. He's been through more reinventions than David Bowie, I'm sure.'

Delia threw her lolly stick and napkin into a handy bin

and said, 'Can we speed this up to the part where you ask me something you want to know?'

'I want you to keep an ear out for any political figures you might be working with. They're not names currently in your strategy folder. Let me know what's said.'

'That's it?' Delia said, suspiciously.

'For now, that's it.'

She sensed that Adam was stringing this out to torment her.

'Apart from one other thing.'

Delia's shoulders sagged.

They'd done a small circuit, bringing them back towards the street again. Adam turned to face her.

'The stunt with Sophie. That sort of thing works once, twice, maybe several times, if you can pull websites out of your backside. Sooner or later, one of these tall tales comes apart. You're left with a serious problem going back to that journalist, or anyone else they've talked to. You get blackballed. This industry is still small enough for reputations to matter.'

'You're telling me this, why?'

'As a word to the unwise.'

Delia looked at the idyllic scene around them. Why was she being lied to all the time? Why had she got herself into the position of telling so many? She felt so . . . soiled by it all. Delia couldn't trust anyone.

She looked at Adam levelly.

'You turn up being snotty with me in Balthazar, you steal a file and hold me to ransom over it. Today it's walks in the park and ice creams and advice. How come?'

226

Adam West didn't have a ready reply, for once. He shrugged.

'I expected to meet someone with the soul of a crow but I increasingly get the feeling you don't know what you've got yourself into. You may turn into a crow yet. For now, I'm prepared to issue a friendly warning.'

'That's generous of you. What I'd like more is for you to release me from this arrangement so I don't get sacked.'

'No can do, I'm afraid.'

'Then you can shove your friendly warnings.'

Adam shrugged and smiled. His phone started to buzz and, fishing it out of his pocket, he answered it, mouthed 'bye' and sauntered off, chatting.

Delia watched him go, trying to decide what she thought of him in return. She felt exploited but not truly angry any more. Adam had joshed her too much for that. But she remained worried at what they were building towards, and felt the need to get ahead of it.

As she walked back to the Tube, Delia had a glimmer of a hopeful thought. Adam West was equally in the position of forewarning her on his angle of attack.

Perhaps she could use him? Delia Moss: triple agent. She wasn't helpless. She was enjoying working with Steph too, she'd not had a friend at the office in years. Peshwari Naan was a solid constant as well, given his ubiquity online.

Back at Emma's, she picked up her pen and sketchpad, grinning to herself as the characters emerged from the canvas.

This was the magic of The Fox – it helped her focus and gather herself, it told an inspirational story. It showed her what to aim for.

# Thirty-Three

When it came to overtime, if you had to do it, you might as well pull it by dining in the latest hot restaurant with its 'reservations currently on lockdown'.

The menu at Apricity was astonishingly expensive in more than one way: thick leaves of cotton-soft paper with gold embossed curly writing.

It began with the enigmatic:

**Apricity (n.) obsolete**
**From the Latin *aprīcitās*, 'warmed by the sun'**

Glad that's clear, Delia thought.

There seemed much more of the menu than was necessary, too. To get to the food, you had to get past *Our Ethos* and *How To Eat* and *Sources & Inspiration*. It quoted 'let food be thy medicine' and stated a mission to 'heal as well as nourish' that Delia thought was taking on responsibilities beyond its jurisdiction.

Kurt squinted at it through his glasses.

'I thought I was coming out for dinner, not joining a cult.'

Once they found the selection of dishes, the menu suddenly became economical with words, as economical as the unadorned straight-edged steel-and-wood dining room.

So you had 'Duck Eggs: Three Ways'.

That was it.

'Boiled, scrambled and fried?' Delia suggested and Kurt guffawed.

'Were you and your fella big on eating out? Foodies?' He sipped his mineral water.

'We liked eating out, I'm not sure I'd say we were foodies. We had a rule of thumb that if a restaurant didn't have a dried flower arrangement in the window, we'd give it a whirl.'

Kurt laughed again.

'You split up because he'd been sleeping with someone else?'

Delia was shocked and wondered if Steph had told Kurt. He registered her surprise and added: 'It was likely going to be you or him playing away, and it wasn't you, because you're here.'

Delia nodded into her own water glass and scanned the menu again.

'You know what you should do? Sleep with someone else.'

Delia suddenly found the details of where Apricity 'hand foraged' its marsh samphire fascinating. 'Mmm?'

'Seriously, Red. It's the only way you put things back

on an even keel. Revenge. An eye for an eye. I'm a big Old Testament man. People have lost sight of how much sense it makes.'

'Maybe because everyone has taken each others' eyes.'

'Haha! Droll. You're a dry one, aren't you?' There was that wolfish look again. 'You're only young. Plenty of grass to flatten yet, girl.'

Delia was deeply relieved when the sommelier arrived with the wine. After pouring, swirling, sipping, nodding, they re-tasked themselves to choosing the food.

'Emu meatballs.' Kurt shook his head. 'I've come halfway round the world to avoid that stringy bollocks. Emus have got long thin legs and run a lot. If you were a cannibal, would you kill Usain Bolt?'

Delia grinned. Kurt's dander was up now. He got the attention of one of the waiting staff, all twenty-something and looking like they'd walked off a runway. Dressed in crisp white shirts, they were wreathed in the sort of beatific smiles people usually wear before asking you if you're aware that He Is Risen.

A honey-haired beauty floated over and politely inclined her head as Kurt tapped the parchment page in front of him.

'It says here "cockerel yoghurt". Help a bitch. How exactly do you milk a cockerel?'

'You massage its coxcomb until it emits liquid, which is then added to our homemade hung yoghurt. It's like a very unusual tangy cheese.'

Kurt's face was a picture.

Delia had to press the menu against her mouth to stop herself from laughing.

'Do you not think in all the many years of humans roaming this earth and feeding themselves, there's a reason why they never thought, "I know, I'll rub a rooster until some shit squirts out?"'

Delia was shaking now. The waitress smiled the smile of someone who knows that the son of God walks among us and all will be light.

'Apricity is a completely unique experience.'

'So was the Vietnam War.'

Kurt glowered over the menu, and he and Delia made their choices by pure guesswork.

'And my wife and I would like another bottle of water,' Kurt winked, and Delia felt mildly alarmed. He'd insisted Delia accompany as 'more age-appropriate' for him than Steph.

A ripple went round the room and one Gideon Coombes stalked into the dining room as casually as if it was his own lounge, taking a table with a rotund male friend in the window. Gideon and his companion were trussed up like Wodehousian dandies: pocket squares and waistcoats.

Staff appeared round them like a swarm of bees and Gideon issued instructions with a flick of his wrist, snapping the menu shut.

'How many people are in on this?' Delia hissed, under her breath.

'Bare minimum,' Kurt replied, at normal volume. 'Make a note. You get a better effect if people are helping without knowing they're helping.'

Delia had to discipline herself not to steal looks at Gideon. Kurt had only told her that there would be a 'shock and awe' stunt during the evening's meal.

Kurt and Delia finished fiddly starters involving jewel-like cubes of pickled vegetable and tendril sprigs of green and skidmarks of umami brown that were pleasant enough, though there wasn't enough of anything.

In truth, they were something of an anti-climax, what with plates being set down in front of them as if they were the answer to the meaning of life.

Delia realised this was why she didn't often go to fussy places: the expectation of huge waiting times and cost always led to slight disappointment that it was, after all, simply food.

Delia stole glances at Gideon, still without food after twenty minutes or so, who was ignoring his friend in favour of yapping into his mobile. He was truly weapons-grade rude.

They sipped their wine and made small talk, though Kurt was completely distracted by thoughts of whatever was to happen next. Ten minutes later there was a minor commotion by the door, and the maître d' could be heard telling someone there had been a mistake.

When he moved, Delia could see a moped driver holding a Domino's pizza box.

Gideon theatrically threw his napkin down, got up and strode over, handing a banknote to the delivery man. He returned to his seat with his pizza.

Gasps. The whole room had downed eating tools and was staring at him in rapt amazement. The maître d' looked as if he was watching a sinking ferry.

Gideon calmly flipped the lid and started chewing on a large slice of pepperoni and ham. He offered it to his friend, and he dug in too.

'Oh my God,' Delia whispered to Kurt, and clapped a hand over her mouth. Kurt was beaming.

The maître d' approached Gideon as one might a large animal in the jungle, and said in hushed tones, but not hushed enough for a silent restaurant: 'Sir, you're not allowed to eat that here.'

Gideon stared at him. 'I simply got so blindingly peckish that I had to do something. Please tell the chef that if his service was faster, I wouldn't have need of this fourteen-inch Meatilicious.'

The maître d' hesitated, obviously calculating the pros and cons between snatching junk food from the hands of a restaurant critic, versus going and alerting his superiors that the dining room now smelled of salami and melted mozzarella.

The maître d' plumped for diffusion of responsibility, and disappeared into the kitchen.

Kurt glanced at Delia and winked again. She'd never seen him look so suffused with delight.

Suddenly, in a whir of chef's whites, a loutishly handsome man with ruddy face, dark sweaty hair in peaks and tattoos of dragons on his forearms came bursting out into diners' view.

'What the fuck do you think you're doing in my restaurant, Pizza Fuck?' Thom Redcar shouted in a Welsh accent at an unperturbed Gideon.

'What does it look like I'm doing? I'm eating. Though

I'm not surprised the sight is novel to you, given the time it takes you to crank out two entrees.'

'The fuck is this?!' bellowed Thom, knocking the pizza to the floor. It splatted in a rather vomitous-looking mess and Gideon got to his feet.

'It's been tiding me through from the olives to the starters. Or as you probably call it, the fasting period.'

Thom prodded a finger into Gideon's Savile Row-shirted chest.

'I'm not a fucking short order cook making you pancakes. What I create here is *art*.'

'Yes, a still life. I bet Van Gogh's *Sunflowers* was speedier than your red-wine-braised Dorset snails. What are you doing, asking them to make their own way here?'

'What? Get the fuck out of here! You're barred! For life!'

'It feels like I've been here for a lifetime, so this isn't a great privation.'

Thom Redcar grabbed him by the lapels and bundled Gideon through the doorway accompanied by more gasps, Gideon's friend waddling behind.

Delia could see a photographer, crouching between the parked cars, capturing the stand-off. Their voices carried through the window.

'Can I have my pizza please? My blood sugar's dangerously low.'

'You want dangerous blood? I'll knock your front teeth in, you mincing streak of piss!' Thom bellowed.

Gideon straightened his spotted bow-tie. A spookily

well-timed sleek car pulled up and Gideon and companion piled into it.

'Yeah and take Downton Flabby with you!'

Thom stood there, long enough for the photographers to get another few shots, one chunky hand aloft, two fingers presented to the retreating Mercedes containing Gideon and his plus one.

He stalked back into the silent dining room, where the staff were rushing round, scraping pizza off the floor.

'He said he wanted his pizza back. Can you put it all in the box and send it to him? Do it with a big red ribbon. Address it to Pizza Fuck, *Evening Standard*.'

The staff nodded.

'And put some pubes on it.'

The staff looked taken aback, obviously wondering if they were going to be notified in gold leaf scroll of the identity of the local supplier.

Thom glared at the other diners, as if they were in some way implicated, and crashed back through the double doors to the kitchen.

An awkward low murmur of conversation restarted.

Kurt muttered, 'He's gone off the script with that last one. I don't think he wants to associate his gaff with rubbing your nasties on the produce.'

A disquieted Delia grasped for conversation.

'Looking forward to our trio of eggs,' she said.

# Thirty-Four

Kurt was spending ten days back in Australia, and Delia was sure he could've powered the 747 with his glee at the success of the Pizza Wheeze.

The carefully planned quotes from Gideon and Thom had been sent to favoured media outlets after the news hit the wires – the story going all the further because there were snaps of Thom squaring up to Gideon in the street.

As luck would have it, a shocked onlooker with a perfect power of recall had been there to report the verbal altercation on the night, word for word. A few clientele had even filmed it on their phones.

An immaculately attired, smirking Gideon had appeared on *The One Show* sofa to discuss whether the cult of celebrity chefs was getting out of hand and if modern service culture had forgotten the customer was always right.

Thom gave pugnacious quotes about how the power of critics had got out of hand and there was no excuse for bad manners, which Delia thought was pretty rich from someone who put pubes on pizzas. (Gideon made sure to tweet a photo of the wreckage of his returned pizza, of course, to keep the fire burning. Delia did not zoom in.)

They disagreed over how long Gideon was made to wait. Bizarrely, the media didn't seem much interested in that detail. The Critic Whose Service Was So Slow He Ordered Fast Food was too good to finick about in the facts too much.

'Doesn't Thom mind this implying his kitchen keeps people waiting?' Delia asked Kurt, before he left.

'Apricity is booked solid until next Christmas, it's not going to have any problems. Yet how many punters in the street had heard the name Thom Redcar before this? And now? There you go. Everyone knows Gideon's a snipe. It's pantomime.' Kurt rubbed his hands together. 'I can't wait to sell the *kiss and make up* story. I've got a pictorial in my head, where Thom's pretending to attack Gideon with a knife while he tucks into a stuffed crust. Think we should offer it to *Observer Food Monthly*.'

Delia felt she was gaining layers of cynicism daily, until they would form a beetle-like hard carapace.

Over the next week, Kurt's absence caused a pleasant lull that saw Delia and Steph go for picnic lunches in the nearby parks. Though curiously, whenever they called Kurt's mobile to leave messages, it didn't ring in that staccato international way of phones across oceans. She and Steph raised eyebrows at each other.

Delia felt if she could've chosen her workmate out of a thousand people, she'd have chosen Scouse Stephanie. Steph kept tail combs in her bag for her wild hair, and used the handles to tap a drum beat on the desk, when there were no spoons to hand. (Delia had promised to see her new band, when Steph said they were ready.)

For lunch, she didn't fankle about with calorie-avoidance salads. She often brought what amounted to a whole cheeseboard with crackers and invited Delia to dig in. And when she laughed, she paused, her mouth fell wide open and she made a honking monotone 'HURRRR!' noise. Delia often found herself feeling very older-sisterish towards her.

One afternoon during Kurt's short sabbatical, they were sitting stretched out on the grass, nibbling a pork pie each, when Steph said:

'Delia. Do you think it's possible Kurt could hack our computers? Or do that thing where you can record the keystrokes?'

'I don't know. Why?'

Steph looked agitated, picking at a stray thread on her lace-up shoes.

'He knows about my private life. Or it feels like he does.'

'How do you mean?'

'The other day he was asking me leading questions about who I was dating.'

'Could be nosiness?'

Steph grimaced. 'He was dead pushy: "Do you like girls, or boys? Or both?"'

Delia felt she was missing something. This sounded like distasteful lechery, not special intel.

'When I didn't answer, he said it was cool nowadays . . .

Then he said Scouse girls were usually dressier than me. I was like, I'm a Wirraler.'

'Rude bastard!'

'We're not all Coleen Rooney copycats. I said to him, you don't look much like Crocodile Dundee.'

'Hah, brilliant!'

They laughed.

Ah. Delia twigged. Kurt had sussed Steph was gay or bi, and Steph was fretting as to how. It hadn't even crossed Delia's mind. She supposed she was quite tomboyish. But so what, in every respect? Kurt was a creep.

'Then he outright asked if I had a girlfriend.'

'How dare he!' Delia said. 'As if you'd want to introduce them anyway. We're hardly going to do plus ones at our work dos.'

Delia gave her a supportive smile and the tension in Steph's shoulders relaxed a little.

'Yeah. I don't seem *that* blatant dykey, do I?'

They both laughed in release of the pressure.

'No! He'll probably ask me the same. He's a perv. Don't let it bother you.'

Amid the sympathy and concern, Delia wondered if Steph had partly brought this up to broach her sexuality. It made Delia feel even more protective, if Kurt was being prurient.

One confidence deserved another.

'If he can see what's on our laptops, I'm in trouble. Remember the freelance journalist I wasn't meant to meet, Adam West? I accidentally left my client folder with him. He read and copied it before he returned it.'

'No . . .?' Steph said, pausing mid-pork pie bite. 'Oops!'

'Yep. In fact, it makes me think Kurt can't be spying. He'd have let me go when it happened, if he'd read it on my emails.'

Delia decided to leave the ransom element out, for now. Steph feeling she had to cover for Delia wasn't fair.

'I've got a friend who knows a lot about computers. I'll ask him what's possible,' Delia concluded. 'By text.'

'There's something off, about that office . . .' Steph said, and as soon as she said it, Delia knew precisely what she meant. The receptionist Joy floated around the place like the ghost of a murdered housekeeper. It felt deserted and as if the walls had ears, at the same time – even when Kurt wasn't there.

In the balmy heat of a July day, Delia shivered.

*Mr Naan. Don't laugh at me. Is it possible my boss can see what myself and my colleague are doing on our laptops, the ones we bring to the office? Delia (I asked for your phone number, so we could use a safe line)*

*Hello, on a new channel! It's possible but it's not very likely. Have you left him alone with your laptops at the same time, both opened any dodgy attachments, or otherwise noticed any signs of malware? PN*

*No & no, and I don't think so. D*

*Then short of carefully angled mirrors, I doubt it. PN*

Without the threat of Kurt suddenly descending on them, Delia even dared to book a Friday off work and invite Ralph to visit. It took some effort to persuade him. In fact, it was like heaving a water hippo through a swamp using shoelaces.

Delia wouldn't have had the conviction to be so emphatic with him, but their mother had let it drop that the chippy – or 'award-winning fish bar of Tyneside', as her mum described it to the neighbours – had been urging Ralph to take his holiday owing. Apparently he was resisting because he 'didn't have anywhere to go'.

Delia insisted he could use Emma's room while she was away in Rome. 'I've changed the sheets, have someone to stay! Better yet, have someone to stay in your bed,' she'd said before she left, while Delia rolled her eyes.

On Friday morning as she was waiting for Ralph to arrive, Delia's phone started to ring. Adam West. He wanted a meeting. She tartly explained she shouldn't have to deal with Adam as she was off work.

'Going anywhere nice?' he said.

'No.' She hesitated, thinking humanising herself with her captor and thus making it harder to metaphorically murder her might be a smart move. 'My brother's visiting from Newcastle.'

'Nice,' Adam said. 'Showing him the sights?'

'Ralph said he wants to go to Madame Tussauds.'

'A culture vulture, eh.'

Delia thought of soft-natured Ralph coming into contact with a Stanley knife like Adam West, and gave a small shudder. There was a rap on the door and Delia went to open it, grateful for the excuse to end the call. Stony-faced Carl from downstairs was wordlessly holding out a Jiffy bag. It had her name on it.

Delia thanked him, warily, remembering Emma's warning.

She didn't know what else to say and he saved her the bother by turning on his heel.

She ripped the envelope open. A bottle of Calvin Klein's Eternity perfume tumbled out, along with a scrap of paper.

*Dee, I thought I'd send you a few things that might make you remember why we matter, so much. Here's the first. Love you, Paul x*

She hesitantly unscrewed the lid and put her nose to the nozzle. It was strange how sense of smell seemed to hack straight into your brain's memory vault, find a long-dormant recollection and activate the associated emotions.

With the sweet odour, Delia was thrown back into the earliest, headiest days of dating Paul, and that time when they spent an hour crawling over each other on the old sofa to a *Talk Talk* album. She read the note again. She remembered how it had felt to think: this person is my future. What an effortless click they'd had. Snap, there you are, you're now in the right place. How Delia had assumed finding a soulmate was going to be tough, then she'd tripped over one in her red wedge heels without even trying.

She doubted Paul remembered the specific name of the

perfume, only the label. He must've had to work his way through them in store, an assistant hovering, until he found it. Paul never shopped: Delia had to practically wrestle threadbare jeans from him.

'I'm thinking about you' – the most simple and yet powerful thing anyone, any gesture, could say.

It made Delia wilt. She'd spent a lot of time wondering if she could take Paul back. Maybe she'd got this quandary the wrong way round. Could she give him up?

When Delia saw the familiar unkempt ginger hair of her brother in the crowd at King's Cross, she felt a lurch of protectiveness. He was wearing a huge rucksack on both shoulders, a Spaceballs t-shirt and a baggy hoodie: his off-duty Forbidden Planet employee garb. He looked deeply uneasy. He'd not been to the capital for decades, since they were kids. He didn't even travel into Newcastle much. Ralph never saw any need: the things he liked were at home. His friends, by and large, were fellow gamers.

She felt even more protective when she heard some lads nearby say 'Ed Sheeran's let himself go' and explode with laughter.

Perhaps Ralph – she'd always wondered this, and it made her stomach contract – didn't leave home much because his early forays outdoors had not been pleasant.

At Ralph's request, they went straight to Madame Tussauds, where Ralph was principally interested in dead Prime Ministers and the Chamber of Horrors. Delia tried to imagine explaining to an alien race why it was considered a leisure pastime to look at wax effigies of men who'd poisoned and dismembered their wives at the turn of the last century.

Madame Tussauds' pleasures exhausted, Delia was at a loss. Ralph submitted to her itinerary of principal tourist occasions, yet he obviously found the humid crush, the tsunami of other bodies pouring towards him on the pavements, difficult. Delia wanted to find a way to make it easier for him, but she feared you didn't undo a lifetime's loner habits in one weekend.

'We should get some lunch!' she said to Ralph as they crossed the bridge from the Southbank, hoping to appeal to his stomach.

He nodded.

'Anything you fancy? My treat,' Delia said.

'Whatever is good,' Ralph said, and Delia could see him struggling manfully to look like he was having fun for her sake, and it made her sad.

'Do you want my homemade fried chicken?' Delia said, and Ralph's eyes lit up. Ralph had always been the most enthusiastic consumer of Delia's cooking. She knew that if she was honest and consulted his feelings instead of hers, he wanted to be indoors.

Within an hour he was joyfully installed in Finsbury Park, large legs outstretched, playing his games on Emma's giant telly while Delia prepared lunch.

'Yes! The parallax error beheads you!'

They ate at the kitchen table, piles of chicken in panko breadcrumbs, the 'Glasgow salad' of chips and ketchup. Delia had done a shop and stuffed the cupboards with Ralph-ish foods. Emma might think she had bulimia.

'Do you live here now or are you coming back?' Ralph asked, on his sixth chicken piece. 'Nice photo of Parsnip.'

Delia beamed. She'd propped the paddling pool picture up in Emma's kitchen window.

'He's watching over me. I'm coming back eventually,' Delia said, taking a chip from the bowl. 'I miss Parsnip. My job is fun but crazy. I lie for a living and newspapers print it. I can only do it for so long without despising myself.'

'Eventually' covered a lot of sins. She hadn't moved lock stock to London. However, right now, she couldn't imagine returning to Newcastle and Paul. She was somewhere between the two, in purgatory.

'What will happen if they find out you're lying?'

'Hmmm. Good question,' Delia said, feeling a wriggle in her guts. 'Also, me and Paul might work it out.' She glanced at Ralph over her next drumstick. 'I'm not sure.'

'Did he say why he was with that other girl?'

'He didn't exactly *explain* it . . .' Delia said. Ralph was astonishingly insightful, in his own quiet, uncomplicated way. That was precisely what Delia needed: to know why. That was missing, and maybe it always would be.

Ralph took in his surroundings. 'It's cool here, isn't it?'

'Very cool. Emma wouldn't have it any other way.'

'Is that The Fox?' Ralph said, in an awed voice, turning his head on one side. Ralph could see a frame where The Fox was being pursued by a masked, unnamed enemy, across London's rooftops.

'Oh, yeah,' Delia said, bashful. She hadn't been as circumspect with putting her drawings away while Emma wasn't at home.

She wasn't embarrassed of her drawings, as such. Well, maybe a little. It was more that The Fox felt like her private hobby, a wonderful secret. She didn't want to let air in and spoil it, just yet. She also had to be careful as sometimes, she used people from her life and superhero-ed or villained them.

'Can I read it?' Ralph said, eyes wide, eyes still on the sketchpads propped on the chair by the sink.

'Sure.'

He wiped his hands on kitchen paper and picked the sketchpad up, taking it through to the front room. Delia put the kettle on and as she put her head round the door, saw that Ralph was sat cross-legged, turning the pages, chuckling to himself, completely absorbed.

It was a lovely moment. It was fulfilling in a way nothing else was. If it could entertain Ralph, could it do the same for others?

'Shall we muck around here this afternoon, go to the local for some early doors pints, come back and watch a stupid film on Netflix?'

Ralph grinned: 'Yeah!' This was more his idea of a holiday.

Later, replete with beer, Type 2 diabetes-inducing food and having seen off a very dumb film with Liam Neeson, Ralph played more games while Delia sat emailing Peshwari Naan.

*It's been six weeks. The time has come to find out your real name. You can't seriously think the council would budget to send me to London as part of a long con to unmask you. D*

*. . . GPWM. (good point well made) It's Joe. I work in the rates department. \*Thumbs\* \*Toots Kazoo\* That do you? PN/J*

*Hello Joe! We meet at last! D*

*Well we don't quite 'meet' now, but we did meet, if you remember. (You don't.) J*

*How did you remember me? Are gingers who look like refugees from an am-dram production of Grease that memorable? D*

*Truthfully? You're pretty. J*

Delia had a little spark of surprise at this, and found herself smiling. It was nice to be told that, at this particular point in her life.

*Thank you! ☺*

She noted the lack of Joe giving her a surname and wondered if the information could be gleaned on the council website. Did she even want to know?

She thought about what Emma said, the risk of virtual love affairs. Delia loved chatting to Peshwari Naan, but as time wore on, she couldn't honestly say she felt herself falling in love, or that holy trinity of attraction, affection and admiration that could turn into love. If it was purely platonic, however, why was she nervous about looking him up? She didn't want to break the spell, she supposed. The disinhibiting power of the internet meant they'd chatted about things she wouldn't usually tell someone on so short an acquaintance, and putting a face to her confidante would likely change things.

Speaking of which . . .

*PS So my brother found the comic I've been writing since I moved to London. He's been very complimentary about it. D*

*WAIT, what? You write a comic?! I wanted to ask if you had a passion outside of PR. PR doesn't seem very 'you' – if that's not too forward from a man who knows you from one bit of buffet small talk and a series of emails. J*

*Ah no it's OK, PR/comms isn't very 'me', it was just something I could do. Yes the dream was always to write comics. I did Graphic Art at university. Then I felt stupid about my comic when I was in my 20s and shelved it and did supposedly 'proper' things for a job instead. Only 'proper' seems to mean completely improper now. It's been nice revisiting it. D*

*What happens in this comic? J*

*A nocturnal Delia superhero alter ego called The Fox, who lives underground, rides her magic bicycle around fighting urban crime at night with her sidekick fox, Reginald. Laughing at me yet? D*

Thank God she was behind a keyboard: that was infinitely easier to type than say.

*IMMENSE! Expecting a big NO, YOU SNOOP! but, can I see it? J*

*If you really want to! Keep expectations low. D*

Delia looked up from her screen, to where Ralph was in communion with the other screen.

'Are you having an alright time?' she said.

'Oh yeah, I like London,' Ralph said, absorbed by the virtual Miami on the TV.

# Thirty-Five

Much as she could enjoy solitude, by the end of Emma's Italy trip, Delia was looking forward to a night when the company wasn't the burble of the television while she made endless cakes with the KitchenAid. Ralph had left on Sunday, with Delia following him to the train carriage door and seeing him seated before she could leave him. She knew she had her parents' tendency to wrap him in cotton wool. It was hard not to.

Delia had accepted that touring the sights wasn't Ralph's preference, so they had a late breakfast and then went to see the latest giant science-fiction action explosion on a big-screen cinema in Leicester Square.

Kurt seemed preoccupied and a little secretive after his week off. Delia was learning more about his temperament: his ups were very up but it seemed he had the downs to compensate. In the days that followed, she and Steph learned to look busy in this new 'we're all ruined!' mood.

If they tried to reassure him that business was good, he

barked that it was OK for them, they were salaried. *Equally, we don't share the spoils of the big wins*, Delia thought.

In this slump, he snapped: 'There's a bar opening on Friday I think we should all go to. Lots of networking to be done.' Delia nodded.

Steph said, nervously: 'I have a band audition on Friday.'

'Wow, that's brilliant,' Delia said hastily, seeing Kurt's eyes darken.

'I said you'd have to pull some evenings,' Kurt said to Steph.

Pause. She looked stricken.

It was completely unfair of him, Delia thought, to expect to claim their Friday evening at a day's notice.

'Is this the band that didn't want to see a female drummer?' Delia said, hoping to emphasise that Steph needed to keep this appointment.

'Yes. I talked them round,' Steph said, casting nervous eyes towards Kurt again.

'Cool! That's great.'

'Alright, she doesn't need you to fake orgasms,' Kurt snapped at Delia, who blanched. 'Do what you will,' he scowled at Steph.

After he left, Steph said: 'I got myself in trouble there, didn't I?'

'If it was that important he'd have mentioned it earlier,' Delia replied, though she suspected Steph was right.

Delia came into work in her favourite scoop-necked purple dress the next day, and a floppy black bow in her hair that

Paul called her 'washerwoman' look. She tried to feel positive about a social occasion with Kurt and a coterie of
snake-skinned scenesters.

Presumably because Kurt didn't queue, they were
whisked by Hackney cab to the bar at not inconsiderable
cost. Kurt was poured into a tight bright blue suit with
brown brogues and wearing choking quantities of a stri-
dently pinecone-scented cologne.

'Cock & Tail' was in a warehouse in Wapping, tricked
out to look like a butcher's shop. There were S-shaped meat
hooks dangling above the bar, the staff wore striped blue and
white aprons, and there was a pig's head with an apple in
its mouth mounted like a hunting trophy stag above the bar.

The overall effect was both queasily tasteless and obnox-
iously pleased with itself.

All the cocktails came with a 'carnivorous twist'. Delia
dodged the Bloody Abattoir Mary that looked like it had
a Peperami as a stirrer and instead went for a Suckle It Pig,
something fizzy that tasted of apple and was served with
crisps like Frazzles as a side order.

Kurt had a Black Velvet Pudding, which came with a
coin of black pudding on the rim in the place of a slice
of fruit. Boak.

'Oh for fuck's sake. I thought this was an *exclusive* event,'
Kurt said, looking towards the door.

Across the room she spied who Kurt was eyeballing; a
lightly ruffled – and admittedly dashing – Adam West
arriving in his beige private dick coat. He was with what
tabloids would term a 'glamorous female companion'.

Delia's nerves prickled. Adam and Kurt in the same space could go very badly for her. She swigged the rest of her drink in one and lifted another from a passing tray. She could feel her courage rising with her blood alcohol levels.

Kurt soon abandoned Delia to work the room. She busied herself by moving on to her third − or was it her fourth? − pig fizz thing, and checking her phone with a frown as if she was a heart surgeon waiting to be paged that an organ had come in for transplant surgery.

'What do you think to the bar, Dana?'

Delia looked up to see Adam, wearing his usual look of delighted self-satisfaction.

'Ah, the old getting my name wrong gag, great to see it again,' Delia said, noticing she was speaking rather thickly, and that a significant amount of caution had left her body. 'I think it's pretty awful to be honest.'

'Agree. This place is simply teeming with harmful parasites.'

'One or two.'

Delia reached for her next drink and looked around the room to give the impression she'd mislaid the five great mates she had here that she'd rather be talking to than Adam West.

'It's one of those slap-my-forehead ideas, isn't it,' he continued. 'Why did no one ever call a bar Cock & Tail before? Oh. Because it's *hugely crass*.' He sucked on the straw in his drink.

Delia focused on him again.

'Yet you're hanging around, inhaling the free booze.'

'Yet I am.'

Adam's girlfriend joined them and Delia's soul shrivelled further.

'Freya. This is Delia Moss, from Twist & Shout. I think you've spoken on the phone.'

Adam threw a satirical glance in Delia's direction and Delia tried not to visibly wince at finding out who she was.

Freya had silken straight toffee hair, a butterscotch St Tropez-boothed body and the close set, dead yellow-amber eyes of a swamp-dwelling reptile. She teetered on spike-covered S&M style shoes that left Delia trying to fathom how she could walk a yard, let alone get herself to Cock & Tail.

Freya threaded an arm around Adam and looked Delia up and down. 'Hi.'

Delia almost laughed. She'd never seen a woman mark territory quite so physically before. It was as if she wound herself round his leg like a cat with its tail. If Freya could've lifted her leg to spray him, she probably would have.

'Delia!' Kurt barked as he passed, leaning in across Adam and Freya. 'Let's circulate and talk to the people who matter, shall we?'

He moved on.

Adam grinned.

'Silver-tongued bastard, isn't he?'

'Who was that twat?' Freya asked.

'"*Who was that twat*?" A question often asked in Kurt Spicer's wake. And hopefully *at* his wake,' said Adam.

'If you'll excuse me, I see people I *need* to talk to,' Delia said, giving this announcement the kind of icy, clipped Bette Davis delivery that people used in films when they needed to escape unwelcome cocktail party company. Adam curled his lip in an O RLY? sardonic way.

In fact, she needed a wee.

It did the job though: when she exited Cock & Tail's rather dank toilets, with one of those trendy, giant spinning lemon-shaped soaps on an arm that were surely unhygienic, Adam and Freya had been re-absorbed into the party and were nowhere to be seen.

Having got herself a fresh drink – these apple things had grown on her – Delia tucked herself well out of view of Kurt, Adam and Freya, right by a huge spiky exotic plant in an earthenware tub.

To her surprise, after tuning out the throb of the music, she realised she could clearly hear the private conversation on the other side of the foliage.

'. . . At first I couldn't make sense of it, then I twigged. Spicer's hired these two wholesome northern girls as the perfect mules to shift his product. They're like the Peru Two,' she heard Adam saying.

'This is the ginger girl who sounds like *Geordie Shore*, dressed like Hilda Ogden?' Freya said.

'Delia Moss.'

'No relative of Kate, with those hips.'

*Oof.*

'Mmm. She doesn't seem to have the faintest idea what's going on.'

'She probably has. Don't be fooled by that salt of the earth thing,' Freya said.

'Seriously. She's just off the train. She's fallen off the hay cart and bumped her head. I know more about her company than she does.'

'So, you're going to sleep with her and try for pillow talk?'

'Hah, *hardly*.'

'Not into "Groundskeeper Willie" hair?'

'I think I'd sooner be into willies.'

There followed some nasty female cackling.

'I have other ways.'

'You surprise me.'

'Kurt's about to move into politics and I'm going to be there to shoot out the tyres on his bandwagon.'

'She's part of your plan?'

'Without knowing. When the moment comes, I'll chuck her to the wolves.'

'I love it when you talk ruthless to me.'

'It's not ruthless if someone deserves it.'

What a *thunderturd*! Delia thought.

Hah, well, ironies: he was saying she was badly informed. She was better informed now, eh? She celebrated with another drink.

# Thirty-Six

Almost an hour later, an inebriated Kurt found Delia and told her he thought he'd set up one or two VIP meetings.

'Great,' Delia said, thinking this was her cue to leave, but her head and legs felt slow.

'You know why you unsettle men?' Kurt said.

Delia took a second to catch up with the abrupt change in the conversation. Kurt hadn't altered his tone or volume.

'Er. No?' said Delia, thinking, *do I?*

'You have that childlike face and a very developed body.'

'Developed body'? Surely that was a phrase only used by paedophile uncles during dubious parlour games?

'We don't know whether we want to protect you or defile you,' Kurt said. He fixed her with what he thought was a meaningful gaze. Delia felt revolted. She needed to get out of this conversation, sharpish. Only nothing about her felt sharp. It was more warm, blunted and fuzzy.

'I've never thought about it.'

'Sure. You're an innocent. There's no shame in being

wet behind the ears,' Kurt said. 'Or for that matter, wet between . . .'

'The ears!'

Adam West appeared next to them. *Oh, great.*

'Kurt. How's tricks? Never was a greeting more apposite.'

'You're interrupting.'

'I know. Hey, loving your work with Marvyn Le Roux. Are you teaching him about disappearing acts?'

'There's an old Aboriginal phrase that makes me think of you, West. It loosely translates as go take a face bath between a wallaby's buttflaps.'

'Lyrical. I'd love to hear it in the original dialect,' Adam said. 'Anyway, I came to tell you the photographer wants a shot of you and another ligger.'

'Get lost,' Kurt growled.

'I'm serious,' Adam said, nodding back towards the photographer. A man with a Nikon round his neck could be seen doing a wave and thumbs up.

Kurt grudgingly left Delia's side and made his way to the far end of the bar.

Adam turned to Delia as soon as Kurt was out of earshot.

'You do realise he's trying to take you home? And what's that aftershave? He smells like a Virgin Active locker room.'

Delia wanted to deliver scorching putdowns about how Adam West's presence wasn't welcome either.

Instead, she felt a fizzing in her stomach and an acrid taste in her mouth. Delia didn't think she was going to be sick, but she couldn't stand there for a moment longer either.

The news finally reached her that she was awe-inspiringly drunk.

'I need some air,' she said, and Adam nodded and steered her out of the door. She lacked the ability to shake him off.

Outside she breathed the colder air of the Docklands deeply, and steadied herself. OK, OK. On top of it now.

'I'm gosh to go back insides,' Delia said to Adam.

'I don't think you want to go back into that den, in the state you're in,' Adam said. 'This is work. Don't show weakness.'

The state she was in! Supercilious git.

Delia had a reply all cued-up in her head: *I am not in any state now if you'll excuse me, I am going back inside.*

Instead a kind of 'pshaaaw' noise came out. OK, still drunk.

'I see you have your bag. What does your coat look like?' Adam said. 'Actually, I know it. It's the one that looks like you killed and skinned a Muppet. Do NOT move.'

Delia watched Adam dart inside. She had a sense that she should marshal the pieces of things that happened into a coherent picture, but didn't have the cognitive skills to complete the jigsaw.

She wondered if it'd be quite clever if she did move, as he'd said not to? The door opened and as a couple of people came out, Delia slipped in after them.

Should she have another drink? She should perhaps try the circulating thing. She felt very bold and confident it'd go well.

Freya from the *Mirror* advanced on her, not someone Delia was aiming to circulate with.

'Be careful around Adam. You know he's slept with *everyone*,' she said.

'He's not slept with me,' Delia slight-slurred.

Freya raised an eyebrow and turned her back on her.

As Delia zeroed in on a drinks tray, she felt a tug on her arm and Adam Who'd Slept With Everyone leaned down, hissing: 'Oi! I thought I told you to stay put, you pissed womble.'

'You're not the bosh of me,' Delia said.

'I will bosh you around for your own good and you'll thank me for it tomorrow.'

Delia protested as he propelled her towards the exit. Outside, Adam thrust her raspberry wool coat into her arms. *Did he say it was like a Fraggle? She should tell him that . . . what should she tell him . . .*

'Now please try to look compos mentis long enough to ensure that a taxi will take you. Concentrate. Look at me . . .'

Adam held her face in his hands and Delia scowled as her eyes swiped from side to side. She looked totally cons . . . consch . . . Conch shell. Hah! How had she never noticed those words sounded quite similar before?

'Give me my face back.' Her voice came out in a bad ventriloquist's *gottle-of-geer.*

Adam hooted with laughter, dropping his hands and shaking his head.

'You are something else.'

Delia had a dim sense that things had possibly gone

very very wrong, and she would feel differently about all this in the morning.

The caramel brown-ish Freya girl from earlier came flying out of Cock & Tail and Adam turned his back on Delia. He had a fraught, hushed conversation with caramel girl that a swaying Delia only part-absorbed.

She caught the odd phrase from the cross, slim woman with her arms folded . . . *what the hell* . . . *well who cares if he is* . . . *thought you were trying to get to him, not get into her knickers.*

Knickers?! Delia wanted to move but everything was taking place underwater.

And a terse riposte from Adam All The Sex, who concluded: *If people think that, then let them. What do I care?*

Eventually Freya went back inside, throwing a toxically filthy look in Delia's direction. Delia lifted her fingers in a heavy wave but it came off strangely.

Adam sighed heavily and put his hand on her shoulder.

'Right then, Drunkst Delia, Destroyer Of Evenings. Let's get out of here.'

Delia had a reply ready to go: *Oh so you know my name after all!* And: *No thanks, I will make my own way.*

But again her mouth defied her, and it came out as: shmmmfff. She shook her head. Adam strode out on to the road and put his hand up, a taxi swung in and Delia was ushered inside.

An arm went round her in the cab and a conversation took place she had no conscious part of, although she heard her own voice. With the vehicle's soporific movement, she was fighting it, but she felt her consciousness slipping, slipping, slipping . . .

'Delia, Delia?' she heard a male voice.

'Mmm . . .'

'Stay with me. Stay away from the light. Or the dark.'

# Thirty-Seven

Delia opened a gummy eyelid, as disorientated as someone returning to consciousness in the recovery ward.

Who was she . . . where was she . . . The room even smelled strange: of a powdery, strident brand of washing powder she didn't use. And dust. And *boy.*

She pushed herself up on her elbows and looked around. She was in a single bed in a narrow room, with a plastic clotheshorse at one end.

Her purple dress lay on the floor.

Oof, her head. And her stomach. Oh God oh God oh no . . . the night before came back to her, in violent, strobing flashbacks. The awful bar . . . Kurt trying to chat her up . . . she left . . . who did she leave with? She was in a cab with *someone*, the 'who' was hazy. She felt psychically sick with apprehensiveness and remorse, a nice partner to the literal sick she felt.

Next to her on the nightstand was a bottle of Coke with 'Drink Me' on a Post-it note, a pack of Ibuprofen with 'Take Me', and a folded piece of paper with 'Read Me.'

A booze trout's version of *Alice in Wonderland*.

Delia shifted bones that creaked and ached, and a skull that felt as if it was full of marbles that had rolled to one side. She unfolded the paper.

*MORNING!*

*How's the head? So I thought you needed to go home last night, but I couldn't get your address out of you. Turns out cab drivers need more than FINSHBURRY PORK! repeated three times, with increasing volume. So much for The Knowledge. I had a choice, either go through your things to find out where you live, or bring you back to mine. I thought as dread rivals we were better off without me diving through your handbag. So here we (you) are. Sorry the box room isn't beautiful. See you in the breakfasting salon at sun up in cotton waffle dressing gowns, for kedgeree and homemade granola.*

*Adam*

Oh no, oh God.

Delia grasped for her handbag on the nightstand and dug out her phone. She went to Google Maps and keyed in Emma's postcode, hitting Get Route. The blue pin dropped, giving her location as just off Clapham High Street. She groaned and looked down again at her underwear. Had he undressed her? What had she said? And done? This was so horrific.

With shaky hands, she unscrewed the cap on the Coke and tipped it to cracked-dry lips. Ahhhhh. The reviving power of sugar and caffeine. The abrasive syrupy fizz flowed over her sandpaper tongue and made a noise as it gurgled down her throat. She wasn't sure if she could handle swallowing the tablets, though. Her stomach was telling her she was on Nil By Solids. She waited a moment and did a throw-and-swig with them.

Delia eased herself out of bed and pulled her dress on. She felt deeply uneasy at waking in bra and pants. They didn't match and she was only patchily depilated.

Her shoes had been kicked off nearby but she thought a stealthy exit might be better accomplished not in heels. She opened a compact mirror in her handbag and surveyed the damage, wincing. Easing the door open, there were noises of someone moving about downstairs but otherwise the coast seemed clear. Delia could see where the bathroom was, just across the landing.

She tip-toed in and closed the door. This was a lad's house, albeit apparently one with a cleaner: the towels were in dark colours, the edge of the bath held bottles of functional and sporty things. Inside the mirrored cabinet were disposable razors and packs of soap.

Delia wet gobbets of loo roll and wiped at her smudged eyes. She splurged some toothpaste onto a forefinger, rubbed it across her teeth and tongue, spat and rinsed. She finger-combed her birds-nested, backcombed hair and tried to pull it into something more like a ponytail.

She had small bits and bobs of 'touch-up' make-up in

her handbag, which could now be deployed in accident recovery: concealer, a lip gloss, perfume miniature, and her liquid liner. When she'd finished re-applying, she looked more terminally ill brothel madam than unidentified corpse.

She padded back to the bedroom, slipped her heels on and found her coat slung over a chair.

Time to make a very fast and dignified-as-possible departure.

She wobbled gingerly down the two flights of shallow stairs and ducked her head round the door of one of the rooms at the bottom.

Adam West was in the kitchen, dressed in t-shirt, jogging bottoms and trainers, holding a cup of coffee. He looked as fresh as a dew-speckled daffodil by comparison, glowing from a run.

'The Kraken awakes!' he said, grinning widely.

'Er. Morning. What happened?' Delia said, testing her voice for the first time. It sounded a bit Kermit.

'Apple schnapps in champagne happened, about ten times. Or *lovely nommy naughty Appletise give me back my special tasty Appletise*, as you said constantly on our way home.'

'Oh, fuuuccc—' Delia rubbed a throbbing temple.

'Spirits in champagne are the speedball of cocktails. Be glad you're only the living dead in Clapham as opposed to dead-dead outside the Viper Room.'

He was going to enjoy this to the full, Delia realised. Of course he was.

'Coffee?' he said, picking up a steaming mug from next to the kettle.

'Thank you,' Delia croaked, taking it, more for something to do and an excuse not to speak while she sipped.

She had no idea what to say to him.

'Thanks for letting me stay,' Delia said, awkwardly.

'My pleasure.'

'Did, uh. Did everyone see us leave together?'

Adam did a joke spitting-my-drink double-take. 'You think I did this to make everyone think I scored? I'm not into the Coma Sutra, thanks.'

Delia wanted to die.

'No! I wasn't saying that. I need to work out if I still have a job.'

'I don't think anyone saw us, no,' Adam said. 'It was an act of immense chivalry on my part and I understood the need for discretion.'

'Why was I not in my dress?' Delia said, a reflex response in the snap of shame, not because she much wanted to know.

Adam's eyes widened in surprised innocence.

'Oh, hang on now, any clothing removal was done by you, after I closed the door. Don't turn this good deed into something sinister or I will get anxious and angry.'

Delia nodded, weakly.

She'd been so catastrophically stupid to get so lashed. How many years at the city council had she carefully extricated herself from the Christmas party by the time the Jägerbombs conga hoved into view? But she came to London and went arse-over-tit.

'Do you usually get that slammed? If I hadn't been there then God knows what would've happened,' Adam said over the rim of his coffee mug.

Delia shivered. The bad blond man had a bloody good point. She couldn't remember the last time she'd been that incapable. Thinner, sad Delia who forgot to eat didn't have the same tolerance as the fatter, happier Delia of old. You didn't admit such vulnerability to the enemy though.

'I would've been fine, I'd have got home . . .'

'You honestly need to be careful. You're not around nice people. Alternate alcoholic drinks with water and combine with caution.'

'Ooh tell us more about the effects of this "alcohol", we're all toothless, playing banjos up in Noo Cas'le!' Delia said. It was impossible to sustain any real ire amidst Adam's delighted laughter.

'Oohooohoo! NO! You know what I meant. Kurt was all over you and he meant business.'

'Oh no, he's just very direct and Aussie . . .' Delia lied.

'I saw him buying condoms in the gents,' Adam said, making an 'oh dear' face.

Delia's skin prickled.

'Maybe that was for something else.'

'Animal water balloons,' Adam said, setting his mug down and pushing himself up on to the breakfast bar. His eyes strayed to the kitchen doorway behind her.

'Oh, Dougie, this is Delia, Delia, Dougie.'

Delia turned to see a rumpled, bulky, bum-fluffed man

of about thirty, in a towelling robe. He looked as if he'd had nearly as hard a night out as Delia had.

'Hello. Nice to meet you,' he said in a Glaswegian accent. He poured Crunchy Nut Cornflakes into a bowl, sploshed chocolate milk on to them and turned to leave. Dougie's incurious demeanour around her suggested to Delia that women in their kitchen he'd not met before wasn't an uncommon occurrence.

'Back to bed?' Adam said.

'Aye. Forever. I'm fucked so I am.'

He shuffled out.

'Dougie went out with some friends from his homeland last night. They call themselves the Willy Wallace warriors. Imagine. Actually, don't.'

'Is it only you and him here?' Delia said. She was sure she'd passed several rooms on her way down.

For the first time since she met Adam, he looked ever so slightly uncomfortable.

'Yeah.'

Was he gay? She'd gotten zero gay vibes, but who knew. He slept with 'everyone' apparently, so maybe Freya meant he was AC/DC.

'Why did you do this really?' she said, with a forced smile. 'To get me into trouble with Kurt, or put me further in your debt?'

'There's thanks for you. Because I knew otherwise you'd wake up with a sore groin as well as a sore head in a Sofitel somewhere. I took pity.'

Delia didn't know what to think.

'I never know whether to believe you.'

'I'll let you into a secret, Delia. I always tell the truth. So you always can.'

Funnily enough, she didn't believe him.

# Thirty-Eight

'I'm going to get going then, which way to the Tube?' Delia said, thinking Adam would want her gone as much as she did.

'Come and sit down for a bit and recover,' Adam said, standing down from the work surface.

'Ah. No . . .' Delia resisted.

'You spent the night here, another fifteen minutes isn't going to make a difference. You look like the bad taxidermy version of yourself.'

'Sod you,' Delia mumbled, but she had to admit she was exhausted by the business of being upright.

'C'mon. Dougie's no company for the next twelve hours at least. Take pity on me in return.'

Delia couldn't really refuse, and carried her coffee to the front room.

It was a true boys' rented house, this. Every soft furnishing was navy blue or army grey. There were big saggy worn blue sofas with removable covers, a pine coffee table covered in sticky rings and a huge flat-screen television, coated in a light patina of greasy dust.

The room was cast into a greenish gloom by the thick overgrown ivy that clung like a wig to the window, although it was a nice alternative to blinds.

Delia sank gratefully onto the nearest settee and wondered just how huge a price in ridicule Adam was going to be extracting for this. Right now she couldn't think about that. Physically surviving this hangover was task enough.

'Can I make a suggestion?' Adam said, on the sofa opposite. 'When I have been beaten by the beer, I like to lie like this,' he swung himself round so he was lying on his back, 'my legs like so,' he rested them on the arms of the sofa. 'I think you'll find the angle very relaxing, and the light from the window is precisely the amount your vampire eyes can cope with.'

He folded his hands on his stomach. 'Try it. I promise you, this position held for five hours straight sorted Dougie after he'd done the *Top Gun* drinking challenge.'

Homoerotic *Top Gun*, eh? 'What does that involve?'

'Oh, I dunno. Judging by Dougie's condition you must drink every time there's a moment of patriotic machismo.'

Delia sighed, and moved herself into an approximation of Adam's position. Her muscles relaxed against the sofa cushions, her heels dangling.

'See!' Adam said. 'You look . . . at peace.'

Delia did a weak shaky gurgle-giggling. 'That's what you say about people in the Chapel of Rest.'

'Haha! "Remember her the way she would've wanted, not like this."'

Adam laughed and Delia thought how intensely he was enjoying himself.

'So . . . this Paul of yours, then,' Adam said, and Delia was given the scariest rollercoaster drop-lurch of realising she had said things of which she had no memory. None. Like general anaesthetic. She had put herself under.

'God, what?!' she said. 'What did I say?'

'Oh, nothing much,' Adam said, soothingly. 'You told me he's been fooling around and it's why you came to London.'

Delia's alcohol-poisoned, clammy skin grew clammier against the gritty fabric of the sofa. It was awful and exposing, not knowing what she'd said.

'When?'

'I got you to drink a glass of water when we got back, and we chatted. Briefly.'

The thought that Delia had said things to him where there was no sift, sort or check mechanism before the words left the brain depot was awe-inspiringly dreadful. She groaned and placed a palm over her eyes.

'Now you're sober and possibly going to remember, can I give you my views on this subject?' Adam said, to Delia groaning. 'The man's-eye view.'

Delia groaned some more. 'Because all men are the same.'

'No, we're not. But I think sometimes women apply the logic of how females think to male behaviour, in order to understand it,' he twisted his head to look at Delia, 'then don't understand it. I won't say another word about this if you don't want me to.'

Delia fancied clawing back some control by telling him

to leave it. On the other, she had a small flicker of curiosity about his opinion.

'Go on,' she said, with a long-suffering exhalation.

'Alright. I think you shouldn't get back together with Paul, for two reasons. First reason, he wanted you to tell him he had to end it with the other woman. I think to not give you a straight answer on whether he was leaving you or not when you found out was a proper shit's trick.'

Oh no. She'd said *loads*.

'He *kind* of did. He wanted me to say we were going to get through it. Which I couldn't.'

'Translation: he wanted you to say you'd be there if he broke it off. Shit's trick, as I said. That's someone who's never going to take responsibility for his actions, or treat you with much respect.'

Delia squirmed. This was more incisive and harsh than she expected. And hearing Paul denigrated hurt her.

'Secondly, he happy-cheated, not sad-cheated. If it's a response to something in the relationship that needs fixing, it can possibly be fixed. Happy cheaters do it for the adventure, and they'll do it again.'

'What do you mean? *Sad* cheating? Like if you cry afterwards, it's OK?'

'I mean,' Adam found a cushion under his backside and moved it behind his head, 'when I've cheated, it was because I wasn't happy and wanted out.'

'Oh, so *you've* cheated,' Delia said. 'Now it's coming out.'

Freya's reference to Adam's vigorous activity levels returned to her brain.

'I've never pretended to be perfect myself. In fact, it's precisely because I'm not that I can offer you some valuable insights. Yes, I've cheated, to sabotage something that wasn't working, when I didn't have the stones to finish it. But I've never been unfaithful to a long-term girlfriend who I still wanted to be with, and expected her to forgive and forget.'

'Maybe Paul doesn't want to be with me and this was his way of escaping.'

'He does want to be with you,' Adam said, dismissively. 'He's in his thirties, I'm sure he knows there aren't many Delias out there. But he wants you on his own terms. He saw the chance of some extra fun and he took it. And why did he take it?'

Delia said nothing, surprised at being described as a scarce resource, a valuable ingredient in a life, like saffron. It wasn't how she thought Adam saw her at all. A ginger tragi-mess oddity in granny clothes, would've been more like it.

'. . . Because he knew you wouldn't leave him.'

'I have left him.'

'You haven't though, have you? You're punishing him and then you'll take him back. Or that's what you said last night . . .'

Delia was at a serious disadvantage in a debate where she had no idea how much Adam knew.

'Mark my words, one day, he will take the chance again. I also doubt this Celine is the first time.'

Delia's self-consciousness twanged and her temper broke.

'God, this is really uncalled for! How can you possibly know that?'

'I'm saying: ten years of good behaviour, a meaningless fling and then back to fidelity is not a pattern of offending I recognise.'

'You seem pretty confident to analyse a complicated situation and a complete stranger from a distance.'

'I'm a good judge of character,' Adam said. 'It's not that complicated, is it? Bottom line is, this is not a guy who's ever going to stop taking you for granted.'

'Thank you,' Delia said, hollowly. 'Just what the hung-over woman needed.'

'Sorry,' Adam said, brightly, adjusting the cushion again, 'I felt it needed saying.'

'In the end,' Delia said, chest tight, 'your reasoning might be sound, but it comes down to loving him. I love him, so I can't just walk away.'

'But he doesn't love you enough. You can't do it for both of you. It doesn't work like that.'

Delia sat bolt upright. 'He doesn't love me enough? You really said that?'

A pause.

'Not from what you've told me, he doesn't.'

'Thanks for that completely brutal, unnecessary thing to say.'

'I'm sorry,' Adam looked startled. He sat up too, registering the alarm in her voice. 'I didn't mean to upset you.'

'What could possibly upset me about telling me my boyfriend doesn't love me?'

'*Enough*, I said enough,' Adam said.

'Have you got any idea how cruel that is? I mean, my brother Ralph has no tact, and he wouldn't say that.'

Adam watched as Delia leapt up and grabbed for her bag and coat. 'Come on, don't storm off.'

'I'm not "storming off", I'm leaving because I don't want to listen to any more vicious things about my hopeless life.'

'I didn't say you were hopeless! You seem like a good girl and you're being taken advantage of . . .'

'A good *girl*?!'

'Argh, woman, sorry!'

'You're such a superior *hey, little lady, let me tell you how the real world works* type of . . . sexist southerner,' Delia spat, not quite knowing why she chose this moment to go feminist and Geordie on his ass, though goodness knows he deserved it.

'In both work and personal matters, you have an uneasy relationship with the truth,' Adam said, expression hardening. He looked more disappointed than angry.

'And you . . .' Delia summoned all her wits to sass him, and her dehydrated brain failed her miserably, 'Are a TWAT.'

Minutes later she was doing the walk of shame down Clapham High Street, among bright-eyed Waitrose advert families out for Saturday brunch, thinking Adam West was an awful human being – apart from the fetching Coke and Nurofen thing.

She also had a sense there was something she didn't know, from the night before, amid all the gruesome things she did know of.

Something she'd forgotten, and needed to remember.

# Thirty-Nine

'Then he said he betted Celine wasn't Paul's first indiscretion!' Delia concluded, indignantly.

For a second, there was a flicker in Emma's composure, and Delia saw she agreed with Adam. Adam West couldn't be right. He just couldn't. He was all that was wrong. It must be because Emma fancied him. Yep, that was it.

Emma was in her White Company grey marl pyjamas on the giant sofa, having returned from Rome in the dead of Saturday night, looking wan. She regaled Delia on Sunday morning with torrid stories of the rigidly spreadsheeted hen do, where every chunk of time was accounted for.

'*3.30 p.m. to 4 p.m., "Relaxing at Hen HQ"*. Thanks for saying we can have a half hour break if we want to! It was like one of those Tough Mudder assault course things with the sweatbands, only at least they last a day, you're paying people to shout at you and you lose weight.'

Emma bought Delia a bottle of Aperol and a glow-in-the-dark plastic Virgin Mary.

'The other bridesmaid India said I was trivialising a

religion and I said oh I didn't realise you were showing proper respect when you were taking selfies making peace signs outside the Vatican.'

Delia laughed and gave thanks she wasn't on the 'Hen Don't', as Emma called it.

Emma perked up and whooped with delight at the sight of the food Delia had loaded the kitchen with.

'These look like . . . homemade chicken nuggets?' Emma said, with awe in her voice, as if discovering a knobbly lump of Inca gold in her fridge.

'I made a batch for Ralph last week and thought you'd like them too. I'm experimenting with a buttermilk and Ritz cracker crusting.'

'*Handsome.* Please never leave.'

They'd taken a picnic to the sofa.

'What's that?' Emma said, as Delia moved an envelope and a set of pictures cut out of magazines.

'Oh . . .' Delia found herself strangely shy. 'It's from Paul. He's sending me things to remind me of our past. We had a conversation once where I got Jean Cocteau, Jacques Cousteau and Jean Michel Jarre mixed up.'

Paul was choosing wisely, and wittily. They'd been on holiday, a village in Greece full of whitewashed villas with cobalt shutters and splashes of amethyst bougainvillea. Paul had concluded: 'Please, please don't bring the Cocteau Twins into this or I may not cope,' while physically holding his sides. They'd laughed till tears ran down their faces and Delia had thought how Paul was her perfect foil, and she was his.

'Nice gesture,' Emma said, with an appraising look that Delia returned steadily, keeping her face neutral.

'You told Adam about Paul?' Emma said now, of the Adam outrage.

'Apparently I ran my mouth when I was out of it. So embarrassing. He shouldn't have been talking to me about personal things, when he knew I was in no state.'

They both paused, as it was obvious it wasn't possible to safely convict Adam on an episode where Delia had zero memory.

For all they knew, Adam was saying 'Mmm, hmmm, anyway . . .' as Delia shrieked about Paul's penile crimes the whole way up the stairs.

'It wasn't his place to say that about Paul,' Emma said, and again Delia noticed the political choice of words.

Could this be true? That with manifold opportunities, Paul had fallen from the wagon once or twice before? He'd mentioned women occasionally, and Delia thought that was a sure sign there was nothing to worry about.

Was Paul that very smartest of liars, those who understand that to make something invisible, you hide it in plain sight? Delia was now dredging the ocean floor of memory to see what debris floated up. Hmmm. The leggy wine merchant woman who Paul laughed was trying to flirt her way into a contract, a few years ago? Becky, was it?

She felt like a detective assigned to a cold-crimes unit, reopening investigations into incidents previously classified as non-suspicious.

She recalled Aled being slightly odd about that Becky,

actually. And when Delia asked Paul why, he said: 'I think Aled's got a bit of a soft spot. Nothing for Gina to worry about. You know what they're like as a couple though, they're not like us. If she got wind it'd be a big deal.'

*They're not like us.* If Delia had a time machine, and confronted Past Delia on why Becky was no threat, Past Delia would laugh in Present Delia's face. One of her pieces of immutable evidence would be: Aled would tell me if Paul was playing away.

*Or maybe he'd tell Paul to knock it on the head, and sit there looking deeply uncomfortable when her name came up.*

Delia shook off thoughts of painful imponderables of the past and returned to the painful ponderables of now.

'This was after Adam manhandled me into a taxi and took me back to his place. Ugh. The people I've got involved with, Emma. I'm glad I met Steph or I'd think I was in the sewer with only rats for company.'

'Although,' Emma began, hesitantly, 'what Adam did was quite nice, though? Taking you home?'

Delia wasn't ready to agree. Taking that at face value, she felt, was naiveté and she'd no doubt figure out his motive at a later date. I mean, it felt cynical given all he'd done, but for all Delia knew he *had* tried it on with her. The fact that she had no memory equally meant she couldn't entirely exonerate him. Caution was advisable. He didn't make sense to her and amid these contradictory pieces of evidence, she needed to hold on to the simple sincerity of her initial dislike.

'He'll have weighed up that it had something in it for

him. That's how he operates. He probably wanted to infuriate Kurt.'

Delia also hadn't forgiven him for spoiling her first flush of enthusiasm for London, and Twist & Shout. Before that bloody folder mistake, she was enjoying herself.

Emma nodded.

'Your boss sounds a total scumsock.'

Delia could only agree. She thought he was a flirt before, but now she saw he might be dangerously predatory. She'd never get pissed around him again, that was for sure.

'I don't want to go to work tomorrow.'

'You and me both,' Emma said. 'Inbox of doom.'

Delia resolved to manage the Kurt situation. She'd got too drunk, from now on she'd be on her guard. Surely he wouldn't try again, now he knew he'd get nowhere with her? And it'd be dropping Steph in it to deal with Kurt alone. No, onwards and sort-of upwards. If she got enough experience at Twist & Shout, it'd stand her in better stead for moving somewhere else.

Nevertheless, Delia had forgotten Sunday night blue dreads were the worst thing in the world.

Newcastle City Council had served up a lot of dull days, but not many terrible ones. Which was one of the reasons she'd stayed so long in that job: *not actively bad* was easier than chasing the dream of *actually any good* in your working life, and ending up with *often awful*.

However, there was a little bright spark in the dark of a long night: an email from the Naan. Delia was still adjusting to thinking of him as Joe. She'd scanned in pages from The Fox, using a printer Emma had left in the box under the stairs. Delia had thought she'd be shy, but as the pages stacked up, she thought: they look good! They look proper.

*Delia, The Fox. I love it. I absolutely \*love\* it. It's brilliant. You've never done anything with it? You've not put it on show anywhere? Why not? J*

*Hi Joe! Thank you! . . . Fear. Dx*

*I don't see what there is to be afraid of. Jx*

*. . . Nor do I, any more. Dx*

*Wellokaythen. Jx*

A name came to her: Fantastic Miss Fox. What about putting the comic online? And seeing if anyone asked, as Ralph once did – 'what happens next'?

# Forty

Delia's nerves mounted as she walked the now-familiar wide streets of Charing Cross. Past the Foyles where she sometimes wasted half an hour at lunchtime, towards the building where she mysteriously never saw another soul other than those in her own company . . .

What was she walking into at Twist & Shout this morning? A bear trap? Kurt was a lot like a bear himself, an Antipodean grizzly. Perhaps Delia was like that poor man in the documentary who was convinced he could make pals of grizzlies, and ended up being turned into a mixed kebab.

Her phone pinged with a text.

*Delia, I'm going to call you in a sex. Please answer, it's important I talk to you before you're in the office. Ax*

*PS SEC ☹ I hate auto correct/Freud*

A kiss? This oily sardine was sending her electronic kisses now? And right on cue, her phone began to ring.

'Ah, you answered! Morning.'

'I didn't have much choice. What do you want, Adam?'

'Listen. Kurt's probably going to ask you about where you went on Friday.'

'Oh, so now you're admitting we were seen together?!'

Minutes before Delia had to walk into the room with Kurt, he coughs the truth. *Bloody Adam bloody West.*

'I don't think we were, but you can never be sure and he'll naturally be suspicious.'

Delia's medium–level stomach turmoil became a faster spin cycle.

'It's in both our interests that he doesn't know. When he asks you, say you saw me leave entwined with Freya. She'll back this up if he talks to her.'

Hah, I bet she will, Delia thought.

'. . . Please do use this line if possible, because it's cost me a hell of a lot of grief to get Freya onside.'

Delia felt some guilt at causing a domestic row, in her rescue.

'I didn't mean to upset your girlfriend.'

'She's *not* my girlfriend,' Adam said, with emphasis.

'Oh yes. She said you'd slept with *everyone*,' Delia said, also with emphasis, enjoying wielding a small piece of revenge.

A short silence and Adam said, tersely: 'Freya does my PR.'

What was the *thing*? The thing she needed to remember?

'OK, I'll say you left with Freya. You *should* be a couple, you know. My gran has a saying: when God makes 'em, he pairs 'em.'

'Ack. Stop it,' Adam said. She could sense him grimace. Delightful role reversal. 'Another thing . . . I did go too far with what I said on Saturday morning. Please accept my apology.'

Delia made a 'hmph' noise.

'Never change careers to become a counsellor, will you.'

Adam laughed with genuine warmth rather than cackly snark.

'Fair point. Dougie's choco Crunchy Nut Cornflakes made a noisy return, by the way. It was sheer hubris, he was only at the Lucozade Sport stage at best. I thought you'd want to know.'

Delia laughed, despite herself.

'Chocolate milk on Crunchy Nut Cornflakes is a serious sugar hit. I'm surprised he wasn't juddering.'

'Oh yeah. Dougie's eating habits fully support Scottish stereotypes. He'd try to put me in batter if I stayed still long enough. He *refries* leftover KFC.'

'Sounds like my brother Ralph. He's been known to pour Bird's custard into a brioche hot dog bun. He says the egg in brioche makes it like a bread and butter pudding.'

'Dear God. That's some next-level shit.'

Why was Delia chatting to Adam? Ah: trying to distract herself from the hubbub of her nerves. He was surprisingly easy to talk to, and she wondered how many people had noted this trait, right before he wooed them into their downfall. That said, she couldn't see how swapping 'food mourn' tales mattered. And given she'd blapped about her broken relationship while mentally absent on booze, there wasn't much point trying to maintain a stiff upper lip.

'. . . Did your brother have a nice time when he was down, by the way? Madame Tussauds, wasn't it?'

Adam obviously did that well-brought-up boy thing of remembering details and making polite inquiries.

'He did, thanks. Ralph especially liked Dr Crippen. He said he reminded him of the chief fryer at the chip shop where he works.'

Delia deliberately put that detail in, to see if Adam would take the chance to mock her brother.

'One of the great homeopaths of all time, Dr Crippen, among stiff competition. Woah, and Ralph has access to a deep-fat fryer? Dougie would be in hog heaven. Don't suppose he likes gaming?'

'Does Ralph like computer games?! He lives for them.'

'This is spooky. Dougie's moved into the fantasy ones. He's currently trying to drink the magic drool of the grey owl of Gahoole, or something. We should've hooked the two of them up. Sounds like we'd soon both be buying hats for the wedding.'

Delia laughed again. She didn't think a character like Adam would be certified safe to be around a gentle Ralph. That said, Dougie did seem in the same genre as her brother: not the kind of merciless show-offs she thought Adam West would associate with.

Delia said goodbye in safe distance of the office, and walked in feeling surprisingly bolstered by the conversation: she was cornered, but she had a plan.

Kurt arrived only minutes after her, BlackBerry clamped to ear. (Delia had remarked on his choice of BlackBerry, instead of iPhone. 'You can't properly encrypt communications on an iPhone. Obama doesn't have an iPhone.' Kurt's explanations often made Delia more confused than if she'd left the thing unknown.)

'. . . Oh fucking hell, what a mess. Where is she? St Barts? OK. There in twenty,' Kurt said, before turning to Delia and Steph.

'Marvyn Le Roux's managed to perforate someone's bowel by messing up a knife-throwing stunt, the complete idiot. I need to get down there and make sure his victim doesn't talk to anyone. You OK to hold the fort?'

They both nodded and for a wonderful moment, Delia thought she'd dodged a bullet. Through someone else catching a knife. Adam wasn't wrong about Marvyn's lack of talent.

'Delia, can I have a word outside, please?'

Delia's breakfast omelette turned over.

Kurt rounded on her in the passageway outside, looking somewhat blotchy and stressed.

'Did you leave with Adam West on Friday?'

Delia performed a mock-horror face.

'No! Of course not.'

'You sure? Someone saw you leaving together.'

Delia did a confused face while her pulse pounded.

'He left with his girlfriend. That tall, thin girl from the *Mirror*? Freya?'

Kurt's eyes narrowed.

'She's his girlfriend?'

'Yes. Or I think so; she told me she was.'

'I hope you're telling me the truth, because consorting with Adam West is an employment-terminating offence at Twist & Shout.'

Delia said: 'Ask her if you don't believe me. She seemed quite possessive.'

Kurt's shoulders relaxed: 'My mistake. I was pretty wasted myself . . .'

'Me too,' Delia said, thinking, maybe here's the place where you apologise for saying vastly inappropriate things to a woman who works for you.

Kurt gave Delia a shrewd look that said: *then we will both pretend that conversation never happened.*

'You and Steph fancy a ShakeShack for lunch? If I can still eat after I've finished hearing about how this girl's intestines have been turned into sushi by Marvyn.'

Delia realised that was as much of an apology as she would get.

'A cheeseburger, yes please! Steph's veggie though. I think they do beanburgers.'

'Fuckin' troublemakers. If God didn't want us to eat animals, why did He make them out of meat?'

Kurt really was into his biblical study.

He stalked off and Delia breathed a sigh of relief. She had to admit, if Adam hadn't forewarned her and prepared an alibi, that could've been considerably worse.

She'd like to carry on telling herself he needn't have extracted her from the situation at the bar at all. But Delia knew she was in denial; she'd drunk her legs off.

And if it was a stark choice between Adam or Kurt carrying her to bed, Delia knew who'd she'd choose. Better the devil that doesn't want to rump you.

Her phone pinged.

*And? Did we squeak through? Ax*

*Just about. He might call Freya but he bought it. Dx*

*Praise be! You owe me, Delphine. Ax*

Adam was right about Freya's support coming at a cost: Delia was also recipient of a very sour text from her.

*I don't know what you're playing at with Adam, but you're out of your depth. Next time you throw yourself at him, you can find your own excuse. Freya CB*

If Delia had ever wondered what kind of person would abbreviate their own double-barrelled surname in a text message, now she knew.

'Delia,' Steph said, hesitantly, once they'd settled to their morning's work, 'What was that about?'

Delia explained, leaving out the part where she in fact did go home with Adam West. Delia could see Steph was working up to talking about something that had troubled her.

'You know Marvyn's not in the Magic Circle?' she said.

'Isn't he?' Delia said. 'I suppose that explains why he's causing GBH.'

'But we've said he is, on all the releases,' Steph said, her look of anguish increasing.

'You surprise me,' Delia said.

She recalled Adam saying there was a time limit for how long the lying would work, and she wondered if they were reaching the end of it. Whilst Delia didn't have long-term ambitions to stay in London, Steph certainly did – should she warn her?

'I asked Kurt what we should do if a journalist finds out if he's not in the Magic Circle. I mean, you can look it up online quite easily . . .'

Delia winced, knowing what was coming wasn't good.

'Kurt said if worst came to worst, we'd say Marvyn lied to us.'

Pause.

'Did we advise Marvyn to say he was in the Magic Circle?'

'Yep,' Steph nodded.

'Pheeeew,' Delia exhaled.

'Kurt said, we'll say he's a bit of a liar and a nutter and he's said all sorts.'

'We'd turn on the client and throw them overboard for taking our advice? We'd start briefing *against* them to journalists?'

Steph nodded.

'What if they found out?' she breathed.

Delia grimaced. She had the clearest sense yet that she

and Steph were becoming more compromised every day. She resolved that the next time she met Adam West, she'd ask him to give it to her straight about Kurt. She needed to know once and for all what she'd got herself into. When they met in Hyde Park she still knew nothing, and they'd not managed a meeting since. Had he decided to let her off the hook?

'I might go into the briefing notes and take it out. Kurt will never notice,' Steph said.

Delia nodded.

A text a little later gave her another shiver.

*FY to your I, Kurt has checked our story with Freya. Beautiful demonstration of trust in his employees, wouldn't you say? Watch yourself. And stay away from Naughty Appletise. Ax*

Half an hour later, Kurt marched in bearing piles of burgers, fries and malted milkshakes, and the news that Marvyn's casualty was not seriously injured.

Delia had to smile, thank him, and try not to dwell on the metaphorical knife lodged between her shoulder blades.

# Forty-One

It was a slow week for penning PR fictions and Delia was relieved. Everything seemed calmer, until a quietly spoken phone call from Paul on Thursday morning roundhouse-kicked her in the ribs.

'Dee, it's Parsnip,' he said. 'I didn't want to bother you until I knew what was happening, but I think he's really ill.'

'You think?'

'They're doing tests.'

Delia's knees went wobbly and the phone felt slippery in her hand. She'd got as far as the passage outside the office and thundered up the stairs, past Joy the receptionist and out through the giant Hobbit front door into the street.

Paul was explaining Parsnip had been acting strangely, so he'd taken him to the vet's the night before. Paul was returning later in the day for the verdict. Did Delia want to be there? Of course she did. She should never have left him.

Delia throbbed with guilt.

She'd abandoned Parsnip as a byproduct of punishing Paul, and without her, he'd sickened. It was possible she'd never see his silly wonky smile ever again. In truth, her self-reproach was as irrational as feeling you had to stay awake to 'fly the plane' but Delia felt it keenly all the same. Paul was busy blaming himself too.

'I should've noticed earlier. He's just such a nice lad he didn't make any fuss. He must've been in so much pain . . .' Paul's voice wavered and there was a pause while he got himself under control.

'They've warned me that he's not in the first flush of youth and his heart's not very strong, if he does need an operation.' Delia knew what was coming and had to stare at a passing car's number plate very hard to staunch the tears. 'It doesn't look good, Dee.'

There was a pause while Paul choked on his own tears and Delia swallowed and swallowed again and commanded herself: *don't cry don't cry you're at work don't cry.*

'I'll be there,' she said, robotically.

'. . . I feel terrible I didn't tell you before so you had more notice. I wanted to have something definite to tell you, and I knew you wouldn't sleep if I rang you last night.'

'It's fine, you did the right thing,' Delia said, taking a deep breath. 'What time is the appointment?'

'Half four.' Delia looked at her watch. She could make it.

'I'm going to come back.'

'Are you sure? Your boss will let you?'

'There are other jobs and only one Parsnip.'

She wasn't letting her dog die thinking she'd left him. Kurt would have to fire her.

Delia called him immediately, ready for battle. When she'd explained she needed to use holiday days for personal reasons, Kurt said, emollient, 'Sure, Red. Take it as sick leave. Hope it's not life or death.'

'My dog's sick. He might die,' she said, tremulously.

'Aw shit. Take as long as you need. Let me know if there's anything I can do.'

Having been braced for impact, Delia was weak with gratitude towards Kurt for this generosity.

Roger at the city council had a real thing about animals not being children and got very annoyed at their colleague Gavin having a day off when his boxer, The CEO, demised. Gavin came back to work and put his collar on his desk and did silent crying when he thought no one was looking.

Delia's heart had gone out to him, even if he had called his dog The CEO.

She didn't know quite how to feel about Kurt now. Why couldn't people be one thing or another?

She rushed back to the flat, threw a case together and was on the train heading north inside an hour. Her phone sat on the flip-down table and she dreaded it buzzing with an unscheduled call from Paul.

She checked her emails instead.

*Delia, I have some additional ideas about what you could do with The Fox site before you go live, if I don't overstep the mark. Jx*

Delia toyed with a few responses and couldn't settle on one: she could meet with Joe if she was back in the city. She just didn't know if she would be up to it.

Eventually she decided to explain the uncertainty, and Joe said nice things. It would be so strange to meet face to face, after such a long build up. A familiar friend, who was simultaneously a total stranger. Delia felt virtually certain there was no romance, despite her early flights of fancy. They'd settled into a groove that felt firmly matey. She'd purposefully mentioned Paul a few times to guide it away from those hopes, should they exist. Delia didn't think they did: she felt no 'build' from Joe that could indicate infatuation, despite him thinking her pretty, or remembering buffet chat. Without being unkind to her former co-workers, the council wasn't PR. It didn't provide a smorgasbord of visual treats, and one gaily dressed ginger female could possibly be quite memorable. In fact, she recognised a lot of her brother Ralph in him – someone very happy to stay where they were comfortable, physically and psychically.

She couldn't worry much about Joe thinking it was a date at the present time, though. Instead she thought about Parsnip in his cage at the vet's and felt marginally better now that she was taking action, heading towards him.

Delia hadn't thought about where she'd stay and decided it was best to sleep in the spare room in Heaton, rather than landing on her parents out of the blue, in an unsettled state.

Paul said he'd pick her up from the station.

As she pulled her trolley down the concourse in Newcastle, she saw him craning to see her face among the arrivals. Car keys swinging in one hand, khaki anorak, hems of jeans trailing over grimy white Adidas Gazelles. Delia had a lurch of old love so strong she nearly dropped the case and ran to him. She was home. Paul was her home.

But this wasn't the time, or the reason.

'You look well,' Paul said to Delia as she reached him, and she saw something of what Emma had said about her departure having an effect. He was regarding her differently, as if she was a beguiling mystery to him again.

'Let me take your case,' he said and Delia demurred and said no, she'd manage.

In the drive in Paul's old jalopy – the silver Golf, held together with duct tape and prayer – they fell back on discussing Parsnip practicalities. Like most beloved pets, Parsnip meant something to them that no one else could understand. Other people saw a raggedy, tattered old canine who bore an uncanny likeness to Dobby the House Elf, ready for the knacker's yard. Paul and Delia saw the former stray who still couldn't believe his dinner was for him, and stopped eating every three seconds to check if anyone was stealing up behind him. He was a dog who snored so loudly they had to turn up the TV. Who never stopped trying to make friends with the Pomeranian on the next street, despite her trying to attack him whenever Parsnip tried to say hello.

Other people had sleek pedigree greyhounds or noble Great Danes. They had bandy Parsnip, who had once drawn a crowd of small children in the park petting him, saying: 'Ugwee dog, ugwee dog' while he looked as pleased as punch.

# Forty-Two

They pulled up in the car park at the vet's and the task ahead became real for Delia. Paul unbuckled his seat belt and held her awkwardly across the gearstick as she covered her eyes with her palm and sobbed.

'Think of it as reassuring him, letting him know we're here. He doesn't know what's going on. It's us who are upset.'

Delia nodded.

'You don't have to go in.'

'I want to. Well, I don't want to . . .'

'I know.'

Paul squeezed her hand. Delia reminded herself that a teenage Paul had to be a pallbearer for his dad's coffin, and told herself to buck the hell up.

She crunched across the gravel to the waiting room, a step behind Paul. Inside, it sounded like a zoo even though they couldn't see a single animal – the room was full of miaowing travel carriers and chirruping cages, and the smell of heavy-duty disinfectant. They were told to take a seat and wait.

Delia distracted herself by reading a memorial collage on the wall about the vet's oldest and deceased feline patient, one Gloria Hambly. The oddly humanoid-titled Gloria was a very angry, imperious-looking apricot Persian who'd pottered on to the grand age of twenty-five. Delia could imagine the Grim Reaper had turned up a few times for the glowering orange Gloria, only to be told to fuck right off.

Eventually a kindly young veterinary surgeon in green scrubs appeared and called them through. They rose to their feet, Delia feeling slightly nauseous.

They were motioned to sit down in a room with a plastic floor, chairs and consulting bench. Delia saw a box of tissues and knew it wasn't good.

Paul slid his arm round Delia and they listened as the young vet explained that the tumour they'd discovered causing the problems was considerable, and inoperable. Parsnip would be in terrible pain before the end if they let nature take its course.

'How long would he have?' Paul said in a thick voice, and Delia was so incredibly glad he was there. His arm tightened round her as he spoke.

'It's hard to say. But it wouldn't be a good death. In this situation, we recommend putting him down.'

Tears filled Delia's eyes, turning the scene in the room into a view from a car windscreen during a flash flood. The vet was a blur of brown, pink and green.

'When can you . . .?' Paul said, and then 'Sorry,' as he steadied himself and Delia knew he was crying too.

'The practice manager isn't here now, we can carry out the procedure tomorrow.'

In that second, Delia thought they could make all the intellectual arguments they liked, but her feelings rejected the idea of what they were doing entirely. They were murdering their pet. The creature that trusted them most in the world, they were handing them over, unwitting, to be killed.

She choked out an apology and scrambled from the room, fleeing past the staring faces in the waiting room and crashing out of the doors into the car park.

Delia heard great shattering, gasping sobs rip from her. She hadn't accepted it was a goodbye until this moment and she wasn't ready for it. Please, not now.

Amid so much uncertainty, the one certainty was that she was about to lose Parsnip, and that could never be fixed or undone.

Paul found Delia and wordlessly put his arms around her. She buried her face in his shirt and inhaled the warm, familiar Paulness as he kissed the top of her head and shushed her and murmured *I know, I know*. He was the only one who knew how she felt.

'Why don't we take him home tonight?' Paul said. 'One last hurrah for the lad?'

'Isn't he . . . doesn't he need painkillers?'

'He's had an injection which has made him drowsy. The vet doesn't think he's in too much discomfort for the time being.'

'How can we make him think he's coming home, when

tomorrow . . .?' Delia lapsed back into more stomach-convulsing crying.

'Listen, listen,' Paul pulled back, brushed strands of Delia's damp hair behind her ears and put steadying hands on her shoulders. 'He's not scared, or sad. Our job is to look after him right to the end. Wrap him in cotton wool and act normal. Don't think about that moment until you have to. Think about how nice it'll be to spend the next twenty-four hours with him. Do it for him. OK?'

Delia nodded and Paul disappeared off into the surgery. He reappeared with an unsteady Parsnip on his lead and Delia tried to staunch the tears at the sight of him, in case he could sense her distress.

She crouched down and kissed his wiry head and whispered 'Hello, you!' faux-brightly, putting her arms round his lumpy, barrel-like middle. She could hear him panting his happiness at seeing her. She looked up and this time it was Paul with tears on his cheeks.

'Get ready, boyo. You're going to have the time of your life,' Paul said, roughly wiping under his eyes with the back of his hand.

# Forty-Three

Not so long ago, it would've taken wild horses to get Delia back into bed with Paul. It turned out she only needed a dying dog.

They slept that night with Parsnip lying like a bolster between them, wheezing and snuffling but clearly delighted to be granted special duvet-whiskering rights, lying with front and back legs thrown out in a 'Paint me like one of your French girls' pose.

He usually had his basket shut in the kitchen, due to his eagerness to get the day started at five a.m. Instead, Delia had cried so much and petted him for so long the previous evening that Parsnip was asleep at dawn, while she greeted it with swollen face, and a 'nail gun in the temple' headache. She lay with the grey-yellow light creeping round the curtains, experiencing the grotty sensation of knowing the chance to get any rest had passed.

Paul once told her that after his parents died, he'd stayed up into the night playing records until he fell asleep through exhaustion, dreading sleep because every time he woke he remembered his reality afresh.

Delia looked over at his sleeping form, one arm slung over Parsnip. Her family had fallen apart. It was hard not to see Celine as a tumour, only without anyone to tell them if it was possible to remove her and leave what remained in decent working condition.

Not that she could fault Paul at the present moment. He was being a rock for them both, and if he was doing any of it with the ulterior motive of winning her back, Delia was too vulnerable to care. He joked about how he'd always said Parsnip looked like Martina Navratilova, he mock-grumbled about the lack of space on the bed. He kept up a stream of fuss and chatter that soothed Delia's spirits.

Despite thinking it was impossible, Delia lost consciousness somewhere between very early and an early start, and awoke to find Paul standing over her, dressed, showered and brandishing a bag full of what looked like pork scratchings.

'C'mon sleepyhead. We're taking Parsnip to the park. I've been to Pets At Home and got him those gross pigs' ears.'

Delia dragged clothes on and pressed a cold flannel to her face, painting her liquid eyeliner on puffy eyes, colouring pallid cheeks with blush and imagining it looked quite *What Ever Happened to Baby Jane?* grotesque.

They walked Parsnip to his favourite picnicking spot and Paul threw out the blanket. The three of them settled down. Parsnip was perfectly peaceful and content, nibbling a pig ear, and Delia was glad of the warmth of the sun on her tired body. The sadness came in waves; her body didn't have the energy to sustain the grief as a constant. It meant she could enjoy the moment.

'You were right,' she said to Paul, 'I'm glad we did this.'

He put his hand on her leg. 'You have to say goodbye properly, however much it hurts.'

'He seems so well . . .' Delia had to say it: 'Are we sure it's the right thing to do? If he could have quality of life for a bit longer . . . I'd stay home with him . . .'

'I asked the vet that stuff when I went back in. I said, give us more of the painkillers and we'll see how he goes. But she told me it's cruel to stagger on. He's an animal, he'll be in horrible pain and he won't be able to tell us when it's too much. We can't let him suffer to make us feel better, Dee. We have to carry the responsibility so he has the best end possible. That was the job we took on. The good, and the bad.'

Delia nodded without speaking, so that she didn't cry. Paul was a good person. With flaws, yes, but this was the man she had loved. That's what people like Adam West didn't get, when they reduced her decision to a box-ticking, binary exercise. *Is this acceptable behaviour? Y/N.*

A few yards away, children were playing on the grass with plastic swords and Delia felt the strange cognitive dissonance of seeing other peoples' lives carrying on when your own was falling apart, as if you were watching them on television in a war zone.

'Ralph loves Parsnip. Should I give him the chance to come over and say goodbye? I don't think his shift starts until this evening,' she said.

Paul agreed and volunteered to pick Ralph up, and Delia was impressed he didn't want to dodge the awkwardness of seeing her family.

It also meant she got time alone with her dog. Back at the house, she wrapped Parsnip in his favourite blanket and cuddled him on the sofa and told him how happy she was to have known him. He nudged her with his nose and blinked his watery eyes.

She whispered choked apologies for what they were going to do and asked for his forgiveness. She tried to take in everything about him, because pets were personalities with habits and quirks and aromas that were utterly unique, and only you and others who'd loved them would remember.

Paul walked back in, bent his head and pecked Delia on the cheek, whispering, 'We came via ASDA,' to her, which seemed odd spy code.

She understood when Ralph followed him, bearing a large cake box with a cellophane window, the sort you get in supermarkets. It had PARSNIP on it in wormy twirls of lime green, a Halloween colour combination with its taramosalata-pink marzipan.

'Ralph,' said Delia, restraining the astonishment in her voice so she didn't sound ungrateful, 'what's that, a Happy Death Day cake?'

'No, it's like, an occasion, isn't it? You still have food after a funeral.'

Paul winked at Delia.

'It's a piece of genius,' Paul said.

Her brother's innocent goodwill made sarcasm inappropriate. Delia was very glad to see him. She pushed her arms round his circumference, mumbling 'Thank you' into his somewhat musty *Guardians of the Galaxy* t-shirt.

'Here, boy!'

Ralph set the cake down and slid it out on its foam circle. Delia stifled a reflexive remark about too much sugar not being good for Parsnip.

Parsnip yelped and slithered down from his seat on the sofa, and started licking the icing while Ralph patted his back.

'Strawberry's your favourite, Uncle Ralph knows.'

Paul grinned at Delia. 'Interesting insight into the babysitting that went on. No wonder Parsnip liked his visits to Hexham, eh.'

Ralph was a tonic. He played with Parsnip, he chatted to him easily, he took photos on his phone of the two of them together. Delia had shrunk from doing this as she wasn't sure she'd ever want to look back on his last day, so she was glad now she had the mementoes safe with Ralph. When it came time for Paul to drive him back, he shook Parsnip's paw and said: 'Very nice knowing you, Mr Parsnip,' and wiped a tear away. 'Enjoy dog heaven and all those cakes.'

Paul and Delia would've carried on allowing Parsnip such wanton gluttony throughout the afternoon, yet it was obvious he was uncharacteristically full, and fading, only wanting to nap. Selfishly, Delia was glad at some concrete evidence of his illness.

Finally, after an hour's innocent sleep for Parsnip, it was time. Delia shut down and measured the process in achievable steps. Get Parsnip to the car. Get to the surgery. Walk into the consulting room, assemble selves, each holding one of Parsnip's scrawny, bony front paws. Kiss him on the cheek, hard, and say goodbye into his nearest ear. Hold him tight and don't look as the needle goes in, even if it means you can feel the last slowing throbs of his bird-weak heart and smell the sugar of the farewell cake on his ratty old ears.

Disentangle your sweaty limbs, hold Paul and both weep openly. Finally: try not to look at the now-lifeless form of a beloved animal on the table.

The vet discussed further business with Paul in hushed tones. They'd discussed burial and Paul wasn't keen.

'You move house and leave them behind,' he said. Delia wondered if it was connected to Paul's dislike of visiting his parents' graves. ('They're not *there*,' he always said, vehemently, in one of the rare moments he showed anger about it.)

Also, you needed to dig deep when preparing the grave, Paul pointed out. He and his brother Michael's childhood guinea pigs – Ant and Dec – had made a macabre reappearance during a rainstorm, surfing the turf. Cremation it was, and Paul would collect the ashes in a few days.

Home in an empty car, both too broken by Parsnip's gigantic absence to speak.

Eating dinner wasn't possible. Inevitably, they sat in their Parsnip-less house and drank too much red wine to blur the sharp edges of their feelings, and ended up in each other's arms. There was no risk of it going further; neither of them were currently capable.

'Delia, you know this is home, don't you? Always. Whatever else. This is your home and no one else's,' Paul said hotly and drunkenly, into her hair.

Delia said yes, she did, and it was.

And with that, without even saying it in so many words, they were back together.

# Forty-Four

Day one of a Parsnip-free house, a Saturday, and Delia
wanted to be out of it. Paul had his escape, the usual one.
The pub had been left for two days and it needed
attention.

He was so effusive in his apologies about having to
work, Delia wondered if he expected her to make some
swipe about him putting the pub first.

After an aimless hour, she messaged Joe to meet up, and
they agreed Brewz and Beanz at one.

She was strangely nervous as she dressed, choosing a
scoop-necked clinging black top and favourite washed-out
pink skirt, making up her weary face with particular care.
He did think she was pretty: the pressure was on. She hoped
the easy, breezy tenor of their electronic exchanges transferred, face to face.

She guessed all internet friendships came to this point
eventually: you had to make it or break it in the real world.

Delia claimed a table in the window, thinking he'd like
that witty nod to their history, and waited. And waited some

more. By half past one she'd gone beyond itchy anticipation and into resigned boredom. She opened a text.

*Did I get the right place / time? I'm here! Dx*

Ten minutes passed.

*Delia, I'm so sorry but something's come up and I can't make it. Apologies for messing you around. Joe x*

Unless his roof had fallen in, he'd stood her up. Was he worried about Paul seeing them? Had he misrepresented himself in some way in their conversations? Was meeting face to face more Delia than he wanted to let himself in for?

She'd not mentioned Parsnip's fate and she was glad; she didn't want the pity vote.

Giving it up as a bad job, she decided to console herself with some fancy Wolford tights from Fenwicks. Then a coffee and a sandwich on her own, preferably while staring at the Tyne and starting a new book.

As she set off through the streets, she was glad to be home, to not feel an interloper like she still did in London.

Hosiery purchased, she wandered the aisles full of colourful cosmetics and their rash promises, absently squirting fruity perfume testers on her wrists until she smelled like a packet of boiled sweets.

Delia was coating herself with something citrusy from Miller Harris when an arrangement of features, half glimpsed over a display of glossily bright toiletry bags, gave her a fright.

They were unknown and known to her at the same time, and for a second Delia was frozen, tester bottle held above exposed inside wrist.

Celine brushed her fine dark hair behind her ear and wandered off towards the cafeteria, and without consciously deciding that she was going to do it, Delia followed her.

Celine headed out the doors and into the street outside, Delia in quickstep pursuit. Celine was wearing a floaty royal-blue dress with camisole straps and a jagged hem, in triangles like bunting, showing off nut-brown, toothbrush-width legs, and gladiator sandals. Delia felt instantly blowsy and matronly by comparison.

Delia trailed Celine down through the shopping centre, losing her here and there, but each time managing to pick up a glimpse of the back of her head again. She didn't ask herself why she was doing it, or when she'd stop. It wasn't as if Celine was likely to be meeting with Paul, on a weekend when Delia was home.

Having headed south into quieter streets, down past Grainger Market, Celine stopped and looked in a window, forcing Delia to also stop and pretend to be transfixed by the contents of a pound shop.

After a minute or so, Delia sensed something wasn't right. You either looked and went in, or looked and moved on. Celine had been standing there too long.

Delia glanced at her and Celine's head turned. She looked directly at her.

'Delia?'

Delia was speechless with shock. Of course – Celine had looked her up online, too.

She was rumbled, caught out trailing her sexual nemesis through the streets like some Mrs Rochester mad wife, let loose from the attic. There was nothing to say, or do, other than to turn on her heel and march off, gathering what was left of her dignity, which was very little. But something glued her to the spot.

Celine pushed her hair behind her ear with a trembling hand.

'Can I buy you a coffee?'

If Celine hadn't looked so terrified, and Delia hadn't felt so foolish, she would've said no.

# Forty-Five

They were near one of Delia's very favourite cafés, The Singing Kettle. While she didn't much want to sully it by using it as a venue for this particular occasion, there was no way they were making polite conversation in step all the way to an anonymous Caffè Nero.

The Singing Kettle was tiny and charming: Gaggia coffee machine, scones under a glass dome by the till, cluttered, clattery, windows steamy. And thankfully, nearly full with a gaggle of chattering day-trippers, so Delia and Celine didn't have to worry about being overheard.

They both ordered flat whites, their creaky awkwardness at odds with the merry manner of the order taker.

'Thank you for doing this,' Celine said. She was well-spoken, with no Newcastle accent, and Delia remembered she was here as a student.

'I'm not sure what it is we're doing,' she said, neutrally, holding her coffee cup in two hands. Was Celine going to issue a *Look, we're together now, it's me he wants, let him go* sort of caution? It didn't feel like it.

'I want to say sorry for everything that's happened,' Celine said.

In 3D, her face wasn't as glacially intimidating as the image Delia had constructed in her mind. Celine was beautiful, but she also had typically twenty-something spot-prone skin, and teeth that were slightly too big for her head.

Delia noted this dispassionately, not cruelly. She had been suckered in by social media's bleachily lit, pouty photographs that are carefully selected to fit your internalised, idealised self-image. The highlights reel – or 'sizzle reel', as Kurt called it.

Delia wondered which of her other ideas about Celine might be wrong.

Celine was trembling with adrenaline, her jaw juddering when she cast her eyes down at the table. Delia felt the fear too, but with nothing to feel guilty about, she was steadier.

'I didn't think of myself as the kind of person who'd do this sort of thing,' Celine said, again doing her hair-tucking tic. She hadn't touched her coffee.

'Paul said the same thing,' Delia was impressed her voice worked so well. 'Maybe the people who do these things never think they'd do this sort of thing. Maybe that's how they *can* do it.'

She said this without spite but Celine looked terrified nonetheless.

'It was like it wasn't real when it was happening. I mean, I know it *was* real . . .'

'Did you know about me from the start?'

Celine nodded.

'Other people told me Paul lived with his girlfriend when I met him. When we . . . got on well, I didn't think about it. I told myself you must have problems for him to be with me . . .'

Celine's head jerked at what she'd said and she obviously feared Delia might slap her.

Instead, Delia found grudging respect for Celine. She was displaying stark and difficult honesty, a quality in short supply around these parts lately. Delia nodded.

'Did Paul tell you we had problems?'

Celine shook her head.

'Not . . . no. He sometimes said you'd drifted apart a bit, but that was when I was asking about you, for my benefit. He didn't want to talk about you. I knew he'd never leave you. When he told me you were getting married, I felt sick. I realised what I'd done – what we'd done – and it wasn't this separate bubble any more.'

'But you asked him to go to Paris?'

Celine blushed fiercely. 'I didn't know if getting married was what he wanted. I said we could talk, go away until it blew over . . .'

*Blew over?* Delia chalked this turn of phrase up to being twenty-four, but Celine had just used up a credit.

'. . . Paul said no and he was getting married.'

'Hah. Well he isn't, now.'

Tears rolled down Celine's cheeks and Delia had no idea what she was meant to do. Comfort her? Gloat? Deliver a sermon?

Celine wiped her tears away and rolled her eyes to the ceiling until she'd got herself under control, doing the 'drying nail polish' finger-waving movement at her face.

'It was so stupid,' she said, her voice so thick it made her words difficult to distinguish. 'I thought *Oh, it's only some fun,* but it's not fun to mess with people's lives and I should never have done it.'

'Did he make you think he was going to leave me?'

'No.' Celine shook her head, without hesitation. 'He always said I should find someone my own age. He was never going to leave you for me.'

'Did you want him to?'

'Sometimes,' Celine said, dabbing under her eyes with the back of her wrist, nose running.

Celine opened her fake quilted Chanel bag and rummaged for tissues, her iPhone with silly chocolate bar case tumbling out, along with her Vaseline tin lip balm. She suddenly looked so terribly young to Delia, and she felt a surge of anger at Paul for hurting two people like this.

The very last thing Delia would've said she wanted to do was a sit down with Celine. And yet, it had helped. Celine didn't frighten her. In fact, Delia was impressed with herself; she'd faced the worst and coped. The pain at the thought of Paul and Celine together had begun to reduce to a dull ache.

'I'm so, so, sorry,' Celine said. 'I can't tell you how sorry I am. It's such a rancid thing to have done. I'm not that girl, you know?'

Delia didn't react, wanting to choose her words carefully.

'I'm not saying that sleeping with someone's boyfriend is right, but it was Paul's fault more than yours,' she said.

Celine nodded.

'I wouldn't blame you for throwing that drink in my face. I would if I was you.'

Delia smiled.

'You don't know how you'll feel until it happens, I've learned.'

She didn't say so, but Delia suddenly realised she could've been a Celine herself, in the right circumstances. If she'd met a confident older man when she was Celine's age; if she'd fallen for him hard, and he obligingly kept the girl-friend out of focus? She would've probably rationalised it was *his* responsibility.

For Celine to be someone Delia couldn't understand, she'd have to be nasty, spiteful, to glory in the pain she'd caused. But a human who'd made a mistake: Delia could relate to that, to her. The casting director of Delia's life's drama had screwed up. She wasn't a proper enemy.

It was Paul who was thirty-five, and knew the impact of what he and Celine were doing. Paul who had made promises to Delia, who came home to the dinner she'd left him in the fridge, and took longer over his post-service shower than usual, before climbing into bed beside her and saying sorry, he was too tired for anything.

Her disgust flared again. Celine regarded her nervously and it occurred to Delia that she was frightened herself, only not of Celine. Delia had answers in front of her. Could she bear to ask them? Should she walk away, having made her decision to reunite with Paul? Surely that would be the easy thing to do – but if she did, she would forever wonder.

'Can I ask you a few things?'

Celine nodded, expression deeply wary.

'Did Paul give you a Valentine's card?'

Celine nodded again, slowly, and Delia felt the faith she'd had in Paul the previous evening start to unwind.

'What did it look like?'

'It had teddy bears on it,' Celine said.

'Did you call him your boyfriend?'

'Yes. He called me The Girl.'

Delia gulped. Pet names? Liar, you *liar*. This was hell. But she'd started, so she'd finish.

'You know the first time that Paul went back to yours?' Delia said. 'Who came on to who? How did it happen?'

Celine's unlined brow knitted.

'Uhm. He came up to me as I was leaving and said if I stayed, he'd make me a Caipirinha. We'd already been flirting and I knew it'd be only us left . . .'

She blushed again. Delia knew this was true; it bore the hallmarks of her own first encounter with Paul.

'He came on to you? Not the other way around? He wasn't outside, locking up, when you approached him?'

Celine shook her head, for the first time looking sorry for Delia, as well as ashamed.

Delia continued: 'When was this?'

'After New Year. January the fourth.'

Of course, Celine would know that date immediately, as Paul would have.

So, his claim that it was Mother's Day wasn't just a simple invention, it was a horribly manipulative one.

For the first time, Delia flinched.

# Forty-Six

Delia stood under the vaulted roof of the train station listening to the distorted, aurally foggy announcements, feeling as if she was in a clearing house.

It was a grim but instructive lesson to find out what she could withstand. If this Delia had told the Old Delia, gleefully planning her marriage proposal, that she would lose both Parsnip and Paul within hours of each other, she'd have collapsed. Yet Delia hadn't collapsed. She was here with her trolley case, waiting for the 3.35 to London King's Cross, with an unshakeable sense of purpose. She wasn't uncertain now.

Her mobile rang, as she knew it would. Her note had simply said she was heading back to London. She picked up the call.

'Why have you gone? I thought you were staying for the weekend.'

'I met Celine.'

Horrorstruck pause.

'What? When?'

'I ran into her in Fenwicks. We went for a coffee.'

'God,' Paul said, and Delia suspected he wasn't quite as sorry he wasn't face to face with her now. '. . . How did that go?'

'It's not the worst thing that's happened this weekend, though that says more about the weekend.'

Paul made a teeth-sucking noise and Delia heard the platform announcement for her train.

'She told me a lot of things that didn't match with things you'd told me, Paul.'

Silence.

'Can you think what they'd be?'

'Delia, look . . .'

'You *did* send her a Valentine's card. You *did* know she called you her boyfriend. You called her *The Girl*. You started the whole thing. And when did it start, Paul?'

'. . . Oh, God, Delia. Listen . . .'

'*When*?!'

'New Year,' Paul said, in a low voice.

'Yet you said Mothering Sunday. I wonder why pick that day, of all days?'

'I'd blurted out three months and that sounded about right if I tracked back, it wasn't . . . Oh my God, it wasn't because . . .'

'Why say three months?'

'I knew I'd fucked up so badly I was going to lose you and I was saying anything that I could to stop that happening. It was over, so the rest was detail and I didn't want the detail to hurt you even more.'

'You don't think I deserved the truth?'

'You did. Absolutely you did. I know that now. I thought off the top of my head, three months sounded less appalling. Delia, I promise. I promise on my life. There's no significance to any of this other than me flailing around, trying to stop you going.'

'"I promise",' words that Delia could no longer put any faith in at all. Jesus, untangling lying was exhausting.

'You started it with her.'

'I got myself in a mess. I'd say it was six of one, half a dozen of the other. I don't know why I did any of this, Delia. Like I said, flirting got out of hand. When you confronted me, I was grasping at straws . . .'

'Bullshit!' Delia was conscious of bystanders' heads jerking up, on the periphery of her vision. 'You've lied so much, you're probably still lying now. You can't have any respect for me at all. We're over, Paul. Go back to Celine. See if she'll grasp at your straw. Though I think she deserves better.'

'Delia, please. If you'd just come back and we could talk—'

Delia took a ragged breath and ended the call, cutting Paul off mid-sentence. That was that. Done with a bang, not a whimper.

After her train glided to a halt, she found a quiet corner of a carriage and opened her laptop. There was an email from Joe. Her spirits lifted, even before she knew what he was saying. Typing was a way of focusing, amid the thunderstorm of her emotions.

*Delia. Profuse apologies for my no-show. Joe*

*Don't worry about it! What happened? Everything OK? Dx*

*I feel so stupid. I chickened out. Are you still here? Joe*

*No, I'm on the train heading back to London. I ran into Paul's Other Woman, we had coffee. Turns out he's an even bigger lying hound than I thought. We've split up for good, I've ended it. Sorry not to see you. No need to be scared of me! I am quite tame, honest. Dx*

*Oh God I'm sorry! Are you OK? Jx*

*Yes. I will be. Are you? Dx*

*Yeah. Ish. OK, this is more explanation than you probably want or need, but, you asked a while back why I'm still at the council when I have a few IT moves. I actually have fairly crippling social anxiety. If I met you, I'd need a month to prepare and I'd walk round the block twenty times. And even then I'd probably not manage to go in. I should've said sooner, but online is where I get to be 'me'. Not the me who sweats and shakes and stutters. And I so like you and did want to meet you, sorry. I'd rather you know this than think I didn't care enough to turn up. Joe*

*That sounds so tough. Don't be sorry, you have nothing to be sorry for. But you can get to your job OK? Have you thought about treatment? (obvs don't mean electro shock things in hospitals on haunted islands) Dx*

*Haha! I might be up for that. I've had it all, CBT, Beta Blockers, the works. It's like I'm my own worst enemy. It's not agoraphobia, I can leave the house. I just can't deal with new people or situations easily. As you know, at the council you don't get much stimulation, in that respect ☺ I can imagine you're backing away slowly now, and I don't blame you . . . Joe*

*Not at all! This is fear, at heart? I have plenty of that. We can keep chatting like this, and only meet if you ever feel you want to. Dx*

She thought about what Emma said about online wooers not being what they seemed, and she was right, if not in the way she imagined. Underachieving keyboard warriors might not be heartbreakers or bank account rinsers. They might simply have a whole inconvenient reality you hadn't factored in to your fantasies.

Only . . . Delia was a sucker for a bird with a broken wing. It was what helped it along with Paul, after all.

The train rocketed past countryside bathed in honeyed afternoon light. As Delia watched the world speed by, she decided then and there that there would be no more half measures. No more London as a waiting room. It was a destination, it was where she was going to build a new life, one on her own. This was her chance for a fresh start.

Her mobile was on silent, on the flip-down tray table. She watched it push itself around with the vibrations of three missed calls, an answerphone message and a text from Paul, like a little mechanical scorpion with a ringer as its sting. Ignoring it, she opened an email to Joe.

*PS Speaking of fear. Let's press GO on Fantastic Miss Fox. It's time I let her out into the world. Dx*

# Forty-Seven

The thing about Emma was, she was so *reassuring*. There was nothing you could throw at her that she couldn't handle, and coolly manage. Panic wasn't in her emotional vocabulary, nor was the kind of knee-trembling doubt that frequently assailed Delia. Her sense of humour was never damaged.

This was why she was so brilliant at her job, Delia thought, apart from the bit where she could marshal the recollection of endless pieces of dry data at will. She'd have 'Leave It With Me' on her gravestone.

So when Delia called and said her dog was dead, her relationship was dead, and could her stay in Finsbury Park be a little longer, there was zero drama. Capable Emma said in that Minnie Mouse voice: absolutely yes, and that she loved her, and it'd all be fine, and did Delia want to chat it out over some very good Chinese food?

While prodding at pallid purses of excellent dim sum in wicker steamers, feeling much better than she thought possible, Delia related what had passed.

Emma was concerned, yet Delia noticed, she wasn't looking the required amount of shocked and outraged about Celine's disclosures, or Paul's weak rationalisations. It was the moment of silent agreement with Adam West, replayed.

'You ended it? For good?' Emma said, carefully.

'Yes.'

'I think this is the right move and you needed to make it. Whatever happens in the future.'

*Whatever happens?*

'You don't think Paul and I are over? It bloody well feels like we are.'

'I don't know, only you know that. But not necessarily. Can I play devil's avocado? I'm not entirely surprised at what Celine told you,' Emma said, sucking on the straw of a giant restorative lemonade. She'd been brought low by a corporate wine-tasting event with management consultants the previous evening.

'Paul lied to me!'

'Paul lied to you all the way through having the affair. Try some of the pork with spring onions, it's amazing.'

'I know. But once I'd found out, to *still* lie? To keep lying then is so insulting. I'll never trust him again. Mmm, that is amazing.'

'He didn't want to lose you.'

'That's not good enough,' Delia said, shaking her head, clacking her chopsticks like jaws as she went in for the kill again. 'To lie at that point is worse than anything to me.'

'Worse than him having sex with someone else?'

Delia grimaced.

'I know it hurts. I can't imagine how much. This is the fallout. But I'm not sure it changes anything.'

Delia looked dubious.

'Can I use the analogy of Bill Clinton's "I did not have sex with that woman"? And Bill and Hill patched it up.'

'He did have sex with that woman?' Delia said, confused.

'I mean the lying, on the spot. You're caught out fooling around and what do you do, in the *oh fuck* moments? You blather your way through it as best you can. Paul wasn't likely to admit things like he'd made the first move. I'm not sure if this is a lawyer attitude or not, but I know that very few people voluntarily make things worse for themselves, if they have a choice. You know, there's the way we all like to think we behave, and then there's the way we actually do.'

Delia pondered. Was it possible she'd used Celine's answers in place of finding her own answer about Paul? That she'd wanted X to mark the spot, to find conclusive evidence that would simply tell her what to do? But if she'd not run into Celine, she would've believed Paul, ultimately because she wanted to. She wouldn't make that mistake again.

'I'm not undermining what you've done; I think your coming to London properly is amazing. Obviously. Self-interest aside,' Emma said.

'No. It's good to have another perspective,' Delia said.

Emma spun the Lazy Susan.

Delia dwelt on what she said. She didn't think the former President's impeachment was the best analogy – there was a bit more at stake for him – nor did she agree with Emma that Paul could be excused for further lying when caught. Emma's realism said everyone works their advantage, whilst Delia was an idealist who thought a truly penitent Paul should've held nothing back. If that was too high an ideal, she was still keeping it.

'I can't believe I'm single! I've been out of circulation for so long,' Delia said, sitting back, stuffed to the greedy gills with dim sum. 'People I slept with before Paul are so long ago they don't count.'

'Oh, don't worry about that,' Emma said, waving her hand. 'It's not as if Cock Number Twelve is a magic key that unlocks the secrets of the erotic universe. Do you know, I've got my second wind – let's stay out.'

They went on for a 'quiet neighbourhood drink' in a narrow, gothicky nearby bar with Emma's gay friend Sebastian. He had a very small round head, with features that looked as if they'd slid to one side, and he did a laugh like *nyuck-nyuck-nyuck*.

Delia had forgotten there was no such thing as quiet drinks with Emma, who had now found her second wind.

'Let's do Picklebacks!' she squeaked. Picklebacks turned out to be pure necromancy: a shot of whisky followed by a shot of brine.

'The saltiness helps take away the taste of the whisky. They're all drinking these in Brooklyn. Along with sipping tequilas,' Emma said, coughing slightly, as if any of part of this statement made sense. Delia declined drinking more gherkin jar water in favour of a lager.

'You drink pints,' Sebastian said approvingly to Delia, 'I love the whole . . .' he danced his hands in the air around Delia's up do and Alice band and sucked on his vanilla flavoured e-fag, '. . . vintage store Lucille Ball thing you have going on. You dress for women, not men.'

'I dress for me . . .' Delia said, '. . . and I'm a woman. So I suppose you're right.'

She liked the idea she'd styled herself with intent. Her life seemed to have happened to her, in many other ways.

'Any more news of Aristocratic Adam?' Emma said, making an overbite face.

'Only that, in my revolution, he would not be spared,' Delia said, borrowing a phrase from Paul and internally chiding herself for it.

Sebastian got the Adam story, including the impromptu B&B after the Cock & Tail.

'If he's as awful as you say, why did he do that?' he asked.

'I don't know,' Delia admitted. 'I can promise you it wasn't carnal interest, he made that very clear. Probably thinks drunken women in public are sinful, due to his breeding.'

'I'd breed with him,' Emma said, stoutly.

Sebastian fiddled with his waxed hair, rolling two pieces at his temples into horns.

'Maybe this man thought it was the right thing to do?' he shrugged. 'There *are* men with principles. Not among any men I've ever met. I saw one once in a film.'

# Forty-Eight

Delia had started to think that she'd never meet a Twist & Shout client from the world of politics, and Adam West's request for information on clients in that sphere would end up being as much use to him as a candyfloss codpiece.

Yet the following Tuesday morning, Kurt muttered that he wanted her to come with him to meet a Parliamentarian, one Lionel Blunt.

As they left the office, the heavens opened with a summer monsoon and they were pelted as they hurried through Soho under umbrellas, getting thoroughly drenched.

When they located Lionel, he was sat underneath an awning outside a bar. Rain was pouring in a sheet from its edge as if he was behind a waterfall. His reason for being al fresco in inclement weather was nothing to do with a love of nature, but a result of him puffing away on a fag, over a late morning schooner of brandy.

He had swept-back salt-and-pepper hair, librarian spectacles on the end of his nose, and a somewhat lived-in three-piece suit. Not as lived in as his walnut face, however, which looked not so much 'lived in' as 'trashed after a gatecrashed party'.

'What kind of fucking world is it,' he said by way of greeting, waving his cigarette, 'when a working man and private individual whose forebears fought in wars for this country, is put out like the fucking dog for wanting to enjoy the fruits of one of our most successful industries?'

'The twats are in charge of the twat farm, LB,' Kurt agreed solemnly, patting paper napkins from a metal dispenser on his hair.

'As my dear mother said when she was on her deathbed, I'm bloody glad I'm off to my box, Lionel, because this world is only getting worse. God rest her soul, how right she was.'

*I wonder if the cause of death was passive inhalation lung cancer*, Delia thought.

'And who is this bird of paradise?' Lionel said, peering down his specs at a mildly revolted and very damp Delia, shaking her brolly out and unpeeling her sodden coat.

'My girl Delia. Grab us some coffees would you, Red?' Kurt said, and Delia's soul wilted at the flagrant sexism. 'And another – Courvoisier, right? – for Blunters.'

As she walked into the coffee shop, she could clearly hear Lionel's voice: 'What an absolutely stupendous pair of natties your secretary has on her. I'd like to see the launch of those torpedoes on my HMS *Dreadnought*.'

Delia's face flared and she shuddered, glad that Kurt's response was lost to traffic noise.

Lionel Blunt was a bon viveur and raconteur – and

other euphemisms for 'functioning alcoholic'. He was also a 'social diarist' and columnist; his weekly 'Blunt Speaking' in the *Telegraph* was what could politely be termed *divisive*.

He had now turned MP for The Albion Party, hoping to soon win a by-election in Eastleigh Central. Pro-hunting, anti-smoking ban, anti-Europe, anti-immigration, pro-saturated fats, the military and cricket, Lionel was a libertarian.

Except, it seemed, when it came to 'These shameless hordes of wrong 'uns and botters, mincing around as bold as brass,' as he described two men with mohawks in fluoro fishnet t-shirts across the street, muttering: 'Thank God there are some real men left in this country to fight our wars.'

Delia liked the idea that our shores would be better protected by asthmatic old roué Lionel.

The forty-five minutes that Delia spent in his company made her feel as though she'd met a relic of the past, and like outdoor toilets and potted tongue, a bit of the past you'd be happy to leave there.

'The trouble is,' Lionel said, swirling his second brandy with the stem of the glass between forefingers, 'the bloody commies in their coloured strides and cheap shoes over at Broadcasting House love to stir up a fuss over nothing. I was at a fête in Amersham last weekend and did a speech. Absolutely roaring reception. Yet the media picks up on one bloody joke and the puritans started shrieking about my plain speaking . . .'

'Which joke . . .?' said Delia.

Lionel ground his fag out, and lit another.

'I said I'd be more in favour of female MPs if there weren't so many heavy-calved matrons of the shire who remind me of my Nanny Bootle. Believe me, if you'd met Nanny Bootle you'd understand why. The woman's face could sour milk. And the less said of the rest of her, the better. Let's just say painting a face on her arse and teaching her to walk backwards would've been a fool's errand.'

Delia's eyes widened. This man was running for political office?

'Don't worry, my darling,' Lionel said, seeing she was disconcerted, patting her knee, cigarette clamped between his teeth. 'You're an irresistible bouncy castle party for any red-blooded gent.'

His eyes slithered south to Delia's chest. 'Don't count on his vote though.' He nodded towards a man in cycling shorts and a crop top bearing the words *Put A Donk On It*.

Delia sat in mute shock. The idea was, to use Kurt language, to 'throw some glitter' and 'valourise' Lionel Blunt's image.

Whatever spectacle Kurt was cooking up to make Lionel more cuddly – Delia thought it was as much use as putting deely-boppers on a crocodile and calling it Miriam – the circle of trust was being kept very small indeed. Even around Delia, they were circumspect about the particulars. Lionel and Kurt discussed timings and location for some future meeting, but no specifics whatsoever.

After the manly handshakes, and Delia enduring a frog-like wet kiss on the back of her hand, she tried to probe her boss to find out precisely what the plans were.

'Wait and see,' Kurt said. 'It might be my best yet.'

For *best*, Delia read *worst*, and swallowed a sense of foreboding.

# Forty-Nine

The unseasonal summer rain continued all week. Delia rather liked the combination of steamy heat, forbidding skies, atmospheric gloom and rainforest downpour. Although it was best admired with a drink, through a window, admittedly.

A text from Adam said it was time to meet, and he wanted to discuss Lionel Blunt. Delia thought, well, good luck – I know barely more than nothing about The Blunt Plan. She just hoped it didn't involve him speaking.

They met in an independent cinema in Borough at seven, Delia accepting Adam's reasoning that that was where one traditionally met to covertly swap information. Despite herself, Delia quite liked the idea of sliding into an empty matinee of *Dial M for Murder*, holding a paper bag.

The Roxy Bar & Screen only delivered on lighting levels, otherwise it was well populated. Delia had invested in a bright yellow raincoat, today thrown over her white cotton sundress she got for a fiver from Oxfam, and felt like a luminescent traffic cop in the middle of the dark room.

Its tables were low lit with lamps, speakeasy-style, and crimson swags of curtain, like the dancing midget set in *Twin Peaks*. A screen at the back played *Scarface* while people knocked back cocktails and ate leaking burgers the size of their heads. Delia made a note to come back here for a better reason. It was one of those pockets of London that made her feel part of things.

She ordered a beer, found a seat in the bar area and pulled her hair to one side, wringing it out like a twisted bedsheet.

Adam appeared on the other side of the murky room. It seemed he'd been holding a newspaper over his head as a makeshift umbrella, and now threw it down and put both hands to his own wet hair. He shrugged himself out of his coat, and pulled the damp shirt underneath away from himself, leaning forward. Delia found herself oddly transfixed by this scene, set to muted movie dialogue. She held her bottle of beer up to indicate 'Got one' and he nodded.

Adam finished at the bar, crossed the room and sat down with his own bottle, slinging the sodden coat onto a spare chair.

'You need towelling off like a dog,' Delia said, without thinking, at low volume.

'"Towelling off like a dog" is on the menu at a sauna near my office,' Adam said, equally quietly. He shot her a grin.

'It's good to see you,' he added.

He said this so simply and sincerely that Delia could only safely reply: 'Hmmm.'

And then continued: 'It's obligatory to see you.'

OK, he might be being more emollient but Adam hadn't played fair from the start. She was here because he'd forced her.

Adam laughed, stifling the sound with a swig of beer.

This was it, this was the problem. Every time she tried to insult Adam and remind them both they were implacable adversaries, he found her amusing. It was him giggling in Hyde Park over useless Scottish magicians, all over again and it totally undermined her. It spoke, Delia decided primly, of a fundamental lack of respect.

'If it's a punishment I best get to the point. Lionel Blunt, then. Go.'

'How do you know we're working with him?'

'Never you mind,' Adam said. 'A girl's got to have some mystery. Blunt's as wholesome as churned farmhouse butter, isn't he?'

Delia screwed up her face. In a raised whisper, she told Adam about some of Lionel's more prehistoric opinions, with vague allusion to his approval of Delia as a Twist & Shout 'asset'.

'Y'see, I know it's no secret I'm not a fan of your boss, but even so, how shit is it that he's letting you be spoken to like that by a male client? Condoning workplace harassment, or what.'

There was a pause. Adam twitched at the label on his beer bottle. 'Has Kurt made any more attempts on your honour?'

Delia shook her head.

'That's something, I guess.'

'We're dating,' Delia said, poker-faced.

Adam's jaw dropped. 'Please to God tell me you're kidding.'

'Haha!' Delia giggled, beer hissing in her gut.

'I know you hate me, I didn't think you hated yourself.'

They both hush-laughed now, Delia checking that no one seemed to mind them potentially interfering with Al Pacino.

She was in danger of liking Adam West, if she didn't keep a close eye on herself. Obviously some sort of Stockholm Syndrome was going on, given that she shouldn't even *be* here.

Delia remonstrated with herself: he knows he's charming and plausible! This is what Men Who Sleep With Everyone do! She might've been long out of the game, yet she could remember the basic rules of engagement. Your Shakespearean archetypes. These men pay a particular interest, slyly start to make you feel special. You're enchanted into taking your clothes off, like some kind of masculine hypnotism. Then the next morning they're whistling 'Another One Bites the Dust' while fastening their cufflinks and promising to add you on their Facebook fan page.

Not that she thought for a second that Adam wanted to sleep with her, but whatever it is Sex Men are pursuing, the methods remain the same.

Turning it back to business, Delia outlined the little she knew about Lionel. Adam noted down a date, time and a location, before clicking his pen and pocketing his notebook.

'If you happen to appear there, it's going to look very dodgy,' Delia said, nerves returning. 'If it's only me, Kurt and Lionel who know, it's not going to take long to work it out. Are you going to intervene?'

'Trust me to be discreet. I got you out of the Cock & Tail corner, didn't I? He won't know it was you.'

'Sounds like a risk.'

'It does carry a risk, but I think you'll be OK. You're going to have to trust me.'

'Why do you have it in for Kurt? It feels quite personal.'

'You're ready for the full unexpurgated Kurt?'

Delia prickled. She wasn't, really.

'So Maryvn Le Roux, the world's most useless magician who couldn't pull a rabbit out of a rabbit hutch . . .'

Delia's eyebrows shot up. Of all Twist & Shout's clients, she thought of him as the most harmless.

'His very wealthy Caledonian family, the McGraws, made their fortune in biscuits. They have a number of additional interests – one of them is a company called Lively Later Life. Retirement complexes. There's a few in Scotland, now looking to expand into England.'

Delia nodded.

'Lively Later Life is bidding to take over the running of two care homes from the local authority in Lionel Blunt's constituency. Surprisingly enough, Lionel Blunt has been busy extolling the virtues of efficient private ownership to local media. If this follows the pattern of escapades Kurt has been involved in previously on the other side of the world, I think I know why. Kurt is acting as go-between and giving bungs to Blunt from the McGraws to help wave their application through. Kurt will also be rewarded himself, obviously. Lively Later Life aren't considered the height of luxury, to put it mildly. Look them up, lots of gory stories about prison conditions. "The McGrawshank Redemption" is one nickname doing the rounds in Fife. Poor Stan and Betty are the losers while everyone else greases their palms with gold. I guess at least they'll never be short of biscuits.'

'Can't you report the conflict of interests, that Lionel Blunt and Marvyn have the same PR?'

Adam shrugged. 'Marvyn has nothing to do with his family's firm. It's mere coincidence, unless you can prove money's changed hands. Which I can't, at the present time. The outcome of the bids is decided next month, so it's on a clock.'

Delia thought about elderly people trapped in grimy cells, and her small part in it, and her innards gave a lurch. 'How do you know what Kurt was doing in Australia?'

Adam sipped some more beer. She had an odd sense of seeing him properly for the first time. Adam's manner was devil-may-care flippant, but the image didn't match up with the interior. She realised he was quite angry, and yes, principled.

'In my youth, I got a trainee job on the business desk at the *Sydney Morning Herald*. I took an interest in Kurt, poked around in a few things he was involved with. Next thing I know, I'm in the deputy editor's office being told I haven't fitted in. I was halfway to the airport when the penny dropped that it was Kurt. Not least because he sent me a farewell message, crowing about it. Presumably he had something on someone at the paper . . . I was so proud of getting that job, too. My visa depended on it, so that was that. It was a real tail-between-legs moment, coming home so soon. I'd been a bit of a tearaway, my mum thought it was a turning point.' Adam paused, to shake off his seriousness. 'Anyway. *Imagine* my delight when he resurfaced here, Debra.'

Delia felt for him. She hadn't thought of Adam as someone with parents and obligations and real proper feelings until now.

'Why didn't you ask me about this at the start? You said you were interested in consumer clients. Then you said you weren't fussed about Marvyn.'

'Ah, well . . .' Adam did one of his boyish grins. 'Excuse my cynicism. I had a suspicion you might turn triple agent on me and tell Kurt what I was inquiring after.'

Delia recalled the Hyde Park meet. Yes, she might've done that.

Adam moved his chair so some people could move on to the table next to them. Their proximity necessitated a shift in the conversation away from sensitive topics.

'Why did you leave journalism?' Delia asked.

'Oh, ouch.'

'Newspapers, I mean!'

'One morning I found myself writing a feature about food exports with the opening line: *The California-led craze for kale isn't dying down anytime soon.* And I thought: *enough.*

This wasn't the kind of crusading reportage I imagined I'd be doing back when I was in my kipper tie and bell bottoms on the *Scunthorpe Target*, sexually harassing secretaries and smoking B&H at my desk.'

'Haha. You were never on the *Scunthorpe Target* . . .?'

'. . . And that's the only part that doesn't ring true?' Adam tipped the bottle neck to his mouth. 'You're such a bitch.'

Delia smiled.

'Can you really make enough money from online journalism?'

'For now, it's enough.' Adam shrugged. 'Early days for the site, small staff.'

'At first I thought you were a shouty kind of blog, but Unspun is more thorough and professional than that?'

'Yes, it isn't just me banging a drum, on WordPress. Thanks for noticing,' Adam said, rolling his eyes, smiling. 'I think of it as the News in Depth bit of a paper. We're not always strictly topical. We can follow our own interests and leads. Hence the name.'

Delia nodded.

'You're all with the questions, suddenly,' Adam said, leaning back and regarding her before taking another swig from his bottle.

'Making conversation, as you say. Who runs it? Who's your boss?'

'He prefers not to be named. He's your stereotypical reclusive billionaire benefactor.' Adam smiled. 'What are your long-term plans, then? Back to Newcastle?'

Delia gulped and shook her head.

'Things definitely over with the ex?' Adam's expression showed he'd spoken his thoughts aloud and he looked momentarily embarrassed. 'Sorry, don't mean to pry.'

Delia gave him a tight smile.

'I had a blinder of a weekend up north where I bumped into my ex's bit on the side. Right after my dog had to be put down.'

For a split second, Delia thought it was safe to mention Parsnip. It took one second more to discover it wasn't. Her eyes brimmed and she was desperately grateful for the low lighting.

'Oh. Shit. Sorry.' Adam put a hand on her arm and then moved it away again immediately.

Delia had to do deep breathing and rapid swallowing to move past the tears and Adam said, in a moment of authentic charm and consideration, 'Should I talk nonsense for a short while? Erm . . . is it safe to show you a cat photo?'

Delia smiled gratefully and nodded vigorously. She watched him scroll through photos, head bent, iPhone in palm, old-fashioned watch with a brown leather strap. Nice hands. He was attractive, she supposed. If you liked that kind of thing.

'So here's my secret love,' Adam said. He turned the phone screen to display an obese tortoiseshell cat being held under its front legs, an acreage of white stomach on show above dangling back legs. 'Stuart.'

Delia was nearing being able to talk again.

'He's a fat knacker my twin sister adopted from a rescue

centre. He stole poppadoms from my hand last time we got takeaway curry. Moments later he runs back in from the kitchen with bright orange whiskers and we realise he's been motorboating the tandoori chicken.'

Delia laughed.

'Another beer?' Adam said politely, when their bottles only had foamy dregs.

'Thanks, but I've got to get off. And this is our last meeting, by the way,' she said, with a smile. 'You've got what you wanted.'

Delia was glad she'd resolved to say this, in advance. She could feel herself getting a little too comfortable with this smooth frenemy. Time to show Adam she wasn't his toy. He was still, however much for a good cause, putting her job at risk.

'Oh,' said Adam frowning, briefly lost for words. '. . . I thought I called time on this?'

'I'm calling time.' Or rather, your bluff.

Adam made a *hmmm* face.

'What if I call Kurt and tell him about the folder?'

'You won't,' Delia said, confident she had this one; she'd done her sums, and Emma had said the same. It had a time limit. 'If you'll save me from his advances, you won't get him to sack me.'

'Remember, I think being employed by him is only marginally more acceptable than being scuttled by him.'

Delia shook her head: 'This is a fair trade, I've done what you asked. Also, I know your secret,' she said.

'Oh?' Adam was wary.

'You're kind.'

He looked surprised.

'A compliment from Delia Moss. There's a first. Nice working with you.' He put out a hand for Delia to shake.

She shook it, and couldn't think of anything better to say than: 'Enjoy the rest of your life.'

Adam looked slightly unsettled, and she got the impression he didn't like Delia calling the shots. Typical male ego.

As she walked to the Tube, spattered with mizzle as the rain made up its mind, an *Evening Standard* bill on a street corner almost stopped Delia in her tracks. It mentioned drug mules. Her mouth dropped open.

*That was it!* The conversation at the Cock & Tail she overheard, that was the thing she needed to remember! Adam had compared her and Steph to the Peru Two!

Hang on . . . Delia came to a complete standstill, as passersby flowed around her. Freya had suggested Adam might sleep with her to get information . . . he'd mocked her as an unlikely prospect . . .

And he'd said something like '*When the time comes, I'll throw her to the wolves. It's no more than she deserves.*'

She'd just told him he was *kind*?

Oh, for five minutes he'd had her. For a moment there, she even thought there was a distant possibility they could be friends, if Delia survived his exposé of Kurt and later, at a time of her own choosing, left Twist & Shout. What he'd said about Kurt was awful, but was it the whole truth?

Delia had always fretted she shouldn't trust Adam. Just because Kurt was bad, didn't make him good. Now, solid proof of his treachery had arrived at last. It was all the more upsetting, having sat there and gaily chatted about his sister's garden fence arrangements for housecat Stuart, feeling bad for him about Australia: Interrupted.

What did Adam have planned for her?

*When the time comes . . .*

Had the time come?

# Fifty

Delia and Kurt clambered from a black cab – Delia didn't think the man ever took public transport – to the meeting point; half past nine by the bronze Boudicca statue on Westminster Bridge.

They took up a position next to a stall full of Union Jack-laden tourist tat – Big Ben keyrings and Buckingham Palace snowglobe paperweights and I HEART LONDON sweatshirts, the real Eye and Houses of Parliament over its shoulder.

Delia only felt as if she was getting to know the capital when she was in Emma's slipstream, learning the patterns by which residents moved around within its vastness. Whenever she was somewhere central, she felt as fish-out-of-water alien as when she visited as a little girl with her aunt and uncle, for face-painting and a trip to the Hard Rock Café.

'Lionel's late,' Kurt said after a few minutes, checking his watch. 'Hope he's not piled into the Rémy Martin with his cornflakes and slept through.'

'Does he do that?' Delia said, and Kurt swivelled *what do you think* sarcastic eyes towards her. 'His last housekeeper left when she found him doing his "morning yoga", naked as a jaybird. He said it was the "Happy Baby" pose. She said an eyeful of Lionel's taint is more Lionel than she's being paid for.'

'. . . Taint?'

'You know. That bit that ain't the front and ain't the back.'

Delia grimaced.

A fidgety ten minutes followed, Kurt scanning up and down the road in both directions.

Delia's heart was beating double time and she cursed Adam West for making what should simply be a day at work – albeit an unconventional one – so laden with foreboding.

A red bus rumbled past and there in the distance across the street, amid a momentary gap in the teeming bodies, Delia saw a flash of dirty-blond hair on a tall-ish man. And a beige coat . . .?

Oh no. Adam West was leaning against the railings on the bridge, watching from a distance, phone in his hand. She had a feeling he was taking photos, but she couldn't be sure. These were the photos that'd end up on his website, and there she'd be, right-hand woman to Kurt when something dreadful was about to unfold: the camera never lies. Kurt would put two and two together about who the tipster was. She felt surging panic.

Kurt was still scanning for the tardy Lionel and it would

be a matter of minutes, or seconds, until his eyes alighted on the same spot and he saw Adam.

There was no way it was going to be plausible that Adam was here by any sort of coincidence. But maybe it was never supposed to be believable? Even if Kurt didn't clock that they were under surveillance, *something* was about to unravel with Lionel Blunt, and if Adam inserted himself into the middle of the action, it'd become clear enough then.

Delia could feel the sweat collecting on her upper lip and under her arms.

In that moment, she realised she was sick and tired of feeling afraid. You know what, *fuck* Adam West for putting her in this position. She'd been skulking around like a cornered animal, letting other people set the terms.

And that conversation with Freya – the ugly, dismissive way he'd spoken about her, then gulled her into thinking they were matey.

Delia still had choices – she could walk away, having taken back some control. She wasn't being caught in some miserable version of a ménage à trois between him and Kurt. Once again, she was caught in the current, rather than picking her own direction. It was the story of her life.

She looked up at Boudicca, riding into battle. Was quitting a PR job really so terrible? What was the worst that could happen about coming clean? She'd be getting public transport home? If you make a mistake, better to admit it. That's what you were told in life. Delia was going to admit her mistake, and find out who she was working for.

'Kurt,' Delia said, 'there's something I have to tell you. You remember the first time I met Adam West, I didn't know who he was?'

'Yeah?'

Delia was sharing Kurt's attention with his BlackBerry. She cleared her throat and spoke confidently and clearly.

'I had the strategy folder with me. I left it behind by mistake and he's been blackmailing me ever since.'

'Blackmailing you? For what? He's banging you?'

She had Kurt's attention now.

'No! For information.'

'Oh right. And what did you tell him?'

'Nothing, other than when and where we were meeting Lionel today.'

Kurt put his head on one side.

'Why are you telling me now?'

'I can see him over there . . .' Delia inclined her head and Kurt's line of sight followed. 'I can't be responsible for him ruining anything. I understand if you sack me.'

'Thing is,' Kurt made a face, 'West's bullshitted you. I'd have never sacked you in the first place. There's nothing in those folders that matters.'

Delia's mouth fell a small way open. 'But . . . you said . . .?'

'Yeah, it's a little thing I do. A test. If the contents get out and about after that, I know not everyone's to be trusted. Not all of the clients inside are actually clients.'

'Oh.'

'Everything Twist & Shout needs is in here,' Kurt tapped his head. 'Or in my little friend who never leaves my side.'

Delia didn't know what that meant but thought an apology here might be the thing.

'I'm so sorry. I was very new when it happened and I didn't know what to do. I'd only just got this job and I really wanted to keep it. I wanted to prove myself before I owned up.'

Kurt narrowed his eyes and shrugged his shoulders. 'Seems like you manned up when it mattered.'

He checked his watch.

'We need to get rid of him before the show starts.'

He cast around. Eventually his vision snagged on something. He turned back to Delia, eyes dancing with malign excitement.

'As I learned as a kid, Red – if you make a mess, you gotta clear it up. Back me up.'

A pair of police officers passed them, one male, one female, in high-vis jackets, giant chirruping walkie-talkies strapped to them.

'Excuse me,' Kurt said, in assertively loud Aussie. 'That guy over there indecently exposed himself to my girlfriend.'

'What . . .?' Delia said under her breath, aghast.

Kurt threw a supportive arm around her.

'She's embarrassed. You've gotta tell people when things like this happen, honey. You can't let sickos get away with it.'

'Who are you saying did this?' the female police officer asked.

Delia swallowed thickly and couldn't immediately reply.

Kurt pointed at Adam, who saw that he'd been 'made' and was looking deeply concerned, frowning, hands in pockets.

'Uhm. Over there. In the light-brown coat. Fair hair,' Delia muttered.

'What happened?' said the male police officer. He got a pocketbook out and starting jotting down details.

Delia had an out-of-body experience, where a version of herself she barely recognised stood on an historic London bridge after the morning's rush hour, falsely accusing an innocent man of waving his pork and beans at her.

'I . . . uhm. I was on that side of the bridge taking a photo of the view on my phone and he was right next to me and I looked down and . . .'

'Filthy bastard,' Kurt said, with vehemence, pulling his arm tighter round Delia and shaking his head.

'Would you be prepared to make a statement?' the male officer said, and Delia nodded, thinking *Oh God what am I doing?* as they noted her name, address and phone number down.

'Don't make her go to the station with that depraved animal!' Kurt said, hotly.

'She can make a statement later. Leave it with us,' the female police officer said. Together they strode across the road to speak to Adam.

'Don't worry, you don't have to make a statement,' Kurt said, arm still round Delia. 'Say you've changed your mind and the sun was in your eyes. Or it was too small to be sure, har har.'

Delia watched in misery as the police officers had what could be sensed as a heated altercation, Adam throwing furious looks back in their direction and pointing. Delia thought: his problem is, he won't have a very good reason for why he's hanging around, or why he won't leave.

Sure enough, the police escorted a vociferously protesting Adam away. He'd been arrested.

'Haha, *burn*. Shouldn't have worn that flasher's mac,' Kurt chuckled. 'Ah, here's Lionel at last! LB, let's get you on to this radio interview. Maybe after we can get a pass to the Commons Bar.'

'Oh good. I feel like a badger's knapsack,' announced a bloodshot Lionel.

# Fifty-One

Delia trailed behind Kurt and Lionel towards the Houses of Parliament, wondering what happened to Adam West and whether he was having a photofit of his Member of Parliament taken.

She'd had to act, she had no choice; that it spiralled out of control once Kurt was involved ought to have been no surprise. Delia should be pleased: she'd vanquished the folder threat *and* pre-empted Adam West's strike. Yet she didn't. She remonstrated with herself: *You're bound to have regrets by getting in first. Yes, it would have been nice to have absolute proof he'd turn you over. The trouble with that is, by that time you'd have* been *turned over.* And this wasn't Old Delia, she was The Fox: controlling her own destiny.

As sanguine as Kurt had been about Delia's mistake, she doubted he'd have felt the same if he'd heard about it from a triumphant Adam West, while Adam acted as wrecking ball to his plans.

Halfway along the bridge, they came to a knot of people blocking their path.

'Excuse me,' Kurt barked, 'we're in a hurry here.'

One of the people said: 'He's going to jump.'

Through the onlookers, they glimpsed a man sitting on the bridge's railings, leaning on one side against its verdigris Victorian street lamps. He was dark-haired, forty or so, dishevelled in a dirty t-shirt.

'Don't do it! Get down!' someone cried, from the crowd.

'I have nothing left! I want to go,' he replied, in a thick accent.

The atmosphere had that car crash rubberneckers' electricity, when something deeply aberrant has occurred in an everyday setting and everyone has dispensed with their usual Britishness to stand around, riveted by the spectacle and united by tension.

Delia's gorge rose at the thought of seeing someone end their life, and she fought the urge to lunge forward and pull the man back to safety. Any attempt at intervention could see him jump, of course.

Then – WHUMP, like a sandbag – it hit her. This was it? This was the stunt? She glanced at Kurt and Lionel, who both looked curious enough about the scene before them. Hmmm. Though they didn't look too bothered about being late for the interview, and these weren't men whose hearts bled for others.

Minutes ticked past as the crowd swelled and police arrived in two patrol cars with lights but no sirens, blocking the traffic on the bridge, an ambulance behind them.

'Get back or I'll jump!' the man shrieked, twisting his head to look at the sudden swarm of yellow jackets.

'No one's going to do anything you don't want them to,' soothed a female police officer. 'Take it easy.'

People produced phones and started silently snapping away, some recording film. Delia wondered if there was any size of human calamity or indignity that people didn't think was fit for recording and posting on social media. Given that she heard a man mutter to his companion: 'Some of them take hours to do it. Come on you've taken it now, let's go,' she had her answer.

'What's your name?' Lionel bellowed, cupping hand to mouth, causing everyone to turn and look at him.

'Bogdan,' said the man.

'Do you smoke, Boglin?' Lionel said.

'*Bogdan*,' Kurt hissed.

'What, smoke?' said the man over his shoulder, straining to see who was addressing him. 'Yes?'

'I've got a damn fine cigar here. Cohiba, the No.1 in *Cigar Aficionado*'s poll of the cigar smokers' cigar. I was saving it for a special occasion. I'd like to give it to you, if I may?'

The police presence looked concerned. An officer said: 'Sir, please don't involve yourself. We're handling this.'

The crowd held its breath.

'A cigar?' Bogdan said.

'Yes.'

'. . . I like cigars.'

'Perhaps if you climb down, sir, you could—' began a police officer.

'I AM NOT GETTING OFF I AM GOING TO DO

IT!' screamed Bogdan, wobbling dangerously as he clung to the railings, giving Delia a seasick stomach, causing the police officer to step back.

'Take it easy, take it easy.'

'I would like a cigar.'

Lionel approached, brandishing the cigar, holding it out at arm's length as if giving a horse with tombstone-sized teeth an apple.

'I'll put it in your trap, stay steady, soldier . . .' he said.

Delia thought Lionel staying steady was more of a worry.

Bogdan opened and closed mandibles over the cigar, and Lionel took a silver nude woman-shaped lighter from his pocket, snapping at it twice before it lit.

When Bogdan inhaled, Lionel took it from his mouth while he exhaled, then replaced it, keeping up a stream of chatter.

'Splendid flavour, no? Only good thing communism has ever produced. What do you do for a living? A builder? Good, noble profession. I'm detecting an accent, from whither do you hail?'

There continued the strange pantomime of Lionel helping a hands-free Bogdan from Macedonia smoke his cigar while they talked, now more quietly.

Word had clearly gone round that this strange thing was occurring on Westminster Bridge and people wearing lanyards and proper-sized cameras were snapping away, along with the iPhone paparazzi.

They seemed to conclude their chat, Lionel gallantly

took the cigar and stubbed out the remainder on the metal, then turned to address the crowd.

'Bogdan, divorce is a terrible thing. Well, if you were married to my ex-wife, it's a blessed release, but that's by the by. If you reconsider your decision today, I'd like to offer you a friendly listening ear whenever you need it, to find you a job, and a lifetime supply of Cohibas. With these—' Lionel swept his arm at the crowd '—fine people as my witnesses. You're a good man and the world can't afford to lose one.'

Bogdan turned back to look down at the Thames.

Collective breath was held as they all wondered if they'd witnessed an MP incite a potential suicide into an actual one. Delia felt fairly confident of the outcome.

'A lifetime supply of Cohibas?' Bogdan said.

'You have my word,' Lionel said.

A pause. Bogdan pushed himself backwards, swung his legs over the railing and set his feet back on the pavement. Lionel hugged him in a hearty, clap-on-the-back way. There was loud applause and cheering as Bogdan was led to the ambulance, with police carefully steering him. Delia felt deeply uneasy. She wished she shared the emotions of the onlookers, thinking this was a rescue.

Kurt sidled up to Bogdan, had a word in his ear and slipped him his business card, before the police shooed him away.

'You're a hero!' a chalkily made-up sixty-something woman was saying to Lionel, 'A hero! You saved a man's life.'

'Not me, my darling. My cigar,' Lionel said, to more adoring laughter from the audience.

'You're going to be late for this interview, Blunty Boy, but for a damn good reason. Your heart's too big, my friend. You suffer from a condition called an enlarged heart,' Kurt said to Lionel, yet also to the crowd.

'Preferable to my piles.'

The crowd corpsed with laughter and Delia wanted to shout STOP! IT'S A TRICK! Too late. She was a collaborator. She was Kurt's right-hand woman and Lionel's lackey. She could plead ignorance and claim she was *only following orders*.

Nevertheless, she was going to be on the wrong side of history.

# Fifty-Two

'So Lenny, something priddy outta the ordinary happened to you on the way to the studio this morning. Can you tell us more?'

The presenter, Stevie, spoke in that faux-chummy quasi-American lilt that seemed mandatory for local radio DJs. He'd also seen fit to christen Lionel with the nickname 'Lenny'. They were in a studio near Parliament and Delia considered that they had no reason to meet on the other side of the bridge, yet it led them to parade past Bogdan. Kurt Spicer had orchestrated the story of the depressed Macedonian immigrant with faithless wife, and Lionel's lifeline cigar, of that Delia had no doubt. Kurt had apparently offered to 'handle' Bogdan's requests for interview to get him the best price, which equally meant 'control access to him'.

Lionel, member of The Albion Party with its range of batty, offensive and regressive policies, would be served only softballs, as he'd swept in on a wave of sentimental acclaim. The DJ had kept the audience going during the wait,

trailing Lionel's delayed arrival with promise of a 'miraculous, heartwarming' story, helpfully relayed by Kurt to a
researcher as they left the bridge.

Lionel was playing down his heroism with a perfect
blend of *aw shucks it was nothing* humility and raffish wit,
while Stevie and his studio crew lapped it up.

'Weren't you worried about stepping in?' Stevie said.
'That's a helluva lot on your shoulders if it'd gone wrong.'

'The thing is, Stephen,' Lionel said, statesmanlike, 'I come
from a generation where we prized action above words. In
these modern times of health and safety gone mad, risk
management, you hear the most awful tales of lifeguards
letting children drown because they didn't have the right
piece of paper to say they could legally pull them out. We
over-sixties don't hold with that. We muck in and get our
hands dirty, for better or for worse. If that means we end
up being blamed for mistakes, so be it.'

'Uh-mazing. Any young 'uns listening could take note
of this, Lenny. You're a breath of fresh air.'

*Oh please*, Delia thought.

'The anti-ciggy lobby bores would disagree with you
there, my friend, but thank you.'

'Haha! Seriously. Inspiring stuff. We'll be talking more
to Lionel Blunt after this, by T'Pau.'

Lionel was no longer seedy old slosh, but a brave, victory-
for-common-sense Churchillian-Gandalf hybrid.

Delia wondered again what Adam would've done to
disrupt proceedings. The image of him being marched away
under arrest came back again and she winced.

When they got back to the office, Kurt fielding calls on his mobile the whole way and jiggling with anticipation at the pictures of Lionel and Bogdan hitting the *Evening Standard*, Delia felt limp as a dishrag. Kurt's presence in the office meant she couldn't even gossip with Steph.

Delia volunteered to get Starbucks as a way of getting out of the room with Kurt, while he bellowed into his phone about Bogdan's delicate psychological state meaning Kurt needed to sit in on any interview, and how he didn't want his fragility 'exploited'. If hypocrisy was hair, Kurt would be the Sasquatch.

As she returned from the coffee shop balancing three tall cardboard cups slotted into a tray, a voice right behind Delia almost made her jump and spill them.

'Afternoon, Delia.'

She turned to see Adam West wearing a murderously angry expression and a pale-blue shirt. Frustratingly, both suited him.

'Don't worry, I'll stay zipped up. I've learned my lesson.'

'Er . . . Hi.'

'Lying to the police, wasting police time. The small detail of completely fucking me over. Congratulations, you're a fully functioning team member at Twist & Shout. You got there in the end, eh?'

Delia trembled, along with the cups. He was going to throw her to the wolves. Quid pro quo.

'Tell me more about how self-serving and false I am, when you're no better.'

'Oh man,' Adam stepped back, '*I'm* no better? This is going to be good. Explain that?'

'You were about to lose me my job. All I was doing was stopping you.'

'I gave you plenty of assurances I wasn't going to do that, if I could help it. However much it'd be doing you a favour.'

'If Kurt's firm goes bust, my job goes with it?'

'Ultimately, yeah. I can't help that. Delia, sorry if you need it spelling out in skywriting but your boss is a dangerous man. I'm not going to apologise for taking him down, but it could happen in a way that kept your name clean.'

'What was your plan today then?'

'I was going to keep a safe distance.'

'I spotted you.'

'You knew to look for me. I'd have only made my presence known when I could plausibly say I'd got the tip-off elsewhere. As a favour to you. And I'm really asking myself why I bothered.'

'When were you going to sell me out, then? Because you were definitely going to do it. "*When the time comes, I'm throwing her under the bus. She deserves it. The ginger minger.*" Sound familiar? It's not a word for word quote but near enough.'

Adam frowned. 'When . . .? What?'

'Cock & Tail, you and Freya. I heard you talking about me.'

Adam seemed taken aback. *Yeah get out of that one*, Delia thought, sourly.

'If you'd only asked me,' he muttered, then louder: 'I was actually bullshitting Freya to protect you in that conversation.'

'Hah! You really do think I'm some northern dimwit. What did you say, I'd fallen off the apple cart?'

Adam made an exasperated hand-to-forehead gesture.

'Freya gets extremely stabby about any woman she thinks I might get to know. If I told her that you didn't know anything, then she'd have nothing on you and leave you alone. I told you before, enemies on nationals aren't something you want.'

'You had no intention of losing me my job?'

'I told you the truth. That it was a risk, but I'd try to limit it. You know, it's possible if you've only overheard a conversation, you don't have the context or the history between the people to make sense of it. If you were concerned, you could've simply *asked me*.'

Adam could slink out of traps like a buttered ferret in a boob tube. Pure contempt and scorn for Delia had radiated from that exchange with Freya.

'The tone of that conversation was absolutely not about having any sort of thought for me. What about the whole, "Huh, as if I'd sleep with HER, vom"?'

'I told you, it wasn't really about work. Freya gets jealous, it's easiest to placate her. If I hadn't played along with her, and not said tough-talking things, she'd have taken it out on you one way or another. I got enough heat for going home with you as it was. Yeah, in fact – tell me this. If I wished you harm, why did I rescue you from Kurt's clutches that night?'

'To have something over me.'

'I already had something over you.'

'. . . Staying at yours made me even more compromised.'

'I made sure Kurt didn't find out.'

'You wanted me in play for the Lionel Blunt thing.'

'You *already were.*'

Delia adjusted her hands on the tray.

'Even if you did that to be nice, it doesn't change the fact that you were using me and I had every reason to protect myself.'

'I believe in my cause; I didn't want you to be collateral if I could help it. I tried to act with some sort of honour, and look where it got me. West End Central police station, answering questions about whether I was "manipulating myself to issue" or simply letting it dangle there.'

Delia momentarily closed her eyes in embarrassment.

'Sorry,' she said, hoarsely.

'You know, I told my sister about you, that I thought you were better than the place you'd found yourself. You know what she said? Lie down with dogs, get fleas. I should've listened. You absolutely played me.'

'YOU played ME! You started the manipulation with the folder!'

'That was to attack Twist & Shout, not you. Does nothing I've told you about Kurt matter to you?'

'Oh what, and I was supposed to blindly trust in every-thing you said?'

'No, you were meant to do your own asking and thinking

and come to a conclusion yourself. It seems you did. Team Kurt all the way.'

'Stop cloaking everything you've done in massive nobility and turning this into a moral judgement on me, when you backed me into a corner.'

'I think it is a judgement, whether you like it or not. It's a grim discovery of what you're capable of, in a corner.'

Delia was stung by the contemptuous dislike in his voice.

'Fun as this has been, I've got to get back to work,' she said.

'Oh, about that. I'm going to pop in and have a chat with your boss about a folder. What do you say to that?'

'I say, knock yourself out. I've already told him and he doesn't care.'

This startled Adam. He paled and didn't speak for several seconds.

'On the bridge, the police said you were a couple . . . You're seeing him, aren't you? What you said at the cinema was true?' A look of authentic revulsion and anger settled on his face, some of the film-Nazi hauteur of old. 'Jesus, to think I felt sorry for you,' he spat. 'To think I bought all that "She's vulnerable and been hurt by her adulterous boyfriend and hasn't worked out how many lies he's told her" stuff that was designed to make me feel white knight-ish towards you. Liars are clearly your thing.'

Delia could correct his mistake, but it felt too much like asking for his approval – a pointless task in the circum-stances anyway.

'As if I was trying to make you feel sorry for me by

telling you about Paul! I couldn't even remember what I'd said the next day.'

'Yet you could remember eavesdropping?'

Delia opened her mouth to explain but Adam ploughed on: 'It's pretty hard to make me think less of human beings than Kurt Spicer already did. But congratulations. You managed it.'

He glared at her with such a potent mixture of rage, disappointment and resentment that Delia couldn't help but feel it.

How had she ended up here? Three months ago she was a good person, in love, in respectable employment, and planning a blameless future. To be replaced by the woman who'd done these grubby things, and chosen so badly in where to place her trust, between Adam and Kurt. She'd never taken long enough to ask herself the pertinent questions, and find honest answers, as Adam said. She'd focused on her own survival, not the bigger picture. The Fox fought for good against evil, not to save her own skin.

'I can't believe I ever trusted a word out of your mouth,' Adam said.

'The feeling's mutual,' Delia said, turned on her heel and left him there.

It wasn't. She finally believed everything he said.

# Fifty-Three

'I've hardly seen you,' Emma announced, at the start of Delia's third month in London. She'd got in at what was nearly Delia's bedtime, drinking apple juice straight from the bottle in the fridge door, looking wrecked. 'We should spend Sunday together. Sundays are the best in London. Whenever I go back to Mum and Dad's village Sundays are like time-travelling back to 1955.'

'You keep saying you're over London, and want to live on a smallholding with chickens,' Delia said.

'I do. I also want three bars on my phone and flat whites and Uniqlo and Bloody Marys at Kopapa. Is that too much to ask?'

'You want to live in the countryside once they've built all the things they have in the city there?'

'Exactly!'

Delia was duly introduced to these Bloody Marys that weekend – spiked with sherry as well as vodka, Emma would've fitted in well in the court of Caligula – over

Turkish eggs with chilli oil and thick charred toast. Kopapa was loud, busy and bright, filled with young people living shiny lives in a tiled, raucous room. Delia didn't think her soul could settle in London, but her belly could be pretty damn happy. She swung her ballet-shoe-clad feet and practically hummed.

'You like?' Emma said, moving a celery stick out of the way of her mouth as she drained her 11 a.m. cocktail. She had blonde rope-twists of her growing-out fringe held away from her cherubic face with kirby grips, and was wearing a cream ruffled top along with a big onyx teardrop necklace, which Delia had bought her two Christmases ago from a craft market. She looked like a twenty-two-year-old intern. How the stress of her work and the pace of her partying didn't tell on her appearance, Delia had no idea.

'Mpppfff,' Delia nodded vigorously with a mouthful of food, the yolk escaping. She would never understand non-enthusiastic eaters.

At that moment, she saw the unmistakeably broom-handleish form of Freya Campbell-Brown, in buttock-skimming mini-dress, bare legs and slouchy fringed ankle boots. She was smoking on the street outside, holding fag aloft between knuckles, other hand clutching her elbow, listening to her companion with a shrewd expression. It wasn't Adam, thank goodness, but a man with quiffed hair like The Fonz, blinding white sneakers and a piercing that left a hole in his earlobe large enough to poke a pencil through. Lionel Blunt would not approve. Freya finished her cigarette, dropped the butt and ground it under her heel.

'Emma, talk! Say something so I don't make eye contact with the woman coming in the door . . .' Delia hissed.

She'd been avoiding telling Emma the latest twist in the Adam West saga. The thought of what had happened between them made her stomach muscles turn into a Venus flytrap.

'Hi.'

Delia heard a hard voice to her left and turned her head to see Freya giving her a Paddington stare.

'Hello.'

'I'm still waiting on a "thanks" for bailing your arse out with your boss?'

Delia gulped. Naked hostility wasn't something she encountered often. The British way was coded hostility you seethed about afterwards.

'Sorry, I didn't ask you to say anything. Adam did it of his own accord.'

'He felt he had to clear up after you. For. Some. Reason.'

Freya's spitting out of the last three words made it clear she meant 'His Penising Reasons'.

'I'm not doing anything with Adam,' Delia said, dumbly, wishing she could find a hundred Mae West-worthy comebacks that weren't this lumpen bare denial.

'Not for want of trying, I'm sure. You have egg on your face,' Freya said, with a quirk of her lip. She runway-strutted back to her seat as Delia rubbed the back of her hand against her cheek.

'Egg on *her* face, more like,' Emma said, fascinated, putting her fork down, her smoked salmon with 'yuzu mayo' suddenly abandoned. 'What was THAT about? Is she seeing him? She practically had static electricity hair like Sigourney Weaver in *Ghostbusters*.'

Delia offered a brief summary of what had happened, concluding: 'Irony being, Adam absolutely despises me now.'

Uncomfortably, she had to concede that Freya's behaviour was further reaffirming Adam's claim that when he misspoke about Delia, he was placating a nuclear warhead of a personality.

'Can I be clear? He *didn't* flash you, so there's no point asking more about that?'

Delia looked up in confusion and saw Emma was making her 'I'm a devil' face.

'This is pure Uni, Delia. You've moved here and got yourself caught in a love triangle in how much time?'

'It's not a love triangle! It's not a love anything. It's me being trapped between two gits,' Delia said, mock-grumpily.

Emma stabbed at the ice at the bottom of her glass with her straw.

'You don't regret coming to London, do you? I know the job's a bit ripe.'

'No! It's kept me sane! It's been great. And I get to see you,' Delia said, trying to convince herself that FlasherMac Gate didn't cancel out the good, like eggy brunches.

Emma smiled. Her time in Finsbury Park had made Delia see how she'd drifted into very intermittent, superficial contact with her best friend. She wouldn't let it happen again. She'd already decided to propose they book a girls' holiday, if Emma could cope with yet more of her.

'It's so incredible to have you living with me in London,' Emma said. 'I never see anyone otherwise.'

'You seem to see loads of people?'

'Nah, not really. It's just wafting about, nothing of any quality,' Emma said, stabbing her ice some more. Delia realised you should see plenty of people you love, because the meaningful conversations don't happen in the first twenty-four hours together, or forty-eight, or even the first few days. They came at moments like this.

'Do you think you'll stay down here?' Emma said.

'I don't know,' Delia said, 'I think it'll be hard to make enough money to have a life and I'll miss Newcastle. But I'm enjoying it for now.'

'You're lucky being from a cool city. If I leave London, I don't have anywhere to go. Well, Bristol, but Tamsin's there.' Emma pulled a face at mention of her forceful sister. 'I hope I meet someone from somewhere good.'

'You can always come back up to Newcastle with me. Show those lawyers how it's done. You could start your own practice! Imagine what kind of house you could buy.'

'Yeah?' Emma perked. 'That'd be amazing.' She paused. 'Somehow, I always thought I'd have a better chance meeting my soulmate here. Economies of scale and all that. Now I think London life doesn't do soulmates. Did I tell you about the SnapChat wanker?'

'The what-what?'

'You know what SnapChat is, right?'

Delia nodded: vaguely. 'It automatically self-destructs, like in Inspector Gadget?'

'A while back I met a nice man on Match Dot Com. We were planning our first date and he was like oh are you on SnapChat? And I said yes I am on SnapChat. He says I want to send you something. I open it and it's a clip of him . . .' Emma did a kind of frantic mime with curled fist, shaking her right hand.

'No?' Delia said. 'No?!'

'YES,' Emma returned to the remains of her salmon.

'Why would he think you'd want to see that?!'

'I don't know. This trading dirty images black market is beyond me. I'm a lawyer, I know people like me end up sifting through them before it ends up in court.'

'Maybe he meant to send it to someone else?'

'He sent me messages afterwards asking what I thought.'

'What did you say?'

'Great watch, is it a real Rolex?'

Delia laughed, although she had a nasty twinge of wondering whether Paul and Celine had done this sort of thing. Her instinct was Paul would run a mile – but that was the Paul of before.

'You can't help think we've lost something, compared to our grandparents' generation. It's bad enough we don't do proper dancing, but wanking videos instead of love letters! Whoever gets a love letter now? Yet they're so much hotter than seeing someone fapping away like a monkey.'

'It's like unwrapping your Christmas presents early,' Delia said, distractedly.

'Hahaha!' Emma squealed. 'A WHITE Christmas . . .'

'Enough!' Delia said, looking into the leftovers of her eggs.

Usually, Emma would sigh at this point and say how lucky Delia was to have her male counterpart in Paul. That was one thing about Delia's new singlehood – she could ask questions without any risk of seeming smug.

'Are you bothered about not having met anyone?'

Emma pushed her lips out in an expression of uncertainty.

'Yeah . . . but also not so much that as, I want the next part of my life to start. If I'm not going to meet anyone here, I need to decide what next. Workwise, I feel as if I've got to the top of the mountain and seen there's nothing up there, you know?'

Delia nodded. 'Well, I don't know, having never been successful,' she laughed, and Emma laughed with her.

'You're very successful. You're successful at being Delia. Did you mean it about me coming to Newcastle?'

'Of course!' Delia near-shrieked.

They spent the afternoon wandering around Borough Market – 'A bit of a cliché now, but I think you'll like it.'

When they got back to the flat, a small, thick envelope for Delia had been propped against Emma's door.

'Huh. Must've arrived yesterday and someone didn't pass it on,' Emma said, handing it over.

Delia recognised the handwriting. Paul was still trying? She didn't know if she wanted him to or not.

She tore the parcel open and a CD single of Oasis's 'Live Forever' tumbled out.

'More Paul mail?' Emma said, 'What's this one?'

Delia held it up.

'He sung it once at karaoke. For me. I'm not going to listen to it. Manipulative arsehole.'

Emma nodded.

It wasn't mentioned for the rest of the evening. Emma got a call from her parents and went upstairs to take it, leaving Delia alone with the stereo. She stared and stared at the cover and eventually weakened to see if it had any effect and slipped the CD in, turning the volume down very low, sitting on the floor and hugging her knees.

The crash of the drums started and Delia breathed hard through her nose to stop tears from starting.

It had been a night at the pub, two years or so after they'd got together. Paul had closed on a Thursday evening to let Aled's sister Rosie hold her hen do. Ordinarily, Paul wouldn't let karaoke within fifty feet of his establishment, but in a typically generous Paul gesture he'd gone all out and let Rosie deck the place in pink, made banana daiquiris, the lot.

Delia came to spectate towards the end of the night and help Paul clear up. The hen do girls had been heckling Paul to step up and sing a song. Paul eventually made a show of letting himself be corralled into it, sheepishly. Delia watched through her fingers, laughing and cringing in equal measure.

After fiddling with the song library, announcing it was full of girls' music, he selected Oasis.

'I'm dedicating this to my girlfriend, Delia,' Paul said,

into the tinny microphone. 'She's somewhere in the crowd. Ah, there she is!' He play-acted a rock-star wave across a throng. 'This one's for you, darling.'

During the opening bars of the song he mussed up his hair, drawing it into his eyes in an approximation of Liam Gallagher's, put his hands behind his back and let rip with a pitch-perfect impersonation of his lairy nasal Mancunian whine. It sounded just like the record.

The hen crowd went wild. Delia's mouth fell open. He could sing? Paul pointed at Delia during the track – and several hens, who had developed 0-to-60 crushes since the song started, turned to look at her.

Song finished, he gave a little bow, resisting entreaties to perform another, blew a kiss to Delia, then the bride-to-be.

After a few minutes he was by her side, arm snaked round her middle.

'Didn't embarrass you too much, did I?' he said.

His expression said he knew that Delia was in as much of a swoon as everyone else in the room with ovaries.

Delia, stretched out on Emma's sofa, could recall every last detail of that moment: the throb of the music, the heat and smell of Paul's skin as he leaned in to kiss her.

The nostalgia choked her.

Alone in Emma's front room, hundreds of miles away, she thought: charm isn't enough any more.

# Fifty-Four

The following week, Kurt was having another one of his black mood spells, which was peculiar given that Twist & Shout alumni were doing very well for themselves.

Lionel Blunt had won his by-election. Delia was horrified that even broadsheets had done 'More to him than meets the eye'-type profiles, with photographs of him saving Bogdan through the bonding power of a bundle of tobacco.

Gideon Coombes had got himself a TV show entirely designed around his special talents, called *Food Sod*. He ate in notoriously bad restaurants and then gave the kitchen team a detailed dressing-down afterwards. Delia had seen five minutes of him verbally decapitating a man who ran a Moroccan in Bridport called 'It's So Moorish!' and had to turn it off.

*Shoo Number Two* bathroom spray was the centre of a day-long Twitter storm when its female-targeted marketing – 'Boys Shouldn't Know When Girls Go' – was spotted by a journalist as a result of their press release, and outed

384

as obscenely sexist. A win–win for Twist & Shout as they weren't responsible for the marketing, but were charged with getting the product attention. A female *Guardian* columnist wrote the think-piece 'Poo: The Last Taboo?' Sales rocketed and the manufacturers were delighted.

Kurt was making a mint from crisis management due to Thom Redcar 'inserting his meat thermometer' into a front-of-house hottie instead of Mrs Redcar. It seemed to mainly involve calling journalists and wheedling, then threatening them, like a bipolar closing-time drunk.

In short, the universe was unfolding as it shouldn't.

The best times in the office were when Kurt did one of his two- or even three-day Lord Lucan disappearing acts, and Delia and Steph had a laugh. Sadly this week he'd brought his brooding disgruntlement back into the office.

When he mercifully shoved off one afternoon, Steph got to her feet and darted out of the room. Delia looked up from her keyboard curiously until she got back.

'He's gone,' Steph said, slightly out of breath, back to the door she'd closed again. 'OK. So he's definitely looking at our computers.'

Delia stopped typing and felt a chill.

'How do you know?'

'I deliberately said one thing to Kurt, and then another to the journalist, and emailed them on my Gmail, not my work account. Then Kurt comes in the next day, and there's an atmosphere . . .'

Delia could see Steph had worked herself into a state

waiting to say this. The thought that Kurt could see the contents of their inboxes was pretty horrifying.

'He has been grumpy . . .' Delia said.

'I know, Delia, but seriously – you know when the air's tight before someone says something that they're busting to say? Like that. Trust me. There's been other things, little things.'

Delia rested her face on the heels of her palms.

'I suppose the reason I thought this was impossible was the Adam West thing, yet that's all out in the open now. You're right, he didn't seem as shocked as I thought.'

Steph nodded, and re-took her seat.

'We're going to have to be so, so careful about what we send now.'

Delia paused over her press release and imagined Kurt sat at some satellite office somewhere, her words filling his screen, and gave a shudder. She texted Joe. She hoped he didn't mind being her unpaid IT helpdesk.

*OK, so my colleague is CERTAIN our boss can see what we're typing on personal email. Any more thoughts? Dx*

*Only that I want to know his secret if so! I've had a poke around since you raised this and honestly, if he is, I am foxed as to how. Foxed! Hah. Stay safe, though. Jx*

Kurt's laptop wallpaper was a photograph of him skydiving, goggles on, cheeks blown out. As time went on, Delia realised that Kurt was an adrenaline junkie in his work, too. What she'd thought of as comfortable lulls, when everything was ticking over nicely, had Kurt pacing his cage. Finally, the moods made sense.

He needed stunts to keep upping the ante; he was restless when not walking the high wire. So she supposed she shouldn't be surprised when he hit a new low.

A recently acquired client, Terri Moody, wrote 'Painful Lives' – fictional misery memoirs about abuse. Her latest, *Please Don't Daddy*, had stormed the bestseller charts. Delia looked at her canon, which included *He Said It Was Our Secret* and Fritzl-inspired *The Miser's Cave*, and couldn't possibly fathom why anyone would want to read them.

'Her problem with the publicity is she's not got any sob story of her own,' Kurt explained. 'She's writing these "A Child Called Shit"-type things about being forced to eat pissed-in porridge, but she's a happily married mum of two in Billericay. You need a narrative. I've not gone down this road before – I wondered if she should get cancer.'

'She should . . . get cancer? She doesn't have cancer?'

'Yeah. Shave her hair, ask her to drop a few pounds. She could write the letters to her kids, do memory boxes and all that. Then go into miraculous remission.'

Delia was speechless with horror.

'What, tell her kids she might die?'

'Nah, they wouldn't know, they're babies. Twins. Ugly ones actually, they look like haggis. Still, no refunds with IVF.'

Delia swallowed hard and tried not to howl. She wanted to wash her brain.

'I don't think we should lie about cancer. It's terrible karma, apart from anything else.'

'Hark at the Delia Llama, here,' Kurt chuckled. 'Sling a press release together about it, I'll talk to Terri in the meantime and see if she's game. Her dad was a proper East End villain, knew The Krays: known as Kenny the Fingers. She's a tough old bird, I reckon she'll go for it.'

The client's willingness was the least of Delia's objections. She was going to cross the Rubicon if she did this; she'd be doing something she couldn't come back from. Everything she'd been party to until now was in poor taste, but this was unequivocally wrong.

She didn't incline her head and share any look with Steph, but she was desperate to talk to her. If she gave her notice over this, it'd leave Steph alone with Kurt. She didn't like the idea; at the very least, she wanted Steph to have warning.

'Red, nip out and get us a Starbucks would you?' Kurt said, moments later, 'I've got a tongue like Gandhi's flip flop.'

Delia asked herself why she was letting herself be treated as the tea girl in her mid-thirties, sighed inwardly and got on with it. On the way there, she thought about Terri posing in a headscarf, and whether this modern villainy was much less awful than whatever antics had earned her father the name Kenny the Fingers.

Not for the first time, as she carried the drinks back, she thought about her fight with Adam West. She kept nervously checking his website, yet there was no article about Twist & Shout. Judging from the length of the comments and the frequency with which links appeared on Twitter, the site was getting a lot of traffic.

She vacillated over whether his reason for castigating her to Freya was enough. If Delia put it in the context of Freya being a bitter ex – something had happened between them, of that she had no doubt – it made some sense. And if you examined actions instead of words, Adam *had* looked after her that evening.

Without that conversation as motivation, what she did on Westminster Bridge looked like simple treachery. But, *but!* she said to herself. Adam was blackmailing you – he wasn't looking down on you from a place on the moral high ground. He was blackmailing because he said his ends justified the means. Did they? Delia had gone round in these circles many times.

She hated being hated by him, that was for sure. He'd said he'd never lie to her, and on careful review, she couldn't find any evidence that he had.

She imagined Adam's reaction to the Terri Moody 'conveniently timed cancer' story, and wondered if even his cynicism would fall short of believing they'd invented a carcinoma.

Delia carried the tray carefully down the steps into the basement, and set Kurt's coffee down in front of him. Steph wasn't at her desk.

'Has Steph gone far?' she said.

'Oh yeah, sorry, I should've said don't get one for her. She's gone.'

'Gone where?'

'Gone. I let her go,' Kurt said, not looking up from his laptop screen.

'She's been sacked?' *In the last ten minutes?* Steph's things had disappeared, the Sainsbury's bag for life she had her trainers in was nowhere to be seen.

Kurt glanced at Delia, irritable.

'Yeah, you want to argue the point? You're the boss now?'

'No, I just . . . why?'

'Nothing special about her. Girls like her are ten a penny. This isn't a bus, we don't carry passengers.'

Steph was also diligent, bright, a fast learner, nice company and popular with the clients. Kurt was a bastard. Delia thought of the conversation they'd had previously about Kurt knowing what they were doing online. Had Steph done something to seal her fate? Why would she keep emailing once she knew – had she tried to bait him? Delia wouldn't know until she could meet her. She pretend-fussed at admin tasks to avoid writing the Terri Moody release and felt like cheering when he finally left.

She texted Steph a very vigorous commiserations and a demand to meet in the pub, and was pleased that Steph had indeed dawdled in the hope of a pint.

When Delia left the building and hurried down the road, Google Maps open on her phone to find the nominated pub, she had the strangest sense of being followed. She turned and scanned the street; nothing. Gaaah, working at KurtCorps was making her a nervy wreck.

Nevertheless, as a precaution she texted Steph to find a very quiet corner of the pub where they couldn't be overheard.

When Delia arrived in the fairly grotty boozer, populated by a smattering of alkies and a Scottie dog tied by its lead to a stool, a pink-cheeked Steph was clearly on her second or third drink. Her shock of curly hair was now loose and Delia had that jolt of seeing someone in their own garb when you'd only previously seen them in work mode.

'This is so appalling, Steph,' she said, over her first beer.

'It was the way he did it, Delia. He said I'd failed to make an impression and I had to go. All I could say was OK. Then he threatened me about the non-disclosure agreement in our contracts. He said it was tied up tighter than a French gynaecologist's wife and if I ever talked about my work at Twist & Shout, he'd take me to court.'

'This is vile. You've done nothing wrong. Your work was excellent.'

'I thought it might happen. We're coming up to three months at the company, where he has to give us notice and we have some rights. He's always preferred you. Also, I didn't tell you this before, but I think you should know . . .'

Delia tensed.

'He asked me a lot of questions about whether you were seeing anyone and if you were online dating. At first I thought it was because he thought you might be seeing that journalist guy, but I reckon he's after you. I think I've seen him looking through your Facebook pictures too. I can't be sure, he closed it quick, but I saw red hair.'

Delia felt sick. She'd accepted a friend request from Kurt early on: some spurious reason given about information about a client on his profile. She reasoned she was never on the site much anyway.

'Oh, God. This was a while back?'

'It was last week.'

Delia squirmed. Kurt had been talking about entertaining a client in Manchester soon and whether Delia could block out an overnight stay, and she now got the jangly fear. She'd hoped Cock & Tail was an aberration.

'Also . . .' Delia paused, assuming Steph would've raised this straight away. It was possible shock and cider had slowed her faculties.

'. . . You said that thing about Kurt knowing what we were doing online? Perhaps that could've prompted him to sack you?'

Steph shook her head. 'Yeah, I only said that to you. I never put a word of it online. In fact I emailed my sister and said how great it was going, to put him off.'

Delia frowned.

'This computer stalking. It doesn't make sense. I've asked my IT friend. He surely he has more abilities than Kurt, and he doesn't see how he's doing it.'

'Well, I tell you, he knows stuff somehow. Whenever I've done anything I wouldn't want him to know – bang – I'm tellin' you, Kurt's eyes were on me the next day.' Steph pointed her index and middle fingers at her own eyes in a forked 'V', then at Delia's, and back at hers again. She got more Scouse when drunk.

'Wait—' Delia was having an unlikely epiphany, while staring at a brass coal scuttle, 'WAIT. What if he's not *seeing* what we're doing online? What if he's hearing us instead?' What if he's bugged the office?'

Steph's mouth fell open.

'It'd explain why he knows some things and not others. It's far more Kurt's style than tech acrobatics, and easier.' Delia thought on. 'Where would he have the microphone?'

They both drummed their fingers on the pub table. Then, eyes wide, locked on each other: 'THE CAT!'

'Oh my God, that creepy waving cat,' Steph said.

It was a fair bet: the office was bare of ornament otherwise.

'Should I move it and see if he reacts?' Delia said.

They agreed she'd try, to confirm the hypothesis.

'Only if I move the cat, right after he's let you go, he might twig we know?' Delia said.

'How about this. Don't move the cat, just take a look at it. See if you can find a microphone. Be careful as it'll make the sound go muffly; make it look like you picked it up to dust it. Then we'll find a way to get him back once we've thought on it.'

Delia clinked her glass to Steph's. She filled Steph in on Adam's information about the care homes and Steph concluded, somewhat furry of speech thanks to the Bulmers, 'We need to do something about him. I don't wanna lose you your job.'

'I wouldn't carry on working for him anyway,' Delia said. 'Not after this.' She'd have gladly stayed out until closing time, but Steph needed to get back to Chelmsford. Delia bid her fond farewell and shared promises to meet for proper drinks soon.

Left alone with the last inch of her beer, Delia took stock. She was working for a principle-free sexual harasser who'd spy on and threaten young members of staff he'd sacked, invent cancers, suicides and sex tapes for the press and plotted to throw clients overboard if his machinations were exposed. Not quite what she'd hoped and dreamed for her new life in the capital.

Delia was ashamed it had taken her so long to realise what she had to do. In an exhilarating rush, the answers came to her, loud and clear.

She hit Adam's number on her phone. No reply, and she didn't want to leave a message. She texted 'Please answer my call', but no reply came.

Delia was going to have to take the fight right to his door.

# Fifty-Five

It was easy enough to find Adam's house again, being as it was only two minutes' walk from Clapham High Street, the windows veiled by all that unpruned ivy. It was a pleasant redbrick ex-council 1960s terrace, on a street full of a schizophrenic mixture of low-rise tower blocks and Georgian semis with sweet-wrapper-shiny sports cars outside.

Delia knocked the door and waited. Dougie answered.

'Hello, is Adam in?' she said, and felt as if she was fifteen years old.

'He's at the shops,' Dougie said. He was less wan than when Delia last saw him, and seemed vaguely disquieted.

'Can I wait for him? I'm Delia. We've met.'

Dougie's frown deepened.

'Adam said if this girl came round I shouldn't let her in. Ginger hair, pretty face and—' Dougie made rolling and cupping hand gestures to indicate generous bosoms.

Delia reddened.

'I'm fairly sure that is you,' Dougie said, solemnly.

'It certainly sounds a bit like me,' Delia agreed, pointing to her fringe, glad of an overcast day and thus the coat shrouding her chest.

'Sorry,' Dougie said.

'Not to worry, I'll wait out here,' Delia said.

Dougie's brow furrowed as he wondered if this was allowed. His eventual shrug said his housemate hadn't added a Sitting On The Low Wall In The Front Garden clause, and Minecraft and a Coors Light were calling.

Delia dropped her bag, sat down and thought: Adam thinks I'm pretty? Though the boobs mime was a bit much.

Adam came wandering down the street with two lumpily misshapen orange Sainsbury's bags only minutes later, and Delia leapt to her feet. He was in a combination of fashionably washed-out grey things and fashionably beat-up brown shoes.

Adam looked startled to see her.

'*Off* my property, thanks very much.'

'I want to talk to you.'

'The feeling isn't mutual.'

'To apologise, and to offer you the chance to give Kurt what he deserves. Do a proper exposé about Twist & Shout and stop the old people's home scam, with me helping.'

'An opportunity to work with Kurt Spicer's girlfriend. Mmm, let me think about that.'

'I'm not his girlfriend.'

'Lovers' tiff? Or do you not put a label on your crazy connection? Slam piece, then.'

'I'm not doing anything like that with Kurt and I never was.'

Adam stepped past her, onto the front path.

'Which Delia am I meeting today? The one with the big sad eyes who might be about to see the error of her ways, or the one who'll make false statements about me committing a sexual offence to police? The one who's helped a stool sample of a man like Lionel Blunt?'

'Kurt's sacked Steph. He's getting the latest client to fake having cancer. We think he's been secretly filming us. I want to work with you to stop him.'

'Now he's done something bad to you and someone you like, you're bothered? Shame for me I didn't fall into the latter category.'

Delia tried to answer but he cut her off.

'You know what I find the least forgivable, Delia? The time I saw you at the cinema, those things you said to me about me being a good guy. You need a toxic soul to play-act something like that. At least with other lies they have a point, they're intended to achieve something. That was optional, lay-it-on-thick lying for the pleasure of ridiculing me.'

This made Delia think of Paul, and the hurt of the grand-standing fibs he told her that were pure embroidery.

'I've been lied to like that and I know how you feel. That isn't what happened. I did mean it when I said you were kind. I hadn't remembered the conversation with Freya, then.'

'Uh?'

'I can explain. Let me come in for five minutes.'

'No thanks, I have a risotto to make,' Adam held up one of his bags, 'and the rest of my life you promised to leave me alone to enjoy.'

Delia darted forward and took Adam's shopping bags from him. He was so surprised he surrendered them. She placed them in the porch and turned to him.

'Here's what happened. The night you saved me from Kurt, my memory was patchy. For example, I did remember Freya telling me you'd slept with everyone, and that was quite late in the evening.'

Adam glowered and clenched his jaw.

'. . . But I don't remember anything I said about Paul. The conversation between you and Freya, it had been lost to the booze fog too. Then after we met at the cinema, on my walk home – *bang*, suddenly it came back to me. I know you say you didn't mean those things and I believe you, but put yourself in my position. If you'd overheard me telling someone I was going to destroy you, wouldn't you take it seriously? The morning on Westminster Bridge, I saw you and I panicked. I thought it was a 'shoot first' situation. I told Kurt about the folder, that you were there and it was my fault. He grabbed the police and said the awful stuff about you flashing me. I admit I went along with it; not my finest hour, but I didn't know what else to do.'

Adam raised and dropped his shoulders in a simultaneous expression of 'OK' and 'so what?'

'Alright, you didn't mean to behave quite as badly as

you came off. It doesn't make me any more keen on a collaboration with you. Sorry.'

'Even if I'm not sleeping with Kurt, and I'm genuinely offering the inside story you wanted to do about Twist & Shout?'

'Even then,' he said, flatly.

Delia had a sudden, dispiriting sense that she'd lost his trust permanently. He now thought of her as Kurt's viperous Lady Macbeth and Delia had been naïve to think there was a talking cure.

'I mean, how do I know this isn't a Kurt plan to fuck me up further? Last time I saw you, you were short on apologies. Now you turn up on my doorstep out of the blue offering to rat on your employer who you're definitely not dating, despite admitting you were last time.'

'I didn't admit any such thing! You accused me and there was no space in that fight to correct you.'

'I don't trust you, and that's not going to change. Farewell, Delia Moss. I hardly knew you.'

Adam fished his house keys out of his pocket, opened the door, carried his bags through and shut it firmly in Delia's face.

She had sloped halfway down the street when she thought: no. I'm not taking that for an answer. I'm going to fight harder.

Delia walked back to the house and rapped hard on the door. Adam opened it in his shirt sleeves, holding a packet of Lurpak.

'What now?'

'This is a bad decision. You're right to be sceptical of me; I would be if I was you. It's taken me a while to get my bearings. I did realise Kurt was bad, but it was like I'd climbed onto a moving vehicle and had to hang on for dear life. I thought you were going to throw me under the wheels. You have to admit, you haven't been an obvious ally from the start, with all the piss-taking and blackmailing. I got my enemies mixed up. It's taken me a while to sort out what I should do, but I've got there. I want to do the right thing. I'm going to take this care homes story to a journalist, even if it isn't you.'

Adam raised an eyebrow.

'It's my story.'

'Exactly. It *should* be you.'

'You're blackmailing me now?'

'I'm doing what's right! If we're going to stop the care homes deal, someone has to do the story.'

Adam's expression was impassive.

'Think up any test you like to prove I am not in cahoots with Kurt, and I'll take it.'

Delia drew breath.

'Also, if you're making risotto, add some of that butter at the end as well as the beginning. It makes the texture better.'

She gave a slight nod, to indicate 'That's me done', and left Adam with these thoughts.

# Fifty-Six

After a difficult day in which she'd travelled all the way to South London to be called a third-rate human being, Delia could at least spend her evening cooking for Emma and chatting to Joe via email, laptop balanced on lap, wine to hand. And there was the small matter of uploading the next stage of Fantastic Miss Fox's adventures. She had an audience. It was a revelation.

*The Fox is getting such brilliant feedback! People love it. I told you they would. Jx*

Joe had put a 'Follow Me On Twitter!' button on the 'Fantastic Miss Fox' website linked to Delia's personal profile and her usually quiet account was beginning to get a steady stream of positivity and praise. Delia thought of what Emma had said at university. She should've listened to her.

*I know! It's made me so happy! People aren't taking the piss, are they? Dx*

*Oh my God, OF COURSE NOT. I'm thinking if the traffic carries on heading upwards, you should think about taking it to a publisher? Hey, it's occurred to me – if you ever fancy it, we could talk about this on Skype? Jx*

*That'd be great. It's OK, with your anxiety? Dx*

*Yeah, very oddly, it's fine. Put a computer in front of me and I can cope with anything, basically.* ☺ *Jx*

*Then that sounds brilliant* ☺ *Dx*

Her mobile started to trill. Adam? Cautiously, Delia thought this was A Good Sign.

'Delia,' he said, briskly. 'I've thought of a test to prove you're not working with Kurt.'

'Yes?'

'Send me a naked picture.'

'How would I get that? I told you, I'm not sleeping with him.'

'Of YOU, not him.'

Delia's mouth fell open.

'How will that prove anything?'

'You don't need to understand my methods. Send it and we'll go from there.'

There was a brief silence as the penny dropped. Delia burst out laughing.

'You utter bugger . . .'

She felt she could hear Adam grinning.

'Worth a punt. You're seriously offering me a story on Twist & Shout?'

Delia got her laughter under control.

'I am.'

'OK, let's meet to talk about it. If I get the merest whiff of triple cross, I'm off. What's the plan?'

Delia had a plan in outline, she only had to clear it with the woman of the house. Fortunately, the woman of the house looked absolutely delighted at the prospect of hosting the event.

'Adam West's coming here? To my flat? As in here? To the flat?'

'If that's alright. Me, him and Steph need a safe place for discussing this business and we can't be sure Kurt won't see us anywhere else.'

'It's very alright. Can I wear a flimsy kimono and accidentally let it fall open?'

'I'd rather you didn't.'

The following evening, Delia answered the door to a fresh-faced Steph, in her cycling gear, shaking her curls out of a yellow plastic helmet. Shortly after, a rather wary-looking and uncharacteristically polite Adam arrived.

It was odd to see him on home territory. Delia got them both cups of tea, seated them on the sofa, took charge and kicked off the agenda. There was a very different dynamic between her and Adam, and Delia was glad of it.

'The idea is that, between us, we find hard evidence on what Kurt's doing in shuttling bungs to Lionel Blunt, and give it to Adam so he can write a piece about Twist & Shout and the care homes. Kurt gets his comeuppance, and we protect geriatrics from him at the same time.'

'How did the Lucky Cat inspection go?'

Delia winced. 'I had to be quick, and like you said, I didn't want it to record anything that'd be a giveaway. There's a solid base with a solar panel in it, which could easily have a microphone in it. I have a feeling it has a camera, too. I looked up other Lucky Cats online and the eyes are usually painted. These have black glass pupils.'

Delia and Steph looked at each other and shuddered.

'I asked Emma about the legalities. You're allowed to secretly film employees if you suspect them of a crime like thieving. So Kurt would carry on lying in court and try to destroy our reputations, I suppose.'

'Almost certainly,' Adam said.

'Thank Christ the loo's got nothing in it except a loo and a very manky bog brush,' Steph said.

'I could say I'm surprised but I'm not,' Adam said, sipping his tea. 'I take it the whistleblower option is out, I mean with regards to either of you giving me an interview?'

'Steph and I signed contracts with non-disclosure clauses,' Delia explained. 'My friend Emma is a lawyer. I asked her to take a look and she said it's not advisable to cross it.'

There was a noise in the hall and Emma appeared in the doorway.

'Did someone mention me?'

Delia almost burst out laughing at what Emma was wearing: a full face of make-up, a black jumpsuit and wedge heels, half a handspan high. She wasn't, to the best of Delia's knowledge, going out anywhere.

Delia composed herself to do introductions: 'Emma – Steph, Adam.'

Adam got to his feet and shook her hand, a possible sign of a private education in Delia's opinion. Paul would be content with a cheery wave.

'Thanks for letting us meet here. Great place.'

'Oh! Thank you!'

Emma suddenly looked like a sheepish toddler who had been told it had done something very clever by grown-ups, the suave 'cocktail hour' air of before somewhat diminished.

'I see you've got drinks. Would you like stronger ones?'

'I think we're fine for now, thanks, Em,' Delia said. 'I was saying, the non-disclosure agreement in our contracts. It doesn't leave much room?'

Emma put her hand on her hip.

'Not if you don't want to be sued and lose. The cases I know of fighting NDAs are usually about ex-employees going to work for competitors. There, the judge is considering your right to work. There's not likely to be as much sympathy for your right to blab, even if you're saying your boss made bad things up or had a cat with secret video recorder eyes.'

'Thanks. A lawyer in the house is useful when you're crime-fighting.'

'A necessary evil,' Emma beamed, and Adam smiled back. *Oh no*, Delia thought, *they're not going to pull each other, are they?* She hadn't decided how she felt about that.

'I'll leave you to it, then,' Emma said, staring solely at Adam as she backed out of the room, wearing a gracious hostess smile.

'Adam, what can we give you instead?' Delia asked.

A lascivious snort came from the hallway that Delia hoped he hadn't heard.

'I need concrete proof that Kurt's acting as go between for Blunt and Lively Later Life. Failing that, catching him in the act of telling a whopping porker about anything, and we'll go from there. One thing I find with investigations is if you pull at a small thread, other things start to unravel.'

Delia and Steph threw around various items that had crossed their desks, but there was no single incident, or piece of evidence they could raise, that was any significant use. Delia had put pens and pads on the coffee table, and she increasingly felt the idea there'd be enough discussion to necessitate making notes was Girl Guide-optimistic.

Kurt was more devious than they'd given him credit for.

'He's been clever about concealing things from us. Every time he made things up it stayed verbal, nothing on the computer system. He doesn't need loyalty. It's the mushroom treatment of keeping us in the dark and throwing crap at us,' Delia said.

'Kurt's got to have incriminating Twist & Shout information stored *somewhere*,' Adam said. 'He's not doing it all on scraps of paper he shreds.'

'He said hard copies were safer than electronic,' Steph said.

'He said a lot of things to us for effect,' Delia said. 'He

also told us those folders were highly confidential. When they were booby-trapped with fictitious clients and he didn't much care what we did with them.'

'We could turn the tables and record him?' Steph said. 'Get him to talk about clients and tape him?'

Delia looked to Adam.

'You said he usually doesn't outline his most dastardly plans beforehand though?' he said. 'I can imagine it taking a while to get anything, and then his lawyers claiming it was your maverick leader's *Put The Mad Ideas Hat On And Sit In A Circle Humming Day* or something.'

'Better than nothing if we can't get anything else, I suppose,' Delia said, deflated. She strained to find something that didn't make this meeting a busted flush.

'Hang on, it's not much, but . . . Kurt made an odd remark, when I told him about my leaving the folder in Balthazar. Something like how his secrets are stored in his "little friend".'

'Did he know any shifty dwarves?' Adam said.

'Wait!' Steph said, holding both palms up. 'One time I forgot my trainers and went back to the office, he was in there with his laptop. It had a USB stick in it. I remember because it was in the shape of a character, I think it was Superman. Kurt pulled it out fast and put it in his pocket, like he didn't want me to see it.'

'Yes! He said his little friend never leaves his side!' Delia said. 'I think I saw it once, too. This *must* be what he meant.'

'Boom,' Adam said, tapping a pen on his knee. 'If there's a smoking gun about the retirement homes deal, that's where it is.'

'If it's always in his pocket, how the hell do I get to it?' Delia said. 'Wait until he's got it in the laptop and goes to make a cup of tea?'

'I don't think he ever put it in the laptop when we were there. Also, Kurt never makes the tea,' Steph said.

'Good points.'

'Not to be Debbie Downer, but even if we get the USB stick, we're not going to get anything from it. The contents will be encrypted, heavily security-protected,' Adam said.

'We'd need some sort of IT genius to break through it?' Delia said.

'Yup.'

'I have an idea.'

# Fifty-Seven

Delia went into the kitchen to put the kettle on and put the laptop on the table while the Skype call connected. It was too self-conscious 'meeting' Joe for the first time with onlookers.

The call was answered and a surprised Delia, stood in Emma's kitchen in London, found herself face to face with a slim man in his thirties dressed in a black t-shirt, in Newcastle, in what looked like a storeroom. Delia was ashamed to admit that it surprised her that he was boyishly attractive, in a *skinny computer geek with pointy angles and unkempt hair* sort of way. She'd been ready for any stripe of seriously eccentric shut-in.

'Hello!' she said. 'Joe!'

'Delia. We meet at last,' Joe's youthful voice, in her native accent, sounded over the tinny speakers on her laptop. He grinned tightly and self-consciously.

'Oh my God! It's you! And me!'

'It is,' Joe said, tucking his hair behind his ears. 'I'm in the garage by the way. In case you think I might be in prison. It's my lair. Yes, OK, I live with my parents.'

Delia guffawed.

Relief at how easy it was to chat washed over her, making her even more voluble. Delia was burbling merrily at the screen as she carried the laptop back into the living room, placing it on the coffee table, facing the sofa.

'This is Joe,' she said a little breathlessly. 'He's got mad skills when it comes to computers.'

'My skills *are* quite sick,' he said. 'Ah, there's all three of you. Hello!'

Delia could sense Joe was not a natural performer but he seemed reasonably at ease in the sanctuary of his garage.

Delia sat in the reflected glow of his expertise as Joe said his hellos to Adam and Steph and then discussed 'Operation Hack USB' in much more authoritative terms than anything Delia had managed so far.

'Everything boils down to passwords these days, up to twenty characters or so,' Joe said. 'The difficulty of the password is generally in proportion to the value of the information to the owner. If it's, say, grumble pictures of your girlfriend, you'll have medium level. If it's something that could see you in prison for a thirty-stretch, it'll be very strong, and so on.'

'Expect the latter,' Adam said.

'Can't you run password-finding software where a million options scroll past and then it finds the password, the cursor stops on it and it clicks and flashes?' Delia said, only half-joking.

Joe grinned. 'That's how we'd do it in a film. Unfortunately the reality is not quite that easy.'

'If we have to guess a password, this is a needle in a haystack, isn't it? Or Shakespeare and the typewriter chimpanzees.'

Adam smiled at her.

'Not *quite*,' Joe said, ruffling his hair with his long-fingered hands and looking about sixteen. 'Firstly, frequency of access is in our favour. This is something he's using often. My guess is he won't have put in lots of underscores and random numerals because it'd be a pain to input. It'll be a phrase. With brute forcing, what we can do is "seed" the attack. With your help, I pull together everything available about Kurt online. Hopefully somewhere there'll be a clue as to what's influenced his choice of password. We run a program, pre-loaded with this research, that then throws everything it has at guessing the password, bam bam bam bam—,' Joe did open and closing hand movements. 'It's a hailstorm assault until something snags. A hailstorm tailored to your target. It'll find its mark eventually.'

Adam and Steph both looked impressed. By contrast, Delia tried not to look disappointed. This still sounded hopelessly impossible, to her untrained ears.

'It could be anything?'

'Technically, yes. But it won't be. Think about your own passwords,' Joe said. 'Did they come from nowhere? Or are they associated with your life: important dates, names, pets, favourite songs?'

'Songs,' Steph put her hand up.

'There you go. If you've got a Spotify or iTunes account, I know what you listen to.'

'There's a lot of hair metal,' Steph said.

'How long would it take?' Delia said.

'Can't say. We could hit oil in fifteen minutes, or it could take two hours.'

Adam shook his head. 'I don't think we should keep it long enough that Kurt notices it's missing and figures out what's happened. We should try to get it back to him before he realises. That'd give us the element of surprise when we publish, and Delia wouldn't be in as much danger. If he realises she's nicked it, all hell will let loose.'

'Then it's pot luck. We'll try for as long as we can safely have it,' Joe said. 'Or you know, you can drug him, drag him to a cellar and hit him with a wrench until he tells you the password.'

'Probably more crime than we want to commit,' Adam said.

'How do we separate Kurt from his trousers so I can get the drive?' Delia said.

Steph stifled a laugh.

'You wouldn't have much trouble doing that.'

Adam side-eyed Delia.

'Much as I want to take Kurt down, I don't want it at the price of you having to go down on him.'

'Second that,' Joe said, cheerily.

'Thanks for the chivalry but I wasn't going to volunteer,' Delia said, slightly offended.

There was a pause while they silently wrestled with the conundrum of Kurt's trousers.

'Hang on, hang on!' Delia said. 'There's a fancy dress

party at the V&A that Kurt suggest we go to on Friday; some vodka launch. We're going to change at work. He'd take his trousers off then?'

Her thoughts ran ahead, almost tripping over themselves. 'He'll take the stick out of his pocket and put it in the costume's pockets. I'm in charge of ordering the fancy dress.'

'What's he going as?'

'A 1920s gangster, pinstripe suit, trilby, tommy gun.' Delia was excited now. 'And Kurt said it didn't have pockets and asked me if I'd carry his BlackBerry! He won't give me the USB, of course. It's not feasible to get the drive out of a trouser pocket. But his *jacket* pocket, if you distracted him, noisy room, drink . . .?'

'What are you going as, a gangster's moll?' Adam said, giving her a satirical look.

'A fox,' Delia said. 'Not as in foxy lady,' she said, hurriedly. 'A literal fox, the animal. I've got an amazing tail with bendy wire in it.'

'The Fox! Two become one!' Joe said. 'That's the coolest thing.'

Delia beamed at him and had a sense of them being a private club of two.

Amazingly, out of the nothing they had an hour earlier, a plot formed, with parts for everyone to play.

Joe would be talking Adam through the code-cracking. Delia was grateful this wasn't her bit, as Joe's account of what he was going to do became even less intelligible.

'To make this work, I'm going to need more processing

power. A lot more. We could rent it from The Cloud, but that would leave a footprint to follow. There's a wholesaler that's gone bankrupt and has loads of old Xbox 360s going on the cheap. I reckon I can cobble them together into a *beastly* server of our own. In my garage. Or the Naan-cave HQ, as Delia knows it.'

She laughed.

'Do what you need to do, and bill me,' Adam said. 'I can put it on the company expenses.'

Joe rang off as Delia thanked him profusely.

'No need,' he grinned. 'This is the shit I smoke.'

'The CIA want to worry about him,' Adam said. 'In theory, with about half a dozen moments ripe for disaster to strike, and scant chance of cracking the password in time, this could just work.' He gave Delia a look of admiration. 'Say I get something I can use. What happens to you?'

'I'm not going back that job after Friday, no matter what. I have some savings, I'll live off them if I can't get anything else straight away. I might even be a barista. I always wanted to know how to make a good coffee.'

Steph nodded and Adam looked at her curiously, as if he hadn't had the full measure of her until now. It was peculiarly gratifying.

As the meeting wound up, Delia thought she better say the thing they might've been thinking.

'How legal is this? Aside from that, how ethical is it to steal? I mean it isn't, obviously . . .' Delia said, looking to Steph. 'I've had pangs of guilt.'

Steph cast her eyes downward.

'None here, sorry. You should've heard him when he sacked me, Delia. He's *nasty*. Also it's not stealing if we give the flash drive back. It's snooping.'

Adam looked from Steph, back to Delia. 'Exactly. The legalities are more for me to worry about if I publish, as I can be sued. There's a public interest defence for snooping. If we don't find anything in the public interest, we don't use anything we find. The website has a lawyer on the payroll to check the safety of these things before we publish.'

'What if Kurt reports us for theft anyway?' Delia said.

'I have a strong feeling he won't want to invite that sort of scrutiny of Twist & Shout. You're leaving, so sacking you isn't a threat. Kurt got me sacked, once upon a time, and he's spying on you, so no sensitive stomach about his right to privacy here. I won't be opening folders with photos of his ex-wife. But Delia, are you sure you want to do this? You're on the front line.'

Delia took a deep breath and squared her shoulders.

'I think sometimes you have to do wrong to do what's right. It's not ruthless if someone deserves it. Right, Adam?'

She waited for him to realise she was quoting.

'You're an even bigger smartarse than me, Dahlia.'

# Fifty-Eight

As Steph reclaimed her bicycle from Emma's hallway down-stairs, Adam hung back, waiting to say something.

'Delia,' he said, 'it's fine us sitting here and coming up with this *Mission Impossible* heist. None of the rest of us have to actually tangle with the twat. You need to be care-ful. This is Kurt's livelihood and he'll be vicious as he needs to be to guard it. I know he's got a soft spot – and a hard place – for you. But it wouldn't mean a thing when push came to shove.'

'I know,' Delia said, with a shiver of nerves. 'I'm not depending on Kurt's affection.'

'If it's not happening on the night, it's not happening. None of us will blame you if you can't get the drive.'

'. . . Thanks.'

Delia tried not to take this as scepticism about her Spy Fox skills. Adam looked at her intently.

'Diving around in his pocket . . . don't go too far. Nothing's worth anything that'll make you feel less human afterwards.'

As much as she knew this was well intentioned, she was faintly angered by it. She'd seized control, and he was still acting like he had the upper hand. She folded her arms.

'You think you have to tell me not to give him a gobble, Adam? Think this could be considered patronising, and insulting?'

'I don't mean *that,* exactly. In the pursuit, when the adrenaline's flowing, strange things can happen. It overtakes you. I've done stupid things when I'm after a story. Ducked under a police cordon, during a fingertip search . . .'

'I'm not about to duck under Kurt's cordon and conduct a fingertip search!'

'I'm not having a go or accusing you of anything, I'm looking out for you. Kurt's not a nice man. He'll go further than anyone else. He's built a career on it.'

'That's why we're all here,' Delia said.

'Seriously. Be careful,' Adam said, and Delia muttered, tersely: 'Yes, thanks. Got it. I will be.'

They parted on rather less warm terms than she might've expected, after the evening's highs.

Emma's upside-down head suddenly popped into view, nearly level with Delia's, making Delia scream with surprise. She was hanging over the upstairs landing from where she'd been listening in, her blonde bob making her look like a naughty schoolgirl after lights out in an Enid Blyton.

'Has he gone?'

'Yes.'

'Oh my God, you two!'

'What?'

'You didn't tell me you were like that together!'

'Like what?'

'Bickery and flirty and close and sexual tension.'

'Yuck! Hardly!'

'You don't think he was being manly and protective about a woman he likes too much?'

'Did you spot the bit where he implied I'm loose as a goose?'

'He *wasn't* implying that. Cor, you have to make everything a cause, you do. That was the heat of his jealousy at the thought of another man's hands on you.'

Delia made a face. 'Your judgement's completely clouded by your randiness.' Delia turned her head to one side. 'Hasn't the blood gone to your head?'

'I'm draining it away from my . . .'

'Stop, STOP!' Delia said and Emma gurgled with laughter, withdrew her head and came halfway down the stairs, sitting on a step.

'You sneaky bitch. That evening we met Sebastian you were all—' Emma made fluttering eyes, pushed her lips forward, '*Why has disapproving man done nice thing for me? Yeah. What a fiendish PUZZLE.*'

'I concede Adam West has *some* decency. He wouldn't be here if I didn't concede that. You're completely off about the rest. In fact –' this was a little disingenuous, but Delia wanted to nip this Emma idea in the bud '– I once overheard him saying he'd sooner turn gay than go for me. So there.'

'Hah! Grandiose denials to throw others off the scent. It's textbook bewitchment.'

Delia sighed.

'He cares about you,' Emma said. She smoothed her dress over her knees, 'It was nice to hear.'

Delia had no reply for that, so she said: 'Come and look at something,' leading her into the living room and the laptop. She opened The Fox comic online.

Emma held her hair back as she peered at the screen: 'Is this the comic you were doing at uni? It looks fantastic. Fantastic Miss Fox, perfect! I'd forgotten how well you can draw. Delia, this is so cool. You've done this since you've been down? You're so sly. No wonder you like foxes.'

'I got it out of storage when I was back at home and started writing it again. I thought I might . . . I've been looking into contacting agents or publishers or something and seeing if anyone professional likes it. What do you think?'

'I think you should definitely, definitely do this.' Emma regarded her. 'You've got your sparkle back, you know. I don't want to take the credit – but I absolutely should have the credit. Coming to London has been good for you.'

'It has,' Delia said, glad she could be entirely honest. 'It really has.' She hugged Emma. 'Christ, you are drenched in perfume.'

Delia was apprehensive about Operation USB Stick, even more so after Adam's cautions, yet she felt peculiarly energised. She was making things happen. She was making choices, standing up for what she believed in, doing good for others and taking risks for the right reasons.

This was a life she was building for herself.

# Fifty-Nine

It was fair to say that Delia had never encountered the problem of 'how to sit down in a black cab when you have a huge fox tail springing from your arse' before. She tried pulling it to one side but there was still a large bushel of bum accessory between her and the seat. She perched, doing an impression of sitting that was more squatting.

'Why the hell do you want to look like a bin-scavenging varmint?' Kurt said, eyeing her from his flip-down seat opposite, one big hand on the handle above the door to steady him, the other holding his *Bugsy Malone* fake firearm.

'I like them,' Delia said, trying not to pitch forward into his lap as the cab took a sharp corner. 'They're mysterious and nocturnal and slink around our world when we're asleep.'

'They're rotten thieves who need to be on the wrong end of a twelve-bore.'

He didn't know how true he spoke.

'Look at my tail though!' Delia said.

'Yeah. You're making the get-up your own, I guess,' Kurt

said, openly scoping her form in a way that would make Lionel Blunt proud.

In fact, Delia was regretting her choice of costume. It had seemed delightfully funny as an idea, but it was cumbersome and embarrassing in actuality.

There was a theme to women's fancy dress, it seemed – if you didn't want a French Maid outfit or similar 'the stripper's arrived' gear, you had to be a Slutty Something. Slutty Heidi, Slutty Witch, Slutty Snow White.

When the fox outfit arrived, it was less cute and more provocative than she'd hoped, being a tube dress made from clingy orange lycra. It was low cut with a chest wig of white fluff underneath, thus drawing maximum attention to her cleavage, while the tail was an open invitation to stare at her behind. Her fiery block of fringe peeped out from under a hood attached to the dress, which had large triangular ears.

Delia was right, the tail was the best feature – a foot-long fountain of russet fluff with a white and black tip, as bushy as a small Christmas tree and engineered to stand up by itself.

Delia had used a kohl pencil to draw a nose and whiskers on her face. She felt ludicrous, and was glad of the black Zorro-face mask over her eyes, so she wasn't instantly recognisable.

In contrast to Delia, Kurt clearly loved his attire; a black double-breasted suit with wide white pinstripes, spats, a black shirt and white tie and black trilby. Cartoonised Al Capone.

Despite saying Delia would have to carry his BlackBerry, he couldn't bear to part with it, and it peeked out of one of his shallow jacket pockets.

She scanned for the outline of the Superman stick in his other pocket, while trying not to be caught – as she emphatically didn't want Kurt to think she was eyeballing his crotch.

He must've swapped the stick into that jacket. *Must have.* Adam was right that there were a lot of ifs and buts and suppositions in their scheme, however. The world usually threw up more variables than you ever allowed for in a planning session.

Kurt himself was one big belligerent variable, a dangerous person who Delia had decided to cross for the greater moral good.

After passing a few bored-looking paparazzi, they were in the domed atrium at the V&A, where their names were crossed off a guest list. Delia cricked her neck gazing at the extraordinary neon green, blue and yellow glass chandelier that tumbled from the ceiling, looking like the tangled innards of some crash-landed alien spacecraft.

Now they were somewhere so magisterial and proper, Delia felt the full force of the plan to rob Kurt. This was scary.

She followed Kurt through the marble tiled hall, steps echoing.

They came out into the courtyard with its oval, lake-sized pond, light glinting on the water in the early evening sunshine. Delia felt as if she was in an episode of *Doctor Who*: the space was thronged with Incredible Hulks, Stormtroopers, fairytale princesses, and Cleopatras. This was certainly a high-end fancy dress do where everyone had gone all out. Delia was only used to half-arsed, cheapo student ones where people turned up in Stetsons and spotted neck ties and mislaid them within a half hour of their arrival.

Waiters in *Phantom of the Opera* masks with trays of Martinis circulated, an ice luge in the shape of a swan dribbled vodka. The brand's inspirational theme slogan of *Become Who You Want To Be* was plastered around the place, to remind everyone why they looked stupid. Delia was glad of her costume now; she was no longer out of place and it made playing tonight's role easier.

She accepted a cocktail, grateful for Dutch courage, and yet equally aware that she needed to stay sharp.

She'd looked up YouTube videos about pickpocketing, thinking how useful and also worrying it was that there were How To videos on crimes nowadays. She learned she needed to distract Kurt by mentioning something else about his person, so his 'area of concentration' was directed elsewhere.

Delia also had to weight his pocket with something equivalent to the drive so he'd think he had it while he didn't have it. She'd almost used a Lil-Lets holder until, doh, she twigged: *buy another Superman-shaped USB drive.* She was paranoid about getting them mixed up, or Kurt spotting hers every time she opened her not-very-Fox-ish handbag: Steph had judged them identical.

One Martini down, she felt emboldened enough to breathe deeply and say: *it's time.* She palmed the empty drive, feeling the clock-tick of her heart.

'Is your pocket square sewn in or did they give you a real one?' she said, leaning over in a supposedly tipsy manner and twitching at the red silk in the upper right-hand side of his jacket.

Kurt's eyes followed her hand.

Simultaneously, she slid her fingers into the jacket pocket nearest her, feeling for the drive – yes! It was there! Oh my goodness! She'd never truly believed that theory would become reality. She swapped one for another, holding Kurt's drive with her fingertips and letting go of the second one in her palm. Her palms were slick with the transgressive, self-conscious guilt of a shoplifter.

Kurt, chin on chest, said: 'It's the real McCoy, should be for this money,' and yanked it out, waving the hanky as demonstration, as Delia withdrew her hand sharply. Amazing – distraction worked like a dream. She got the impression she could've been less dexterous and still got away with it.

She didn't dare look at what she had in her hand, her fingers closed tight like a vice over the ridged plastic bullet.

'Just nipping to the loo,' she announced gaily, voice brittle. 'Is the gun getting in the way, shall I see if they can cloakroom it?'

'Nah, I kinda like it,' Kurt said, miming machine-gunning the guests. *Lovely.*

Making sure she hadn't been followed, Delia headed for the toilets, texting Steph with nervously clumsy fingers.

*I have it.*

# Sixty

Delia pretended to be touching up her whiskers at a mirror. She felt a light tap on her shoulder and a shorter version of the killer from *Scream* stood at her elbow.

They'd agreed Steph's costume needed to be both completely anonymous and easily removable, as Adam was holed up in a rented office across the road. Drawing large amounts of attention once she was outside the V&A wasn't ideal.

Delia slipped the tiny superhero into her black gloved hand and hoped she'd dealt with the right cloaked slasher. She felt as if she was in the movies, only instead of the events happening to someone else onscreen and being resolved by the credits, she was right at the centre of the tornado.

She made her way back to Kurt and set into her second Martini, not listening to a word of a work conversation between him and a man from *Avatar*, complete with dread-locks, electric blue body paint and giant spear.

Delia still couldn't believe the switch had gone so

smoothly. In a different version of the plan, that'd be it, done – they'd discussed whether or not to leave Kurt with the decoy USB. As appealing as it had been to only do the switch once, they'd come to the conclusion that Kurt would realise he'd got a dud very soon after leaving the party. Adam thought leaving him any time to mount legal actions and get injunctions before he published his article would be a bad idea. Or, something worse.

'If he guesses what we've done, I wouldn't put it past him to have someone come and take a baseball bat and smash my hard drive up, and they might have a go at smashing me up while they're at it. I mean, we've not exactly played fair, so we'd have trouble going to the police. He needs to know right at the point I'm ready to post the article about Lively Later Life and no sooner. Publication is protection.'

The thought of Adam getting a pasting after a scheme Delia had dreamed up had been horrible to contemplate, and she acquiesced to the logic. It still didn't guard against Kurt suddenly deciding he was leaving the party and it happening anyway, another variable that gave Delia a gippy gut.

Having told herself to go steady with the booze, she already felt slightly blurry and off-kilter. She remembered the wisdom that Martinis were like boobs – one was not enough and three too many – and only pretended to sip this one.

Time ticked past, and Delia knew they must have used most of the hour maximum they'd allowed for the hacking.

It had been one thing to agree in principle that it might fail. In the event, Delia had to admit it was incredibly dispiriting to think they might be empty-handed, and she still had to perform the switch again.

She felt her phone bip in her bag.

It had been at least forty-five minutes. This was obviously going to tell her to prepare to take delivery of an uncracked stick.

*BINGO. IN. Bloody hell, your boy is good. On its way back to you. Ax*

Delia had to absorb this air-punching news without betraying a flicker of emotion. She'd never quite believed they could do it. She knew Joe was good but this should see him get an award.

Delia waited five minutes and excused herself to the ladies again. Inside, the *Scream* killer with warm gloved palms pushed the talisman into her hand, as Delia pretended to touch up her vulpine nose. Despite Steph's face being entirely obscured and Delia's being heavily disguised, she could feel the moment that passed between them.

Once back at Kurt's side, she struggled to stay level and make conversation when she was on a euphoria-, adrenaline- and Martini-high. Perhaps master criminals who turned over casinos and stole famous art did it for this sort of illicit buzz, as well as the money.

Nevertheless, with the end in sight, Delia surprised herself by her hesitation in doing the swap back. She was almost home. She'd proved to herself she could do it. In a way, the second part was harder. There was more at stake now.

Prevaricating, she let time pass. She felt her mobile buzz with texts. She didn't want Kurt to wonder why she was checking her phone constantly, and left them ten minutes before looking.

*Is everything alright? Sx*

*Did it go OK? Ax*

They were obviously fretting she'd been grabbed by the wrist by Kurt and he was attempting Sharia Law with a rubber meat cleaver prop.

What should she use as distraction? It couldn't be the hanky the second time. It'd have to be something in their eye line.

'I hope that Klansman isn't a Twist & Shout client,' she said, conversationally. Kurt had mentioned that Gideon Coombes was here, somewhere, under a layer of panstick or a wig. He wouldn't be speaking to him as he 'didn't believe in fraternising with clients in a social setting'.

Kurt glanced over. Delia quickly delved into his pocket, grabbed the spare and dropped the drive. And yet – unexpected variable – Kurt glanced back and said: 'I think it's a shit ghost.'

The movement meant his body pushed closer to the pocket, and the pressure of her hand, holding the decoy drive, was greater than intended. He would very likely have felt the contact and Delia had a split second to decide what to do. She couldn't think of anything other than to pull her hand out swiftly and pretend she'd been intending to clasp him at the waist, praying desperately he hadn't sensed precisely where her hand had been.

'I'm going to get off, anyway,' she said, leaning up to peck him on the cheek, as if the whole thing had been an overfamiliar, over-refreshed way of saying farewell.

It was an odd moment, with Delia seemingly behaving completely out of character, and she could see Kurt trying to make sense of it.

'Wanna go somewhere quieter? I could be into that,' he said, reciprocating with his hand on her waist.

Ordinarily, Delia would've knocked him right back. Here, she was trapped in the charade where she'd suddenly become inappropriately tactile towards him. If she broke the spell, he might wake up to what she had been doing.

'I best get off. Early start in the morning. I'm off to Newcastle. A christening.' *A christening?*

Still, it tied with her plan to call him on Monday and say she was gone for good.

'It's not early if you don't go to sleep.'

With revulsion, Delia realised Kurt was moving his hand up her ribcage. 'Never thought a woman with chest hair could look this good.'

'Haha,' Delia forced a laugh and moved his hand away, trying for a coy but knowing smile. She still had the spare drive clasped tightly in her left hand. 'See you on Monday.'

Kurt's eyes narrowed.

'Hot and cold, eh? Are you asking me to do a spot of fox hunting? What's with the . . .?'

As Delia backed away, she collided with a passing masked waiter. Or more accurately, her giant appendage did. The size and volume of her tail meant she effortlessly took out a whole tray of Martinis which went crashing to the ground, spattering an Elmo from *Sesame Street* and an Eve, in flesh-coloured bodysuit with fig leaves, who shouted things that didn't sound either very kids TV or Garden of Eden.

As she whipped round, the drive flew from her hand. *Oh fuck oh fuck oh fuck oh fuck oh no* . . . her body was hopefully obscuring Kurt's view. She had to retrieve it before he saw the stick, or all was lost.

The waiter waved his hands angrily and dismissively at a flapping Delia, crouching down over the wreckage of broken glass and Queen Green olives on cocktail sticks. Delia watched in horror as with a gloved hand, he briskly swept up the stick with the rest of the detritus, back onto the tray.

Regroup, regroup, think, she told herself: there was nothing on that stick. As long as Kurt didn't see it, it didn't matter if it got thrown in a bin. She stayed directly between Kurt and the waiter, blocking Kurt's line of sight. The waiter had the tray on both palms and was striding back towards the main building.

'Bye, Kurt!' Delia called, barely looking at him, threading her way out through the multicoloured, multi-species crowd to the interior of the V&A, and then to freedom.

# Sixty-One

Delia burst into the road outside, euphoric, like she'd managed a prison break. She texted Adam and Steph that she was on her way to the meeting point, a few streets away, untying her mask and taking the hood down. It was pretty embarrassing being in public with a giant white-tipped tail bouncing behind her, yet there were bigger things at hand.

Heartbeat ticking at 'managed panic', she glanced over her shoulder a few times. As far as she could tell, she was on her own. *Success?* She wouldn't believe it until there was high five-ing and chest bounces.

Steph was there in plain clothes, having stuffed her costume in a rucksack, her unruly long hair gathered back in a crocodile clip.

'Did we do it? We got the information?' Delia said, and Steph grinned from ear-to-ear while nodding. 'Where's Adam?'

'You didn't see him?' she said.

'What?'

434

'We were worried you'd been caught when you didn't text back so he went into the party. He looked like one of the waiters.'

'No . . .? I didn't even know Adam had a costume! Or an invite.'

'He brought one on the off-chance he needed it. He said he'd go in and look for you. I was going to go too but he asked me to look after his laptop.' Steph held up a bag.

'There he is,' she pointed as Adam rounded the opposite corner, holding his mask.

'You know, with any plan, you think "I hope we don't end up having to use the back-up plan," he said. 'I *stink* of vodka Martini. I think this is yours, madam?'

He proffered the Superman stick. He and Delia gazed at each other, him amused, her stunned.

'What? Where were you?'

'I was the waiter chucking the drinks around.'

'I thought my tail knocked that over.'

'I ran into you on purpose. I saw you getting groped and thought I'd lend a hand. As it were.'

Delia had lost track. 'Sorry. Yes. But we broke in? You got the goods from the flash drive?'

'Took us right up to the wire but, yep. That lad is skilled to a scary degree.'

'I wish you could've seen it, Delia,' Steph said. 'We felt like something in a movie. It was Adam pacing around: *We don't have much time left, dammit*!'

'It's all backed up?' Delia said.

'It's on my laptop, and Joe copied it too,' Adam says.

'I can't believe it worked!' Delia said, looking to each of them.

'Oh. It might've gone less well than we thought,' Adam said, face falling.

He was looking over Delia and Steph's shoulders, his expression anxious. Delia turned to see Kurt, looking like he'd willingly play a key role in any St. Valentine's Day massacre, if only his gun weren't a replica.

Delia's body went shaky.

'Guess what *you*—' he jabbed a forefinger at Delia, '—now have in common with *her*.' He pointed at Steph.

Delia, Adam and Steph stood frozen to the spot, aghast.

'Think I can't work out what's happening, when you're suddenly all over me?' he said to Delia. 'You can thank this prick,' he gestured at Adam, 'for confirming it.'

'Fairly sure *you* were all over *me*,' Delia said, trying to imbue her speech with considerably more confidence than she felt.

Kurt pulled the USB stick from his pocket and every pair of eyes moved to it.

'This what you were after, when you were feeling me up?' he waggled it, and put it back in his pocket. 'Thought so. Unlucky. It'd be less than useless even if you were good enough to take it from me. I've got a level of encryption on there that'd give the NSA a migraine.'

Delia looked to Adam and then to Steph. They stared at each other and then looked back at Kurt, who took their speechlessness as their being utterly bested, as opposed to mute relief.

'This was his idea, to get him a scoop, I take it,' Kurt gestured towards Adam. 'Fucking hell, women are stupid.'

'Actually, it was my idea. I think what you do, and how you treat people, is despicable. You can't complain when underhand tactics are used against you,' Delia said.

Kurt reeled back in mock-amusement.

'Oh darling, you think I'm some big bad guy? In this city? Bless you. You should go back to that place you're from and get on with firing out babies. You're custom-built for it, after all.'

Adam took a step forward.

'You've sacked her. Let's call it an evening, shall we?'

Kurt ignored him in favour of Delia.

'Don't kid yourself you're any better, darling. You're a worse whore than me.'

Adam burst out laughing.

'Is there a central plank to that argument? Other than you?'

'You should've seen her rummaging around just now. She had her hands on it. Yeah, I don't think she was going to tell you about that.'

Adam said nothing and Delia parried with, 'Kurt, unfortunately, everyone here knows you make things up.'

Kurt addressed Adam.

'If you publish one single full stop about me on your boring blog, I will sue you so hard your teeth will rattle and you'll be pawning the fillings. I warn you, this is the last time we run into each other. Or you'll regret it.'

'Agreed.'

'Honestly,' Kurt shook his head at Delia and Steph, 'you can't get the staff nowadays. I give a pair of losers from the sticks a chance, and this is how you repay me.'

All of a sudden, Steph shouted, loud enough to startle them all, going more Scouse than ever under stress: 'Oh why don't you just DO ONE, you arsehole!'

Kurt smirked. He got the drive from his pocket again, kissed it, replaced it. Gave them the finger on each hand as he backed away, turned and sauntered off.

'I don't know about you, but I'm going to miss him,' Adam said.

They all burst out laughing in a release of tension.

'How did he find us?' Delia said.

'Must've recognised me and followed. Sorry,' Adam rubbed his neck.

'It doesn't matter. He doesn't realise what happened.'

Steph checked the time and said she had to be off to band practice. She shook hands with Adam and hugged Delia: 'Keep in touch.'

'You've got what you need?' Delia said to Adam.

'From the merest scan of the contents, I suspect I'll need counselling once I've delved around in Kurt's Top Secret files.'

Adam stuck a spirits-sticky hand out for Delia to shake.

'Amazing work this evening. You were brilliant.'

Delia shook it.

'Finally, I have his respect!'

'You always had my respect,' he said. 'Just my disapproval as well.'

438

He smiled and Delia launched herself at him for a victory hug, a strange hug where they were separated an inch by her chest fur. Adam held it for longer than Delia expected, and gave her a concerted, valedictory squeeze.

As they stepped back, she saw a look on his face she couldn't immediately decipher, and she knew she'd replay later.

'Your whiskers,' he said, grinning. He leaned round: 'And that tail . . .'

'Shaddap!' Delia said, colouring.

Adam was looking at her with a challenge in his eyes that Delia couldn't quite identify. She felt shakier still, also kind of hot and queasily excited and off-kilter.

'I'd suggest a celebratory drink, but,' Adam gestured at himself. 'Perhaps go for one when we won't look like cosplayers and furries and I don't reek of spirits?'

'Deal,' Delia said, shaking her tail.

She was on her way home when Adam texted.

*Hah, forgot to tell you what the password was! I Fucking Hate My Ex Wife. Stay classy, your ex-boss. Ax*

# Sixty-Two

'Here's a quiz. What Did Kurt Spicer Do Next, then, Daria?'
Adam said.

Delia smiled at the sound of his voice and balanced her mobile between ear and shoulder while she clamped the sketchpad under her arm more tightly. She was walking along The Serpentine in the sunshine. Being — hopefully short-term — unemployed was so far pretty great.

'That's a broad canvas.'

The USB stick had yielded everything Adam had needed, and then some. His site had published a piece about the politician, the magician and the very dodgy PR man who bound them together. The rest of the media picked up on it, Lionel Blunt faced questions in the house and a police investigation, and Lively Later Life withdrew from the care homes bid. Exactly how the 'documents seen' by Adam came into his possession was left vague to 'protect his source'.

Adam reported to Delia that when he'd called Kurt on the eve of publication and asked him for a quote, Kurt at first went ballistic and fulminated, threatened and blustered.

Then he quietened down as it dawned on Kurt that if Adam had seen what was on the stick, he was truly shagged and best off not antagonising Adam further.

One of the many revolting findings in Kurt's Pandora's Box wasn't just that he promoted his clients' interests, but actively discredited and smeared those who he identified as their enemies. Or engaged in 'throwing shade' at them, as Kurt kept calling it in his communications.

Surveillance was second nature – he was busy tapping phones and hacking emails to find compromising material, so no wonder he was spying on his own employees. Any guilt Delia had felt about what they did had entirely dissipated and Kurt's ability to complain about breach of privacy was void.

'The depth of his depravity no longer surprises me,' Delia said.

'It's the girth of his depravity I find surprising,' Adam said, and Delia burst out laughing, feeling a flush of unguarded affection. Somehow, they'd become honest-to-goodness friends. How had that happened?

'Kurt's legged it,' Adam said.

'Has he? Where?'

'Fled back to Australia.'

'No!'

'Yes, poor old Down Under. At least they're used to felons.'

'I can't believe he's simply gone.'

'It's his way. He's done Scarlet Pimpernels before, from what I can glean. He'll turn up somewhere else, probably with a different name. He's Interpol's problem now. Or more likely, the Australian media's. The main thing is, if you and Steph were worried about any trouble he might make for you, I think you can sleep easy. He's on the other side of the world and likely to stay there for a good long time. He won't come after me when he knows I have endless ammunition.'

Delia was touched Adam was thinking about them. In truth, she had been looking over her shoulder, and knowing Kurt was on the other side of the world was a huge relief. And Steph had already got herself a junior account manager job with a decent firm. Delia had been concerned for her, in case Kurt tried to spoil it.

'We did the right thing, didn't we?' Delia said.

'The right thing's always a matter of opinion,' Adam said. 'I reckon when we're on our deathbeds, we'll think the day we titted around at the V&A was one of the more productive ones.'

Delia smiled and shifted the phone to her other ear.

'On our deathbeds? I've got an image of camp beds, side by side.'

'If I'd said our deathbed, singular, that'd sound weirder.'

'We'd only die together if we'd drunk from an ice luge that Kurt had got to.'

'I don't know. Maybe a future adventure takes us to a Venetian palazzo with a historic but highly unsound infrastructure. We get brained by falling masonry.'

'Sorry to say, but I think this is my first and last job with you, Adam. I can't take the heat.'

'That's a shame. I thought we made a good team.'

'Hah! See you around,' Delia said, laughing.

'Depend upon it. Oh, your comic drawings are brilliant by the way.'

'You've seen them?' Delia said, 'How come?'

'Ahem, I am an investigative journalist. Seriously. I'm impressed. You're extremely creative. I think you gave Kurt too much of a jawline, mind.'

Delia laughed.

She got back to Emma's flat to find a package waiting for her on the table in the hallway. The Paul parcels continued. She felt apprehensive, discomposed. As she ignored entreaties by voicemail and text to speak to him, it was the only avenue of contact left open.

In the quiet of the flat, she shook out the contents and untied the green ribbon on the gift inside.

Inside was a cheese with ash-grey rind in wax paper from Valvona & Crolla, a treasure trove of a delicatessen that Delia had become obsessed with on a trip to Edinburgh. 'The Salami Cavern' she called it, until Paul pointed out that sounded like a double entendre.

There was a note.

*Did I get the right one? Did it survive the journey? I remember I was impressed at all the wild food you ate when we got together. Remember the Swedish herrings you bought, and when you opened the tin, Parsnip hid? Anyway. Please come home, Delia. I love you. Px*

Home. But why was home where he was?

# Sixty-Three

Delia had organised drinks with Adam and Steph, and this felt a minor miracle to her. She knew people in London! Enough people to fill a two-man tent!

Three new friends, if you counted Joe, up north. Delia thanked him effusively for the V&A efforts. She wanted to do something in return for him. He'd said there was something, but he was too shy to say on Skype. 'Nothing pervy!' he stressed, as Delia boggled slightly.

Minutes later, he texted:

Just carry on being a friend and chatting with me. Your company has brightened up my days, Fantastic Miss Delia! One day we'll meet in the flesh, promise. I'm working up to it. PN (I'll always be PN to you, won't I ☺) x

Delia promised Joe. Yet by the time the occasion to drink offline with the rest of the V&A gang arrived, she had a job getting in the way.

Or, sort of. She was working in a bistro-bar in Soho. It

was the kind of place where, if you asked for nuts, you got a Kilner jar of unshelled pistachios instead of packets of KP. It served 'sliders and sharers' on chopping boards, the menu written in lipstick on a mirror. The room was full of coconut trees and too-loud music from a DJ, and the walls glistened with moisture when it got two-thirds full.

Delia knew her way around this environment blindfold thanks to often helping Paul when he was shorthanded. She'd seen a sign in the window the previous week asking for summer staff and popped in, on impulse, thinking they'd say 'Aren't you thirty-three?!' instead of 'Please God yes, can you start tonight?'

Delia was enjoying it: the simplicity of hard toil with no mental effort involved, and no moral quandary. They usually needed her from midday to six, after which she got back to Emma's, had a cool shower and picked up her sketchpad.

When she called Adam to apologise for a Saturday shift clashing with their plans, he suggested they meet at her place to 'keep her company' and she could join them when she knocked off.

Delia agreed, and only realised she might feel silly when she was pouring his lager, her hair coiled in Heidi plaits and sweat pooling in her bra, underneath her apron.

'Don't you dare laugh at me,' she said pre-emptively, as Adam rested pale-shirted elbows on the bar, watching her work.

'I'm not laughing at you, Delia Moss. I'm slightly in awe of you.'

'Hah! Awed enough to finally learn my name.' She took the flat of a palette knife and swiped the head from the lager, as if she was bricklaying. Adam was surveying her fondly. Delia felt shy, yet pleased.

'I'm serious. You never stop surprising me.'

Delia's co-workers behind the bar were two lissom twenty-something gap-year travellers, Dutch and Irish, respectively, and both fans of the short-short. Most men's eyes strayed to their behinds when they bent down to the bottle fridges, or reached up to the optics. Delia had been enjoying relative invisibility next to them. Yet with Adam she felt she had his sole scrutiny; his eyes never flickered in their direction. She turned to get Steph's rosé from the fridge and made sure she knelt down, rather than leaning over as she did.

'It's not irritating, us being here?' Adam said, taking a first sip of his drink as she sploshed the wine out.

'Not at all. It's nice.'

Adam gathered the glasses together.

'OK, well. We'll pace ourselves so we still make sense by the time you clock off.'

Looking towards the table in the corner, Delia felt pangs at not being able to take proper care of two people she'd brought together – yet they seemed to be coping fine without her.

Delia watched Adam chatting with Steph. He was speaking animatedly, gesticulating to illustrate the anecdote he was telling. You didn't often get to simply watch someone. Delia found herself gazing at him, cataloguing his mannerisms: the way he rubbed his hair, how he pressed his palm to his forehead when expressing dismay, the fact he listened properly when others spoke, chin angled downwards.

This was the funny thing about Adam: the more she got to know him, the less handsome, and more attractive he became. She often forgot he was so perfectly arranged, because he was just Adam. When he laughed, his face contorted into goofy joy. She loved the way he'd shoot her a direct look after deadpanning, and then crumple with delight if she laughed with him.

He kept glancing over at her, a confidential expression on his face, as if they were sharing a private joke.

It was then that it happened; something Delia had thought might happen, eventually. It made her reveries ridiculous, left her feelings oddly bruised. A blonde woman with spirally hair and a strong, good-looking face walked in. She had tortoiseshell sunglasses on her head, a sweepy maxi dress and carried herself with regal bearing. Adam threw an arm round her neck, trapping her in the angle of his elbow and kissing the top of her head, introducing her to Steph with evident enthusiasm.

Delia was very glad she had to stay in whirling motion to serve the throng of customers. For God's sake, why now? She saw Adam was being proprietorially considerate, leaping up to find her a chair. It wasn't an occasion for plus ones, it was unofficially their celebration of the V&A caper. *Insensitive.*

Once the sexy Amazonian interloper was settled, Adam was straight up to the bar, leaning in to half-shout a request for a slimline G&T over the music.

'Can I introduce you to Alice? I'd love you to meet her,' he added, as Delia concentrated on trowelling crushed ice into a dishwasher-warm glass to cool it down.

She didn't know what to say, other than: 'Uh, OK,' throwing away the ice and squirting soda from a siphon aggressively, as if she was firing a gun.

'Don't worry about her having any attitude with you. She knows what the score is between us.'

'Why would she have attitude with me? Like Freya did? You can really pick them, can't you?' Disappointment made Delia lairier-Geordie than usual.

'Alright. Sorry I asked,' Adam said, eyes widening. 'Alice is no Freya. Also I didn't pick her . . .'

'Whatever.' She turned and pumped a measure of gin into the glass, asking over her shoulder, 'Single or double?'

'Make it large, in the circumstances,' Adam muttered.

Delia flipped the lid on the tonic bottle and placed the drink on the bar mat. 'Anything else?'

'An explanation of what I've done wrong would be . . . wait. You realise Alice is my *sister*, yes?'

Whoops.

'Oh,' Delia said, light dawning. Yes! Relief. But also, oh no.

She'd forgotten the wedge of lime and was glad of being able to turn her back to get some. Delia wanted to disappear into the cellar and never come back. God, she'd sounded like a jealous girlfriend. Or a spurned one. That was a part she had no intention of playing ever again. Why did she feel so territorial, and so touchy? Had the experience with Paul left her without layers of skin?

She expected Adam to look fairly offended or angry when she risked catching his eye again as she took his money, he only looked perplexed, and maybe curious.

'Uhm,' he paused, and did the head rubbing thing, as she handed over the change, 'I've been meaning to say. I feel bad for shutting the door on you at dinner time, that time.'

'Did you?'

'Yes. When you did an *As God Is My Witness* plea at my door while I was holding a packet of porcini mushrooms.'

Delia laughed, more heartily out of relief that Adam wasn't attacking her. 'It was butter.'

'Ah yeah, butter. If you can bear to trek out to Clapham, I'll cook for you to make it up. If Dougie joins us, I forewarn you he puts gallons of sriracha on everything. It's quite stomach-turning.'

Delia said that sounded lovely and popped a stirrer in Alice's drink, trying not to wince with shame at what had just passed between them. There had been a heat to her words that she couldn't explain, to him or to herself.

She was deeply apprehensive when it came time to unwind the apron and join them; nevertheless, their lengthy head-start on the drinking made for an easy atmosphere.

Delia made even more of an effort with Alice than she might have, determined to drench her with loveliness after Adam's tales of Twist & Shout. Though it turned out she didn't need to be nervous: Alice was warm, intelligent and unaffectedly friendly. Delia imagined they could be friends.

When Delia thanked her for putting up with the venue, she said: 'I couldn't pass up a chance to meet the famous Delia, who I've heard so much about.' Adam balled up a paper napkin and threw it at Alice. Delia glowed.

Half an hour later, Emma and Sebastian called by and things got even more raucous. Delia was fairly exhausted by the time they spilled out into the street at ten o' clock. She'd never get used to how far you were from your bed in London.

On the way home, Delia and Emma got into a drunken loop debate about the significance of the evening's developments.

'A date! You're going on a date!' Emma said, when Delia told her about Adam's offer of dinner. She stopped and grabbed her hand so hard as they walked to the Underground that it felt as if she'd crushed the bones.

'It's not a date! Dougie's going to be there!'

'It's a date!'

'Dougie!'

'DATE!'

'DOUGIE.'

Emma put her fingers in her ears.

'DATE, IDST!'

'What does IDST mean?'

'If Denied, Still True.'

'Emma, we're thirty-three years old.'

# Sixty-Four

Delia stood at the door in Clapham in a summer dress with swallows on it and new cheapo pistachio heels, having peeled the stickers off the soles on the Tube. She was holding a bottle of homemade blackberry vodka in lieu of wine and telling herself it wasn't a date, because Dougie would be there.

Adam answered the door in a white t-shirt, smelling of smoke and holding tongs, thanking her for the booze. 'Dougie's gone AWOL, I'm afraid.'

Argh, date then? No – she followed Adam down the narrow hallway to the kitchen, and saw the small round dining room table was laid for three.

The door to the back garden was open and the odour of firelighter bricks and charred spicy meat was billowing through it.

'I thought barbecue, to be manly. Like all dads through time I've fucked it up and cremated everything.'

Adam wiped his sweaty forehead on his t-shirt sleeve and Delia inspected the ashen, disintegrating turd-like things on the rack and started laughing.

'Luckily I have chops too. Oh shit, you're not vegetarian, are you?'

'Hahaha no, carnivore all the way,' Delia said. 'I say just rip its horns off and wipe its arse.'

Adam burst out laughing.

'I haven't had time to do the potato salad. Oh, Delia, this is a disaster.'

If there was one emergency Delia could help with, it was a culinary one.

'I'll make that, you concentrate on this,' pointing at the grill.

She took over in the kitchen and in half an hour, they were sitting down to a very decent meal, half cut on cold beers and fresh air. Adam left the door open, as planes intermittently zoomed overhead.

'We're on the Heathrow flight path,' he said, glancing up. 'Why is this potato salad so good?'

'Red onion, lemon juice and gherkin, fine dice. Cuts through the clagginess of this much mayonnaise.' Delia nibbled a chop and thought what comfortable company Adam had become.

'Why did you pick Clapham?' Delia asked.

'It's where I landed when I moved here and you tend to stay where you land. It wasn't as much of an arsehole jamboree then. The local's still good though.'

Adam explained that Dougie was a few doors up in the Bread & Roses pub with his Scottish friends, and would probably crash through the door at any moment. Delia couldn't believe she'd ever thought this would be awkward.

Alright, she was quite drunk, but she and Adam were chatting, laughing, bickering and debating like old hands.

That said, she wished she'd been a little less relaxed when she went upstairs to the loo. Delia hadn't spotted the transparent shower curtain trailing out of the bath and had stepped on it as she walked away, ripping the rail part of the way out of the ceiling, a small shower of plaster coming down with it.

After she went back downstairs and coughed to it, Adam was unconcerned, refusing her offer to pay for the damage. The disagreement escalated.

'Adam, I insist. In fact, forget it. I don't need your approval. I'll post the cash to you inside a sock.'

'Don't! I don't want to take a shift's wages from you.'

'I'm not a charity case,' Delia said. 'Seriously. Why should you and Dougie pay?'

'The landlord's easygoing.'

'He lets you bash the house up?' Delia said, smiling.

Adam gripped the edge of the table and exhaled. 'Your nickname should be Tenacious D. Alright, look. The landlord, he's me. *I'm* telling you I don't want your money.'

A forkful into a very decent cheesecake – Adam admitted he'd bought it, plated it and thrown some icing sugar over it – Delia paused. 'How can you be the landlord?'

'It's my house. I own it.'

'Is that true? Why not say so before?'

'It's a general policy. I don't want randoms trying to move in. I don't mean you.'

Delia swallowed some cake. 'Isn't renting out rooms a

great source of income though? Online journalism can't be hugely well paid.'

Adam sighed. 'Too many questions.'

'Sorry,' Delia said, embarrassed. Speculating about his salary was over the line. 'I didn't mean to be so . . . northern and blunt.'

Adam regarded her over his dessert, pushed his plate away and blew out a breath.

'I don't know if I should tell you this. This information can't be un-known.'

Delia found herself unexpectedly nervous. She liked the Adam she was having vanilla cheesecake with, who'd bothered to light candles on the windowsill and put Stevie Wonder on the CD player. He and Dougie kept rooms free for what, hosting swinging nights? Sheltering criminals?

'I'm rich.'

'OK.'

'My Dad was a hedge-fund manager in the City, set up his own company. It did very well. He gave up work before fifty. My sister and I had trust funds we came into at twenty-one. Large ones.'

Delia regarded him.

'Ooh. Like, millions?'

'Yes.'

This wasn't bad news, exactly, yet Delia felt a gulf between them had gotten wider. Clapham already seemed far too brash-preppy and full of popped rugby collars for her. With this, she realised she was truly out of her depth.

'See,' Adam said. 'You're already adjusting how you think about me. This is why I never tell people.' He fixed her with a look. 'I mean it, Delia, please don't tell anyone else. Dougie knows, that's it. I guarantee if you do, I can see it in their faces within seconds. You get attuned.'

'I promise I won't.'

Delia turned it all over in her head and examined her feelings. Adam's crisp self-assurance wasn't what she was used to. She'd guessed it was partly borne of a private education. Now she pictured him on yachts, as well as attending Hogwarts. They had so little in common . . .

'You used to work for those papers? None of that's made up?' she said.

'I've done those jobs and got the scars to prove it.'

'And Alice is a teacher?'

'Alice is a full-time, knackered, overworked, summer holidays-loving, Education Secretary-hating, certified authentic 100 per cent teacher in Tower Hamlets.'

'She's rich too?'

Adam nodded.

'What happened was – my parents divorced when we were teenagers. We grew up in Surrey, went to university, had normal if privileged lives, and then *bam*. My dad announces the trust funds, before he disappears to France with Wife No. 2. My mum was dead against it. However, my dad did tell us, in incredibly vehement terms, not to tell anyone, as a condition of receiving it. I'm glad he did because I didn't understand why, back then.'

Adam drew breath.

'At first, I thought, what's to worry about – it was all my Christmases at once. Alice was doubtful. Twenty-one-year-old Adam decided to live like a dissolute Saudi prince. I travelled, I bought stupid gadgets. I had a stupid tiny red car that weighed as much as a Coke can, and I crumpled it like one too.'

Delia grimaced.

'Yeah, every dickhead cliché I'm afraid,' Adam said, misconstruing why Delia had grimaced at the thought of him crashing a car. 'I told Alice she was mad to enrol on her PGCE. She's since told me she was worried I'd become an irretrievable arsehole. One day I woke up and noticed something that I'd been hiding from myself with the excess. I was incredibly bored, and isolated.'

'Isolated?' Delia said. 'Couldn't you buy company? Or *a* company.'

'Think about it, Delia,' Adam said, getting up to pull the back door shut. Delia didn't know if he did it because it had grown chill in the twilight, or due to the secrecy of the discussion. 'Think about what never having to work again means. Being nothing like anyone you'll ever meet. It's like living in zero gravity. My friends were in their first jobs, learning stuff, meeting people. There I was, lying on a couch, throwing Wotsits into my mouth, fast becoming a very dull person. I realised, the only way this is going to work is if I do what Alice had already sussed we had to do. Behave as if the money didn't exist, until we needed it for something important.'

'It shouldn't matter so much. Emma out-earns me to

the power of seven, and it's never affected us. You work, you're not some parasite,' Delia said.

'That's the problem. Think that through. You're complaining about work in the pub. Sooner or later someone says bitterly: "I don't know why you don't leave, it's alright for you." Admiration for your work ethic is a short hop away from resentment. You're taking a job from someone else. You get a promotion, ahead of a mate. Imagine how annoyed they are then? They need that extra income to get a mortgage. Say it's pre-payday, everyone's short – why have you only got your rounds, why not get them all? You feel guilty, but when you buy the rounds, they end up hating you for that. You're tight if you don't, and flash if you do. Soon they're avoiding you, because the normal rules don't apply and it's uncomfortable. Eventually they *want* you to piss off to Boujis and drink Treasure Chest cocktails and play polo and stick with your own.'

He suddenly looked alarmed. 'Shit, this isn't meant to be a Poor Me. I'm incredibly lucky, obviously. I'm just over-compensating in case you think this means I'm some vile swaggering hooray.'

'Hah. No!'

Delia put her head on one side. She could see it, when he put it like that.

'Neither you or Alice ever tell *anyone*?' Delia said, feeling some burgeoning pride in being among the trusted few.

'No one. Not even when drunk.'

'Not girlfriends?'

'Especially not girlfriends.'

'Not Freya?'

Adam raised an eyebrow. 'Not a girlfriend. And no.'

Delia's pride flickered again. It was an honour to be told? He did make it sound as if she was a complete anomaly. What category was she in? Tech heist co-conspirator? Bathroom wrecker?

'Why especially not girlfriends?'

'I didn't ever want to wonder if the loot swung it for me. An ego thing.'

Delia laughed.

'I think with the right person, that wouldn't even be a question,' she said. 'You'd want to trust them with it. When you fall for someone, you want them to know everything about you.'

'Yes,' Adam said. 'You're right.'

He took a large swig of his drink.

Delia sighed. 'I never considered being insanely loaded was this complicated.'

'It's not, if you hand it over to accountants, pay yourself a reasonable salary and largely ignore it.'

'That's how you fund the website?'

'Yeah,' Adam said, clearing the plates, waving away Delia's attempts to help, 'With power comes responsibility and all that. You give to charity, but it's passive. When I got very disillusioned with the state of the press generally, I thought, you have a unique chance to do this differently. I have a trade I can always go back to if it fails miserably. Rich boys love their doomed vanity ventures – at least this one has an honourable aim. It's not some awful Mayfair club night.'

Delia added this up, turned it over.

'I don't want to turn into some trustafarian,' Adam started, as he dumped the crockery in the sink and sat back down.

'Adam,' Delia said. 'You're a southern posh boy who probably hangs his sunglasses on his shirt.'

'. . . A funny thing you discover with money. It's much better at easing pain than giving pleasure. Think of a "best moment" in your life so far . . .'

Delia put her head on one side and thought of her and Emma drinking cider in taffeta gowns and elbow-length gloves. Adam gave her an odd, intense look.

'Thinking of one?'

'Yep.'

'Did it cost much money?'

Delia put a hand up and waggled her fingers as she counted off the pounds. 'Hardly any.'

'What is it? Do I want to know?' Adam said.

'Grad ball.'

Adam's intense look went.

'OK. There you go. How often is that answer "An Alain Ducasse restaurant"? Or "skiing in Meribel"? Almost never. Being stoned on a day you skived off lectures and laughing with a friend 'til you hurt. Cost: your PlayStation, a bag of weed and the trouble you got into later for knowing nothing about the Reformation.'

Delia nodded.

'The best things in life are free,' Delia concluded, doing a 'cliché' face and jazz hands.

'Ah, but they are,' Adam said. There was that unreadable look again. 'Such as, the bottles of champagne I got at an awards ceremony a couple of months ago. Want to help me drink them?'

'Hmmm. Champagne was my downfall in AppletiseGate.'

'Delia Moss's life struggle – repeatedly forced to drink free champagne.'

'I could do a misery memoir. *Please, Barman, Stop.*'

# Sixty-Five

'What does Dougie do for a job?' Delia asked, as Adam unwound the wire on the neck of a bottle of Moët at the Formica breakfast bar.

'He works for Coutts. You know, the Royals' bank? You have to have a quarter of a million liquid to open an account. Before you ask, no I don't have an account.'

'That's so not what I expected.'

'Seems the most unlikely job imaginable for him, doesn't it? He's got a mad head for numbers. Although he's always overdrawn. Dougie is what's known as a curate's egg. Nice lad.'

Adam pulled out the cork and slopped fizzy into wine glasses, while Delia surreptitiously eyed the kitchen. She thought of the things she'd do with it if she owned it. Paint, furniture re-think . . . she couldn't help it, home-making was in her blood. Still, it certainly looked like a rented home, so Adam's disguise was working.

They clinked and took their drinks to the saggy sofas in the front room.

'You and the hacker wizard guy, you know each other well?' Adam asked.

Delia filled in the Peshwari Naan folklore, leaving out Joe's problems in meeting face to face, which she wasn't sure she was licensed to share.

'You have a . . . special rapport,' Adam said, lightly, sipping his drink.

'It's not like that.'

'Like what, exactly?'

Delia shrugged and smiled. She wanted to turn the attention away from herself.

'You're not seeing anyone?' she said.

'Nope.'

'No one as in *everyone at the same time*? Freya did say . . .' Delia smirked.

'You're never going to let me forget that, are you?'

'Most men wouldn't mind being spoken of as successful with women.'

'Well I do. It makes me sound like an indiscriminate seedy praying mantis. Which was of course her intention.'

'Aren't you, then?' Delia said.

'I've been single for a while and I did what single men do. Freya was massively overstating the case.'

'Freya's one of the everyone, I take it?'

Adam nodded and Delia was surprised to find that, despite trying to tease him, it backfired on her. She twinged at the confirmation, and discovered she'd been hoping for a denial. Must be because she'd started to think of Adam as her kind of person, not Freya's.

'Only a one-off thing but she wanted a relationship, and I didn't. We stayed friends. Not friends with benefits, I hasten to add. Friends with drawbacks.'

'She makes life hell for your girlfriends?'

'She would if she could, but I've not had one since forever. The thing is . . .' Adam rubbed at his hair, 'I say this, knowing full well how bad it'll sound. I've not met many people I've liked enough to commit to. I thought I was in love a couple of times, got embroiled, and then realised I wasn't in love – or at least not enough. It caused a lot of hurt. So I thought I'd rest relationships. Better to be honest about how much you want, then move on. It's not what I planned or necessarily wanted, it's what's happened.'

'You've never been in love?'

'Enamoured, maybe . . . but no. Nothing deep and lasting. Obviously.'

He was what, mid-thirties? Didn't sound like he was designed for it, then. Delia could easily imagine that any woman vesting her romantic hopes and dreams in Adam would be like keeping custard in a colander. She didn't doubt many had tried. It made her feel dismayed, somehow.

'I see you with a Jemima Khan-type,' Delia said, trying to lighten herself.

Adam guffawed.

'Jemima Khan? Nothing like my remit. More likely to boff the Aga Khan.'

'Or Shere Khan?' Delia said.

'Amir Khan.'

'Genghis Khan.'

'*Wrath of Khan.*'

They laughed.

'I'm uncomfortable with labels like *incredible swordsman* and *skilful eroticist*. I don't like stereotyping.'

Delia laughed til she gurgled and Adam looked pleased.

'Do you mind me asking if you've seen anyone, since you moved here?' Adam said.

'No,' Delia snorted.

'It's not that absurd an idea,' Adam said.

'This is going to sound pathetic. The idea of being . . . *with* someone who isn't Paul still freaks me out. It's as if I still belong to Paul.'

'What, you'd feel you were cheating on him?'

Delia's skin heated. She wouldn't have said this, sober. 'Yeah.'

'That's silly. He didn't feel very exclusive about your rights over his nudger, did he?'

Delia giggled at 'nudger' and was surprised – the whip-crack snap of pain at thinking of Paul and Celine together wasn't there. Time *was* a healer.

'Stop living for him. Your body isn't his, it's yours.'

'I'm *scared* by sleeping with someone else. What if he wants—'

Delia fell silent.

'Wants . . .?' Adam did a 'carry on' hand gesture.

Delia started giggling and couldn't stop, the words coming out strangled. It felt good to offload to Adam.

'Say . . . *bum sex, up front*?' she mouthed the words.

Adam squinted.

'Tell him it's quite difficult to have bum sex up front.'
Delia giggled.

'You know what I mean!' she said, mock-mournfully.
'I'm so uncool.'

'If you don't like something, you say so,' Adam said.
'What am I missing?'

'Then he goes away and tells everyone on the internet
he's had the most boring sex of his life with me.'

'If he does that sort of thing, I'd question why you
were sleeping with him in the first place. Who is this, by
the way? Someone I know? Is he going to brute force a
seed attack on you?'

'No! A hypothetical man.'

'A hypothetical bum-sex bully online over-sharer. I see
why you're concerned. This entirely made-up man you've
had imaginary sex with is quite the non-existent dick.'

Delia was shaking with laughter now.

'*Or.* You could sleep with a man who wants you to enjoy
it, and doesn't check in as Mayor Of Your Ass on Foursquare.'

'How will I know when this prospect presents himself?'
Delia said. 'How do you tell a good one from the bad
ones? Like the squirrels testing the nuts in *Charlie and the
Chocolate Fact—*'

'He'll kiss you like this.'

Adam moved across, tipped Delia's chin towards him,
bent his head and kissed her. It was perfectly judged – not
pushy or too full on, but definitely full of intent.

Delia was initially motionless, in shock, immobile. Then
she found herself responding. Quite a lot.

When she did, Adam stopped, pulled back a little, looked into her eyes and moved in to kiss her again, unhurriedly, as if they sat together kissing like this all the time.

Delia felt as simultaneously terror-struck and turned on as a teenager necking when she was meant to be babysitting. *Was this shameless opportunism? Did their friendship mean so little? Did he think he was going to . . . how dare he . . . why was she . . . oh God she was definitely kissing him a bit too enthusiastically to blame him when it stopped . . .*

Adam broke off again. They gazed at each other, chests rising and falling, breaths coming quite heavily.

He waved his hand: 'Or you know, something *like* that.'

Delia gasped: 'Why did you do that?'

'I'd reached the point where I couldn't not do it. Shouldn't I have?'

Delia stared at him. He returned her gaze steadily. She was confused and self-conscious rather than offended, but offence was the easier pose to strike.

'You thought you'd have a bash because we've established I'm desperate, and you're a lothario? I thought we were friends.'

'We are. I was hoping we could be more.'

He was looking at Delia directly, and being braver than her.

She gulped and tested her reaction to the news that Adam found her attractive.

'I never thought you liked me. Like that?' she said.

This was daft, she thought, as soon as she said it. Adam

obviously liked her enough, and her body had Thames-at-Millennium fireworks going off inside it.

Why did she need assurances it wouldn't spoil the friendship? This was a chance to approach sex the way other people did, ones who hadn't spent a decade with the same person.

'Seriously? I thought there had been a fair few clues. Like rescuing you from Kurt.'

'I thought you thought it was the right thing to do!'

'Haha. I did. It just so happened it was also what I wanted to do, given the debilitating size of my crush on you.'

Delia flushed at this. Emma had been right all along?

She looked at Adam to gauge if he was being truthful. He seemed bashful and even shy in that moment, shirt slightly unbuttoned, hair mussed-up and eyes a little starry with champagne and . . . desire? The house was quiet, still no sign of Dougie. Delia examined how she felt about how they might spend the next few hours.

The answer from her body was an emphatic *Yes please, do it*, and her intellect didn't seem much at war with it either. Her emotions were running to catch up. God, why bring emotions into it? Why was she second-guessing this? That kiss was *incredible*. Her emotions asked her to consider if she was going to get hurt.

*Be honest about how much you want, then move on.* She'd be naïve to think anything more than a fling was on offer here. He was someone who slept with everyone. But if she was going to conquer the fear-demon of The First One After Paul, Adam could be a classy choice.

She sat forward and kissed Adam again. He put his hand on the back of her head this time, and deepened it. Delia's stomach did that up-down swoop you get when you lean back on swings.

She climbed onto his lap, planting her knees either side of his legs. Who was this person? She liked her.

'Delia,' Adam said, coming up for air, hands on her waist, minutes later, 'Delia?'

'What?' she whispered. Weird how sex moves suddenly necessitated whispering.

'Are you OK with this? You're sure?'

She sat back, heels digging in to her thighs, and smiled.

'Is this some sort of arch seducer, pick-up king tactic, getting me to officially say it was my idea? *State any objections for the record*?'

'No,' Adam said, gripping her waist more tightly, expression serious. 'It obviously started as my idea. When I say I like you, I mean I like you a lot. I'd be gutted if you regret this and bolt. I don't want this now, if now means it won't happen again. Does that make sense?'

Actually, it didn't. Was he spinning her a line to close the deal? Delia was hardly acting like a deal that needed closing. Only, he'd admitted he had a short attention span with women, and what he said he felt at the outset didn't last. Delia decided she didn't care. Tonight, she wanted him.

'Listen,' Adam began, in a low voice. 'About what I said earlier . . .'

'Shhh, I feel fine about this. More than fine,' Delia said, leaning in to kiss again.

But when things had got heavy enough that Adam made murmured suggestions of going upstairs, she wished her nerve had held, as she blurted: 'Wait. Can I get drunker first?'

Adam said: 'Oh fucking hell, THANKS!' and they both collapsed in laughter.

'Only because I'm a trifle rusty.'

'Is that your porn-star name?'

They both laughed until they ached. It helped ease the tension.

'One epidural, coming up,' Adam said, pushing himself off the couch and heading for the kitchen, and Delia found herself grinning at thin air.

Adam brought the bottle through to top them up. Their eyes met over the glasses after the first sip, and the champagne was soon ignored in favour of grappling again. Delia found she couldn't keep her hands, or mouth, off him.

They barely spoke again, until they were stumbling through his bedroom and Adam whispered something urgently that surprised her.

'Do you really still feel like you belong to Paul?'

'No,' Delia lied.

# Sixty-Six

Delia had expended a lot of emotional energy worrying about what if sex with someone else was rubbish. What she hadn't considered was how disconcerting it would be if it was amazing.

She and Paul had been pretty good. It had been more solidly enjoyable than thrilling, if she was honest. There was a 'Get in, get the job done, clear up and get off on time' attitude to it with him. You'd recommend Paul's workman-like, efficient services without qualm. Whereas an Adam performance review would involve giggling, wistful sighing, a foolish smile and pinwheel eyes.

They were good together. *Maybe this is what they mean by chemistry*, Delia thought. She'd thought it was a myth.

She'd expected Adam to feel like Not Paul and the Not Paulness to freak her out, for there to be attacks of disorientation or self-recrimination. But they never happened. Although Adam was different — taller, leaner, fairer, more communicative, but less into complaining about being pushed off the bed — he wasn't unfamiliar.

'You know how you've been with *loads* of people,' Delia said, as they lay side by side in the afterglow.

His bedroom was more classic male décor: a pine double bed, dark bedclothes, military-grey carpet, a sink with sparse masculine toiletries, a cork pinboard covered in tickets, postcards and the odd photo of his sister and the fat cat. Delia was glad of the desk lamp with the blue shade that cast subdued light.

'What?' Adam said, sharply. She glanced over. She thought he'd come back with another quip about being South London's premier salami salesman, but he didn't look comfortable at the line of inquiry.

'Is it quite hard not to compare? Compare The Market Dot Com? Do you find yourself thinking "Her hip action reminds me of that bird from Kettering I met in Ibiza in 2006" and so on?' Delia said.

Adam abruptly shifted on the pillows to look at her full in the face. He was such a ridiculously handsome creature, he could plausibly audition for James Bond. Only he was scowling as if he was playing a scene where he'd been told that the arms dealer with the iguana on his shoulder had won their deadly game of blackjack.

'Jesus, what a thing to say at this moment. What does that mean? "Did I think of other people while I was with you?" Absolutely not, why would I? Did you think of Paul, with me?'

'No!' said Delia, quickly, a little stung to have misjudged post-coital chat so badly, when she was congratulating herself that this whole 'sex with people who aren't Paul' thing was like falling off a log.

'You sure?' Adam said. 'Funny thing to ask otherwise.'

'I was making a casual observation about our relative experience,' Delia said. 'Never mind.' It was more than that. She was jealous, it rankled her and she was determined to show that it didn't.

'Experience isn't a tally,' Adam said. 'I've not spent a decade with someone, or proposed to them.'

Delia thought about this.

'I guess not.'

'I worry about what you think of me. I did say I didn't see this as scoring?'

'I know,' Delia said, and shifted her arm so it was draped over his chest. He was serious? She didn't quite believe it, though she was happy to believe it for now.

They lay in silence for a while.

'Your hair is incredible,' Adam said, stroking it as it fanned over the pillow. 'A red-golden colour you usually only see in paintings.'

'You like it?'

'Why is everything nice always met with surprise, with you?' Adam said, but warmly this time. 'You're beautiful.'

Delia twanged with pleasure at hearing this: *beautiful*.

'Not everyone likes ginger nuts,' she said, then wished she'd used different terminology.

'I'm not sure I'd like ginger *nuts*,' Adam said, and they laughed. Adam moved away from her a little, and cast his eyes downward. Delia had crossed the frontier of fear and was now in the previously unknown country of being able to be naked with new person. In the abstract, being naked was a gigantic deal. And yet it turned out that a bra and pants were a fairly small amount of material and could be on or could be off without the sky falling in.

Their eyes met, in an intoxicated way, and Delia thought she needed to prepare for round two.

'I might use the loo,' she said, thinking she was glad of the low lighting if she was going to have to get up in front of him. Naked lying down wasn't the same game as naked walking around.

She sat up, and at the same time heard the rumble of a voice on the other side of the door saying: 'Adam?'

The handle cranked and the door started opening. With ninja-like reactions, Adam flung himself across Delia and pinned her back down on to the bed with the upper half of his body, shouting: 'Dougie will you please LEARN TO KNOCK!'

'Oh shit, sorry,' she heard Dougie say. Pause. 'Is that . . . Delia?'

'YES IT'S BLOODY DELIA GO AWAY.'

'Hi, Dougie,' Delia squeaked, muffled, from underneath Adam.

'Hello! You two made up then?' Dougie sounded piddled.

'No, we're in the middle of an argument! What the fuck does it look like?!' Adam spluttered.

'Did I stay out late enough?'

Delia burst into laughter.

'Not late enough for my liking, no. BYE.'

The door shut and Adam groaned, 'Jesus and Joseph,'

moving off Delia so she could breathe again, through her laughter.

'That was very gallant,' Delia said, pulling the sheets up to her armpits, in case Dougie remembered something else.

'Don't mention it. I don't want images of my Delia stored on Dougie's mental hard drive.'

*My* Delia? Her stomach fluttered. What had happened between them, exactly? Much as she wanted to be with Adam, she felt like she needed a very long walk on her own, to start figuring this out. It had moved too fast to land, yet.

'So. What happens next?' Adam said.

Delia paused.

'. . . You know where Dougie won't be, next weekend?' Adam continued, sitting up and resting his chin on his hand. 'Paris.'

Delia was startled.

'Paris?' she repeated, dully.

'Yes,' Adam said, tucking a strand of Delia's hair behind her ear. 'Would you like to go?'

'Why?' Delia said.

'It'd be fun. I'd get to spend whole days and nights with you. And I refer you to my earlier point about Dougie not being there.'

'Have you been there before?'

'Yeah, my dad lives in France,' Adam paused. 'I haven't been there with another woman, if that's what you mean.'

'It's not that . . .' Delia said. 'It's a nice idea.'

Adam smiled, a little sadly. 'Not sensing a whole heap of enthusiasm, if I'm honest.'

'No! It would be great . . . but Celine wanted to go there for a "make or break" weekend with Paul, that's all. Strange associations.'

Adam slumped back on the pillows, and fell silent.

'You know what I would like to do? A weekend in London,' Delia said.

Adam squinted.

'Show me all your favourite places here. Give me a tour. We can stay in a hotel. A Dougie-less hotel?'

'That could work. We can start with a date? I know a very nice French restaurant where the maître d' owes me a favour.'

'Oh aye?'

'MALE maître d'!'

'Oh aye!'

Adam mock-huffed and she kissed his cheek and said it sounded lovely.

Downstairs, the television suddenly blared out and Dougie could be heard mumbling: 'Rhodesia! Zimbabwe! It's Zimbabwe!'

'Oh, no. He's on those quiz chat lines where a woman in hotpants gets you to call a premium-rate number again. His bank statement is like a list of indictable offences.'

'I can't believe you told him I had big norks, by the way. When I came round that time, and Dougie wouldn't let me in. You'd given him my vital statistics?'

'I had to think of characteristics that would stand out

for Dougie. Personally, I've been far too busy concentrating on your personality to ponder your norks. The bigness or otherwise of them is neither here nor there, to me.'

Delia wiggled the sheet down.

'They're here.'

'. . . Oh yeah. Hadn't noticed.'

Adam lunged and Round Two kicked off, punctuated by an offstage scream of: 'CALCIUM CARBONATE!'

# Sixty-Seven

Delia flew back in the door, dying to tell Emma, in broad-brush outline terms, of the vigorous ransacking she'd had and thorough plundering she'd done the night before.

She was aglow, exhilarated. She felt as if she was soft clay and she could still see Adam's fingerprints on her. They'd barely slept and she was on an adrenaline high. Could this be the start of . . .? She didn't know. She was in the air, flying, suspended between one place and another. What had Adam said – 'neither here nor there'? That described Delia's state perfectly.

Surprisingly, Emma wore a look of consternation rather than anticipation of Delia's tale of having been out all night. She was emphatically shaking her head and making 'fingertip across neck' slashing gestures.

'I called you and left a message, didn't you get it?' she said in a high, brittle voice.

Delia frowned. 'Oh. I haven't looked at my phone.'

She'd been on the Tube wearing a sappy happy face, blasting music on her iPod and grinning loopily at strangers.

She slipped it out of her pocket now and saw she had many missed calls, an answerphone symbol and three unread texts.

'I've been at Adam's,' she said, knowing this was somehow the thing Emma didn't want her to say and yet not able to stop herself.

Emma did a 'pulling rope knot tight at side of neck and tongue lolling out' gesture.

'Paul's here to see you,' she added, in a *More Tea, Vicar?* sprightly way.

Paul appeared in the sitting-room doorway, hands shoved in pockets.

Delia and he eyed each other, equally surprised and wary. His gaze travelled over her dress and low heels and pale, slept-in, semi-made-up face. She took in his unusually smart attire, new dark blue jumper, jeans. Even the flashes of white on the Gazelles were Tippex-bright, not puddle grey.

'I'm going to leave you two to it!' Emma said, bustling around and grabbing her handbag.

Delia was going to reflex-reply: 'You don't have to,' but that was plainly quite silly and she couldn't think of anything else to say in the seconds it took for Emma to gather herself to depart.

'Thanks, Bez,' Paul said and she trilled 'no problem!' as she clattered away down the stairs. Bez, he was back to Bezzing her? It was Paul's nickname for her, based on Berry, and showed he'd been sat on her sofa for longer than five minutes. Paul was a big one for nicknames.

Once they were alone, a chilly silence settled over the pair of them like a fine layer of snow.

'So,' Paul said, eventually, and Delia could see he was shocked and hurt at her dirty stop-out status, yet trying to stay level. 'Who's Adam?'

'A friend,' Delia said. Why did she feel guilty? She had no reason to feel guilty.

Another pause.

Delia had wanted to know everything when Paul had been with someone else. Although Paul didn't have the same rights to interrogate her, Delia felt he wouldn't want to know even if he did. He grimaced. A moment passed and he said:

'Sorry for landing on you like this. Sometimes the phone isn't showing enough respect, you know?'

Delia nodded. Also, she'd had a policy of ignoring Paul's calls, and he'd obviously thought better than to mention this. He must've got the red eye to be in London at this hour.

'Can I talk to you?' he said.

Delia dropped her bag and followed him to the front room. Sun was streaming in through Emma's majestic curtains, casting pools of light on the honeyed floorboards. They sat at either ends of the giant L-shaped couch.

'Uhm,' Paul cleared his throat. 'I've done some thinking since I last saw you. It's been a quiet house, without you, or the boy . . .'

He shared a look with Delia and she shook her head: not now, and Paul nodded back and ploughed on.

'I realised that to have any chance of you forgiving me, you needed to know why I did what I did. I didn't have an answer for you, because I wouldn't ask myself what my reasons were. I want to find a better phrase than *soul searching*, but it's all I'm coming up with.'

He gave Delia a wan smile and put his palms together.

'OK. Here goes. When my folks died . . .'

Delia stiffened. He better not try for the sympathy vote. He'd irrevocably cheapened that in his lying over the Valentine's card.

'. . . You know how the official story goes that Michael was a mess, and I held it together? It wasn't quite as simple as that. I looked like I was keeping it together, and I was . . . more or less. Until I got kicked out of school.'

'You got expelled?'

This was news to Delia. 'Not suited to academia, didn't do A-levels, got a bar job' was the version she had.

'I used to get good grades, then I got in with a bad crowd and used to go drinking at lunch, that sort of thing. I was only a few months from finishing but it put the kibosh on staying there for sixth form, or going to university.'

'Oh.'

'I didn't tell my uncle and aunt what had happened. I managed to get to the letter before they did. When the head called their house, I got to the phone first and put Michael on, made him pretend to be my uncle. Instead of facing up to trashing my life, I thought I was an absolute Ferris Bueller, cock of the walk. I carried on pretending I was going to school, leaving the house each day and wandering around, getting into mischief.'

'What, you were shagging around at sixteen?' Delia said.

'No, hah. Teenage Me wishes. Hanging round offys, shoplifting. Then one day I got caught thieving, got arrested and it all came out. My uncle and aunt were gutted. I made them feel they'd let my parents down.' Paul swallowed and steadied himself. 'They said the worst of it is, you lied to us. The problem was, I didn't want people to see me falling apart. I had a lot of pride and I got very clever at hiding my feelings. I'm too good at putting on an act, you know?'

Delia nodded. This, she did know.

'Anyway,' Paul rubbed his face, and Delia wondered how it was possible she could have known Paul for so long and not known any of this, 'I'd been avoiding the shrinks after the accident because, trust me, everyone is asking you how you're feeling every five minutes and you just want to go kick a ball around. After the arrest, I had to have counselling. They said I'd had a depressive episode.'

'Paul,' Delia said carefully, 'I'm not saying this in an uncaring way, but you're talking about twenty years ago. How did that affect you sleeping with Celine?'

Paul looked at her directly, bracing his hands on either side of him on the couch.

'No, I'm thirty-five. Nothing can excuse what I did, Dee. But if it helps you understand, I'm trying to explain that at the end of last year, the shutters came down. I felt the same way as when I was skiving school, lying to people who loved me. It's weird, you wouldn't think the twenty-year anniversary would mean much and I didn't think it would either. Given how I've behaved, it obviously does matter. This is going to sound strange, but I've never got over the fact my parents are not coming back. Even now, some small part of me thinks they're going to walk in the door and say: "Surprise! There, that made you and Mike stand on your own two feet, didn't it?"'

Delia looked at Paul and saw his expression, the way the muscles had tightened, a look she'd never seen before, and knew this was sincere. *Every day, you can choose to be happy.* How had she never been perceptive enough to see that survival techniques could also mean denial? It was because she too had fallen in love with the persona Paul sold to the world.

'. . . The counsellor told me I would have these episodes of spinning out again, and I'd need to get help when I saw the clouds gathering. Of course, I didn't. I thought, I've got my girl and the pub and the dog and I'll style it out, with my usual arrogance. Even though I was having these dark thoughts about ageing and dying, feeling hollow inside. Wondering why the staff seemed so horrifically *young* to me, these days.'

He did a mock-shudder.

Delia was surprised. Very. Bouncy, effervescent, Where's the Party Paul?

Paul took a deep breath. 'What happened with Celine. I can't imagine the amount of insult and grief I caused you. I mean, you've – and I—'

Delia squirmed and Paul wisely abandoned the Adam analogy.

'. . . It wasn't anything to do with sex or not being happy at home, Dee. I have – had – everything I want in you and I'd never give that up willingly. It was a distraction. This ridiculous thing started and when I was doing that, I didn't have to think about my other problems. I gave myself a different problem to avoid the real one. *Uncharacteristic risk-taking behaviour*, is what my counsellor called it. Like psychic self-harm.'

He was seeing a counsellor again?

'Girls coming in and flirting with bar staff happens often enough, as you know. It wasn't that she was anything special or different compared to you. It's just that, this time, I wasn't my right self.'

Delia looked at her hands in her lap.

'Have there been others apart from Celine?' Delia said, simply, looking up.

'Other women?'

'Yes.'

'No, never. Ever. Why would you think there were?'

'My friend,' Delia said. 'He said men like you never cheat once.'

Delia felt oddly like she was betraying Adam by passing this on, despite the fact there was scant chance she was spoiling a potential friendship between the two of them. Still, Adam said Paul happy-cheated, not sad-cheated. It would seem that was wrong.

'*Men like me*,' Paul said, brow furrowing. 'I'd like to meet this paragon of virtue. Is he on a plinth, holding a bow and arrow? No others. Absolutely not.'

'You've lied to me a lot.'

'I have.'

Delia felt they were at factory settings, stripped bare to the essential components: were they still in working order?

'The lies you told me, after I found out. They hurt me the worst of all.'

Paul's eyes were shiny.

'I saw the love of my life about to walk out and I thought complete honesty would mean losing you forever. It's taken me until now to see that complete honesty was my only hope.'

Paul wiped his eyes on a sleeve of his jumper.

'Delia. That's it. That's the whole story of how I was so stupid as to risk everything that mattered to me, on something so meaningless.'

Delia believed him. She finally understood it. She had no anger left. Only sadness.

# Sixty-Eight

'There's something else as well,' Paul said. 'Given I'm here to beg you for another chance, I'm not doing the best sales pitch here . . .'

Delia didn't know how to feel. She didn't know what she felt.

Paul rubbed his palms on his jeans.

'You've heard that thing about how counsellors are not there to judge you and it's about helping you talk through things yourself, and so on? Well, for fuck's sake, I'd get the one who breaks the rules, wouldn't I? This one's really chatty. She's given me tough feedback and no mistake.'

Paul grinned and Delia gave him a grudging small smile.

'We talked about my attitude to marriage and kids. You know what she said? She said I've been subconsciously resisting them and staying a perpetual man-child, to be the boy my parents left. Like I'm waiting, or something.'

This made Delia's throat muscles lock.

'It made me see how unfair I've been. Expecting you to fit round me, to wait for me.'

485

Paul pushed his hips off the sofa, fumbled in his jeans pocket and took something out, palming it.

He opened a ring box. Inside, sat the emerald and diamond Art Deco design that Delia had picked out. She had no idea how he'd found it.

Paul turned towards her.

'This isn't the place, or possibly the time, to say these words. You deserve something romantic, done properly, the way you did for me. I want you to take this as a kind of pre-proposal, to know that I am ready to do the down-on-one-knee if you are ready to hear it. Delia, I love you. More than words can say. I want to be together for the rest of our lives. I want to marry you. The sooner the better.'

Delia gazed at the ring in wonder.

'How did you—?'

Paul flushed with pleasure at her reaction.

'Is it the one? I know there's that antique jewellery place you like and I thought you might've been in. I described you to the shopkeeper and she remembered you. We went through five or six rings she said you looked at and when I saw this, I was like THAT'S the one. That's my Delia's taste. I've had it sized against some rings you left at home.'

Delia was impressed. This was what ten years together could do. Paul knew her better than anyone.

The ring glinted and sparkled in the light of the room. Delia exhaled.

'Paul, I can't go back to how we were. I lived my life around you and for you. I've found my old self again and I don't want to lose that.'

'What you've done since . . . since we broke up is incredible, making a life down here. Are you saying you want to stay in London?'

Delia shook her head. 'It's not about geography. It's about carrying on being in charge of myself. If I come back, I won't be that person I was again, always waiting for you, following your lead.'

'You want to be a team,' Paul said. 'I get that. So do I.'

'Do you want to put this back together because you really love me and want to be with me, or because you don't know what else to do?'

'I'm surprised you even ask that. Who wouldn't want to be with you? Yes, of course. Delia, I don't say this in terms of giving you an ultimatum, as you can always come home. But if there's no chance, it's for the best you tell me. The not-knowing is killing me. And you seem settled, here . . .'

He trailed off, Adam the elephant in the room again.

Delia thought of all the Pauls she had known.

The Paul who always let her mix cocktails behind his bar and let her waste stock as she sloshed spirits around, mopping up her spillages without complaint. The Paul who sat at a dining table with her family and respectfully discussed the chippy with Ralph as if they were both small business owners. The Paul who rubbed her feet when she'd been wearing ridiculous shoes, who fixed her bike, who wolfed down her cooking and told people she'd missed her vocation as a chef. The Paul who called her, in his moments of most private, soppiest affection, Strawberry Shortcake, after a luridly copper-wire haired doll from an '80s cartoon. *I think you're the same as me . . .* Paul and Delia, Delia and Paul. He'd been a great boyfriend, for the most part.

Were all those Pauls erased by the Paul who'd had sex with another woman and lied about it? The Paul who had always been trying to impress her in his own way, she saw now, and couldn't let the swagger drop when he was low. She'd wanted him to play the hero. It was a two-way deal, a pact.

There was so much more good than bad. Their history spoke for itself – she couldn't let that go. She still loved Paul.

She nodded, slowly. 'OK. Let's try again. No engagement for now. I want to come back to Newcastle.'

Paul leaned over and put his arms round her and they sat like that for a moment, buried in each other's shoulders, Delia wondering if she had Adam's scent on her. *Adam.* That had been a wonderful fantasy – strange and new and exciting – but this was her reality.

'By the way, I asked Emma for her blessing in asking you to marry me,' Paul said, disentangling. 'I hope you don't mind. I couldn't ask your dad in these circumstances and I wanted sign off from someone you love.'

'And she gave you her blessing?'

'Are you kidding? She bollocked me rigid. *Then* gave me it.'

Delia burst out laughing. The tension in the room uncoiled as they made practical arrangements and talked about lighter things, planned a dinner out with Emma.

'Also, I have to see my friend and tell him I'm leaving,' Delia said eventually, forcing her voice to stay confident.

Paul bit his lip and jerked his head in an 'OK' nod.

'Sometimes the phone isn't showing enough respect,' she added.

'I'll keep the ring for now,' Paul said, slipping the box back into his pocket.

# Sixty-Nine

Delia didn't know the official terminology for what she was about to do. Could you break up with someone you weren't exactly 'with'? Was she about to make a fool of herself, revealing her copy of the dating rules handbook was archaic?

She felt as if she'd been blindfolded and spun in that party game where you staggered off and tried to regain your balance and your bearings. She'd left this house only hours ago, in a completely different mood. The blazing sunshine that accompanied her task of schlepping over to Clapham felt wrong. Once again, seismic shifts could take place in your life, but existence in general had the audacity to carry on as normal.

Delia wanted rain. The art director of real life had messed up.

Adam answered the door and Delia tried not to dwell on the look of apprehension he was wearing. She obviously hadn't called to ask for 'a chat' instead of a date so they could put Paris back on the table.

'Hi. Can we talk upstairs?' Delia said.

Adam said nothing, only nodded, and Delia was tense with the difficulty of what she was about to do. To make matters worse, he put his hand in hers and led her up to his room, whilst Delia tried not to focus on how that felt.

Once inside, he pushed the door shut, folded his arms and leaned back against the wardrobe. His expression told her that he roughly knew the shape of what was coming.

Delia knotted her fingers.

'Uhm. Paul came to see me.'

Pause. She expected something here, yet Adam said nothing.

'We're getting back together,' Delia concluded, slightly hoarse.

'Getting or got?'

'Got.'

Adam put his chin on his chest.

'Sorry,' Delia added.

There was a poisoned silence. Adam cleared his throat and moved his back, standing up straighter.

'Fast work,' he said.

Delia could hardly deny the timing was vulgar. Moving on to a second man while your body was still reverberating from the seeing-to you'd had from the first.

'He's over the whole "having sex with another woman" thing, then?'

Delia couldn't go into the details of bereavement or depression.

'I can't explain now, but he had his reasons.'

'I'm sure he did.'

'He promised me it'll never happen again.'

'Of course he did.'

'Look. Adam. I haven't done this lightly. I'm not a doormat.'

'I didn't say you were.'

In the face of his dangerous quiet, Delia floundered.

'He's made a big gesture. He proposed, with a ring. He asked Emma for her blessing.'

'Your *mate*?'

'Yes.'

'He got your friend to say you should marry him?' Adam said, finally showing anger, turning his eyes to the heavens. Delia noticed he was so white he looked pale green. 'Manipulative bastard.'

'I don't think he intended it like that. He's making amends.'

Delia tried to speak and her windpipe wobbled. Tears threatened to start and she made an effort to control herself. It wasn't fair on Adam to weep and turn herself into the victim of the piece.

'You're forgiving him for how he's treated you?' Adam said. 'Actually, don't answer that, as you clearly are. OK. Whatever I say doesn't matter.' Adam shook his head. A tear rolled down his cheek and he didn't brush it away.

'We weren't . . . we were just having fun though, weren't we?' Delia blurted, startled.

'So it seems,' Adam said, shrugging his shoulders, yet his voice was shaky. She'd never seen him vulnerable. 'You're moving up north?'

'Yes.'

Adam shook his head and looked away, and Delia got the feeling he couldn't trust himself to speak.

She was stunned, and ashamed. She'd deliberately not dwelt very hard on how he'd react. She knew she wouldn't have his heartfelt congratulations, yet despite the warm words she'd had no time to assess how strong Adam's feelings truly were. Yes, he'd said things, but people did, when they fancied someone. Him now shrugging *Oh dear that's a shame we could've had some good times, have a safe journey* had been a distinct possibility.

This was the most touching discovery, made in the most agonising way – he really did like her. Delia swallowed hard. It wasn't awkward. It was quietly devastating.

'When do you go?' he asked.

'Tomorrow,' Delia said. 'I'm packed. I don't have many things here.'

'Evidently,' Adam said, raising empty eyes to meet hers.

'Adam, I'm so sorry—'

He shook his head.

'Don't apologise. You want that more than you want this. There's nothing more to say.'

Silence again. In fact, there was so much more to say. Delia wanted to tell Adam about what he had done for her, and what he had come to mean to her. How she'd come to London at her life's lowest ebb. How his transformation from enemy to this incredible friend – and now incredible shag, as it turned out – had been the very best of it.

That he'd changed her life and restored her faith in male human beings, and that she'd come round to thinking he looked good in pink. She would never, ever forget him.

Understandably, all that mattered to Adam was that she was leaving with Paul.

This was it. She would never speak to him again, never laugh with him, never hold him? It felt wrong. Surely it wasn't meant to be like this? Weren't they both meant to waltz away with warm memories, couldn't they keep in touch? She hardly needed to ask. She wished she'd known the price at the point of purchase. That sex meant a full stop to the friendship. It had become something else last night, something that was over before it had begun.

Knowing a last time was a last time was unbearable.

Delia gazed at him and tried to commit his face to memory. She wanted to draw it. She could see he'd rather she left.

'Goodbye, Adam.'

'Yeah. Bye,' Adam said, in such a low voice she could barely catch it. Arms folded, he stared at the floor again, not looking at her.

Delia left the room, feeling as if her nerves were on the outside of her body and she'd been turned inside out, like balling a sock.

She fled past the kitchen, where Dougie was beating drums along to the radio with a spatula on the sideboard, the sound of a frying pan spitting and sizzling on the hob as percussion.

'Hey Delia! How's life?'

'Good,' Delia said, blankly, at a loss for what else to say, and not knowing if she was telling the truth or not.

# Seventy

Delia was home again. She sailed through the streets as if she owned the place on her red bicycle, chatting to people in local shops, her accent becoming a shade stronger. The colder air up here had started to smell like autumn was on its way.

She cleaned her house from top to bottom, she cooked using her own pans. She pulled dresses she'd not worn for months from her wardrobe, she did her eyeliner looking in her old 50s-style dressing table with the oval mirror.

She went for drinks with Paul at their local, they had takeaway curries in front of the television, she drank coffee from her favourite mug. Things were still different between them, it was a tentative re-coupledom. Delia told herself that it was a fresh start, which meant they were dating again, finding their way back into it. There would be an evening soon when it'd click and make sense; you couldn't rush it.

She and Paul scattered Parsnip's ashes in the Tyne, holding hands.

'I miss him,' Delia said. They agreed they weren't anywhere near ready for another dog, they only wanted Parsnip. Could they be ready for other things though? As they walked away, wiping their eyes, a young father was wrestling a squealy toddler who was demanding a wee by a wall on Dean Street. They looked at each other and grinned. A moment of understanding passed between them.

A few days later, Paul asked Delia to come to the pub at the end of service. She found the lights still on and everyone gone. There was a sign up saying they were closing early due to 'Personal Reasons.'

'Is everything OK?' she said, worried.

She saw two flutes on the bar, and a bottle of pink Laurent-Perrier next to them, a vast bouquet of her favourite pink peonies next to that. Delia's hero David Bowie came over the sound system – 'Be My Wife' – and Paul came out from behind the bar, holding a small velvet box.

He went down on one knee and slid the ring on to Delia's finger while she found herself unable to stop laughing uncontrollably, feeling as if they were playing a grown-up's game. They got woozy on drink, discussing wedding plans in his deserted pub with the drip trays piled in the sink and the tills turned off. That night they consummated their reunion.

Delia told herself that this was what she wanted, and moving forward was essential: the moment of happy certainty where her feelings fell into place was somewhere on the horizon: strive for it.

The next day she went through job adverts and

highlighted ones she could do, made a list, an agenda for action. She wasn't worried about getting another job. She'd survived Twist & Shout, so anything was possible. It felt different now she had resurrected her part-time passion of The Fox. Who knew, maybe eventually it would grow into a full-time passion? It was a comforting thought.

Delia tried not to think about things that hurt her to recall, things that didn't help, about someone far away. He'd get over it. He said he'd hurt other people. He'd have hurt her the same way, very probably, if she'd hung around long enough and let herself start to believe in it. She tried not to think about him, but he crept into her thoughts constantly, like spreading ink on paper. She kept making mental notes, observations for anecdotes and conversations she'd never have with him, except in her head.

Most of all she tried not to notice that she no longer got the urge to throw her arms around Paul and kiss him. It'd come back. It was on its way. Delia had made her choice.

Delia used the silver jalopy to go to Hexham and show her politely wary parents the ring. ('Not a big wedding,' Delia reassured them, and they smiled the fixed smiles of people who thought any wedding wouldn't be small enough for them. Delia never needed to wonder where she got her homebody urges from.)

Flashing the ring wasn't why she looked forward to her first visit. She'd also brought her laptop. She got Ralph on his own, through the pretext of being interested in his latest game.

'You know you told me The Fox was good?' she said, peeling the wrapper from a yellow French Fancy, as Ralph played his latest game. 'I put it online. People seem to really like it. So I sent it to some publishers. You know, like small indie ones. I've got a meeting with one about it, in Leeds. They might publish it.'

She flipped open her laptop and showed Ralph the Fantastic Miss Fox site.

'In a book?' Ralph said, entranced by the pictures on the screen. 'A book you could buy?'

Delia nodded, swallowing icing. 'All because of what you said to me in this room a few months ago. I wouldn't have dared to do it otherwise.'

Ralph looked gratified. 'Cool. I was only telling you the truth.'

'I know, you always tell the truth,' Delia said. 'If it's published, I will dedicate it to you. Is that helicopter going to crash?'

'Yeah,' Ralph said, re-tasking himself to the game and picking up the console again. 'It's OK, it's not us. We shot it down.'

'I was thinking. I've been through things since then that I never thought I could get through. Having the break-up with Paul. Moving to London. Doing a scary job. Meeting scary people. Stopping a scary person doing bad things. It made me realise – Mum and Dad, they're great. But I think they made us love home a little bit too much. We both get scared of the world outside, sometimes?'

Ralph seemed to be listening, as well as driving the

onscreen action. Delia had no idea how this was going across.

'I did get through it all though, Ralph, and I'm better for it. Like you said to me about The Fox – *you're in charge*. You're in charge too. You don't have to stay at the chippy, or stay at home. If you're scared, it's alright. Because you're scared doesn't mean you'll fail. If there's anything you want to do, tell me. I want to help you in return.'

Ralph scratched his mop of ginger hair. 'I thought about reviewing games.' He looked at Delia, uneasily. 'On YouTube. But you know, loads of people do it. No one would want to watch me, I don't think.'

'That's a brilliant idea! Ralph, you should do that! You're really entertaining when you talk about games. I love listening to you. You'd be a cult hit.'

'I do have some good opinions. This regular in the shop, John, he always asks me what I think and we had some really good talks, until the boss complained. Now John has haddock instead of saveloys. We cook them fresh and it gives us longer to chat.'

Delia beamed at her brother.

Ralph turned back to the screen. 'I don't know I'd make anything worth watching.'

Delia's mind whirred. 'What could help? Someone who could help you make the videos and start a following? Like they did for me and The Fox site?'

'Yeah, I guess.'

'Ralph, I know someone! Just the person.'

She knew Ralph would be wary of presenting his idea

to a stranger, so she rattled on: 'He's got a phobia of meeting new people though. Well, more socialising. But he can talk on Skype. He could tell you about the things he helped me with, it was uh-may-zing. He cracked a super-tough encryption code and everything. Can I introduce you? Only on my laptop.'

Ralph's eyes widened at 'cracking code' and Delia knew she had him. Also, a fellow bedroom ghost would intimidate him a lot less.

Minutes later, with his permission, she'd made the call and Joe in his garage was present in Ralph's bedroom in Hexham.

'Hello!' Joe said tucking hair behind ears. 'There's two of you. Red flags.'

They were soon chatting like fast friends, as Delia encouraged Joe to relate the V&A yarn. They exchanged details and Joe pledged that not only would he help Ralph, he'd hugely enjoy it.

Delia left Hexham with a skip to her step, practically hugging herself. She'd known Joe and she met for a reason, so they could help each other. Now perhaps, she'd incepted a fruitful relationship that would benefit her brother and the Naan.

Well, it was either the start of a beautiful friendship, or they'd fall down the rabbit hole of endless gaming together and end up with castaway beards and curly toenails.

In keeping with her resolve never to let them drift again, Delia had booked a week's holiday in Barcelona with Emma. The plan was a riot of tapas, sherry and Gaudí.

'I miss you being down here so much,' Emma said, when she called to confirm the flights were booked. 'I've been looking at Rightmove. What if I DID move back to Newcastle? Would I cramp your style? Could I set up my own firm? I'm picturing that bit in *Sliding Doors* when Gwyneth Paltrow starts a successful PR company just by asking a bank for some money, doing some roller painting and then having a sexy launch party with flowers in her hair.'

'It will be exactly like that,' Delia said, laughing. 'Apart from a bank giving you any money. That film's quite old.'

'You've inspired me, Deels. You came down here and absolutely kicked arse. It makes me think I can do anything, too.'

'*I* inspired *you*?'

'Yes. You're Fantastic Miss Fox.'

Delia's eyes welled up. She'd mothballed The Fox because she thought it was frivolous and childish. Instead it was always telling her what she needed most: courage.

# Seventy-One

Delia had been back in Newcastle for three weeks when she sifted through the mail alone on a Saturday morning.

She almost missed the thin, creased envelope, addressed to her in unfamiliar handwriting, and it very nearly died a quick, unceremonious death, slung in the recycling, sandwiched between a Land's End catalogue and the offer of 4.8% APR credit. She fished it back out and tore the envelope.

It was a card with a print from the Tate Gallery, a painting of a young woman with shining titian hair. Delia opened it. Both sides full of close written black biro.

*Dear Delia,*
*Hello again. I didn't say much last time I saw you. Sorry about that. Those words were all my jealous heart could bear. I'm going to manage a few more here. This doesn't need a reply, I should stress. It's a gesture from me, to you, because I can't leave things the way they ended.*

*First of all, I miss you. My God, do I miss you. Like the*

colour's leached out of the film. I am sick and tired and bored and sad about walking into rooms that don't have Delia in, but it looks like I'll have to get used to that happening for the rest of my life.

Secondly, I'm in love with you. Did you know I fell in love with you? Probably not. I didn't exactly give off strong and consistent 'I'm in love with you' signals.

And you thought I was only after something casual. I don't blame you for thinking that, given who I was before I met you.

I wasn't. I already knew I was head over heels and trying to work out how best to let you know how serious I was, without completely freaking you out with the extent of my adoration.

I mean, take things I'd always thought weren't for me: marriage, babies, domesticity. Add 'with Delia' to the equation and suddenly they looked incredibly appealing. I finally got it. All those times laughing at people who told me when The One turned up, I'd just know, then there you were, and I did.

I wanted arguments over shelving units in Ikea, Christmas dinner in paper hats with your parents, Boxing Day playing video games with Ralph, and our names to always be used as a pair. (Like Hepburn and Tracy. Or Cannon and Ball.)

Also, while I'm not making it a competition – I'd never sleep with another woman behind your back. (I'm making it a competition.)

Once you told me you were leaving for Paul, I thought, why admit any of this? Why wound my pride further?

Then I realised, it does matter. You should know how much feeling you inspired, and I should have the courage to tell you.

*Even when there's no hope of it changing anything. Even when it wasn't mutual.*

*None of this is intended to, or should, make you feel guilty, by the way. You can no more help who you're in love with than I can.*

*Part of me wishes so hard I'd said this to your face, in the hope it might've changed things. I thought it was too soon. I was going to try to get away with mumbling a lot of it in the darkness at three in the morning, further along the line. But there was no further along the line, and I think deep down I always knew there wouldn't be.*

*Dearest, wonderful, best, funniest Delia, with that lovely voice I'll never hear again – goodbye. I will always be a little bit lonelier without you.*

*Please take care of yourself, so I can think of you happy. And if he ever makes you sad again, I will feed him ladlefuls of his own boiling blood.*

*Adam x*

Delia read and re-read the words first in disbelief, then in joy, then in an ecstatic sort of pain, until they warped and blurred through her hot tears. It was astonishing to think these passionate words were about her, that she'd unconsciously managed to make someone feel this strongly.

'You bastard,' she said in a choke-sob-laugh aloud, to the card.

He was in love with her? Adam was meant to be a fling. She didn't belong in his world, nor he in hers. Why did nothing make sense? Why did her chest feel like it was burning, her legs like liquid? Her stomach seemed to have disappeared entirely.

If nothing else, Adam had proved that money didn't give you life's most valuable things. This card had cost next to nothing, other than Adam's pride.

It meant the world to her.

# Seventy-Two

Delia walked from room to room in a daze, holding her card, re-reading it. Eventually, with a goitre-sized lump in her throat, she called Emma.

'Oh, Em. I don't know what to do. Adam sent me this incredible . . . I feel stupid saying *love letter*, but it was. Card. Telling me he was mad about me and wanted this whole life together and never got the chance to tell me. That he's in love with me.'

'Wow! Really? He actually used the L-word?'

'Yes, he used lots of words. He said he wanted to settle down with me.' Delia's body hummed with so many emotions: delight, gratitude, regret, incredulity, happiness, sadness. Guilt.

'You had no idea before? He never said?'

'Not exactly. He was hinting at liking me a lot, he told me he didn't want a one-night stand and wanted to start seeing each other. We slept together and then if you remember, Paul came back the very next day.'

'Oof. One night with you and he's turned into a love-letter writer. You must have an incredible pelvic floor.'

'I'm feeling sick with the need to see him. I thought it would go away, but it hasn't. It's got worse. What do I do?'

'Do? Is there something to do?'

'I don't know.'

Emma paused.

'OK. You know I think he's a fierce piece of arse. Part of me wants to say *go for it*. Like "Just drive!" at the end of Thelma and Louise. But, let's not forget they drove into the Grand Canyon.'

Delia laughed, weakly.

'I'm going to be the best friend I can be,' Emma said. 'By being sensible about this. However hard it is, have a glass of wine and a weep and put that card somewhere that Paul won't find it. Or somewhere he *will* find it, as it might remind him how lucky he is. And move on.'

'You don't think Adam means it?'

'I think he means it. However, I think there's a difference between meaning it and it working out between you.'

'We're too different?'

Emma blew out a breath.

'Not exactly. I think it's a huge gamble. You want a family, and you know the deal with Paul.'

'I thought I did before, remember?'

'Yes, but he's promised you he's sorted himself out, or you wouldn't have gone back. Adam's an unknown quantity. I mean, are we sure that this isn't an extreme reaction because he isn't used to women dumping him? Not that I'm saying he can't simply be smitten with you. This is about his nature.'

Delia thought this was a fair point, if a little ego-denting. Without intending to, she had turned the tables. It might be quite a novel experience for him.

'What's his relationship history? Much monogamy? Or high body count and trail of devastation and grieving people behind him, like a serial killer?'

'Sketchy, I think. He told me he'd never been in love. And yes, he's been around . . .'

'It's a brave–slash–foolish woman who trusts she's going to be the game changer, Deels. Believe me, I've been that woman. Eventually you realise the women before you thought they were that woman too.'

*I thought I was in love a couple of times, got embroiled, realised I wasn't in love, or not enough. Caused hurt . . .*

'Though Adam's obviously besotted. You know I spotted that before you did,' Emma said. 'He can be entirely sincere and still not a safe bet.'

'Hah – Adam said Paul would never be a safe bet. That his type of cheating would happen again.'

'Did he say this around the time when he was trying to go to bed with you, by any chance?'

Delia had to admit it had broadly coincided.

'You want to be in Newcastle, too?'

Delia murmured agreement. She appreciated she was asking for a gear shift from Emma, when not so long ago, her best friend was congratulating her on her engagement as 'the way the world should be: with Paul and Delia together'.

'Bottom line, I think throwing your lot in to be with

Adam is the most massive risk,' Emma said. 'I've seen you go through so much and come through it. I'd hate for it to go wrong a second time. He's gorgeous, I know. That means he gets plenty of female attention. Would you honestly want to spend your life fending other Emmas off?'

Delia laughed.

'He'd never lie to me,' Delia said. She meant it. For all Adam could be mistaken for glib, there was something very nailed-down about him. If a truth was ugly, he'd still give it to her. *And a few things besides . . .* argh, don't be consumed in a fug of lust, she thought. Great sex doesn't make it a great idea. *Although it makes a bit of a great idea,* a voice said. She and Paul hadn't been very lively in bed since she moved back in. Delia was still fearful of thinking of him with Celine, in the act. Was it also fear of something else?

'Paul has the pub and the house. You know how his life works. Adam's this freelancer with no secure income, and an ability to piss people off.'

'Oh, he's completely set financially,' Delia said, biting her lip, 'He has savings.'

It meant an awful lot to keep Adam's secret, so she said no more. Delia now knew for sure it had been a major thing to tell her. It gave her another hard pang. That whole conversation had been a way of hinting to her that she was important to him in a way no one else had been. He'd nearly said so in so many words, and she'd blithely missed the significance.

'Falling in love is one thing. Staying together is arguing over whose turn it was to get dishwasher tablets. Ask yourself if you want the upheaval of having those arguments with a different man.'

Emma had a lot of right on her side. Emma was judging the situation without heart, head and loins consumed with adolescent-level Adam longing. Delia was old enough to know tempestuous infatuation was a drug that wore off, and it was what was left when it cleared that counted.

'Also, I want to be your bridesmaid. Don't steal it away from me a second time.'

Delia smiled: 'I promise you, you'll always be my bridesmaid.'

After she rung off, Delia noticed Emma hadn't asked the key question.

Maybe because she knew the answer. Maybe because – and Delia thought this was more likely – she'd say the answer wasn't helpful in making a wise decision anyway.

The thing was, right now, working out the answer to that question felt like the only thing that mattered.

Delia couldn't respond to Adam. She didn't know what she'd say. She picked up her pencil again.

# Seventy-Three

Life moved on and there was going to be new life in their Newcastle circle. Delia had been nervous about meeting Aled and Gina for the first time since her and Paul's break, and she guessed they'd feel apprehensive too.

As it turned out, Paul and Delia's reunion wasn't the top item of news. They would be bringing an extra mystery guest.

It meant their usual boozy, rowdy dinner was moved to a lunch, making it easier on a morning-sick Gina. Delia went through the pre-Aled-and-Gina-visit rituals: putting flowers in tank vases, getting the better glasses out, refilling the candle holders. Cleaning up covert Parsnip pee was no longer on the agenda, and Delia felt a little bereft there were no puddles of urine hidden in corners of their house. The things you missed.

Delia was trying a Turkish recipe with a spicy tomato sauce and baked eggs, putting a heavy skillet under the grill until it bubbled.

As she stared out of the window, she thought about the

things she'd never cook for Adam. There was an untrodden path back in London, one she'd started down and abandoned.

Lost experiences and unknown things that had previously merited pained curiosity had, since his card, flared into outright yearning.

There was a date they never went on, to Clos Maggiore in Covent Garden. She'd looked it up. The dining room had an open fire and a roof made from white blossom, exactly Delia's type of kitsch. She stared at the round tables with the linen cloths and imagined the evening that had never happened, the conversation they never had. Their not being able to stop thinking about how they were going home together and seeing that thought in each other's eyes all evening. The walk home through the streets holding hands, testing how it felt to belong to each other for the first time.

'Weird not having Snippy the Piss Kangaroo here, isn't it,' Paul walked in behind her. 'Aled always used to bring him those buttons.'

'You alright?' he said, seeing Delia's face as she turned, pausing.

'Yes, why?'

'You look a million miles away.'

*No, only about three hundred.*

'Oh. It's . . . Aled and Gina. They were a bit crap to me when it all happened. Aled called me and wound me up about Paris, and Gina only bothered with a text.'

Paul looked uncomfortable.

'They would've been trying to be considerate, Dee, it was awkward. It was my fault. Really. Don't think the worse of them.'

He squeezed her shoulder and Delia feigned a smile.

'Five minutes inside the door, and you'll forget all about it and so will they.'

As it turned out, Delia hadn't forgotten it after five minutes, or fifteen, or fifty.

They looked like the same Aled and Gina – exact physical opposites with his black hair and heft, her wiry frame and peroxide pixie cut – but everything else was different.

They avoided her eyes and asked nothing about her London sojourn, keeping up a constant burble of shop talk with Paul.

Delia had been a welcome addition to the gang as Paul's fun, easygoing girlfriend who made the great food. As a person in her own right, someone who they were unsure around after her mistreatment, who made them feel guilty: *that* Delia had to be subtly ignored until normal service was restored. Delia had discovered that some friendships got longer without getting deeper.

She retreated into her own thoughts, filling glasses and offering plates round to give the illusion of participation.

Gina showed them the sonogram picture and Delia thought about how Adam had said he wanted kids with her. Ikea arguments. Christmas lunch in paper hats. To get to know Ralph. To be a couple. The idea gave her shivers, the nice sort.

Aled joked about how many times they'd had to do

it in a month to conceive. Delia thought about how it felt to do it that many times with Adam in a night, bodies entwined and him whispering heated things in her ear. She thought those things he said on the night about what she did for him might be part of his standard patter, but he must've truly meant them . . .

'What the fuck is a budget babymoon?' Paul was saying. 'We've got a honeymoon to afford, don't tell me there's more expense round the corner.'

He looked to Delia for her smile at the reference to family plans.

Delia's imagination went to Paris; a trip on the Eurostar, a walk along the Seine at night, red wine at a café with those wicker chairs . . .

'Delia? Delia?' Paul's voice cut through. 'Earth to Delia?'

'Yes?'

'I was saying, that place we went in Yorkshire that time. Where was it?'

'Oh! Swaledale?'

'Swaledale, that's it. Beautiful. Al was saying they're going Ponce Camping.'

'Glamping,' Gina corrected him.

'If you don't suffer, it isn't camping,' Paul said. 'Dee doesn't camp. She's a home comforts girl. Don't get me started on the time she tried to pack a hairdryer for Glastonbury.'

He nudged her and she smiled obligingly. Aled and Gina pretended to smile the way they would've once smiled. Delia thought how the old double act with Paul as the irreverent-yet-devoted antagonist to her sweet long-suffering stoic didn't work any more. She'd wanted to believe it had been here to return to, like walking back into a room full of your possessions, left untouched.

Aled and Gina left in a shower of positive sentiments and promises to have Paul and Delia round and Delia knew they were dying to get to the car and dissect whether she'd seemed herself, if it was doomed, whether either of them had put a foot in it and mentioned France or infidelity or Celine Dion. Then they'd sigh and say magnanimously *Oh well, hope it works out for them* and feel glad it wasn't them.

Delia busied herself with the washing up. She'd noticed when she did housework, the activity made the sensations inside ease. It was as if she had a bag of knives inside, and sometimes their sharpness poked her.

'Great to see them, wasn't it? Like old times,' Paul said, saying exactly what she wasn't thinking. He slid his arms around her, from behind.

'Kind of makes you envious, the baby fever. They're going to have a six-month-old at our wedding,' he continued. They'd set a date, though they'd yet to decide on a venue.

'Oh yeah. Hadn't worked it out.'

'Unless you want a no-babies rule? We always said we'd do it proper old-school relaxed, a total free for all. Kids racing round with cake all over their face.'

'Definitely. I mean, if they scream the place down during the ceremony, that's not ideal,' Delia said, absently.

'We need a registrar with a voice like Brian Blessed, who can start competing with them.'

Delia concentrated on a tough spot on the pan, then put the wire wool pad down and turned to him.

'Paul,' she said, peeling the pink Marigolds off. 'You know when you came to see me at Emma's? You asked if I wanted to stay in London? What would you have done if I'd said yes?'

'Uh.' Paul stroked his upper lip as if smoothing a moustache. 'Try to persuade you out of it, I guess. Do you know how much it costs to live there? You need to be an oligarch to have a garden.'

'But what if I'd said I was staying?' Delia persisted.

'I don't know. I can't dig the pub up and take it, can I?'

Delia noticed the order of priority, her wishes versus the pub's needs. Paul possibly regretted what he'd said.

'We'd have worked something out. If that had been your heart's desire,' he said, not completely convincing.

'Mmm.'

'Why, do you want to be in London?' Paul said, again reviewing the meaning of what they were saying, at a slight delay.

'No,' Delia said, honestly. 'But I need to talk to you.'

# Seventy-Four

It was Delia's turn to answer an avalanche of questions, and accept the hurt her answers would cause. It wasn't that she didn't love him. It wasn't that she'd got cold feet about a wedding. It wasn't, in the end, because he'd slept with another woman. It was because she'd changed, in the time they were apart, and she'd discovered it was irrevocable.

She was no longer that person on the bridge who proposed to Paul, who'd have done anything to make their life together work, even when she'd sensed him drifting away. Feeling the way you were supposed to couldn't be accomplished through sheer force of will, Delia knew that now. She wanted love which was mutual, and equal. Even if Paul could finally give that to her, she discovered, she could no longer reciprocate.

Did she have that, with this Adam?

Delia replied truthfully: she hoped so. But while Adam had helped her to wake up to her reality, he didn't create it. What she and Paul had was past, whether she and Adam worked or not.

She held Paul while he cried and let him say it wasn't over, he wasn't giving up. Above all, even more than his sadness, she could tell Paul was astonished. He found it hard to accept the powerlessness of the situation. There was nothing he could offer, nothing he could say or do. He couldn't be impotent – it didn't work this way. In his worldview, he would always be leading man and she was his love interest.

*What happens next?* She could provide the answer.

Now, at last, Delia thought of herself as the hero of her own life. A hero on the train from Newcastle to King's Cross, armed with the knowledge that risk, when it meant fear, wasn't a reason for not doing something. She hadn't followed her artistic dreams because of risk of failure, when the consequences of not trying were far worse than any rejection.

The question of whether Paul would hurt her by cheating again was the wrong question, as was whether Adam was too great a gamble. Nothing worthwhile was without risk. You had to decide whether your feelings were strong enough to make it a risk worth taking.

Delia got to the house in Clapham late. It was a balmy night, and she felt a contained hysteria surge inside her as she knocked the door.

How did you say to someone, as greeting: *I've pushed all the chips on red. Here I am, I am yours, I hope you meant it. I hope you didn't write to me in a fit of alcohol-soaked emotion and then wake up in the morning and think: thank goodness I won't be running into her on the Piccadilly Line.*

Dougie answered, understandably looking taken aback.

'Is Adam in?' Delia said, sweetly, as if it was normal to be standing on someone's doorstep at nearly ten at night with a trolley case and no appointment.

'He's out,' Dougie said.

'Can I wait for him?'

'Sure,' Dougie said, shuffling aside to let her in. 'He'll be on his mobile, too?'

It was hardly a conversation for the phone.

'I want to surprise him.'

They sat and had a beer together on the saggy sofas and chatted, Delia feeling guilty that pleasant, earnest Dougie had to make conversation with this twitchy woman, her eyes constantly darting to the clock on the wall.

As the minutes ticked into an hour, Delia couldn't fail to notice neither of them were mentioning where Adam might be, at nearing midnight on a Saturday.

'I'll let you turn in,' Delia said, after Dougie's second stifled yawn. 'I'll wait in Adam's room, if that's alright?'

Dougie made politely neutral noises and she didn't blame him for being thoroughly clueless by now about what Delia's trespassing rights were.

It felt oddly intrusive to be in Adam's bedroom without an invitation. She tried not to touch anything or do anything that could be remotely construed as prying. She rolled her trolley case out of sight of the door, thinking it could look presumptuous.

More oppressive, now she was alone, was the thought circling round her head that got louder and louder: *where is he? Where is he?* Delia was getting images in her head she didn't want there. Even worse, her imagination kept defaulting to Freya.

She laid down on the bed and closed her eyes. It made her brain's sex tape of Adam and Freya having hair-tossing, back-clawing softcore intercourse even clearer, so she opened them again. What if he was doing that? If he'd reverted back to type? They weren't together, she had no claim over him that made it unfaithful. If he was mowing through women like a tractor to endure heartbreak, however, it wasn't a great indicator of how he'd deal with any relationship problems.

Also, there was nothing in that card to her to say she was welcome back into his life. It had very much spoken of what *could be*, which was inevitable when she'd announced her intention of marriage and moved hundreds of miles away.

A few short hours ago she'd have said that that card didn't strike a single false note. In the solitude of a deserted bedroom that Adam apparently had no need of tonight, she fretted that Emma had read between the lines much more efficiently, unlike a dumbfounded Delia. Perhaps it was full of lavish things you could declare to someone you were confident you'd never see again. A cheque you'd never have to cash.

There was no guarantee he'd come back this weekend. Maybe he'd gone away! His dad in France? No. Dougie would know if he had.

Delia wasn't going to fall asleep. She'd just put her legs on the bed and her head on a pillow that smelled faintly yet wonderfully of Adam aftershave and . . . oh. Fall asleep.

# Seventy-Five

Delia woke with a start to the sound of the front door slamming and thought *fffffuuucccck*. She scrabbled out of the bed. The LED display on the alarm clock said 7.41 a.m. Adam had stayed over somewhere. The thought hurt like hell.

Oh no. What if he was *with* the woman, what if he'd brought her back? She hadn't considered that grotesque possibility. She couldn't hear any voices though. Her pounding heart slowed slightly.

Mercifully, Adam must have been checking his mail or putting the kettle on or something because Delia had a few minutes' grace to brush her teeth and get her hair more in order. She looked warily at her tired reflection and heard him bounding up the stairs, two at a time, then he barged into the room.

He made a stifled yelp of surprise at the sight of Delia and stepped back.

'Hello,' Delia said, doing a quick raise of one palm.

Adam stood motionless, still staring.

'Dougie let me in, last night,' she went on. 'I ended up sleeping here while I was waiting. I hope that's alright.'

Adam still said nothing. He was wearing a black coat she'd not seen before. His life moving on, even in as much as selecting new outerwear, jolted her. He'd lost weight, which did even greater things for his cheekbones and made his eyes tired.

Adam didn't look the way he had in her head. What else might be different?

Why wasn't he saying anything? *Where had he been?*

Delia had a demented moment of irrational fear that the card to her had been an elegant forgery.

'Why are you here?' Adam said. He didn't sound welcoming. He'd definitely been with another woman.

'I wanted to talk to you.'

'Delia,' Adam said, and he rubbed his hair, his lovely dirty-blond hair. 'That's nice, but. If you're here to check I'm OK, I'm not that OK. Not to sound like a bitter bastard: you can't help me with this, at all. Please don't twist the knife by checking in on me as a friend, and then leaving again. You leaving is something I only want to experience once.'

'Does spending nights out at other people's places help?' Delia said, carefully.

Adam frowned. 'What?'

'I'm thinking . . . given the hour . . .?' There was a loaded pause.

Adam said: 'Hang on. You move to the other end of the country to marry someone and I'm not allowed to spend a night out?'

'You are allowed,' Delia said, voice thick, eyes glassy. 'Also, I've left Paul.'

Adam stared at her, taking this in.

'Well, allowed or not, I can't think of anything I'd less like to do than sleep with someone who isn't you. I've been at my sister's in Leytonstone. Drinking red wine until a stupid hour, being maudlin and self-pitying.'

'Really?' Delia said. She felt a hot tear of exultant relief slide down her face, which wasn't the way she'd planned on doing this.

'Really,' Adam said, looking perplexed. 'Why have you left Paul?'

'Because I didn't want to marry him. You're not pleased to see me?' Delia asked.

'I'm overwhelmed to see you. But whether that's a good or bad overwhelmed is conditional on what you're here to say,' Adam said, more gently.

Delia took a deep breath.

'I came to tell you I'm in love with you, too,' she said.

Adam swallowed and cleared his throat.

'OK, now I wish I hadn't been so arsey.'

He grinned and Delia let out a sob-laugh.

'Although you realise this is rank madness. You've never been in love before. What if you realise next month it was another fad?'

'Jeez, I know I once told you I bought a wanker's car but I'm not Toad of Toad Hall,' Adam said. The shared joy and anticipation fizzed and snapped between them as they both laughed. It was hands down the happiest moment of

Delia's life. 'Delia. You've spent most of the time I've known you hung up on someone else. You don't have the monopoly on insecurity. I wouldn't say I felt those things about you without being very sure I mean them, and will carry on meaning them.'

She nodded.

'. . . The things about wanting a life together. I know we've barely started out, I don't want to rush it. But I'm thirty-three.'

'I'm thirty-four, so I win.'

'Yes but you're a man. You can keep ejaculating indefinitely.'

'I'm guessing we're into the part of the speech you didn't plan?'

'No, this is all from my notes,' Delia said, and Adam grinned a grin that lit her up. 'Staying in love isn't the same as falling in love. It won't be dressed-as-giant-animal spy antics and doing it three-and-a-half times in one night and restaurants with flower canopies. It's arguing over whose turn it was to buy dishwasher tablets.'

'I get Ocado deliveries. You should look into it. Also, *half*? Show your working.'

Delia laughed. 'I'm serious!'

'So am I. I know what you're saying. I don't want intense and unreal and short-lived. I want all day, every day normal. I want the same chance you gave Paul.'

That was what Delia needed to hear.

Adam said: 'Come here please,' and pulled her into an embrace so hard it almost winded her, then they kissed.

It was the greatest, most thrilling, most promising kiss of Delia's life, one that tasted of red wine and toothpaste and a new life where this was the person she always kissed.

'Thank you for coming back. Thank you so much,' Adam said into her hair as he held her tightly.

'Sorry it took me this long. I'd only just begun working us out when Paul appeared . . .'

Adam pulled back and his expression tightened at mention of Paul.

'Things are definitely over between you this time?'

'Yes.'

'There is one thing, though,' Delia said.

'Oh?'

'I'm not sure I want to live in London. Would you move to Newcastle?'

'In a heartbeat.'

Delia was slightly stunned. Adam seemed as much a London landscape fixture as the red buses.

'You'd do that?'

'Sure. I could rent this room out. I've only been there once years ago, seems a good city. If quite cold. Why not? Give it a go.'

'I can't believe you'd do that for me. You'd leave your home for me?'

'Home is you,' Adam said, putting his hand to her face.

Outside the window, the city was starting to wake up to a cloudy late summer day. There had been heavy rain overnight, it would leave the greenery looking jungly and make the streets smell steamy. Most people had been asleep and missed it. Delia and Adam had listened to it for an hour, wrapped around each other.

'Adam?'

'Delia.'

'When did you know you were in love with me? I can sort of better imagine you *being* in love with me than saying to yourself: wait! Guess what. I think I've fallen for that ginger PR bird. *Davina.* You always thought I was silly.'

'No, I thought your *job* was silly. I thought *you* were the most intriguing, infuriating, interesting person I'd ever met. Every time I spent any time with you, it wasn't enough.'

'Apart from when you were tongue-lashing me, thinking I was Kurt's knock-off.'

'Ugh, that was horrible. I kicked a lot of furniture and swore constantly and played a lot of aggressive contact sports afterwards. I went to see my sister and in the middle of a tirade of abuse about your moral degeneracy, I said: *It's so messed-up she's with him. She should be with me.* There it was. I didn't even know I was going to say it.'

'Haha! What did Alice say?'

'She said, oh dear, you've fallen in love with her, you idiot. I said no, no, no, absolutely not. I'm simply experiencing an overpowering level of irrational emotion that makes me want to roll a rock over the door like a Flintstone and imprison her, until she realises she must choose me. I won't be a cruel jailer, she will get fed and can take supervised baths. My sister said, yeah, that's love. You?'

'It was when you told me you were rich. I saw your sensitive side.'

They laughed.

'I knew I was in love with you when I thought about you every forty-eight seconds. Adam tinnitus. I couldn't be walking down the aisle, wondering about how you were spending your weekend.'

Adam said 'hah', but Delia sensed it was still too fresh in the memory to mention the wedding plans.

She spoke more carefully. 'When I read your card, I couldn't stop re-reading it. Eventually I admitted, this isn't only about how he feels about you, this is how you feel about him. You said to me, *You can't help who you're in love with.* You meant you didn't blame me for being with Paul. Instead it exactly described why I should be with you.'

'Wow. It wasn't written with the hope of you coming back. It was a straight goodbye.'

'I know. That's why it was so effective,' Delia smiled.

She knew that even if it didn't work out with Adam, she would never regret taking this chance. It was already worth it.

'Not that it's a competition, but would you have ever come looking for me, if I hadn't written to you?' he said.

'I know for sure I would have,' Delia said, her eyes momentarily dazzled by the light glowing through the red curtains, so Adam was only a silhouette in the blue of the room.

'You do? How?'

'I'd started writing you into my story.'

# The End

# Read on for more from Delia, Adam and Mhairi...

# Q&A with *Mhairi*

### What inspired you to write *It's Not Me, It's You*?

I think people expect a sort of thunderbolt, flashing-lottery-finger answer to this question, as if there's a divine intervention moment of inspiration saying, 'Here it is, here's your book', which sadly isn't the case. For me, it tends to be a composite of things. Delia was a heroine I'd had in my head vividly for a long time, and I knew I wanted to use Newcastle as a setting, because I love it there. And then once I knew Delia was a Geordie it all came together. And I wanted to write the classic 'find out someone's cheating on you' plot and work through it when it isn't as straightforward as binning the bad guy. How do you come back from that when you still love each other and want to make it work? Paul isn't just a bad guy, it would be too easy for Delia to walk away. He's ultimately a good guy who's done an awful thing and it's a journey for him and Delia to figure out how they got there. So for me, it's plot, setting and only then the situation I want to put them in.

### What was the inspiration behind The Fox?

In Delia's secret comic, she has a superhero alter ego called The Fox. The Fox patrols Newcastle by night with her faithful fox sidekick, Reginald, fighting crime. The idea came from watching *Buffy* and realising that you could use genres to tell an emotionally resonant story. *Buffy* is really clever structurally and brilliantly grown up and emotionally mature in the stories it tells, much more so than many 'adult' dramas. With *INMIY*, my heroine had lost courage, lost direction and lost hope – so what if she had a superhero pole star? A Buffy-ish avatar? I loved the idea of Delia having a higher version of herself – where she can be the Delia she wants to be. The Fox's courage is emblematic of what she needs in real life.

**Where did you get the idea for Paul's mis-sent text to Delia?**

Hah! This idea actually came from a friend of mine who was ranting about a boss at work and she accidently sent it to the boss rather than her friend. And she was so brave – far braver than me – that when she realised what she'd done she hit 'call', rang her boss, confessed to it and fortunately managed to clear the air. And being a writer, as soon as I heard that anecdote, I did that thefty-Gollum-writer thing, where I thought 'oooo that's a good inciting incident!' Technology: awful when it trips you up; a gift to women's fiction writers. I took my friend's lemons and made Lemontinis.

**What have you learnt while writing your novels?**

The best way to sum up my learning is: it gets easier but it doesn't get easy. And I suspect that if it was easy then I'd worry that I was doing something very wrong. Loyal readers want you busting a ball and doing your very best, and rightly so.

**What readers say again and again is how relatable your heroines are. How do you feel about that?**

I absolutely love that. I'm so pleased. I think reflecting actual human dilemma and real emotional experiences is important in women's fiction. If you're writing about relationships – I mean in the broadest sense there, not necessarily romantic ones – then say something about relationships. Pay attention to your problems and complications and those of people around you! It's all material! (My friends must be so sick of when they're confiding in me and I get that gleam in my eye... my bloodshot beady eye...) If I'm honest, pure escapism alone doesn't appeal to me. I love a high concept romantic comedy, but I want to see some truth in it. When I came to write chick lit, I was fed up with stories where the heroine *suddenly* finds herself a PA to a millionaire rock star in Cancun or whatever. I felt like part of the genre had stopped speaking to me, and my life, and my friends' lives. But writing about authentic problems and temptations, the sort of things we discuss when we're a bottle of wine down, really excited me. When Emma counsels Delia against Adam at the end of *INMIY*, I don't think Emma's wrong, as such. She's presenting the 'cons' to Delia of him as a choice. But in life, you can't always achieve happiness by relying on other people to tell you what you should do, or playing it safe. That's Delia's hard-won wisdom. I was once given a brilliant piece of advice (much better than 'write what you know' which can be too restrictive) – *lie about anything except emotions*. Get that right, and you can do anything else you want: you've nailed what matters to the universal human experience (hark at me. *Alright, George Eliot*) to the floor. So while there are fantastical elements to Delia's story, she still goes through what I hope is a realistic journey to acceptance and understanding, of both herself and Paul. I didn't want to short-sell that element. It's not all laughs, it's not credit cards and rock stars and designer shopping and the tap of a magic fiction fairy wand solving it all for her.

**Another thing you're known for is how genuinely laugh-out-loud your novels are. How do you keep the LOLs coming?**

Thank you! I didn't start off trying to write books that were funny! I started off – and I think this is true of a lot of people – thinking that writing novels is a serious business. There is an awful first draft of *You Had Me At Hello*, which is really bleak and grim and it just went horribly wrong. Even now, I can't bring myself to look at it. And my mum said, 'well maybe the reason that it's not working is that you're funny.' (Am I, Mum? *Am I?*) I realised no-one thinks, 'Hey, I can be funny' – not outside trying to make it as a stand up, anyway – so I hadn't approached the writing as if I could do that. Then when I rewrote *YHMAH*, I relaxed and started to let my characters say funny things, just to make myself laugh, and that was how it came about. So I don't do 'humour' self-consciously. It's weird, I think it'd go wrong if I did sit down and say: I shall craft a lolocaust! I think of it as the characters entertaining me. I sound a trifle nutty now…

**What did you want to be when you grew up?**

My earliest plan was to be a space princess with blue hair. Then I wanted to be a witch – witches were cool, they got to dabble in magic, they got to make potions and they had black hats. But then as I got older I realised that being a witch wasn't actually a career choice. So then it was being a writer. I always used to write stories as a kid: my mum saved one called *The Adventures of Snaily Snail* which I think shows my early gift for naming characters! Most people write stories when they're kids, so it's not like I think it was pre-ordained – I just knew I loved writing and making up stories. I went into journalism because it seemed the obvious job if you love writing, and it quickly became apparent I was a natural feature writer rather than newshound. I used to love nothing more than having a great interview in my notepad and coming back to the office knowing I could spend a whole day on a 1,000 word piece. Being sent to a disaster zone and asked to file a few paragraphs over the phone? Nothing about that appealed to me at all. Not least the impact on my lunch break.

**You're very prolific on Twitter and you've incorporated a lot of texting and emailing into all your books. What do you think of the spread of social media in the last few years?**

Argh, I tell you what, Twitter has to be toned down during intensive writing phases! Well, as a writer, I think you can't get away from social media in rom coms now. Or if you want to swerve it, you've got to (as they say) address it to dismiss it. If your heroine is wailing 'I'll never see him again' you can't dodge the fact he may well be in her Facebook friends. That's the one thing it's screwed up actually – the 'Before Sunset' sense of parting forever, it's just not the same when you can fire up the Stalkomatic 3000 and hunt for activity online. But I'm generally a big fan of the storytelling opportunities that social media affords. In *INMIY*, Delia has to track down a message board troll, Peshwari Naan. Emma says of people who meet on social media: 'it's smoke and mirrors, they could turn out to be anyone.' This is something friends who internet date talk about – there's a way you 'sell' yourself in the medium which can be highly misleading. As we later find out, the Naan is a keyboard warrior with problems socialising in real life. It's useful to think of it as a type of Freshers' Week – everyone's enjoying the liberation of being whoever they want to be. You're meeting a projected version, or only one aspect of the whole. This has got a bit deep! But yes, I'm a huge fan of it. The idea that I can just log on and chat to people anywhere, I love that. It has freed friendships from the tyranny of geography!

**What was your 'it's not me, it's you' moment in real life?**

[I'm going to define this as 'thing that other people do that you just don't understand'.] I was asked in a Q&A what the one quality was that I would never ever give a character, which I think is a great question! I mean there are obvious things: racism, sexism, voting UKIP – all of those things are complete boner-killers – but then I thought: being tight-fisted is actually a huge one. Imagine a hero who was really stingy! A friend of mine went out for a curry recently with a large group of friends, and at the end of the meal, one person was there with a calculator working out exactly what she had. As my friend said, 'she got forensic about the price of her bhaji'. And I find that really odd – surely you go out to have a nice time, not to come home patting yourself on the back for having saved four pounds, but having everyone else hate you a tiny bit! If you were that short of cash, you wouldn't go? So that's my INMIY moment: what's the point in being tight in those situations? Can someone explain it to me?

**What do you think the worst clichés in rom coms are?**

I hate the cliché that a woman has a good job and therefore must be punished for it. I don't understand how we're still doing this in 2015. Like in *The Proposal* – Sandra Bullock is a top flight literary agent with Ryan Reynolds as her tea boy, but she must be punished for her success by being an awful person. Then she goes on a weekend with his family to fulfil the sham wedding plot and she is the kind of idiot who doesn't understand that Louboutins weren't built for climbing into boats so she must be ridiculed and mocked for this. It drives me mad. How is this still going on? Another thing that winds me up is when Mr Wrong is a complete and utter irredeemable tool. Is our heroine so dim that she didn't notice? It makes her a bit of an idiot. I also hate the 'I shop therefore I am' thing. I mean don't get me wrong, I love the *Pretty Woman* montage, it's great, but I think we've got to the point where shopping-as-character-trait is fairly grim. Women aren't defined by what they buy!

**Tell us about your typical working day.**

I'm glad I've been asked as I'd like to share best practice if I may. I suggest waking up at maybe 10-10.30am with your hair all over the place, preferably a bit hungover. If you're sensible, you've left a bit of your make-up on, so you can just fill in the gaps, then you spend about two hours on Twitter arguing with people about things that don't matter. By this point, it's lunchtime, so time to microwave a pouch of something and eat that while reading *Guardian* food blogs about really good cooking in posh restaurants. Then it's early afternoon, so time to answer your emails – make sure you reply to lots of friends, in great detail, taking the time to be really funny. Then by about 3pm you haven't written a word of your book, so spend about 40 minutes tapping away sweatily. By then it's 4 or 5pm and your friends in office jobs have started to think about the end of the day so it's time to email to see if they want to go to the pub tonight. Then you have a brief editing phase, where you look at the work that you've done, feel intense dismay at its evident crapulence, but soon get distracted by your friends planning the pub trip. Then it's time to leave for the pub.

Are HarperCollins going to read this?

# YOU TOLD US SOME OF YOUR

The British Summertime

*Tell us your 'IT'S NOT ME IT'S YOU' moment*

Got kicked out of tennis club, aged 4, for talking about dinosaurs too much.

It wasn't me, it was THEM

*Tell us your 'IT'S NOT ME IT'S YOU' moment*

When your version of cleaning up is moving a plate from the table to the counter above the dishwasher.

*Tell us your 'IT'S NOT ME IT'S YOU' moment*

As a male, I never get the opportunity to say 'It's not me it's you' because apparently it's always me...

*Tell us your 'IT'S NOT ME IT'S YOU' moment*

# TS NOT ME ITS YOU MOMENTS

Being mistaken for other bald men that look nothing like me

Tell us your 'ITS NOT ME ITS YOU' moment

HE ATE THE LAST PORK PIE

Tell us your 'ITS NOT ME ITS YOU' moment

It's not okay to internet date when you have a girlfriend of <u>2 years</u>

#itsnotmeitsyou

Tell us your 'ITS NOT ME ITS YOU' moment

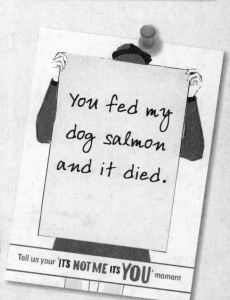

You fed my dog salmon and it died.

Tell us your 'ITS NOT ME ITS YOU' moment

# Cocktail Recipes

## The Mhairitini (vah-ree-tee-nee)

*Created for the launch of
It's Not Me, It's You*

Add all the ingredients to a shaker, shake well and strain into a martini glass. Garnish with a cherry and drink while reading this book.

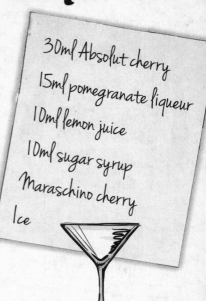

30ml Absolut cherry

15ml pomegranate liqueur

10ml lemon juice

10ml sugar syrup

Maraschino cherry

Ice

## Delia's Vintage Delight

45ml sloe gin

15ml elderflower gin

10ml sugar syrup

Soda water to top up

Ice

Add all ingredients except the soda water to a cocktail shaker. Shake. Strain into a beautiful vintage tea cup, top with soda water and drink with pinkie finger extended.

# Emma's Tinder Shot

*Guaranteed to make your swiping less selective*

Wipe the lime around the mouth of the glass, fill it nearly to the brim with the vodka, and add a splash of Red Bull. Down it. Warning: too many of these may lead to unreliable right-swipes.

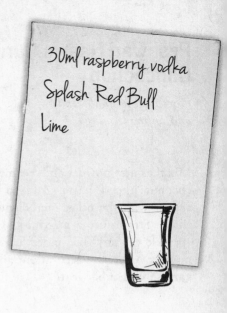

30ml raspberry vodka
Splash Red Bull
Lime

# Adam's Millionaire Sidecar

*For the refined gentleman*

Add all ingredients to a cocktail shaker and shake well. Strain into a martini glass and garnish with an orange slice. Drink like you're P Diddy.

30ml cognac
15ml triple sec
15ml Goldschläger
10ml lemon juice
Ice
Orange slice to garnish

## Peshwari Naan's Curry Concoction

*Goes well with all kinds of spicy food and online trolling*

Mix the curry powder and creamed coconut into a paste. Add to a shaker with the other ingredients, shake. Strain into a martini glass, sprinkle a tiny bit more curry powder over as decoration and garnish with a bay leaf.

3/4 tsp mild curry powder

1 tsp creamed coconut

45ml gin

10ml lemon juice

Ice

Bay leaf to garnish

30ml rum

30ml midori

30ml pineapple juice

30ml mango juice

Soda water

Ice

## Kurt's Poison

*For the discerning villain*

Add all ingredients to the shaker, top with soda water and give it a good shake. Pour everything, including the ice, into a high ball. Drink while working on your masterplan for world domination.

Rachel and Ben. Ben and Rachel.
It was them against the world.
Until it all fell apart...

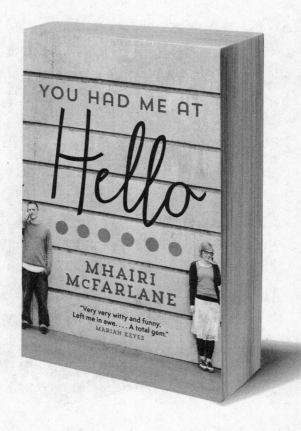

Hilarious, heartbreaking and everything in between,
you'll be hooked from their first 'hello'.

Anna Alessi – history expert, possessor of a lot of hair and an occasionally filthy mouth – seeks nice man for intelligent conversation and Mills & Boon moments.

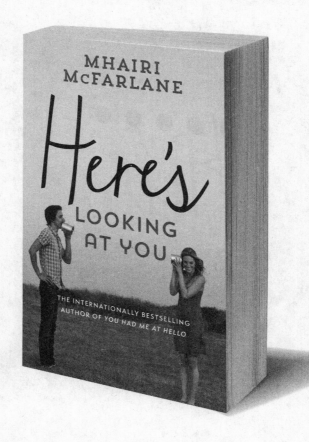

Hilarious and poignant, you'll be laughing one minute and crying the next.

# Find Mhairi online!

It's no secret that Mhairi is a huge fan of social media!
She can be found online, chattering away daily, so find
her on Facebook or follow her on Twitter now!
She would love to hear from you.

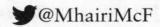

**f** /MhairiMcFarlaneAuthor

🐦 @MhairiMcF

Keep up to date on all the latest news about Mhairi
and her novels by visiting her website

www.mhairimcfarlane.com

# The W6 Book Café

Want to hear more from your favourite **women's fiction** authors?

Eager to read **exclusive extracts** before the books even hit the shops?

Keen to join a monthly online **Book Group**?

Join us at **The W6 Book Café**, home to HarperFiction's best-loved authors

 Find us on Facebook **W6BookCafe**

Follow us on Twitter **@W6BookCafe**